ONE
Summer
AT THE RANCH

REBECCA
WINTERS

ONE Summer COLLECTION

June 2016

July 2016

July 2016

August 2016

August 2016

September 2016

ONE
Summer
AT THE RANCH

REBECCA
WINTERS

DONNA
ALWARD

CHRISTINE
RIMMER

MILLS & BOON

First Published in Great Britain 2016
By Mills & Boon, an imprint of HarperCollins*Publishers*
1 London Bridge Street, London, SE1 9GF

ONE SUMMER AT THE RANCH © 2016 Harlequin Books S.A.

The Wyoming Cowboy © 2013 Rebecca Winters
A Family for the Rugged Rancher © 2011 Donna Alward
The Man Who Had Everything © 2007 Christine Rimmer

ISBN: 978-0-263-92234-9

09-0816

Our policy is to use papers that are natural, renewable and recyclable products and made from wood grown in sustainable forests.
The logging and manufacturing processes conform to the legal environmental regulations of the country of origin.

Printed and bound in Spain
by CPI, Barcelona

THE WYOMING COWBOY

REBECCA WINTERS

*I want to dedicate this series to the courageous
men and women serving in our armed forces
who've willingly put their lives in harm's way to
keep the rest of us safe. God bless all of you.*

Rebecca Winters, whose family of four children
has now swelled to include five beautiful
grandchildren, lives in Salt Lake City, Utah, in
the land of the Rocky Mountains. With canyons
and high alpine meadows full of wildflowers,
she never runs out of places to explore. They,
plus her favourite vacation spots in Europe, often
end up as backgrounds for her romance novels,
because writing is her passion, along with her
family and church.

Rebecca loves to hear from readers. If you
wish to e-mail her, please visit her website:
www.cleanromances.com

Chapter One

MARCH 1
Pulmonary Unit
Walter Reed National Military Medical Center
Bethesda, Maryland

Carson Lundgren was sitting in the hospital ward's common room watching the final moments of the NASCAR race when he heard a disturbance. Annoyed, he turned his head to see Dr. Rimer passing out a document to the eight vets assembled. What in blazes was going on?

"Ray? You're closest to the TV. Would you mind shutting it off?"

Ray nodded and put an end to one of the few distractions the men looked forward to.

"Thank you. You'll all be going home tomorrow, so I urge you gentlemen to read this and take what you can from it to heart. It's a good letter written by a former serviceman. I like a lot of things it says. While you're doing that, I'll go find our special guest and bring him in."

Special guest?

The guys eyed each other with resignation. Who

knew how long this would take? They were all anxious to watch the end of the race. Carson looked down
to scan the page.

*Consider how different and difficult it is to go from
a life of service, where every day has a mission,
and someone depends on you to make life-and-
death decisions, to a life with civilians who are
making decisions about what client to call back
first or what is the best outfit to wear to work.*

Life would be different, all right. In Carson's case he
didn't need to worry about choosing the proper clothes.
He was going back to his Wyoming ranch, where a shirt
and jeans had been his uniform before he'd signed up
for the Marines. It would be his uniform again, now
that he was out of the service.

*In the beginning it feels as if you are so much
more experienced than the people around you,
and in a lot of ways you are. But that kind of
thinking will only further alienate you from others. Practicing humility is the best possible advice I can give to help with reintegration into
civilian life.*

Carson did feel more "experienced." He'd seen things
in the war that he could never explain to people who
hadn't gone through the same thing.

*Veterans need to recognize that even a short tour
in a combat zone can have an effect on them.*

While it takes everyone some time to recover after coming home, those who have seen, or been directly affected by a traumatic or horrific event (using your own definition or a generally accepted definition of such an event), need to be able to reconcile that it may have an impact on their lives and relationships with others after the deployment is over.

Since Carson had no family and his grandfather was dead, he didn't need to worry about that.

Seeking help is not a sign of weakness, no more than asking your buddy to cover your backside. The body may heal from scars and wounds readily, but the scars and wounds of trauma can last much longer and are more difficult to heal.

Difficult? A caustic laugh escaped from him. The cough he'd developed in Afghanistan would never go away, and no one could convince him otherwise.

I promise that, in time, you will see that your civilian counterparts are skilled and have a perspective that you may not have ever considered. And through a respect for what they do and what they have done, you will learn that you, too, are valued and respected.

Carson had always respected the ranch staff and knew he could count on their support.

*Just as you are on edge in the beginning, they too
may be a little unsure of how to treat you and how
to act around you.*

They'd treat him just the same as always.

*So, take the first step. Be patient, be kind and be
humble, and you will see that the transition is
much easier.*

"Gentlemen?" Dr. Rimer came back in the room
where most of them were coughing because of the
same affliction. He was followed by a five-star general
decked out in full-dress uniform. Carson glanced at his
buddies, Ross and Buck, wondering what was going on.

"I'm pleased and honored to introduce General Al-
dous Cook. He's anxious to talk to you men recovering
in the unit. He's been asked to do some investigating for
the Senate committee examining the troubling findings
of the *Millennium Cohort Study of 2009*."

The eight of them got to their feet and saluted him
before shaking his hand.

The General smiled. "Be seated, gentlemen. I'm honored to be in your presence and want to thank you for
your invaluable service to our country." He cleared his
throat. "I understand you're all going home tomorrow
and have a great deal on your minds so I'll make this
quick.

"As you're well aware, a significant number of
returning American veterans like yourselves have
reported respiratory problems that started during deployment to Iraq and Afghanistan. The study of 2009
revealed that fourteen percent of the deployed troops

reported new breathing problems, compared with ten percent among those who hadn't deployed.

"Though the percentage difference seems small when extrapolated for the two million troops who've been deployed since 2001, the survey suggested that at least 80,000 additional soldiers have developed post-deployment breathing problems.

"There's a fierce debate under way over just how long-lasting and severe these problems really are. We're tracking the numbers accrued among the troops based in Southern Afghanistan since 2009, particularly the Marines.

"After ruling out other factors, it's apparent that the powerful dust storms, plus the fine dust from metals, toxins and burn pits used to incinerate garbage at military bases, are the potential culprits. Steps need to be taken to reduce the hazards, and I'm concerned that this exposure isn't getting the serious review it needs.

"Dr. Rimer has indicated you've all improved since you've been here, but we'll continue to track your progress. He assures me that with time, most of you will overcome your coughing and shortness of breath."

Tell us another fairy tale, General.

"My concern is that every one of you receives the post-deployment care you need for as long as you need it. I'm fighting for you in the congressional hearings."

Along with the others, Carson stood up and applauded. At least the General had bothered to come to the hospital in person and make an attempt to get at the root of the problem. Carson admired him for that. The General chatted with each of them for a few minutes, then left. With the end of the NASCAR race now missed, everyone left the lounge except Carson and his two roommates, Ross and Buck.

They hadn't known each other until six weeks ago, when the three of them had been flown here from their various divisions and diagnosed with acute dyspnea. But even if they were hacking, coughing and wheezing, at least they'd arrived at the hospital on their own two feet. It tore them up that some of their buddies—especially those who'd been married with families—hadn't made it through the war.

The behavioral psychologist who'd been working with them suggested that, once they were discharged, they should find a positive way to work through their survivor's guilt.

In addition to the guilt Carson already struggled with for personal reasons, he was barely functioning. During the long hours of the night when they couldn't sleep, they'd talked about the wives and children who'd lost husbands and fathers from their own squads. If the three of them could think of a way to help those families, maybe they could forgive themselves for coming home alive.

At one point in their nocturnal discussions, Carson threw out an idea that began to percolate and gain ground. "What if we invited the fatherless kids to my ranch for a summer vacation? The ranch has lots of outdoor activities for kids who may not have spent much time out-of-doors. We could take them fishing and camping, not to mention horseback riding and hiking."

Ross sat up in his bed. "All of those are good confidence builders. Heaven knows those children will have lost some confidence. How many kids are you talking about?"

"I don't know."

"Do you have enough room for guests?"

"No. We'd have to live in the ranch house, so that wouldn't work. We'd have to put up some cabins."

"I could build them with your help," Buck offered. "Construction is what I was raised to do."

"I'm afraid I don't have much money."

Buck said, "I have a little I've put away."

"I have some, too," Ross chimed in. "Looking down the road, we'd have to hire and pay a cook and provide maid service."

Encouraged, Carson said, "No matter what, we'll have to start out small."

"Their moms will have to bring them."

"You're right, Buck. How long should they come for?"

"This is a bit of an experiment, so how about we try a week with one family and see how it goes?"

"For working mothers, I think a week sounds about right," Ross theorized. "One thing we can do is help the kids if they need to talk about death, since we've been through a lot of grief counseling ourselves."

"Good point. That's one thing we know how to do. What ages are we talking about?"

"I'm thinking about my nieces and nephews," Buck murmured. "How about little guys who are really missing their dads? Like six on up to maybe ten."

Carson nodded. "That sounds about right. They'd be school age. Younger than six might be too young."

"Agreed," they all concurred.

Before long, enthusiasm for the project they envisioned wouldn't let them alone. They soon found themselves plotting to turn Carson's ranch into a dude ranch where tourists could come along with the families of fatherless children. They would establish a fund to take care of the costs. If their pilot program went well through the summer, they'd talk about keeping it open year-round.

Their plan was a good one and sounded feasible, except for one thing. None of them had gone home yet. Anything could happen when Buck and Ross were reunited with their families. Their parents had dreams for them when their beloved sons returned to their former lives. For that reason, Carson wasn't holding his breath—what little he had at the moment. He had to admit the inhalers were helping. When he'd first been brought in, he'd been gasping for every breath and thought each was his last.

Of the three men, Carson was the only one who didn't have living family. The grandfather who'd raised him had passed away five months ago of a surprise heart attack, leaving the ranch and its problems to him. Not even his grandfather's doctor had seen it coming. Carson had flown home on emergency family leave to bury him.

In that regard, he wouldn't have to run their brainchild past the older man he'd abandoned when he'd entered the military. At the time he hadn't seen it as abandonment. They'd corresponded and phoned whenever possible, but in the end Carson wasn't there for his grandfather when the chips were down. Now it was too late to make it up to the man he'd loved.

"Tomorrow's the big day, guys." Once they were all discharged from the hospital in the morning, he knew anything could happen to change his friends' focus.

Buck nodded. "I'll join you before the week is out."

Maybe. But knowing Buck was the oldest son in a large, close-knit family who wanted and needed him back in the construction business, maybe not. "Give me a call and I'll pick you up at the airport. What about you, Ross?"

"Three days at the most."

"You think?"

He eyed him narrowly. "I *know.*"

Put like that, Carson could believe him, but his family who'd made their mark in oil for generations would have its way of pressuring the favorite son who'd made it home from the war. His politician father had long laid hopes for him set in stone. Time would tell if their master plan would get off the ground.

"I can hear the carts arriving with our dinner. Let's get back to the room and eat before our final session with the shrink."

It couldn't come soon enough for any of them. The war had been their world for a long time. Tomorrow they'd leave it forever. But fear clutched him in the gut that it would never leave them.

MAY 2
Sandusky, Ohio

AT THREE O'CLOCK, Tracy Baretta left her office to pick up Johnny from elementary school. When she joined the line of cars waiting for the kids to come out, she hoped she'd see Clara Brewster. Her son, Nate, was a cute boy who'd invited Johnny to his birthday party last month. Johnny hadn't wanted to go, but Tracy had made him.

Maybe Nate would like to come home with her and Johnny to play, but she didn't see him or his mom. Her disappointment changed to a dull pain when she had to wait until all the kids had been picked up before her skinny, dark-haired first grader exited the school doors alone.

He purposely hung back from the others. His behavior had her worried sick. She'd been setting up some playdates with a few of the other boys in his first-grade class, but they hadn't worked out well.

Johnny preferred to be alone and stay home with her after school. He'd become a very quiet child since Tony's death and was way too attached to her. The psychologist told her to keep finding ways to get him to interact with other kids and not take no for an answer, but she wasn't gaining ground.

He got in the rear seat with his backpack and strapped himself in. She looked over her shoulder at him. "How was school today, honey?"

"We had a substitute."

"Was she fun?"

"It was a man. I didn't like him."

She eyed him in the rearview mirror. "Why do you say that?"

"He made me sit with Danny."

"Isn't he a nice boy?"

"He calls me squirt."

His tear-filled voice brought out every savage maternal instinct to protect him. Praying for inspiration she said, "Do you want to know something?"

"What?"

"Your father was one of the shortest kids in his class when he was your age. By high school he was five feet ten." The perfect size for Tracy. "That'll happen to you, too. Do you think your father was a squirt?"

"No," he muttered.

"Then forget what Danny said. When we go to Grandma's house, she'll show you lots of pictures to make you feel better."

Of course Johnny couldn't forget. Silence filled the car for the rest of the drive home to their small rental house. She parked in front of the garage. While he scrambled out of the back, she retrieved the mail and they entered through the front door.

Once inside, he raced for the kitchen. "Wash your hands before you eat anything!" He was always hungry for sweets after school.

While her six-year-old grumbled and ran into the bathroom, Tracy went to the kitchen and poured him a glass of milk before she sorted through the mail, mostly ads and bills. Among the assortment she saw a hand-written envelope addressed to Mrs. Anthony Baretta. It had a Jackson, Wyoming, postmark.

She didn't know anyone in Wyoming. Her glance took in the return address. Lundgren's Teton Valley Dude Ranch was printed inside the logo of a mountain peak.

A dude ranch? She'd heard of them all her life, but she'd never been to one. Truth be told, she'd never traveled west of the Mississippi. Every trip had been to Florida, the East Coast, New York City, the Jersey Shore or Toronto. Tony had promised Johnny that when he got out of the service next year, they'd take a big driving trip west, all the way to Disneyland. Another pain shot through her.

She took a deep breath, curious to know who would be writing to her from Wyoming. After slitting the envelope open, she pulled out the handwritten letter.

Dear Mrs. Baretta,
My name is Carson Lundgren. You don't know me
from Adam. I served as a marine in Afghanistan
before I got out of the service.

The word Afghanistan swam before her eyes. *Tony.*
She closed them tightly to stop the tears and sank down
on one of the kitchen chairs. Her husband had been
gone eleven months, yet she knew she would always
experience this crushing pain when she thought of him.

"Mom? Can I have a peanut-butter cookie?" He'd
drunk his milk.

"How about string cheese or an apple instead?"

"No-o," he moaned.

"Johnny—" she said in a firm voice.

"Can I have some for dinner?"

"If you eat everything else first."

"Okay." She heard him rummage in the fridge for the
cheese before he left the kitchen to watch his favorite
afternoon cartoons.

When he'd disappeared into the living room, she
wiped her eyes and continued reading.

Buck Summerhays and Ross Livingston, former
marines, are in business with me on the Teton
Valley Dude Ranch. We put our heads together
and decided to contact the families of the fallen
soldiers from our various units.

Your courageous husband, Anthony Baretta,
served our country with honor and distinction.
Now, we'd like to honor him by offering you and
your son John an all-expenses-paid, one-week va-

*cation at the dude ranch anytime in June, July or
August. We'll pay for your airfare and any other
travel expenses.*

Tracy's eyes widened in total wonder.

*You're welcome to contact your husband's divi-
sion commander. His office helped us obtain your
address. If you're interested and have questions,
please phone our office at the number below.
We've also listed our website. Visit it to see the
brochure we've prepared. We'll be happy to email
you any additional information.*

*Please know how anxious we are to give some-
thing back to you after Anthony's great sacrifice.
With warmest regards,
Carson Lundgren*

His words made her throat swell with emotion. With
the letter still open, she phoned the commander's office
and learned that the offer was completely legitimate.
His assistant had nothing but praise for such a worthy
cause and hoped she and her son would be able to take
advantage of it.

Tracy's thoughts flew to her plans for the summer.
When school was out, it was decided she and Johnny
would spend six weeks in Cleveland with Tony's parents. They saw Tony in their grandson and were living
for a long visit. So was Tracy, who'd been orphaned at
eighteen and had no other family.

Luckily, she had June and the first half of July off
from her job as technology facilitator for the Sandusky

school district. Both she and Johnny needed a huge dose of family love, and they would get it. Grandma planned for them to stay in Tony's old room with all his stuff. Johnny would adore that.

The Barettas were a big Italian-American family with aunts, uncles and lots of cousins. Two of Johnny's uncles were policemen and the other three were firefighters, like their father. *Like Tony, before he'd joined the Marines to help pay for a college education.*

Their loving kindness had saved her life, and Johnny's, when news of the tragedy had come. He needed that love and support more than ever. She wondered what his reaction would be when he heard what this new invitation was about.

But before she did anything else, she called her sister-in-law Natalie to feel her out. When Tracy read her the letter, Natalie cried, "You've got to be kidding me! A dude ranch? Oh, my gosh, Tracy. You'll have the time of your life. Ask Ruth. She went to one in Montana with my folks a few years ago. Remember?"

"Vaguely."

"Yeah. It was a working ranch and they helped feed animals and went on trail rides and stuff. She got to help herd some cows."

"I don't think this is that kind of a ranch, but I don't know for sure. The thing is, Johnny's been difficult for so long, I don't think he'd even like the idea of it."

"If you want, I'll tell Cory about it. I could have him call Johnny and tell him he's thinks it would be super cool."

"That might work. Johnny loves Cory and usually goes along with anything his favorite cousin says."

"Cory will want to go with him. But seriously, Tracy, I can't believe what a wonderful thing these ex-marines have decided to do. You hear a lot of talk about remembering our fallen heroes, but this is the first time I've heard of a group of soldiers doing something like this."

"I know. Believe me, I'm blown away by this letter. If Tony knew, he'd be so touched." The tears came. She couldn't stop them. "There's just one problem. The folks are expecting Johnny and me to visit there as soon as school is out. Since my vacation is over in mid-July, I would have to make arrangements to do this trip before then."

"True." Natalie's voice trailed. "It will cut into the time you planned with Mom and Dad Baretta."

"Yes. You know how they're looking forward to spending time with Johnny."

"Well, don't say anything to them until you find out if he wants to go."

"You're right. First things first. I'll let you know what happens. Thanks for being there and being my best friend."

"Ditto to you. *Ciao*."

Deciding there was no time like the present to find out, Tracy picked up the letter and walked into the living room. Johnny was spread out on the floor with his turtle pillow-pet watching *Tom and Jerry*.

"Honey, do you mind if I shut off the TV? There's something I want to talk to you about."

He turned to look at her out of eyes as dark a brown as Tony's. She picked up the remote and turned the set off before sitting down on the couch. "We just got an invitation in the mail to do something we've never done before. It was sent by some men who used to be marines, like your father."

That seemed to pique his interest enough to sit up cross-legged. "Are they going to have a party?" In his child's world, an invitation meant a party. Since Tony's death he'd shied away from them. He seemed to have lost his confidence. It killed her.

"No. Let me read this to you."

He sat quietly until she'd finished. "What's a dude ranch?"

"It's a place to go horseback riding and probably lots of other things."

Her son had never been on a horse. Neither had she. "You mean like a cowboy?" She nodded. "Where is it?"

"In Wyoming."

"Where's that?"

"If you're interested, I'll show you on the computer."

"Okay."

He followed her into her bedroom where she had her laptop. In a second she'd brought up a map of the United States. "We live here, in Ohio." She pointed to Cleveland. "Now, watch my finger. You have to cross Indiana, Illinois, Iowa and South Dakota to get to Wyoming, right here."

She could hear his mind working. "How long would we be gone?"

"A week."

"That's a long time." His voice wobbled. "I don't want to go."

Tracy had been afraid of that answer, but she understood. It meant leaving the only security he'd ever known. Going to stay with his aunt Natalie and play with his cousin Cory, or having an overnighter on the weekend with his grandparents, who only lived an hour away, was different.

"We don't have to. These men know your daddy died and they'd like to do something nice for you, but it's your decision, Johnny. Before I turn off the computer, would you like to see some pictures Mr. Lundgren sent so you could see what it looks like?"

He sighed. "I guess."

Tracy typed in the web address and clicked. Up popped a colored photograph of the Teton Mountain Range with a few pockets of snow. The scene was so spectacular she let out a slight gasp. In the bottom of the picture was the layout of the Teton Valley Dude Ranch surrounded by sage.

A "whoa" from Johnny told her his attention had been captured. She read the description below the picture out loud.

"The dude ranch is located along the legendary Snake River in the shadow of the magnificent Teton Mountain Range. It's just five miles from the town of Jackson, a sophisticated mountain resort. Fifteen minutes away are world-class skiing areas.

"This 1,700-acre ranch operates as a cattle ranch with its own elk and deer herds, eagles and bears. There's fishing along the three miles of the Snake. At elevations from 6,200 to 7,300 feet, summers bring average temperatures of eighty degrees and low humidity.

"Mountaineering, fly-fishing, white-water rafting, wildlife expeditions, horseback riding, photo safaris, hiking and camping trips, stargazing, bird watching, ballooning, a visit to the rodeo, are all included when you stay on the ranch. Among the amenities you'll enjoy are a game room, a swimming pool, a babysitting service, laundry services and the use of a car for local transportation."

Johnny nudged her. "What's white water?"

She'd been deep in thought. "There's a picture here of some people in a raft running the rapids. Take a look."

His eyes widened. "You mean we'd do that if we went there?"

"If we wanted to."

He looked up at her. "When would we go?"

So he *was* interested. She felt a sudden lift of her spirits. "How about as soon as school is out? After our trip is over, we'll fly back to Cleveland and stay with Grandma and Grandpa for a month. Why don't you think about it, and let me know tonight before you go to bed?"

"Can I see the rest of the pictures?"

"Sure. You know how to work the computer. While you do that, I'm going to start dinner." With her fingers crossed, she got up from her swivel chair so he could sit and look at everything. He needed something to bring him out of his shell. Maybe a trip like this would help.

A half hour later he came running into the kitchen where she'd made spaghetti. "Mom—you should see the elks. They have giant horns!"

"You mean antlers."

"Oh, yeah. I forgot."

She hunkered down and gave him a hug. "It's pretty exciting stuff, huh."

He stared at her with a solemn expression. "Do you want to go?"

Oh, my precious son. "If *you* do."

JUNE 7
Jackson, Wyoming

IT WAS LATE Friday afternoon when the small plane from Salt Lake City, Utah, started to make its descent. The pilot came on over the intercom. "Ladies and gentlemen, you're about to land at the only commercial airport located inside a U.S. national park."

Johnny reached for Tracy's hand.

"We're flying over the Greater Yellowstone region with forests, mountains, wilderness areas and lakes as far as the eye can see. Ahead is the majestic Teton Range. You'll see the Snake River and the plains around it in a patchwork of colors."

Tracy found it all glorious beyond description, but when the Grand Teton came into view, knifing into the atmosphere, every passenger was struck dumb with awe.

"If you'll look below, we're coming up on Jackson Hole."

Seeing it for the first time, Tracy could understand the reason for its name. It was a narrow valley surrounded by mountains and probably presented a challenge for the pilot to land safely. She clung to Johnny's hand. Before long, their plane touched down on the tarmac and taxied to the gate.

After it came to a stop, she unclasped their seat belts. "Are you all right, honey?"

He nodded. "That was scary."

"I agree, but we're here safe and sound now." She reached for her purse above the seat. "Let's go."

They followed the other eight passengers out the exit to the tiny terminal. The second they entered the one-story building, she heard a deep male voice call her name.

Tracy looked to her left and saw a tall, lean cowboy in jeans and a Western shirt. With his hard-muscled physique, he stood out from everyone else around him. This was no actor from a Western movie set. From his well-worn black Stetson to his cowboy boots, everything about him shouted authentic.

Johnny hugged her side. "Who's that?" he whispered.

The thirtyish-looking stranger must have heard him because he walked over and reached out to shake Johnny's hand. "My name's Carson Lundgren. I'm the man who sent your mom the letter inviting you to the ranch. You have to be John." His eyes traveled over Tracy's son with a compassion she could feel.

He nodded.

"Have you found your stomach yet, or is it still up in the air?" His question made Johnny laugh. He couldn't have said anything to break the ice faster. "I'll tell you a secret. When I was your age and my grandpa took me on my first plane ride around the Teton Valley, I didn't find my stomach for a week, but you get used to it."

While her son was studying him in amazement, his hot blue gaze switched to Tracy. Her medium height meant she had to look up at him. He removed his hat, revealing a head of dark blond hair, attractively disheveled.

"Mrs. Baretta, it's a pleasure to meet you and your son."

"We're excited to be here, Mr. Lundgren, and honored by the invitation. Please call us Johnny and Tracy."

"Terrific. You can call me Carson." He coughed for a

few seconds. "Forgive me. I do that quite often. Something I picked up overseas. It's not contagious."

Johnny's head tipped back to look at him. "You used to be a marine like my dad, huh?"

"Yup. I have a picture of him and his buddies." He pulled a wallet from his pocket. Inside was a small packet of photos. He handed one to Johnny. "I didn't know him, because I'd just been transferred in from another detail when the picture was taken. But I learned Tony Baretta came from a long line of firefighters and had the reputation of being the toughest marine in the unit. You can keep it."

"Thanks." His young voice trembled. "I loved him."

"Of course you did, just like I loved my grandpa."

"What about your dad?"

"My parents were killed in a freak flood when I was a baby. My grandparents raised me. After my grandma died, it was just Grandpa and me."

"Didn't you have cousins?"

"Nope. How about you?"

He looked at Tracy. "How many do I have, Mom?"

"Let me think. Twenty-two-and-a-half at the present counting."

Carson's brows lifted. "You're lucky. I would have given anything for just one."

That sounded like a lonely statement. Tracy looked over Johnny's shoulder while he studied the photograph. She counted a dozen soldiers in uniform. When she found Tony, her eyes glazed over.

Johnny's next remark surprised her because it wasn't about his father. "You look different in a helmet."

"We were just a bunch of metal heads." Johnny

laughed again. "None of us liked them much, but the gear kept us protected."

"I like your cowboy hat better," Johnny said before putting the picture in his pocket.

Carson grinned. The rugged rancher was one striking male. "Shall we get you a hat like it on our way to the ranch?"

"Could we?" Tracy hadn't seen him exhibit this kind of excitement in over a year.

"Of course. You can't live on a dude ranch without your duds."

"What are duds?"

"Everything I'm wearing plus a lot of other things."

"What other things?"

"Chaps and gloves for bull riding."

"Do you ride *bulls?*" Johnny's eyes grew huge.

"I used to when I was training for the rodeo."

"Can I see one?"

"Sure. I'm planning on taking you to the Jackson rodeo on the last night you're here. You'll see barrel racing and steer wrestling too."

"Mom!" Johnny cried out with uncontained excitement.

"Come on, partner. Let's get your luggage and we'll go shopping."

"As long as you let me pay for everything," Tracy interjected.

He shook his head. "While you're here, we take care of everything for the kids."

"I can't allow that," she insisted. "A free vacation is one thing, but I'll be buying whatever Johnny wants or needs while we're here."

His blue eyes flickered before he shoved his hat back on. "Yes, ma'am."

Johnny had to hurry to keep up with the larger-than-life cowboy whose long powerful legs reached the baggage claim in a few strides.

"I bet you're hungry. Do you like buffalo burgers?"

"Buffalo?"

Tracy tried to hide her smile. Her son turned to her. "Mom? Are there really buffalo burgers?"

"Yes, but I've never eaten one."

He looked at Carson. "Are they good?"

"Do you like hamburgers?"

"Yes."

"Then you don't have anything to worry about." His lips twitched when he glanced at Tracy. "Which bags are yours?"

"The two blue ones and the matching shoulder bag."

"Here you go." He handed Johnny the shoulder bag and he reached for the other two. "The van's right outside." Her son had to be surprised, but she noticed he carried the bag like a man and kept up with Carson.

They walked outside into a beautiful, still evening. She loved the dry air, but could tell they were at a much higher elevation than they were used to. The mountain range loomed over the valley, so close she felt dwarfed by it.

Their host shot her a concerned glance. "Are you all right, Tracy?"

"I'm fine."

"The air's thinner than you're used to in Ohio."

"It isn't that as much as the mountains. They're so close to us, I feel like they're pressing in."

"I had the same feeling in reverse when we reached

Afghanistan and I got off the plane with no mountains in sight where we landed. I felt like I was in a constant state of free-fall. Without landmarks, it took me a while to get my bearings."

"Coming from a paradise like this, I can't even imagine it. Tony and I grew up on Lake Erie. He told me that after he got there, with no water in sight, he went into shock."

"We all did," Carson murmured. "On every level."

She hadn't talked to anyone about Tony's war experiences in a long time and hadn't wanted to. But this was different, because Carson had made a connection by being there, too. With that photo in his pocket, her son wouldn't forget, either.

He guided them to the dark green van. It was easy to spot, with the same logo on the side she'd seen on the envelope. He stowed their luggage in the rear, then helped her and Johnny into the backseat.

"First we'll head to the Silver Dollar Grill for some grub."

"What's grub?"

"That's what the ranch hands call food. After that, we'll drive over to the Boot Corral and get you outfitted. I think they even sell some mustangs."

"What are those?"

"Cap guns. When I was little I had a mustang and played like I was Hopalong Cassidy."

"Who was he?"

"Hoppy was a straight shooter and my favorite cowboy."

His dark head jerked around to Tracy. "Did you ever see Hoppy?"

Her quick-study son was soaking up all this fascinating information like a sponge. "When I was a little girl my father had some old Western movies and we'd watch them. Hoppy was the good guy who always played fair. He had white hair and wore a black cowboy hat."

"Hey—" He looked at Carson. "So do you!" Johnny cried in delight.

"Yup. I wanted to be just like him."

Tracy smiled. "He had two partners. One old duffer was called Gabby, and the young one was called Lucky. I was crazy about Lucky. He was tall and good-looking."

Johnny giggled.

"All the girls loved Lucky," Carson commented. "That was mushy stuff."

"Yeah," her son agreed with him.

"Now we know where Lucky got his name, don't we." Carson winked at her. "I have a couple of old Western movies on CD, and you can see him in action."

"Can we watch it tonight?"

"No, young man," Tracy intervened. "When we get to the ranch, we're both going straight to bed. It's been a long day."

"Your mom's right, Johnny. Tonight we'll load you up with one of those mustangs Hoppy used to use and all the ammo you want. In a few days, when I take you out riding, we'll scout for bad guys."

"I've never been on a horse."

"Never?"

"No."

Those blue eyes flicked to Tracy. "How about you?"

She shook her head. "I'm afraid we're a pair of the greenest greenhorns you ever met. When I saw your dude ranch logo on the envelope, I never dreamed Johnny and I would end up spending time on one."

His chuckle slid in under the radar to resonate through her. "With a couple of lessons that problem will be rectified and you can explore to your heart's content. There's no place like it on Earth. My grandfather used to tell me that, but it wasn't until I came home for his funeral last November that I realized what he meant." She heard the tremor in his voice.

He'd had a recent loss, too. Tracy sensed he was still suffering.

Carson broke their gaze and looked back at Johnny. "We have four ponies. I think I know the one that will be yours while you're here."

"Yippee!" Until this moment Tracy hadn't thought her son's face would ever light up like that again.

"You can name her," he added.

Johnny looked perplexed. "I don't know any girl names for a horse."

"You think about it tonight, and tell me tomorrow."

"Okay."

Carson smiled at both of them before closing the door. She heard him cough again before he walked around the car and got in behind the wheel. Something he'd picked up after being deployed, he'd said.

"What makes you cough so much?"

He looked over at Johnny. "There were a lot of contaminants in the air in Afghanistan. Stuff like smoke and toxins. Some of the soldiers breathed too many bad fumes and our lungs were injured. When I got sick, I was sent to a hospital in Maryland for special treatment. That's where I met Ross and Buck. We became such good friends, we decided to go into business together after we got home."

"Oh. Does it hurt?" Johnny almost whispered the last word.

"It did in the beginning, but not so much now. We're a lot better than we used to be."

"I'm glad."

Her sweet boy.

"Me too, son."

War was a ghastly reality of life. Carson and his friends were some of the fortunate ones who came home alive. She admired them for getting on with living despite their problem, for unselfishly wanting to make a difference in her life and Johnny's. What generous, remarkable men....

As he drove them toward the town, she stared out the window. With night coming on, the Tetons formed a giant silhouette against the growing darkness. She shivered in reaction.

Instead of Johnny, who carried on an animated conversation with their host about horses and breeds, *she* was the one who felt oddly troubled for being so far away from home and everything familiar to her. This new world had taken her by surprise in ways she couldn't understand or explain.

Chapter Two

Carson pulled the van in front of the newly erected cabin designated for the Baretta family. He'd asked one of the girls from town who did housekeeping to keep the lights on after she left. Earlier he'd made certain there were snacks for the Barettas, and in the minifridge he'd stored plenty of juices and sodas.

It had grown quiet during the drive from Jackson to the ranch. When he looked in the rearview mirror, he saw Johnny was fast asleep. The cute little guy had finally conked out.

Carson got out and opened the rear door of the van. His gaze met Tracy's. He handed her the key. "If you'll open the door, I'll carry him inside."

She gathered the sacks with their purchases and hurried ahead of him. The front room consisted of a living room with a couch and chairs and a fireplace. On one wall was an entertainment center with a TV, DVD player and a supply of family movies for the guests. Against the other wall was a rectangular table and chairs. A coffeemaker and a microwave sat on one end near the minifridge.

The back hallway divided into two bedrooms and a bathroom. He swept past her to one of the bedrooms and deposited Johnny on one of the twin beds. He didn't weigh a lot. The boy was built like his father and had the brunette hair and brown eyes of his Italian ancestry.

He was Tony Baretta's son, all right. You wouldn't think he belonged to his blonde mother until you saw his facial features. Pure northern European, like hers. An appealing combination.

As for Tracy Baretta with her gray-green eyes, she was just plain appealing. Unexpectedly lovely. Womanly.

In the guys' desire to make this week memorable for their family, he simply hadn't counted on...*her.*

While she started taking off Johnny's shoes, Carson went back outside to bring in the luggage. "If you need anything, just pick up the phone and one of the staff will answer, day or night. Tomorrow morning, walk over to the main ranch house. We serve breakfast there from six to nine in the big dining room. Lunch is from twelve to two and dinner from five to eight.

"I'll watch for you and introduce you to the guys. They're anxious to meet you. After that, we'll plan your day. For your information, different sets of tourists are staying in the other cabins, but you're the only family here at our invitation for this coming week. In another month we're expecting our next family."

She followed him to the front door of the cabin. "Thank you for everything, Carson." Her voice cracked. "To be honest, I'm overwhelmed. You and your friends are so good to do what you're doing. I could never repay you for this." Tears glistened in her eyes. "From the time you met us at the airport, my son has been a different child. That picture meant everything to him."

To her, too, he wagered.

"Losing your husband has been a traumatic experience for you. My friends and I know that. Even though anyone in the military, and their family, is aware that death can come, no one's ready for it. When our division heard about Tony, we all suffered because he left a wife and child. We're like brothers out there. When one gets hurt, we all hurt."

She nodded. "Tony talked a lot about his buddies. He was so proud to serve with you."

"That goes both ways. There's no way we can bring him back to you, but we'd like to put a smile back on your son's face, if only for a little while. I promise that while you're here, we'll treat him with sensitivity and try to keep him as happy and safe as is humanly possible."

She smiled warmly. "I know you will." He could feel her sincerity.

"We have other guests coming to the ranch all the time, but you and Johnny are our special visitors. No one knows that we've nicknamed this place the Daddy Dude Ranch. What we hope to do is try to lend ourselves out as dads to take some of the burden off you."

Her hazel eyes glistened with tears. "You've already done that. Did you see Johnny in that shop earlier, walking around in those Western clothes with that huge smile on his face? He put that cowboy hat on just the way you wear yours and tried walking like you do in his new cowboy boots. I never saw anything so cute in my life."

"You're right about that." Carson thought he'd never seen anything so beautiful as the woman standing in front of him.

"That mustang we bought was like giving him a bag of Oreos with just the centers."

Carson chuckled. "He likes those?"

"He has a terrible sweet tooth."

"Didn't we all?"

"Probably. Let me say once again how honored I feel that you picked our family. It was a great thrill to receive your letter. Already I can tell Johnny is thriving on this kind of attention. What you're doing is inspirational."

From the light behind them, he could pick out gold and silver filaments in the hair she wore fastened at her nape. Opposites had attracted to produce Johnny. Carson was having trouble concentrating on their conversation.

"Thank you, Tracy. He's a terrific boy."

"For a man who's never had children, you're so good with him. Where did you learn those skills?"

"That's because my grandfather was the best and put up with me and my friends. If it rubbed off on me, then I'm glad."

"So am I. Johnny's having a marvelous time."

"I had a wonderful evening, too, believe me. If I didn't say it before, welcome to the Teton Valley Ranch. Now I'll wish you good-night."

He left quickly and headed for the van. It was a short drive to the main house where he'd been raised. He pulled in back and entered through the rear door. Ross was still in the den working on the accounts when Carson walked down the hall.

"Hey—" Ross called to him. "How did everything go with the Baretta family?"

"Hang on while I grab a cup of coffee and I'll tell you."

"I could use one, too. I'll come with you." They walked down another hall to the kitchen, both coughing up a storm en route.

"Where's Buck?"

"In town, getting some more materials to do repairs on the bunkhouse. He should have been back by now."

"Unless he made a stop at Bubba's Barbecue to see you-know-who."

"Since his last date with Nicole after she got off work, I don't think he's interested after all. She called here twice today. He didn't return the calls."

"Why am I not surprised?" Buck was a confirmed bachelor, as were they all.

Carson grabbed a donut. The cook, who lived in town, had gone home for the night. They had the kitchen to themselves. No sooner had he brewed a fresh pot of coffee than they heard Buck coughing before he appeared in the doorway.

In a minute the three of them filled their mugs and sat down at the old oak table where Carson had eaten most of the meals in his life with his grandparents. Until he'd gone into the Marines. But he didn't want to think about that right now. The guys wanted to know how things had gone at the airport.

"Johnny Baretta is the cutest little six-year-old you ever saw in your life." He filled them in on the details. "He swallowed a couple of bites of that buffalo burger like a man."

They smiled. "How about his mom?" Buck asked.

Carson took a long swig of his coffee. How to answer them... "Nice."

Ross burst into laughter. "That's it? Nice?"

No. That *wasn't* it. "When you meet her in the morn-

ing at breakfast, you can make your own assessment."
He knew exactly how they'd react. "She's very grateful."

Both men eyed him with speculation. Buck drained
his mug. "What's the plan for tomorrow?"

"After breakfast I'll take them over to the barn and
give them a riding lesson. Later in the day I thought
they'd appreciate a drive around the ranch to get their
bearings, and we'll go from there. What about you?"

"I'm going to get the repairs done on the bunkhouse
in the morning. Then I'll be taking the Holden party
on an overnight campout. We'll be back the next day."

Ross got up from the table to wash their mugs.
"The Harris party is planning to do some fly fishing.
If Johnny wants to join us, come and find me."

"That boy is game for anything." Tony Baretta had
been a lucky man in many ways. He shouldn't have been
the one to get killed by a roadside bomb. Carson could
still hear Johnny say, *I loved my dad.* The sound of the
boy's broken heart would always haunt him.

He pushed himself away from the table, causing
Buck to give him a second glance. "What's up?"

Carson grimaced. "When we thought up this idea, we
hadn't met these people. It was pure hell to look into that
little guy's eyes last night and see the sadness. I hadn't
counted on caring so m—" Another coughing spell attacked him, preventing him from finishing his thought.

He needed his inhaler and headed for the hall. "I'll
see you two in the morning." Ross would do a security
check and lock up.

Carson had taken over his grandfather's room on the
ground floor. The other two had bedrooms on the second floor. It was a temporary arrangement. At the end of
the summer they'd assess their dude ranch experiment.

If they decided it wasn't working, either or both of them could still work on the ranch and make Wyoming their permanent home. He'd already told them they could build their own houses on the property.

Once he reached the bedroom, he inhaled his medication and then took a shower followed by a sleeping pill. Tonight he needed to be knocked out. His old friend "guilt" was back with a double punch. He couldn't make up to his grandfather for the years away, and no power on earth could bring Johnny's father back.

Carson must have been out of his mind to think a week on the ranch was going to make a dent in that boy's pain. He knew for sure Tracy was barely functioning, but she was a mother who'd do anything to help her child get on with living. She had that hidden strength women were famous for. He could only admire her and lament his lack of it.

After getting into bed, he lay back against the pillow with a troubled sigh. He realized it was too late to decide not to go through with the dude ranch idea for the fallen soldiers' families. He and the guys had put three months of hard labor into their project to get everything ready. The Barettas had already arrived and were now asleep in one of the new cabins.

They had their work cut out for them, but Carson was afraid they'd fall short of their desire to make a difference. In fact he was *terrified*.

THE NEXT MORNING Tracy pulled on a pair of jeans and a sage-colored cotton sweater. It had a crew neck and long sleeves. She'd done some shopping before this trip. If it got hot later in the day, she'd switch to a blouse. The cowboy boots she'd bought last evening felt strange and would take some getting used to.

After giving her hair a good brush, she fastened it at the nape with a tortoise-shell clip. Once she'd put on lotion and applied lipstick, a shade between coral and pink, she was ready for the day.

"Who's hungry for breakfast?" she asked, coming out of the bathroom into the sunny room with its yellow and white motif. But it was a silly question because Johnny didn't hear her. He'd been dressed for half an hour in his new duds, complete with a black cowboy hat and boots, and was busy loading his mustang again. Already he'd gone through a couple of rolls of caps, waking her up with a start.

She'd bought him three dozen rolls to keep him supplied, but at this rate he'd go through them by the end of the day. It was a good thing the cabins weren't too close together.

Tracy slipped the key in her pocket. "Come on, honey." She opened the door and immediately let out a gasp as she came face-to-face with the Grand Teton. In the morning sun it looked so different from last night when she'd had the sensation of it closing in on her. Against an impossibly blue sky, she'd never seen anything as glorious in her life.

Between the vista of mountains and the strong scent of sage filling the dry air, Tracy felt as if they'd been transported to another world. Even Johnny stopped fiddling with his cap gun to look. "Those sure are tall mountains!"

"They're magnificent!"

She locked the door and they started walking along the dirt road to the sprawling two-story ranch house in the distance. It was the kind you saw in pictures of the Old West, owned by some legendary cattle king.

"I hope they have cereal."

Tracy hoped they didn't. He needed to get off candy and sugar-coated cereal, his favorites when he could get away with it. His grandmother made all kinds of fabulous pasta, but he only liked boring mac and cheese out of the box. "Carson mentioned eggs, bacon and buckwheat pancakes."

"What's buckwheat?"

She smiled. "You'll have to ask him." The poor man had already answered a hundred questions last evening. She'd been surprised at his patience with her son.

Her eyes took in the tourist log cabins where she saw cars parked. Many of the outbuildings were farther away. Last night, Carson had pointed out the ranch manager's complex with homes and bunkhouses. He'd mentioned a shed for machinery and hay, a calving barn, horse barn and corrals, but it had been too dark to pick everything out. To Tracy the hundred-year-old ranch resembled a small city.

At least a dozen vehicles, from trucks, vans, and four-wheel-drives to a Jeep without a top and several cars, were parked at the rear of the ranch house. She kept walking with Johnny to the front, admiring the workmanship and the weathered timbers. The house had several decks, with a grove of trees to the side to provide shade. The first Lundgren knew what he was doing, to stake out his claim in this paradise.

They rounded the corner and walked up the steps to the entrance. An office was located to the left of the rustic foyer. At a glance to the right, the huge great room with a stone fireplace led into a big dining room with wagon-wheel chandeliers.

"Hi! Can I help you?"

Johnny walked over to the college-aged girl behind the counter. "Hi! We're waiting for Carson."

The friendly brunette leaned over to smile at him. "You must be Johnny Baretta from Ohio."

"Yup. What's your name?"

"Susan. Anything you need, you ask me. Mr. Lundgren told me to tell you to go right on through to the dining room and he'd meet you there."

"Thank you," Tracy spoke for both of them.

"Welcome to the ranch, Mrs. Baretta."

"We're thrilled to be here. Come on, honey."

They were almost to the dining room when a handsome, fit-looking man, probably Carson's age and height, came forward. Though he wore a plaid shirt and jeans, with his shorter cropped black hair she could imagine him in Marine gear. His brown eyes played over her with male interest before they lit on Johnny.

"I'm Ross Livingston, Carson's friend. You must be the brave guy who ate a buffalo burger last night."

"Well…" He looked at Tracy. "Not all of it," Johnny answered honestly. "It was too big."

"I know, and I'm impressed you got through most of it."

Tracy laughed and he joined her, provoking the same kind of cough she'd heard come out of Carson. "Excuse me," he said after it had subsided. "It's not contagious in case you were worried."

"We're not. Carson already explained."

"Good. He got detained on the phone, but he should

be here in a minute. Come into the dining room with me, Johnny, and we'll get you served."

They followed him. "Do you know if they have cereal?"

"Sure. What kind do you like?"

"Froot Loops."

"You're in luck."

"Goody!"

Tracy refrained from bursting his bubble. Tomorrow they'd choose something else.

Ross guided them across dark, vintage hardwood floors in keeping with the Western flavor to an empty table with a red-and-white-checked cloth. A vase of fresh white daisies had been placed on each table. She found this setting charming.

When he helped them to be seated, he took a chair and handed them Saturday's menu from the holder. "In a minute the waitress will come to take your order."

She scanned the menu.

"Mom? Do they have hot chocolate?"

Tracy couldn't lie. "Yes."

"Then that's what I want with my cereal."

"I'll let you have it if you'll eat some meat. There's sausage, bacon or ham."

"And brook trout," Ross interjected, smiling into her eyes as he said it.

She chuckled. "I think after the buffalo burger, we'll hold off on the fish for another day."

As he broke into laughter, the waitress came to the table, but she hadn't come alone. Their host had arrived without his hat, wearing another Western shirt in a tan color. The chiseled angles of his hard-boned features drew her gaze for the second time in twelve hours. He was all male.

"Carson!"

"Hey, partner—" He sat down next to Ross and made the introductions.

"Where's your hat?"

"I'll put it on after breakfast."

"I want to keep mine on."

"Except that it might be hard to eat with it," Tracy declared. "Let me put it on the empty chair until after."

"Okay."

The waitress took their orders and left.

Ross got up from the table. "Hey, Johnny, while you're waiting for your food, I'll take you out to the foyer and show you something amazing before I leave. Since I've already eaten, I have a group of guests waiting for me to take them fishing."

"What is it?" Ross had aroused his curiosity.

"Come with me and see."

"I'll be right back, Mom."

"Okay."

As they walked away, she heard Ross say, "I'm glad you came, Johnny. We're going to have a lot of fun while you and your mom are here."

"Your friend is nice," Tracy told Carson.

He studied her features for a moment, seeming to reflect on what she'd said. "He's the best. Right now he's showing Johnny the big moose head that was mounted years before I was born. It's the granddaddy of them all, but you don't see it until you're leaving to go outside."

"He's fascinated by the big animals."

"Did your husband hunt, or any of your family?"

"No."

"I've never been much of a hunter, either, but my grandfather allowed licensed hunters to use the land during the hunting season, so I do, too. I much prefer to see the elk and deer alive. There's great opportunity here to photograph the animals. I'll show Johnny lots of spots. He can hide in the trees and take pictures of squirrels and rabbits, all the cute little forest creatures."

"He'll go crazy."

"That's the idea."

To her consternation, Tracy found herself studying his rugged features and looked away. "There's so much to do here, it's hard to know where to start. When I read your brochure on the internet, I couldn't believe it."

He had an amazing white smile. "Most people can't do it all. They find something they love and stick to it. That'll be the trick with Johnny. We'll try him out on several things and see what he likes most."

"Mom—" He came running back into the dining room, bringing her back to the present. "You've got to see this moose! It's humongous!" That was Cory's favorite word.

"I promise I'll get a look at it when we go outside."

"Its head is as big as the Pierce's minicar!"

Carson threw back his head and laughed so hard, everyone in the room looked over. As for Tracy, she felt his rich male belly laugh clear through her stomach to her toes. The laugh set off another of his coughing spells. His blue eyes zeroed in on her. "Who are the Pierces?"

"Our neighbors down the street in Sandusky."

Johnny sat back down. "Ross thinks he looks like a supersize Bullwinkle."

"He's that, all right."

Tracy smiled at him. "I have a feeling you and Ross

are both big teases. Can I presume your other friend is just as bad?"

"He has his moments," he drawled. "You'll meet Buck tomorrow when he's back from taking some guests on an overnight campout."

"Can we go on one of those?"

Carson's brilliant blue gaze switched to Johnny. "I'm planning on it."

Johnny's face lit up. "I want to see that elk with the giant antlers."

"You liked that picture?"

"Yeah. It was awesome."

"I couldn't agree more, but I don't know if he's still around. My grandpa took that picture a few years ago. Tell you what. When we're out driving and hiking, we'll look for him."

The waitress came with their food. Tracy's omelet was superb. She ate all of it and was gratified to see Johnny finish his ham. Carson put away steak and eggs, then got up from the table.

"Give me five minutes and I'll meet you out in front in the Jeep. We'll drive over to the barn." He coughed for a moment. "Normally we'd walk, but I'm planning to give you a tour of the property after your riding lesson. It'll save time. The restrooms are down the hall from the front desk."

"Thank you. The breakfast was delicious by the way."

"I'm glad you enjoyed it." He turned to leave.

"See you in a minute, Carson! Don't forget your hat!"

That kid made him chuckle. He'd done a lot of it since last evening. More than he'd done in a long time.

He walked through the doors to the kitchen and nodded to the staff. After putting some bottled water and half a dozen oranges and plums in a bag, he headed down another hall to the bedroom for his Stetson.

Making certain he had his cell on him, he headed out the rear door of the ranch with more energy than usual. Susan would phone him if there were any problems. After stashing the bag in the backseat, he started the engine and took off.

Try as he might, when he drove around the gravel drive to the front, he couldn't take his eyes off Tracy Baretta. From the length of her sinuous body to her blond hair gleaming in the morning sun, she was a knockout. But she didn't seem to know it. That was part of her attraction.

"There's nothing wrong with looking," his grandfather used to say to him. "But if a woman's off-limits, then that's the way you keep it." Carson had adopted that motto and it had kept him out of a hell of a lot of trouble.

This woman was Tony Baretta's widow and still grieving for him.

Shut it off, Lundgren.

Johnny started toward him. "Can I ride in front with you?"

"You bet." He jumped out and went around to open both doors for them, trying to take his own advice as he helped Tracy into the backseat.

Once they got going, Johnny let out a whoop of excitement. "I've never ridden in a Jeep before. This is more fun than riding on a fire engine."

"I don't believe it."

"It's true!"

Carson glanced at him. "I've never been on one."

"If you come back to Ohio, my uncles will let you go on their ladder truck."

"Sounds pretty exciting. But wait till you ride a horse. You'll love it so much, you won't want to do anything else."

"What's your horse's name?"

"I've had a lot of them. My latest one is a gelding named Blueberry. He's a blue roan."

Johnny giggled. "You have a blue horse?"

"Seeing's believing. Wait till you meet your palomino. She's a creamy gold color with a white mane and tail." *Almost as beautiful as your mother.* "Have you thought of a name yet?"

"No."

"That's okay. It'll come to you."

They headed for the barn. He'd talked to Bert ahead of time. The pony had been put in the corral so Johnny would see it first off. He drove the Jeep around till they came to the entrance to the corral. There stood the pony in the sun. Carson stopped the Jeep.

"Oh, Johnny—look at that adorable pony!"

The boy stared for the longest time before scrambling out of the front seat. He'd left his mustang behind.

"Wait!" His mother hurried after him, but he'd already reached the fencing before she caught up to him.

Carson joined them. "Isn't she a little beauty?"

Johnny's head jerked toward him. The excitement on his face was worth a thousand words. "I'm going to call her Goldie."

"That's the perfect name for her." The pony walked right over to them. "Good morning, Goldie. This is Johnny. He's flown a long way to meet you."

Carson lifted the boy so he could reach over the

railing. "You notice that pretty white marking? That's her forelock. Watch what happens when I rub it. She's gentle and likes being touched."

The pony nickered and nudged closer. "See?"

Johnny giggled and carefully put out his hand to imitate Carson's gesture. He got the same reaction from Goldie who moved her head up and down, nickering more intensely this time.

"She loves it and wants you to do it some more."

As he patted the horse with increasing confidence, Tracy flashed Carson a smile. It came from her eyes as well as her mouth. That was a first.

He dragged his glance away with reluctance. "Come into the barn with me, Johnny. We'll go in the tack room to pick out her saddle."

"Tack room?"

Carson shared another smile with Tracy. "It's a room where we keep the saddles and bridles for the horses."

"Oh." Johnny jumped down. "We'll be right back, Mom."

Carson had a hunch the boy was hooked. You never knew. Some kids showed little interest or were too scared and didn't want to ride. This little guy was tough. *Like his father.*

"I'll be waiting."

Johnny asked a dozen questions while they gathered everything, impressing Carson with his bright mind that wanted to learn. This was a new world for Carson who, as an adult, had never spent time taking care of anyone's child. He found Johnny totally entertaining and quite wonderful.

As a kid, Carson had grown up around the children whose parents worked on the ranch, and of course, the neighbor's kids. A couple of the boys, including his best friend Jean-Paul, wanted to be rodeo champions. So did Carson, whose grandfather had been a champion and taught him everything he knew.

In between chores and school, they'd spent their free time on the back of a horse, learning how to be bull-doggers and bull riders. As they grew older there were girls, and later on women, prize money and championships. But it still wasn't enough. He'd wanted to get out and see the world. He'd joined the Marines on a whim, wanting a new arena.

Through it all, Carson had taken and taken, never giving anything back. The pain over his own selfishness would never go away, but Johnny's enthusiasm wouldn't allow him time to wallow in it.

He carried the equipment to the corral and put the bridle on Goldie. Johnny stood by him, watching in fascination. "Here you go. Hold the reins while I get her saddled."

The pony moved forward and nudged Johnny. He laughed and was probably scared to death, but he held on. "She likes you or she wouldn't do that. You'll get used to it."

Carson threw on the blanket, then the saddle. "Okay. Now I'd like you to walk around the corral leading Goldie. Just walk normally, holding on to the reins. She'll follow. It will help her to learn to trust you, because she's nervous. Do you want me to walk with you, or do you want to do it yourself?"

He thought for a minute. "I can do it."

"Fine."

The whole time this went on, Carson was aware of his mother watching in silence from the fence as her brave son did a slow walk around the enclosure without a misstep. At one point she took some pictures with her cell phone.

"Great job, Johnny. Now walk her to that feeding bag. Dig in and pull out a handful of oats. If you hold them out to her with your hand flat, she'll eat them without hurting you, but it'll tickle."

Johnny laughed nervously, but he did what Carson told him to do. In a minute he was giggling while the pony enjoyed her treat. "It feels funny." He heard Tracy laugh from the sidelines.

"You've made a friend for life, Johnny. Think you're ready to get up on her?" The boy nodded. "Okay." Now the next lesson was about to begin. "I'm going to seat you in the saddle, then I'll adjust the stirrups." Carson lifted him. "You hold on to the reins and the pommel. Are you all right? I know it seems a long way up. Did you ever fall off the tricky bars at school?"

"Yes."

"Well, this is a lot safer because you've got this pony under you and she loves you. She doesn't want you to fall. Okay if I let go of you?"

"Okay," he said in a shaky voice.

Carson took a few steps back, ready to catch him if he suddenly wanted to get off. But he didn't. "Good man."

"You look like a real cowboy!" his mother called out. "I'm so proud of you!"

"Thanks."

Moving to the front of the pony Carson said, "I'm going to take hold of the bridle and walk Goldie. You keep holding on to the pommel so you can feel what it's like to ride her. Does that sound okay to you?"

Johnny nodded, but was biting his lip.

"We'll only go a few feet, then we'll stop."

"Okay," the boy murmured.

Carson started to walk. Goldie cooperated. When he stopped, she stopped. "How did that feel? Do you want to keep going?"

"Yes."

"Good for you. I've seen ten-year-olds out here who started bawling their heads off for their moms about now." He moved again and just kept going until they'd circled the corral. "You just passed your first lesson with flying colors, Johnny." He heard clapping and cheers from Tracy.

A big smile broke out on his face. "Thanks. Can I go around by myself now?"

That's what he'd been hoping to hear, but you never knew. "Why not? Let me show you how to hold the reins. If she goes too fast, just pull back on them a little. Ready?" He nodded.

"I'm going to give Goldie a little tap on her hind quarters to get her going. Okay?"

"Yup."

Suddenly they were off at the same speed as before, but without his help. Carson walked over to the fence where Tracy was hanging over it.

"Hey—I'm doing it. I'm riding!" he cried out.

"You sure are," she called back. "I can't believe it!"

"It's easy, Mom." He circled one more time. "Now it's your turn."

Carson saw the expression on her face and chuckled. "Yeah, Mom. It's easy. Now it's time for you. Better not let your son show you up."

"He already has. I'm quaking in my new leather boots."

"I shivered my first time, too, but I promise it will be okay. Annie's a gentle, sure-footed mare."

She got down off the fence and walked around to enter the corral. Carson waited until Goldie had come up to him before he removed the boy's feet from the stirrups and pulled him off. "Give her a rub on the forelock, then she'll know you had a good time."

Johnny did his bidding without any hesitation. "Can I give her some more oats?"

"Of course." He handed him the reins. "Go ahead. You know what to do."

While he walked her over to the feed bag, Carson called to Bert to bring out Annie, and then he made the introductions. "Bert Rawlins, this is Tracy Baretta. Bert has been running the stable for years."

Tracy shook his hand. "It's a pleasure to meet you."

"The feeling's mutual, ma'am. Annie's saddled and ready to go."

Carson reached for the reins and handed them to Tracy. "Let's see how good a teacher I am."

There was more green than gray in her eyes today. They were suspiciously bright. "You already know. My son's over there feeding that pony like he's been living on this ranch for a month."

Nothing could have pleased Carson more. He watched her move in front of the bay and rub her forelock. She nickered on cue.

"This is my first time, Annie. Don't let me down." Pulling on the reins, she started walking around the corral just as her son had done.

Carson decided the brown horse with the black mane

and tail provided the perfect foil for her gleaming blond hair. When she came around, he helped her into the saddle and adjusted her stirrups. "Would you like me to walk you around?"

"I think I'll be all right." What did they say about a mother walking into a burning building for her child?

He handed her the reins and gave the horse's rump a tap. Annie knew what to do and started walking. Halfway around the arena, Carson knew Tracy would be all right.

"Hey, Mom—it's fun, huh?"

"It will be when I've had a few more lessons."

Annie kept walking toward Carson. He looked up at Tracy. "Want to go around one more time, pulling on the reins to the right or left?"

"Sure."

He was sure she didn't, but she was game.

"This time, give her a nudge with your heels and she'll go."

The second she made contact, Annie started out. It surprised Tracy, knocking her off balance, but she righted herself in a hurry.

"If she's going too fast, pull on the reins and she'll slow down."

Little by little she made it around the enclosure, urging the horse in one direction, then another.

"You're doing great, Mom!"

"You both are. I think that will be all for today."

Carson signaled Bert to take care of the horses. "Come on, Johnny." He walked over to help Tracy, but she was too quick for him. She flung her leg over and got down on her own. Whether she did it without thinking or didn't want help, he didn't know.

"Are we going for a Jeep ride now?"

"Would you like that, partner?"

"Yes. Then can we come back to see Goldie? I think she'll miss me."

Johnny was showing the first signs of a horse lover. Either it was in you, or it wasn't. "I'm sure she will."

The three of them got back in the Jeep. For the next hour, he gave them a tour of the property so they could get their bearings. Johnny talked up a storm while a quieter Tracy sat back and took in the sights. As they neared the ranch house, his cell phone rang. The caller ID indicated it was the district ranger for the Bridger-Teton National Forest.

"Excuse me for a minute. I have to take this," he said to them before answering. "Dave? What's up?"

"There's a man-made fire started up on the western edge of the forest bordering your property."

Carson grimaced. Tourist season always brought on a slew of forest fires.

"I've assembled two crews and am asking for any volunteers who can help stamp it out to meet up at the shadow rock trailhead," Dave continued. "There's not much wind. I think we can contain it before it spreads."

Before hanging up, Carson said, "I'll rustle up as many of the hands as I can and we'll be there shortly."

This would happen today, of all days. The hell of it was, with his disease, he didn't dare help fight the fire. Smoke was his enemy. All he could do was bring help and wear his oxygen apparatus.

Johnny looked at him. "Do you think I can take an-other ride on Goldie after dinner? I want to turn her in different directions and do stuff with her."

"I suppose that's up to your mother." Carson's gaze flicked to Tracy. "Did you hear that, Mom? What do you say?"

Chapter Three

Tracy heard it. In fact, she heard and saw so many things already, she was starting to experience turmoil. Johnny was eating up all the attention Carson showered on him. It would continue nonstop until next Saturday when they flew home.

With all their own family and work responsibilities, none of Johnny's uncles could give him this kind of time. Not even Tony had spent every waking hour with their son in the due course of a day. No father did, unless they were on vacation. Even then there were other distractions.

Few fathers had the skills or showed the infinite patience of this ex-marine rancher who seemed to be going above and beyond any expectations. He had to be a dream come true for her son, who'd been emotionally starving for a male role model since Tony's death.

When she'd accepted the invitation to come to the ranch, she hadn't realized these former soldiers would spend their own personal time this way. She had assumed the ranch staff would offer activities to entertain them. Period.

This was different.
Carson was different.

By giving Johnny that photo of his father, Carson had formed a bond with her son that wasn't going to go away. Carson might not see what was happening, but every moment invested for Johnny's sake increased her son's interest.

Tracy couldn't allow that to happen. Before long they'd be leaving this place, never to return. Johnny was still dealing with his father's death. They didn't need another crisis after they got home. She had to do something quickly to fix things before he got too attached to this incredible man. Tracy had to acknowledge that, so far, he *was* incredible, which was exactly what made her so uneasy.

While he'd driven them around the breathtaking property, giving them fruit and water, she'd sat in the back of the Jeep planning what she would say to Carson when she could get him alone. Another lesson at the corral after dinner was not an option.

Tonight after they'd eaten, she and Johnny would watch a movie in their cabin until he fell asleep. Then she'd phone Carson and have an important talk with him. Once he understood her concerns, he would make certain his partners spent equal time with Johnny. By the time he pulled up in front of their cabin to let them out, she felt more relaxed about her decision.

"I kept you longer than planned, but we're still in time for lunch."

Johnny looked up at him. "What are you going to have, Carson?"

"I think a grilled cheese sandwich and a salad."

"Me, too."

Since when? Tracy mused.

Carson tipped his Stetson. "See you two inside."

She slid out, not wanting to analyze why what he just did gave her a strange feeling in her tummy, as Johnny was wont to say. "Come on, honey. Don't forget your mustang."

To her relief, Carson drove off. "Let's use the restroom first, then maybe we'll find some other kids and you can play with them."

A few minutes later they entered the dining room. Ross was seated at a larger table with some tourists, including a couple of children. He waved her over. "Come and sit with us, Tracy. We're all going to do some more fishing after we eat and hope you'll join us."

Bless you, Ross.

"Johnny? Meet Sam Harris, who's seven, and Rachel Harris, who's nine. They're from Florida. This is Johnny Baretta from Ohio. He's six."

"I'm almost seven!"

Tracy smiled. "That's true. Your birthday is in a month." He'd be one of the older ones in his class in the fall.

After they sat down, Ross finished introducing her to Monica and Ralph Harris, who were marine biologists. The Tetons had to be a complete change of scenery for them, too.

Soon the waitress came over and took everyone's order. Carson still hadn't come. Tracy knew Johnny was looking for him.

Sam, the towheaded boy, glanced at Johnny. "How long are you here for?"

"A week."

"Same here. Then our parents have to get back to work."

"Oh."

"Where's your dad?" Rachel asked.

Johnny had faced this question many times, but Tracy knew it was always painful for him. "He died in the war."

"That's too bad," she said, sounding genuinely sad. "Do you like to fish?"

"My dad took me a couple of times."

"We'll catch our limit this afternoon," Ross chimed in, no doubt anxious to change the topic of conversation.

By the time lunch arrived, Carson had come into the dining room and walked over to their table, but he didn't sit down. Ross introduced him to everyone while they ate. "Mr. Lundgren's great-great-grandfather purchased this land in 1908 and made it into the Teton Valley Ranch."

"The ranch house was a lot smaller than this in the beginning," Carson informed them.

"You're sure lucky to live here," Sam uttered.

"We're lucky you came to visit."

Carson always knew the right thing to say to make everyone feel good.

"To my regret, something's come up and I won't be able to join you this afternoon, but Ross is an expert and will show all of you where to catch the biggest fish. When you bring them in, we'll ask the cook to fix them for your dinner. There's no better-tasting trout than a German brown."

"He ought to know," Ross interjected. "He was fishing the Snake with his grandpa when he was just a toddler."

Everyone laughed except Johnny, who'd become exceptionally quiet.

"Enjoy your day. See you later," Carson said. His

glance included Tracy and Johnny before he hurried out of the dining room.

"Where's he going?" her son whispered.

"I don't know, honey." Something had come up. Though he'd shown nothing tangible, she'd felt his tension. "He runs this ranch with his friends and has a lot of other things to do." *Thank heaven.*

"Do we have to go fishing?" He'd only eaten half of his grilled cheese and didn't touch the green salad, which was no surprise.

"Yes." Her automatic instinct had been to say no, because she was afraid to push him too hard. But right now she decided to take the psychologist's advice and practice a little tough love. "It'll be fun for both of us. I've never been fly fishing and want to try it."

"Okay," he finally muttered. At least he hadn't fought her on it. "But I bet I don't catch one."

"I bet you do. Think how fun it will be to phone your grandparents tonight and tell them everything."

This was the way their vacation was supposed to be. Doing all sorts of activities with different people. Unfortunately, Carson had gotten there first and had spoiled her son. Nothing and no one was more exciting than he was, even Tracy recognized that.

Ross got up from the table. "I'll bring the van in front and we'll go." He came around to her side. "Is everything all right?" He'd assumed there'd been a hard moment at the table for Johnny. He'd assumed correctly, but for the wrong reason. She couldn't tell Ross what was really going on inside Johnny, not when these wonderful marines were doing everything in their power to bring her son some happiness.

She smiled at him. For once this wasn't about Tony,

or Johnny's sensitivity to a child's question. This was about Carson. "Everything's fine. Honestly. See you in a minute."

Sam got out of his chair and came over to Johnny, who was putting another roll of caps into his mustang. "Where did you get that cap gun?"

"In Jackson. Carson took us."

He turned to his parents. "Can we go into town and buy one?"

"I want one, too," Rachel chimed in.

Their mother gave Tracy that "what are you going to do?" look. Tracy liked her. "Maybe after we're through fishing."

Tracy took her son aside. "Why don't you go out front and let them shoot your gun for a minute?"

"Do I have to?"

"No, but it's a good way to make friends, don't you think?"

A big sigh escaped. "I guess." He turned to Sam. "Do you guys want to try shooting some caps outside?"

"Heck, yes!"

They both ran out and Rachel followed. Tracy walked over to the parents who thanked her.

"I'm glad Johnny has someone to play with. After dinner we could all drive into town and take you to the Boot Corral. You can get a cap gun and cowboy hats there, in fact, everything Western."

"That's a wonderful idea!"

"I'm afraid my son would sleep in all his gear and new cowboy boots if I let him."

Both Harrises grinned as they headed out of the dining room for the foyer. "This is a fabulous place," Ralph commented. "I wish we could stay a month."

Tracy understood how he felt. She was grateful his children would be here for Johnny. If she could drum up enough activities that included them until they flew home, maybe a talk with Carson wasn't necessary. She needed to let things play out naturally before she got paranoid. No doubt other families with children would be staying here, too, and her worries would go away.

The next time Johnny brought up Carson's name, she'd impress upon him that the owner of the ranch had too many responsibilities to be on hand all hours of the day.

Unfortunately, his name surfaced after their wonderful trout dinner when they'd all decided to go into town and do some shopping.

"I don't want to go, Mom. Carson's going to give me another lesson on Goldie."

"But he's not here, honey. We'll have to wait until tomorrow. Tell you what. After we get back from town, you and the kids can go swimming. How does that sound?"

He thought about it for a minute before he said, "Okay." Convincing him was like pulling teeth, but he liked the Harris children well enough to give in.

As it turned out, once they were back from town loaded with hats, guns and more ammo than they could use in a week, they realized it was too cool outside to swim. Monica suggested they play Ping-Pong in the game room off the dining room.

Tracy agreed and told Johnny to go along with them. She'd come back to the ranch house as soon as she'd freshened up. When she walked in the bedroom for their jackets, her cell phone rang. She checked the caller ID. It had to be her mother-in-law calling.

"Hello, Sylvia?"

"No, it's Natalie. We came over for dinner before we leave on our trip in the morning. I'm using her phone to call because I can't find mine. How are you doing by now? Or, more to the point, how's Giovanni? Is he begging to go back home? I've wondered how he would handle things. I guess you realize our father-in-law is worried about him."

That was no news. Since Tony's death, his father had tried to step in as father and grandfather.

"If you want to know the truth, things are going so well it's got me scared."

"What do you mean?"

"Mr. Lundgren might be a former marine, but he's the owner of this ranch and is this amazing cowboy who's showing Johnny the time of his life. My son has a new hero."

"Already?"

"I'm afraid so. You wouldn't recognize him."

"Why afraid?"

"That was a wrong choice of words."

"I don't think so. How old is this guy?"

Natalie always got to the crux. "Maybe twenty-nine, thirty. I don't know."

"Is he a hunk?"

"Nat—"

"He *is!*"

"Listen. I'd love to talk more, but I don't have time. This nice couple with two children is watching out for Johnny in the game room and he's waiting for me."

"You mean he's playing on his own without *you?*"

"I know that sounds unbelievable. In a nutshell, he's

had his first horseback ride on the most beautiful golden pony you've ever seen, and he's in love with her."

"Her?"

"He named her Goldie. You should see him riding around in the saddle like a pro, all decked out in Western gear and a cowboy hat. We'll bring the same outfit home for Cory."

"You actually got him over his fear long enough to ride a horse?" She sounded incredulous. Tracy understood. Since Tony's death, Johnny showed reluctance to try anything new.

"Mr. Lundgren gave him his first lesson."

"How did he accomplish that?"

Tracy told her about the photo of his father Carson had given him at the airport. "That was the magic connection that built his trust."

"You're right. He sounds like some wonderful guy. What's his wife like?"

Tracy gripped the phone tighter. "He's not married. Now, I really have to go. Have a great time on your trip to New York. We'll talk when I get back. Give our love to the family. *Ciao,* Nat."

There were no words to describe the ex-marine that would do him justice, so it was better not to try. No sooner had she disconnected than the phone on the bedside table started ringing. She assumed it was the front desk calling. Maybe it was Monica. She picked up. "Hello?"

"Hi, Tracy. It's Carson. Am I disturbing you?"

His deep voice rumbled through her. She sank down on her twin bed. After discussing him with Natalie, she needed the support. "Not at all. I was just on my way over to the ranch house to play Ping-Pong with the others."

"That sounds fun," he said before he started coughing. "I'm sorry about today. I'd fully intended to take you fishing and give Johnny another horseback riding lesson."

She gripped the phone a little tighter. "Please don't worry about that. Ross did the honors. Even *I* caught a twelve-incher. It was my first time fly fishing. I must admit it was a real thrill to feel that tug and reel it in."

"How did it taste?"

"Absolutely delicious."

"That's good," he murmured before coughing again.

She moistened her lips nervously for no good reason. "I take it you had to deal with an emergency."

"You could say that. A couple of college kids out backpacking in the forest didn't do a good enough job of putting out their campfire. It took several crews of rangers and forest service workers to keep it from spreading too far onto ranch property."

Her breath caught. That was why she'd felt his tension at the table. "How much did it burn?"

"Only a few acres this time."

"*This* time?"

"It happens every year." Suddenly he was hacking again. "Some fires are more devastating than others."

"Does that mean you were breathing smoke all day?"

"No. I rounded up the hands and drove them to the fire in shifts, but I took oxygen with me."

"Even so, you shouldn't have been near there with your problem," she said before she realized her voice was shaking.

"There was no one else to do the job. Undeserving as I am, I have to try to save what my grandfather willed to me."

She got to her feet. "What do you mean by undeserving?"

"Forget my ramblings. It slipped out by accident."

"And I heard it, which means you inhaled too much smoke today and don't feel well. You ought to be in bed."

"A good night's sleep is all I need. I'll let you go so you can join your son. It would be better not to tell him about the fire."

"Agreed." She couldn't let him hang up yet. "Carson, how long were you in the hospital?"

"About five weeks. From the end of January to the beginning of March."

"Were you all suffering from the same illness?"

"On our ward, yes."

His cough worried her. "Are you getting better?"

"We're certainly better than we were when we were flown in."

"I mean, are you going to get well?"

"We don't know."

She frowned. "You mean the doctor can't tell you?"

"Not really. They're doing studies on us. The day before we left the hospital, a general came to talk to us about asking Congress for the funding to help our cause."

"The Congress doesn't do enough," she muttered.

"Well, at least he came to our floor and said he's rooting for us, so that's better than nothing."

"Then you could have a lifelong ailment."

"That's right, but we can live with it, even if no one

else can. The ranch house gets pretty noisy when the three of us have a coughing fit together."

He tried to make light of it, but she wasn't laughing. "You're very brave."

"If you want to talk brave, let's talk about your husband. Why did he join the Marines?"

"His best friend went into the military and got killed by friendly gunfire. It tore Tony apart. He decided to join up to finish what his friend had started. We were already married, but I could tell he wanted it more than anything. We were lucky to go to Japan together before he was deployed to Afghanistan. It doesn't happen often that a marine can go there with his wife."

"You're right."

"During 9/11 I saw those firefighters run into those torched buildings and I wondered how they did it. Then I met Tony and understood. It's in his genes, I guess."

"Those genes saved lives, Tracy. That's why you can't talk about him in the same breath you talk about me and the guys. We're no heroes."

But they were.

"You shouldn't have gone near that fire today."

"That's the second time you've said it."

"I'm sorry. Johnny's been worried about you, too."

"Tracy," he said in a deep voice, "I appreciate your concern more than you know. I haven't had anyone worry about me in a long time. Thanks for caring. We'll see each other at breakfast. Good night."

He hung up too fast for her to wish him the same. Afraid he'd be up all night coughing, she knew that if she didn't hurry to the game room she'd brood over his condition. And his state of mind, which was none of her business and shouldn't be her concern. But to her chagrin, she couldn't think about anything else on her way to the ranch house.

CARSON HAD MEDICATED himself before going to bed, but he woke up late Sunday morning feeling only slightly better. It wasn't just his physical condition due to the smoke he'd inhaled the day before, despite the oxygen. When he'd phoned Tracy last night, he hadn't realized how vulnerable he'd been at the time. His sickness had worn him down and caused him to reveal a little of his inner turmoil, something he regretted.

She was a guest on the ranch. He was supposed to be helping to lift her burden for the week instead of talking about himself.

He grabbed his cell phone to call his ranch foreman and get an update on the progress with the fencing in the upper pasture. After they chatted for a few minutes, he dragged his body out of bed to shower and shave.

Once dressed, he walked through the ranch house to the kitchen and poured himself some coffee. He talked to the cook and kitchen help while he drank it, then entered the dining room and discovered a few guests still eating, but no sign of Tracy or Johnny. Ross would know what was going on.

Carson went to the office, but the place was empty. Since Buck wouldn't be back until lunchtime, he headed for the foyer to talk to Susan. "How's everything going?"

"Great!"

"Have you seen Ross?"

"Yes. Another couple of groups went fishing with him. Did you know that by this evening we'll be all booked up?"

"That's the kind of news I like to hear."

Like most ranches, the cattle operation on the Teton Valley Ranch had little, if any, margin. But the value of the land kept rising faster than the liability from raising cattle. It was either sell the hay, grass and cows to someone else, or borrow on the land when the market was down. In time he hoped the dude ranch idea would bring in its own source of revenue.

"Johnny Baretta was asking about you this morning. He can't wait for another horseback riding lesson."

That news pleased him even more. "Do you have any idea where he and his mother might be?"

"I heard him and the Harris children talking about going swimming. You should have seen how cute they all looked in their cowboy outfits when they came in for breakfast."

"I can imagine. Talk to you later."

He walked outside and headed around the other side of the house to the pool area. The swimming pool had been Buck's idea and was a real winner for children and people who simply wanted to laze about. The kids' shouts of laughter reached his ears before he came upon the two families enjoying the water.

"Carson!"

Johnny's shriek of excitement took him by surprise and touched him. "Hey, partner."

The boy scrambled out of the pool and came running over to him. Above his dark, wet hair he saw Tracy's silvery-gold head as she trod water. Their eyes met for a brief moment, causing a totally foreign adrenaline rush. "Can we go horseback riding now?"

"That's the plan," he said before breaking the eye contact.

Like clockwork, the other two children hurried over to him dripping water. "Will you take us riding, too?"

He chuckled. It brought on another coughing spell. "Of course. Anyone who wants a lesson, meet me at the corral in fifteen minutes!" he called out so the parents would hear him. They waved back in acknowledgment. As he turned to leave, he heard Rachel ask Johnny why Carson coughed so much.

"Because he breathed all this bad stuff in the war."

"What kind of stuff?" Sam wanted to know.

"Smoke and other junk."

"Ew. I hope I never have to go."

"I wish my dad had never joined the Marines." Johnny's mournful comment tore Carson apart.

He hurried back inside the ranch house to grab a bite of breakfast in the kitchen. While he downed bacon and eggs, he phoned Bert and asked him to start saddling Goldie and two of the other ponies.

After they hung up, he packed some food and drinks in a basket. In a minute, he left through the back door and placed the basket in the back of the truck, then climbed in. The interior still smelled of acrid smoke.

If the kids wanted some fun after their lesson, he'd let them get in the back and he'd drive them to the pasture to see the cattle. When he'd been a boy, he'd enjoyed walking around the new calves and figured they would, too.

When he reached the barn, he saddled Annie, but held off getting more horses ready for the Harrises. They might not want to ride, only watch their children.

Another lesson for Tracy and her son ought to be enough for them to take a short ride down by the Snake

River tomorrow. With enough practice, they'd be able to enjoy half-day rides around the property.

If Johnny could handle it, they'd camp out in the Bridger-Teton forest where there were breathtaking vistas of the surrounding country. Even if the journey would be bittersweet, he longed to show them his favorite places. Since joining the Marines, he hadn't done any of this.

Once Annie's bridle was on, he grasped the reins and walked her outside to the corral where Bert had assembled the ponies. In the distance, he saw the children running along the dirt road toward them. All three were dressed in their cowboy outfits.

Johnny reached him first. "Do you think Goldie missed me?"

"Why don't you give her forelock a rub and find out?"

Without hesitation he approached the golden palomino. "Hi, Goldie. It's me." He reached out to touch her. The pony nickered and nudged him affectionately. "Hey—" He turned to Carson. "Did you see that? She really likes me!"

While Burt grinned, Carson burst into laughter. It ended in a coughing spasm, but he didn't care. "She sure does."

"I'm going to feed her some oats." Seizing the reins without fear, he walked her over to the feed bag.

Knowing Bert would keep an eye on him, Carson approached the fence. Beneath the brim of his Stetson, his gaze fell on Tracy whose damp hair was caught back with a hair band. This morning she wore a tangerine-colored knit top and jeans her beautiful figure did amazing things for. "Are you ready for your next lesson?"

"I think so." Her smoky green eyes smiled at him before she entered the corral.

"Would you like some help mounting?"

"Thank you, but I'd like to see if I can do this on my own first."

This was the second time she hadn't wanted him to get too close. The first time he might have imagined it, but the second time led him to believe she was avoiding contact. He forced himself to look at the Harrises, who'd just come walking up.

"Should I ask Bert to saddle some horses for you?"

They shook their heads. Ralph leaned over the fence. "We've been riding before. Right now, we just want to see how the kids do."

"Understood." He turned to Johnny. "Hey, partner—why don't you help me show Rachel and Sam what you do before you get on."

"Sure! Which pony do you guys want?"

"That was a good question to ask them, Johnny."

Sam cried, "Can I have the brown one with the black tail?"

"Bruno is a great choice."

"I like the one with the little ears and big eyes. It's so cute."

Carson nodded. "That dappled gray filly is all yours, Rachel. Her name is Mitzi."

The children loved the names.

"Okay, Johnny. What do they do now?"

"They have to rub their noses so the ponies will know they like them."

The next few minutes were pure revelation as Tracy's son took the kids through the drill, step by step, until they were ready to mount.

Ridiculous as it was, Carson felt a tug on his emotions because Johnny had learned his lesson so quickly and was being such a perfect riding instructor. He glanced at Tracy several times. Without her saying anything, he knew she was bursting with motherly pride.

Soon all four of them were astride their horses. They circled the corral several times and played Follow the Leader in figure eights, Johnny's idea. Carson lounged against the fence next to the Harrises, entertained by the children who appeared to be having a terrific time. Since Tracy rode with them, Carson had a legitimate reason to study her without seeming obvious.

He threw out a few suggestions here and there, to help them use their reins properly, but for the most part, the lesson was a big success. Eventually he called a halt.

"It's time for a rest," he announced and was met with sounds of protest. "Bert will help you down. I know it's fun, but you need a break and so do the ponies. I'll give you another lesson before dinner. Right now, I thought you might like to ride to the upper pasture with me and see some Texas Longhorns."

Johnny looked perplexed. "What are those?"

"Beef cattle."

"We're not in Texas!" Sam pointed out.

"Nope, but they were brought from there to this part of the country years ago. Want to get a look at the herd?"

"Yeah!" they said with a collective voice.

He turned to the Harrises. "I'll bring them back for lunch. You can come along, or you're welcome do something else."

Ralph smiled. "If you don't mind, I think we'd like to take a walk."

"Good. Then we'll meet you back at the ranch around one o'clock."

While they talked to their children about being on their best behavior, Carson walked over to Tracy who'd once again gotten off her horse without assistance. "Are you going to ride with us?"

"Please, Mom?" Johnny's brown eyes beseeched her.

Apparently she had reservations. Maybe she hadn't been around other men since her husband's funeral and didn't feel comfortable with him or any man yet. Operating on that assumption he said, "I was going to let the kids ride in the truck bed. If you're with them, you can keep a close eye on what goes on. Those bales of hay will make a good seat for you."

She averted her eyes. "That ought to be a lot of fun."

Johnny jumped up and down with glee. "Hey, guys— we're going to ride in the back of the truck!" The other two sounded equally excited.

Pleased she'd capitulated, Carson walked over to the truck and lowered the tailgate. One by one he lifted the children inside. Before she could refuse him, he picked her up by the waist and set her down carefully. Their arms brushed against each other in the process, sending warmth through his body. After she scrambled to her feet, he closed the tailgate and hurried around to the cab.

With his pulse still racing, he started the engine and took off down the road, passing the Harrises. The children sat on the bales and clung to the sides of the truck while they called out and waved. Through the truck's rear window, Carson caught glimpses of her profile as she took in the scenery. Haunted by her utter femininity, he tried to concentrate on something else. Anything else.

There'd been a slew of women in his life from his teens on. One or two had held his interest through part of a summer, but much to his grandfather's displeasure, he'd never had the urge to settle down. It had been the same in the military.

Carson couldn't relate to the Anthony Barettas of this world, who were already happily married when deployed. Though foreign women held a certain fascination for Carson, those feelings were overshadowed by his interest in exotic places and the need to experience a different thrill.

Then came the day when his restlessness for new adventures took a literal hit from the deathly stench of war. Suffocation sucked the life out of him, extinguishing former pleasures, even his desire to be with a woman. Of no use to the military any longer, he'd been discharged early but had returned to the ranch too late to make up to his grandfather for the lost time.

Since he'd flown home from Maryland, the idea of inviting the Baretta family and others like them to the ranch had been the only thing helping him hold on to his sanity. Giving them a little pleasure might help vindicate his worthless existence, if only for a time.

Never in his wildest imagination did he expect Tony Baretta's widow to be the woman who would arouse feelings that, to his shock, must have been lying dormant since he'd become an adult.

Somehow, in his gut, he'd sensed her importance in his life from the moment they'd met at the airport. Nothing remotely like this had ever happened to him before. He couldn't explain what was going on inside him, let alone his interest in one little boy. But whatever he was experiencing was so real he could taste it and feel it.

Next Saturday they'd be flying back to Ohio. He already felt empty at the thought of it, which made no sense at all.

Chapter Four

After passing through heavily scented sage and rolling meadows, the truck wound its way up the slopes of the forest. The smell of the hay bales mingled with the fresh fragrance of the pines, filling the dry air with their distinctive perfume.

To the delight of both Tracy and the children, they spotted elk and moose along the way. Carson slowed down the truck so they could get a good look. Rabbits hopped through the undergrowth. The birdsong was so noisy among the trees, it was like a virtual aviary. Squirrels scrambled through the boughs of the pines. Chipmunks chattered. Bees zoomed back and forth.

Tracy looked all around her. The earth was alive.

Life was burgeoning on every front. She could feel it creeping into her, bringing on new sensations that were almost painful in their intensity, sensations she'd thought never to experience again.

For so long she'd felt like the flower in the little vase Johnny had brought home from school for Mother's Day. The pink rose had done its best, but after a week it had dried up. She kept it in the kitchen window as a reminder of her son's sweet gift. Every time she looked at it, she saw herself in the wasted stem and pitiful-looking petals—a woman who was all dried up and incapable of being revived.

Or so she'd thought....

After following a long curve through the trees, they came out on another slope of grassy meadow where she lost count of the cattle after reaching the two hundred mark. They came in every color. In the distance she saw a few hands and a border collie keeping an eye on the herd. Carson brought the truck to a stop and got out.

"Oh," Rachel half crooned. "Some of the mothers have babies."

Tracy had seen them. With puffy white clouds dotting the sky above the alpine pasture, it was a serene, heavenly sight of animals in harmony with nature. "They're adorable."

Carson walked around to undo the tailgate. Beneath his cowboy hat, his eyes glowed like blue topaz as he glanced at her. "Every animal, whether it be a pony or a calf, represents a miracle of nature. Don't you think?"

"Yes," she murmured, unexpectedly moved by his words and the beauty of her surroundings.

Johnny's giggle brought her head around. "Look at the funny calf. She's running away."

"Buster won't let her get far." Carson lowered the children to the ground. Tracy stayed put on her bale of hay. "Wouldn't you like to walk around with us?"

"They won't hurt you, Mom."

She chuckled. "I know. But from up here I can get some pictures of you guys first." Tracy pulled out her cell phone to make her point. "I'll join you in a minute." She didn't want Carson's help getting down. To her chagrin she still felt his touch from earlier when he'd lifted her in.

After she'd snapped half a dozen shots, she sat down on the tailgate and jumped to the ground. The children had followed Carson, who walked them through the herd, answering their myriad questions. Why were some of the calves speckled and their mothers weren't? How come they drank so much water? He was a born teacher, exhibiting more patience than she possessed.

Soon the dog ran up to them, delighting the kids. Tracy trailed behind, trying not to be too startled when some of the cows decided to move to a different spot or made long lowing sounds.

Carson cornered one of the beige-colored calves and held it so the children could pet it. Their expressions were so priceless, she pulled out her camera and took a couple of more pictures for herself and the Harrises, who would love to see these.

The hour passed quickly. When he finally announced it was time to get back to the ranch house, the children didn't want to go. He promised them they could come again in a few days.

"Do you think that calf will remember us?" Johnny wanted to know. All the children had to run to keep up with his long strides. Luckily their cowboy hats were held on with ties and didn't fall off.

As Tracy looked at Carson waiting for his answer, their gazes collided. "I wouldn't be surprised. The real question is, will you remember which calf you played with?"

"Sure," Sam piped up. "It had brown eyes."

A half smile appeared on Carson's mouth, drawing Tracy's attention when it shouldn't have. "I'm afraid they all have brown eyes. Every once in a while a blue-eyed calf is born here, but their irises turn brown after a couple of months."

Rachel stared up at him. "Do you think there might be one with blue eyes in this herd?"

"Maybe. Tell you what. The next time I bring you up here, you guys can check all the calves' eyes. I'll give you a prize if you can find a blue pair."

"Hooray!" the children cried.

On that exciting note, he lifted them into the truck and shut the tailgate without reaching for Tracy.

Perhaps he wasn't thinking when he did it, but it meant she'd be riding in the cab with him. He must have been reading her mind because he said, "Riding on top of a hay bale might work one way, but you've got more horseback riding to do and deserve a break." Flashing her a quick smile, he turned to the kids.

"That basket in the corner has water and fruit for you guys. How about handing your mom a bottle, Johnny?"

"Okay. Do you want one, too?"

"I sure do. Thanks. Your mom's going to ride in front with me. That means everyone sits down the whole time and holds on tight to the side."

"We will," they said in unison.

"That's good. We don't want any accidents."

"Please be careful," Tracy urged the kids.

"Mom—we're not babies!"

Carson's chuckle turned into a coughing spell as he helped her into the passenger side of the truck. Their fingers brushed when he handed her the bottle of water. This awareness of him was ridiculous, but all she could do was pretend otherwise.

He shut the door and went around to the driver's

side. She could still smell residual smoke from yesterday's forest fire. Carson should have been spared that.

Before he got in, he drank from his bottle. She watched the muscles working in his bronzed throat. He must have been thirsty, because he drained it. After tossing it in the basket in back, he slid behind the wheel.

She drank half of hers, not so much from thirst but because she needed to occupy herself with some activity. "What do you call the color of that calf the children were petting?"

"Slate dun."

"I knew it couldn't be beige."

In her peripheral vision, she noticed him grin. "In a herd of Longhorns you'll see about every color of the rainbow represented, including stripes and spots."

"Thank you for giving us this experience." She took a deep breath of mountain air. "There's so much to learn. Johnny's going to go home loaded with information and impress his relatives. That's saying a lot since they always sound like they know everything about everything and don't hold back expressing it."

His chuckle filled the cab. "Is he homesick yet?"

"I thought he would be. When we were flying into Jackson, I was afraid he would want to turn right around and go back. But nothing could be further from the truth. The second he caught sight of the tall dude who told him he'd take him shopping for some duds like his, he's been a changed child. For your information, tall doesn't run in the Baretta family. Neither does a Western twang."

He darted her a quick glance. "Johnny wasn't outgoing before?"

"He was…until Tony died. Since then he's been in

a reclusive state. The psychologist has been working with me to try to bring him out of his shell. When I get back to Ohio, I'm going to give him your business card and tell him to send all his trauma patients to the Teton Valley Dude Ranch. It's already doing wonders for his psyche."

"That's gratifying to hear, but let's not talk about your going home yet. You just barely got here. I'm glad we're alone so you can tell me what kinds of things he wants to do the most. I don't want him to be frightened of anything."

"Well, I can tell you right now he's crazy about Goldie and would probably spend all his days riding, pretending he's a cowboy."

"He seems to be a natural around her."

"That's because of the way you introduced him to horseback riding. You've given him back some of the confidence he's lost this last year. That was a masterful stroke when you handed him the reins and suggested he walk the pony around first so she would get used to him. In your subtle way, you sent the hint that Goldie was nervous, thereby taking the fear from Johnny.

"I held my breath waiting for him to drop the reins and run over to me. To my shock, he carried on like a trouper. When he was riding her around, he wore the biggest smile I've seen in over a year. That's your doing, Carson. You have no idea the wonders you've accomplished with him already. I'm afraid you're going to get tired of my thanking you all the time."

"That's not going to happen. If my grandpa could hear our conversation, he'd be gratified by your compliment since he was the one who taught me everything I know about horses and kids."

She bit her lip. "You miss him terribly, don't you?"

"Yes. He and my grandmother were kind, wonderful people. They didn't deserve to be burdened with a headstrong, selfish grandson so early in life."

Tracy took another drink of water. "There's that word *deserve* again. Don't you know every child is selfish? The whole world revolves around them until they grow up and hopefully learn what life's really about."

His hands tightened on the steering wheel. "Except I grew up too late. I should never have left him alone."

"Did he try to keep you from going into the Marines?"

"No. Just the opposite in fact," he said before another coughing spell ensued.

"He sounds like a wise man who knew you had to find your own path. Tony's two brothers who wanted to be police officers instead of firemen got a lot of flack from the rest of the family, especially from their father. He thought there was no other way to live, but two of his sons had other ideas. It has left resentments that seem to deepen."

"That's too bad. How did he handle Tony going into the Marines?"

"He didn't like it. But by then Tony was a firefighter and planned to come back to it when he got out of the service. As long as his sons fell in line, he was happy. To this day, he's still angry with the other two. He needed to take lessons from your grandfather."

"Unfortunately nothing removes my guilt. I was his only family left."

"It sounds like he wanted *you* to be happy. That was more important to him. He took on a sacred trust when he took over your upbringing. I feel the same way now that Tony's gone. It's up to me to guide my son. I'm terrified I'll make mistakes. What worries me is the struggle Johnny's going to have later on."

"In what way?"

"His grandfather will expect him to grow up and take his place among the Baretta firefighters. Imagine his shock when we go home and Johnny announces he's going to be a cowboy like his friend Carson when he grows up."

Her comment seemed to remove some of the stress lines around his mouth that could grow hard or soft depending on his emotions. "These are early days, Tracy. Your son's going to go through a dozen different stages before he becomes a man."

She moaned. "Let's hope he doesn't end up suffering from your problem."

His brows furrowed. "What do you mean?"

Tracy looked through the back window to make sure the children were all right.

"I've been keeping an eye on them," he murmured, reading her mind again. Of course he had. He had a handle on everything, inspiring confidence in everyone, old or young.

"I don't want Johnny to be afraid to reach out for his dreams for fear of leaving me on my own. He's especially aware of it since learning I lost my parents at eighteen. Sometimes he shows signs of being overly protective. A few months ago he told me he would never leave me and planned to take care of me all my life."

"There's a sweetness in that boy."

"Don't I know it, but I refuse to exploit it. That's one of the main reasons why I decided to accept your invitation to come to the ranch. If I don't help him to live life the way he should, then I'm failing as a mother. You and your friends have done a greater service for our family than you can possibly imagine. I know I said this before. You were inspired, and I—I'm indebted to you." Her voice caught.

He sat back in the seat. "After so much heartache, do you have any idea how much I admire you for carrying on? Tell me something. How did you continue to function after your parents were killed? I can't imagine losing them both at the same time."

"We had fantastic neighbors and friends at our church. Between them and my close friends, they became my support group and helped me while I was in college. Then I met Tony and was swept into his family."

He cast her a glance. "Swept off your feet, too?"

She nodded. "Natalie, my sister-in-law who's married to Joe, one of the out-of-favor police officers in the family, has become my closest friend. They have an eight-year-old son, Cory, who gets along famously with Johnny. I've been very blessed, so I can't complain."

After a silence Carson said, "What's the other reason you decided to accept our offer?"

"To be honest, I was becoming as much of a recluse as Johnny." She told him about the Mother's Day flower. "Your letter jerked me out of the limbo I'd been wallowing in. Once I caught sight of the Tetons in the brochure, I lost my breath. Like your stomach that flew around in the air for a week after your first flight with your grandpa, I haven't been able to get my breath back since."

"After a visit to the Tetons, some people remain in that state."

"Especially you, who came home from war struggling for yours. You and your friends have paid a heavy price. I admire you more than you know."

She'd been struggling, too, but it was from trying to keep her distance from him, which was turning out to be impossible. Tracy didn't understand everything going on inside him, but she realized that keeping her distance from him would be the wrong thing to do at the moment. Johnny was beginning to thrive. In a strange way she recognized they were all emotionally crippled because of the war and needed each other to get stronger.

"Do you mind if I ask you a personal question?"

"Go ahead."

"Why isn't there a Mrs. Lundgren?"

"You wouldn't like to hear the truth."

"Try me."

"The psychiatrist at the hospital did an evaluation on all of us. That was his first question to me. When I told him I preferred new adventures to being tied down, he told me I was an angry man."

"Angry—*you?*"

Carson laughed. "That was my response, too. He told me that was a crock. He said I'd been angry all my life because my parents died. That anger took the form of flight, whether it was sports, travel, the military. He said I was too angry to settle down. But with this illness that cramped my style, it was time I came to grips with it and let it go, or I'd self-destruct."

"And have you let it go?"

"I'm trying, but when I think of what I did to my grandfather, I can't forgive myself. There's so much I've wanted to say to him."

"Don't you think he knew why you were struggling? Did he ever try to talk to you about it?"

"Thousands of times, but I always told him we'd talk later. Of course that never happened. Then the opportunity was gone."

"As my in-laws used to tell me when I wallowed in grief over my parents' death, 'You'll be together in heaven and can talk everything over then, Tracy.' I've come to believe that. One day you'll have that talk with your grandfather."

"I'd like to believe it, but you've got more faith than I have."

Tracy sat there, pained for him and unable to do anything about it. Quiet reigned inside the cab as they drove through the sage. The children, on the other hand, were whooping it up, firing their cap guns. Johnny was becoming her exuberant child again. She had to pray it wasn't solely because of Carson.

The Harris family couldn't have come to the ranch at a better time. Tracy would involve them in as many activities as possible, because every new distraction helped.

As they drove around to the front of the ranch house, a cowboy with an impressive physique whom she hadn't seen before stood talking to some guests. He had to be the third ex-marine.

The moment he saw Carson, he left them and walked over to the truck. He removed his hat and peered in his friend's open window, allowing his green eyes to take her in. He wore his curly light-brown hair longer than the other two men and was every bit as attractive.

"Welcome to the ranch, Mrs. Baretta. We've been looking forward to your visit." His remark ended with the usual cough. The sound of it wounded Tracy because she knew at what cost they'd served their country.

"Tracy? This is Buck Summerhays. Now you've met all three amigos."

"It's a privilege, Mr. Summerhays. Johnny and I can't thank you enough for making us so welcome."

"The honor of meeting Tony Baretta's family is ours. Call me Buck."

Carson opened the door. "Come on. I want you to meet Johnny and the other two children."

While he got out, Tracy hurriedly opened her door and jumped down, not wanting any assistance. Everyone congregated at the rear of the truck. The men helped the children down, and Carson made the introductions.

Buck shut the tailgate before turning to everyone. "Where have you dudes been?"

"To see the cows," Sam spoke up.

Rachel nodded. "Next time we're going to look for calves with blue eyes. Carson's going to give us a prize if we find one."

His lips twitched. "Is that so." His gaze fell on Johnny. "Now that you've been to the pasture, what do you want to do this afternoon after lunch?"

"I'd like to ride Goldie some more."

"Who's that?"

"My pony."

"Ah." His twinkling eyes sent Carson a silent message. "I was thinking I'd take you guys on a float trip down the river."

"That sounds exciting," Tracy intervened. "How about we all do that with Buck? After dinner you can have another horseback ride before bed."

"Yeah!"

Johnny wasn't quite as enthusiastic as the other two, but he didn't put up an argument for which she was thankful. "Then come on. Let's go in and wash our hands really well. After that we'll find your parents and eat." She herded the children inside the ranch house so the men could talk in private.

CARSON NOTICED BUCK'S eyes linger on Tracy as she disappeared inside the doors. He knew what his buddy was going to say before he said it.

"You're a cool one." He switched his gaze to Carson with a secretive smile. "*Nice* has to be the understatement of all time."

"Her son's nice, too."

"I can see that." Suddenly his expression sobered. "Tony Baretta shouldn't have had to die."

His throat swelled with emotion for their suffering. "Amen." After more coughing he said, "I'll park the truck around back."

"I'll come with you."

In a minute they'd washed up and entered the kitchen to eat lunch.

"How was the pack trip?"

"It went without a hitch, but I noticed there are a lot of tourists already."

"There'll be a ton more as we get into summer."

They devoured their club sandwiches. "I'm thinking that on this first float trip we'll stay away from any rapids. If they enjoy it, then we'll do a more adventurous one in a few days."

"Sounds good."

"Ross is busy fishing with another group for the afternoon. Are you going to come?" Buck eyed Carson over the rim of his coffee cup.

"No. I need to lie down for a couple of hours."

Buck frowned. "Come to think of it, you don't seem yourself. What's going on?"

Carson brought him up to speed on the forest fire. "I kept the mask on as much as possible, but I still took in too much smoke."

"You shouldn't have gone near there."

"That's what Tracy said." He could still hear the concern in her voice.

His buddy's brows lifted in surprise. "Did you tell her about the fire?"

"I had to so she wouldn't think I was abandoning Johnny. When I called her to explain, I was hacking almost as badly as when we were first brought into the hospital. If I ever needed proof of how bad it is for us, yesterday did it. None of us should ever get anywhere close to a fire if we can possibly help it."

"Tell me about it. Last night I had a few coughing spasms myself and realized I needed to stay away from the campfire."

"We need to take oxygen and inhalers with us everywhere, in case we're caught in a bad situation."

"Agreed."

"Tell Johnny and the kids I have ranch business and will meet them at the corral after dinner for another lesson. Let Willy know I'm here if an emergency arises." The part-time apprentice mechanic from Jackson alternated shifts with Susan and Patty at the front desk for the extra money.

"Will do. Take it easy." He looked worried.

Carson got up from the table. "I've learned my lesson. See you tonight."

He left the kitchen and headed for his bedroom. Though he was a little more tired than usual after yesterday's incident, he was using it as an excuse to stay away from Tracy. Carson felt like he was on a seesaw with her.

Sometimes she seemed to invite more intimate conversation, particularly when she talked about not wanting to manipulate her son's feelings. Despite the blow that had changed her life, she had a healthy desire to be the best mom possible. He felt her love for Johnny, and it humbled him.

But other times, she'd keep her distance. He didn't know how to penetrate that invisible wall she threw up, no doubt to protect herself.

She'd married into a family that kept her and Johnny close. If she'd done any dating since her husband's death, it couldn't have made much of an impact. Otherwise, she wouldn't have left Ohio to come here for a week.

He stretched out on the bed. The more he thought about it, the more he was convinced this was her first experience being around a man again in such an isolated environment. A few more days together and he'd find out if she saw him in any other light than her host while she was on vacation.

This was new territory for him, too. He needed to take it slow and easy. Like the stallion he'd broken in at nineteen, you had to become friends first. The trick was to watch and key in to all the signals before you made any kind of move. One wrong step and the opportunity could be lost for a long time. Maybe forever.

And there was Johnny.

It was one thing to be the man who taught him how to horseback ride. But it was something else again if he sensed someone was trying to get close to his mother.

She'd said Johnny showed signs of being overly protective.

No man would ever be able to replace his father. It would take her son's approval and tremendous courage on Carson's part before he could begin to establish a personal relationship with her, even if she were willing.

Last but not least would be the great obstacle of the Baretta family, who would resent another man infiltrating their ranks. Worse would be their fear of Carson influencing Tony's son. He was their beloved flesh and blood.

Frustrated, he turned on his side. His thoughts went back to a certain conversation his grandfather had initiated.

"What are you looking for in a woman?"

"That's the whole point. I'm not."

"You don't want children some day?"

"I don't know."

"One of the things I love most about you is your honesty, Carson. Wherever the military takes you, don't ever lose that quality no matter what."

"Grandpa, are you really okay about my becoming a marine?"

"The only thing I can imagine being worse than your staying home for me when you want to be elsewhere, would be for me to have to leave the ranch when it's the only place I want to be. Does that answer your question?"

Oh yes, it answered it, all right. Carson had gone to do his tour of duty until it was cut short because he could no longer perform. Then he'd come home to the birthright his grandfather had bequeathed him without asking anything in return.

What tragic irony to be back for good, wanting to tell his grandfather that, at last, he could answer those questions. He wanted that talk so badly, tears stung his eyes. But it was too late to tell him what this woman and her son already meant to him.

When he couldn't stand it any longer, he got up to shower and change clothes. There was always ranch business that required his attention. Work had proved to be the panacea to keep most of his demons at bay. But when he left his room, instead of heading for the den, he turned in the other direction and kept on walking right out the back door to his truck.

After reaching the barn, he saddled Blueberry. On his way out he saw Bert and told him he'd be back at seven to give the children another riding lesson. The other man said he'd have the ponies ready.

Carson thanked him and rode off. His horse needed the exercise, and needing the release, Carson rode hard to a rise overlooking the Snake River. In his opinion, this spot on the property captured the view of the grand-daddy Teton at its most magnificent angle. He'd often wondered why his ancestor, Silas Lundgren, hadn't chosen to build the original ranch house here.

While he sat astride Blueberry, his mind's eye could imagine a house of glass, bringing the elements inside every room. Not a large house. Just the right size for a family to grow. Maybe a loft a little boy and his dog would love. From their perch they could watch a storm settle in over the Tetons, or follow the dive of an eagle intent on its prey.

The master bedroom would have the same view, with the added splendor of a grassy meadow filled with wild-flowers coming right up to the windows. While she marveled over the sight, he would marvel over *her,* morning, noon and night.

A cough eventually forced him to let go of his vision. When he checked his watch, he saw it was almost seven o'clock. He had to give his horse another workout in order not to be too late.

As he came galloping up to the corral, he saw Tracy's hair gleaming in the evening rays of the sun. She was surrounded by both families, mounted and ready for another lesson. He brought Blueberry to a sliding stop.

"Wow—" Johnny exclaimed from the top of Goldie. "Will you teach me how to do that? It was awesome!"

Chapter Five

The man and horse truly were one.

Talk about rugged elegance personified in its purest form!

Except for Johnny, everyone else sitting on their mounts was speechless. Tracy realized she was staring and looked away, but she'd never get that picture of him out of her mind. The quintessential cowboy had been indelibly inscribed there.

"If you'll follow me," came his deep voice, "we'll take a short ride past the cabins. On the way back, I have a surprise for you."

"Won't you tell us?" Sam called to him.

"No," his sister chided him. "Then it won't be a surprise."

Tracy exchanged an amused glance with the Harrises. The three of them rode behind the children. Johnny caught up to Carson. Two cowboys—one short, one tall—both wearing black Stetsons. She would love to hear their conversation, but the only sound drifting back was the occasional cough.

To see her son riding so proudly on his pony next to his mentor brought tears to her eyes. They'd been here such a short time, yet already he was loving this and showed no fear. Coming to the Tetons had been the right thing to do!

In the last twelve hours she hadn't heard him talk once about his father. In truth, Tony hadn't been actively in her thoughts, either. Neither she nor Johnny had memories here. The new setting and experiences had pushed the past to the background for a little while. As Natalie had reminded her, this was what the right kind of vacation was supposed to do for you.

Tracy hadn't believed it was possible, but this evening she was confronted with living proof that Johnny was enjoying life again. So was she. The old adage about a mother being as happy as her saddest child could have been coined with her and her son in mind. But not tonight. *Not tonight.*

At one point, Carson turned his horse around. Flashing everyone a glance he said, "We're going to head back now. The first person to figure out my surprise gets to choose the video for us to watch in the game room afterward."

The children cried out with excitement and urged their horses around, which took a little doing. Carson gave them some pointers. Tracy listened to his instructions so she wouldn't be the only one who had trouble handling her horse.

Pretty soon they were all facing west. Sam's hand went up like he was in school. Johnny's hand followed too late.

"Tell us what you think, Sam."

"The mountains have turned into giants!"

"That's what *I* was going to say," Johnny muttered. Tracy hoped he wouldn't pout.

Carson's horse danced in place. "They do look pretty imposing, but I'm still waiting for the special answer."

"*I* know."

"Go ahead, Rachel."

"The sun has gone down behind them, lighting up the whole sky with colors."

"Congratulations! It's the greatest sight this side of the Continental Divide." Carson lifted his hat in a sweeping gesture, delighting her. "The lovely young cowgirl on Mitzi wins the prize."

After the grownups clapped, Monica let out a sigh. "It's probably the most beautiful sunset I've ever seen, and we've watched thousands of them over the ocean in Florida, haven't we, Ralph."

"You can say that again."

Tracy agreed with them, especially the way the orangey-pink tones painted Carson's face before his hat went back on.

A sly smile broke the corner of his mouth. "First person to reach the corral wins a new currycomb."

Sam's brows wrinkled. "A curry what?"

"A kind of comb to clean your ponies after a ride. They love it."

"Come on!" Johnny shouted and made some clicking sounds with his tongue the way Carson had shown him. Goldie obeyed and started walking. In her heart of hearts, Tracy wanted her son to win.

In the end, the ponies hurried after Goldie. They kept up with each other and rode in together. Carson smiled at them. "You *all* win."

"Yay!"

While Bert helped the children down and unsaddled their ponies, Carson went into the barn and brought them each their prizes. Once he'd dismounted, he removed the tack from his horse and showed them how to move the round metal combs in circles. They got to work with a diligence any parents could be proud of. Then they watered the horses and gave them oats.

He was a master teacher. Tonight they'd learned lessons they'd never forget—how to appreciate a beautiful sunset, how to care for an animal, how to handle competition. The list went on and on, increasing her admiration for him.

"Who wants a ride back to the house?"

"We do!"

"Then come on." He punctuated it with a cough. "There's room for everyone in the back."

The men lifted the children. While Ralph helped Monica, Carson picked up Tracy. This time the contact of their thighs brushing against each other flowed through her like a current of electricity. She tried to suppress her gasp but feared he'd heard it.

On the short trip through the sage, the kids sang. They sounded happy, and Tracy started singing with them. It took her back to her youth. She'd had a pretty idyllic childhood. When Carson pulled the truck up in front of the house, she didn't want the moment to end.

Ralph moved first and helped everyone down, including Tracy. That was good. She didn't dare get that close to Carson again tonight. He'd kept the engine idling and said he'd see them in a minute before he took off around the back of the house. Everyone hurried inside to wash up.

Soon Carson joined them, bringing sodas from the kitchen. He sat on one of the leather chairs while the rest of them gathered round the big screen on two large leather couches. Fortunately, they had the game room to themselves.

To the boys' disappointment, Rachel chose *The Princess Bride,* but Tracy enjoyed it and got the feeling all the grownups did, too. Before it was over, both Sam and Johnny's eyes had closed. Ralph took his son home, leaving Rachel to finish the film with her mom.

Carson eyed Tracy. "Johnny's had a big day, too. I'll walk you to your cabin."

Her heart jumped at the idea of being alone with him, but to turn him down would cause attention. Instead, she said good-night to the others and followed him out of the ranch house while he held Johnny's hand. Her son was pretty groggy all the way to the cabin.

Tracy had to laugh when he staggered into the bedroom. Carson looked on with a smile as she got him changed into pajamas and tucked him into bed without a visit to the bathroom. "My son is zonked."

He nodded. "Johnny's gone nonstop all day. This altitude wears a man out."

She turned off the light and they went into the front room where another bout of coughing ensued. Tracy darted him an anxious glance. "You should be in bed, too."

Carson cocked his head. "Is that your polite way of trying to get me to leave?"

She hadn't expected that question. "No—" she answered rather too emotionally, revealing her guilt. "Not at all."

"Good, because I rested earlier and now I'm not tired." He removed his hat and tossed it on the table.

"Please help yourself to any of the snacks." She

folded her legs under her and sank down on the end of the couch.

"Don't mind if I do." He reached for the pine nuts. The next thing she knew, he'd lounged back in one of the overstuffed chairs, extending his long legs. "We need to have a little talk."

Alarmed, she sat forward. "Is there something wrong?"

"I don't know. You tell me." Between narrowed lids his eyes burned a hot blue, searing her insides.

"I don't understand."

He stopped munching. "I think you do. You need to be honest with me. Are you uncomfortable around me?"

She swallowed with difficulty, looking everywhere except at him. "If I've made you feel that way, then it's purely unintentional. I'm so sorry."

"So you do admit there's a problem."

Tracy got to her feet. "Not with you," she murmured.

"Johnny, then?"

Her eyes widened. "How can you even ask me that?"

The question seemed to please him because the muscles in his face relaxed. "Does your family wish you hadn't come?"

"I know my in-laws were astounded you and your friends had made such an opportunity available in honor of their son. They were really touched, but I believe they thought Johnny would want to turn right around and come home."

One brow dipped. "Is that what you thought, too?"

"When I first told Johnny about the letter, he said he didn't want to go. I knew why. Wyoming sounded too far away."

"What did you do to change his mind?"

"I asked him if he at least wanted to see the brochure you sent. He agreed to take a look. The second he saw that photo of the Tetons, he was blown away."

Their gazes fused. "Those mountains have a profound effect on everyone."

"Then he wanted to know about white water. But something extraordinary happened when he saw that gigantic elk with the huge *horns*..." Carson chuckled. "He looked at me and I felt his soul peer into mine before he asked me if I wanted to go. He always asks me first how I feel when he wants something but is afraid to tell me.

"I still wasn't sure how he'd feel after he got here. In retrospect, even if he'd wanted to turn right around, that airplane trip from Salt Lake would have put him off flying for a while."

Carson's smile widened, giving her heart another workout.

"My sister-in-law Natalie thought it was a fantastic opportunity and urged me to accept the invitation, but I don't know how my in-laws really felt about my taking their grandson to another part of the continent."

The tension grew. "Now that you've ruled out all of that, we're back to my original question, the one you still haven't answered."

Naturally he hadn't forgotten where this conversation had been headed and wouldn't leave the cabin while he waited for the truth. "As you've probably divined, *I'm* the problem."

"Why?"

He had a side to him that could be blunt and direct when the occasion demanded. It caught her off guard. "I guess there was one thing I hadn't thought about before we left. After we arrived here, it took me by surprise."

"Explain what you mean." He wasn't going to let this go.

She took a fortifying breath. "I assumed we'd be coming to a vacation spot with all the activities mentioned, but it has turned out to be…more."

"In what regard?"

"I—I didn't expect the one-on-one treatment," her voice faltered.

"From me and my buddies?"

"Yes."

He got to his feet. "But that was the whole point."

Tracy nodded. "I realize that now. But for some reason, I didn't think your business enterprise meant it would be a hands-on experience involving you so personally."

His brows met in a frown. "A dude ranch is meant to cater to the individual. If the three of us weren't here, there'd be others giving you the same attention. After losing your husband, does it bother you to be around other males again? Is that what this is about? I've half suspected as much."

She felt her face growing red as an apple.

"Have you even been out with a man since he died?"

"I've been to faculty functions with men, but they've always been in groups."

"In other words, no, you haven't."

"No," she whispered.

"And now you're suddenly thrown together with three bachelors practically 24/7." He put his hands on his hips in a totally male stance. "I get it. And I'll tell you something."

At this juncture, she felt like too much of a fool to know what to say, so she let him talk.

"I haven't been out with a woman since I was transported from the Middle East to Walter Reed Medical Center. When we were discharged, I felt like I was going home to die. The only thing that kept me going was this plan I dreamed up with Ross and Buck to bring a little happiness to the families who were suffering the loss of a husband and father.

"Lady—when I saw you walk through the airport terminal, I was as unprepared as you were. It was one thing to visualize Anthony Baretta's widow and his son in my mind, but quite another to be confronted with the sight of you in the flesh."

Tracy lowered her head. "After thinking of you in the abstract, the sight of you was pretty overwhelming, too," she confessed. "I guess we'd been picturing three marines in uniform whom we'd get to meet at some point during our stay so we could thank you. Instead, we were greeted by the king of the cowboys, as Johnny refers to you in private. He wasn't prepared, either, and clung to me for a long moment."

"I remember," he said in a husky-sounding voice before another cough came on. "From a distance, he was your husband's replica. That is, until I saw both your faces close up."

She eyed him covertly. Close up or at a distance, Carson Lundgren was no man's replica. He was an original with a stature to match the mountains outside the cabin door. "I'm glad we had this conversation. I feel much better about everything."

"So do I. From now on we each understand where the other is coming from. It'll make everything easier."

Not necessarily. Not while her pulse was racing too hard.

"Pardon the expression, but you and Johnny are our guinea pigs in this venture. The next family we've invited will be arriving next month. Because of you, we'll be much better prepared for the emotional upheaval created by war, whatever it is. Thank you for being honest with me. It means more than you know."

"Thank you for a wonderful day."

His eyes deepened in color. "There's more to come tomorrow, if you're up for it. But after Johnny's experience flying into Jackson, maybe not."

She took an extra breath. "You're talking about a hot-air-balloon ride? The kind mentioned in your brochure?"

"It's an unprecedented way to experience the Teton Valley. Buck will be taking some groups up."

"I'd love to go, but I'll have to feel out Johnny in the morning before breakfast. If it's mentioned at the table and the other children want to g—"

"I hear you," he broke in. "Johnny might be afraid, but will be too scared to admit it. I don't want to put him under any pressure. When you know how he feels, call the front desk. They'll put you through to me. If necessary, I'll give Buck a heads-up."

"Thank you. You have unusual understanding of children."

"I was a child once and had my share of fears to deal with. Peer pressure was a killer. I'm thinking that if he doesn't like the balloon idea, then we'll take a longer horseback ride tomorrow and enjoy an overnight campout on the property." He put his hat back on, ready to leave. For once she wasn't ready to let him go, but she had to.

"I can tell you right now he'll be in ecstasy over that option."

"Good. If it turns out to be successful, then he'll probably be ready to do another one in Teton Park. We'll take the horses up to String Lake. It's a great place to swim and hike around."

"Sounds heavenly."

She had to remember that he was working out the rest of their vacation agenda rather than making a date with her. Yet that's what it felt like. Her reaction was ridiculous considering she was a mother of twenty-seven instead of some vulnerable nineteen-year-old.

The only time she'd ever felt like this before was when she'd driven to Cleveland with some of her girl-friends from college. They were having a picnic at Lakefront State Park when a crew of firefighters had pulled up to eat their lunch and toss a football around. The cutest guy in the group started flirting with her. Mr. Personality. He could talk his way in or out of anything. Tony was a mover who told her after one date that he was going to marry her.

When she thought of Carson, there was no point of comparison because he wasn't pursuing her. That was why she was a fool trying to make one.

"All we've talked about is Johnny's pleasure. Since this vacation is for you, too, why don't you tell me something you'd like to do while you're here?"

She laughed gently. "If he's happy, then that's what makes me happy, but I have to admit I enjoy riding. I had no idea I'd like it this much. You're a great teacher."

"That's nice to hear."

"It's true." After a brief pause because she suddenly felt tongue-tied, she wished him goodnight. He tipped his hat and left.

Tracy closed the door behind him and locked it. Though he'd walked away as if he was glad the air had been cleared, she was afraid she'd offended him. It was humiliating to realize he'd figured out her lame hang-up about being around a man again before she'd articulated it.

To make certain she didn't get the wrong idea about him, Carson had revealed his own surprise at meeting *her*. Then, in the nicest way possible, he'd let her have it by spelling it out she wasn't the only one suffering emotional fallout from the war.

When she finally got into bed, she felt worse than a fool.

When Tracy stepped out of the shower, she could hear Johnny talking to someone. Throwing on a robe, she walked into the bedroom just as he put her cell phone on the bedside table.

"Who was that, honey?"

"Grandma and Grandpa."

"Why didn't you tell me?"

"Because you were in the bathroom. They said they'd call back tomorrow morning 'cos they were in a hurry."

"How are they?"

"Fine. They want to see me ride Goldie. I told them Carson's been teaching me and took us to get my cowboy outfit and cap gun." He ran over and gave her an exuberant hug. "I'm having the best time of my whole life!"

"I'm so glad."

"When are we going home?"

Uh-oh. "Next Saturday morning. Why? Are you missing them too much?"

"No. What's today?"

"Monday." Time was flying.

She could hear him counting in his head. "So we have five more days?"

"Yes."

"Goody! I don't want to go home. I can't leave Goldie."

Tracy knew he'd said it in the heat of the moment, and she was happy about it, but the implication for what it might portend for the future stole some of her happiness.

Though home would be wonderfully familiar to her son after they got back, he would suffer his first attack of culture shock, because nothing in Sandusky or Cleveland compared remotely to Wyoming's Teton Valley.

"Mom? Do you like it here?"

That was one of his trick questions. He needed to find out what *she* really thought before he expressed exactly what *he* thought. No doubt her in-laws had asked him the same question.

She ruffled his hair. "What do you think? I got on a horse, didn't I?"

"Yes," he answered in a quiet tone.

Something else was definitely on his mind, but she didn't know if he was ready to broach it yet, so she asked him a question. "How would you like to go up in a hot-air balloon today and see the whole area?"

Tracy had to wait a long time for the answer she knew was coming. "Do you?" That lackluster question told her everything.

"I don't know. There are so many things to do here, it's hard to pick. We could fish or swim, or go on a hike."

No response.

"Maybe we ought to have a break and drive into town to do some sightseeing. I'll buy you some more caps."

"I don't want to do that," he muttered.

"Or…we could go horseback riding. I like it."

He shot up in her bed. His dark brown eyes had ignited. "I *love* it."

His reaction was no surprise, but the intensity of it had come from some part deep inside of him. "Then it's settled. Hurry and have your bath. After we're dressed we'll have breakfast and walk over to the corral."

Johnny pressed a big kiss right on her mouth. That told her everything she needed to know before he scrambled out of her bed to the bathroom. When he was out of earshot, she called the front desk and was quickly put through to Carson.

"Good morning, Tracy." His voice sounded an octave lower, sending vibrations through her. Maybe it was due to his coughing, or maybe he sounded like that when he first awakened. "What's the verdict for today?"

She smiled. "Surely you don't need to ask."

"Well that answer suits me just fine, since there's nothing I'd rather do than be on the back of a horse. I'll tell Buck to go on without you. After you've eaten breakfast, I'll come by the cabin. You'll need saddlebags to pack your things to stay overnight and go swimming."

"Swimming?"

"Yes. We'll be camping next to a small lake on the property. If Johnny has a camera, tell him to bring it.

He'll have a field day taking pictures of the wildlife I was talking to you about."

An unbidden thrill of excitement ran through her. "We'll hurry."

FORTY-FIVE MINUTES later Carson swung by the cabin in the Jeep, having sent some of the hands to the lake to make preparations for everyone. Johnny was outside shooting off caps.

"Carson!" Like a heat-seeking missile, Tracy's boy came running in his cowboy hat. "Mom said we're going on a campout!" He clasped him around the waist, hugging him with such surprising strength, his hat fell off. Johnny had never been this demonstrative before.

Without hesitation, Carson hugged him back. "We sure are, partner," he answered in an unsteady voice, loving the feel of those young arms clinging to him. Nothing had ever felt so good.

As he started coughing, he looked up and saw Tracy on the porch step, but was unable to read her expression. She'd told him Johnny was protective of her. Without saying more than that, Carson got the point. Her son had a tendency to guard her.

But she couldn't have missed witnessing his exuberance with Carson just now. It had probably shocked her as much as it had him. Needing to return the situation to normal as fast as possible, he reached in the back of the Jeep and handed Johnny some gear.

"These saddlebags are for your stuff. The bigger one is for your mom. Will you take them into the cabin so she can pack what you need?"

"Sure."

"Remember to bring a jacket."

He flashed him a huge smile. "I will. I'll be right back."

Carson kept his distance and lounged against the side of the Jeep to wait. Pretty soon they came out. Johnny carried both bags and handed them to Carson to put in the back. It warmed his heart to see the boy was a quick learner.

"Can I ride in front, Mom?"

"If it's all right with Carson."

"Anything goes around here. Come on." He opened both passenger doors for them, avoiding eye contact with her. So much for the talk they'd had last night. Considering he was more aware of her than ever, it had accomplished absolutely nothing. "We'll drive to the barn and mount up."

"How come Rachel and Sam didn't come to breakfast?"

In the rearview mirror he noticed a pair of hazel eyes fastened on him.

"They ate early and went on an activity with Buck. He'll bring them to the camp later, but they won't be riding up with us."

"Hooray!"

"Johnny—" his mother scolded. "That wasn't nice to say."

"I'm sorry, but their ponies always come right up to mine."

Carson glanced at him in surprise. "So you noticed." He had natural horse sense. Everything the boy said and did pleased him.

"Yeah. They get in the way."

"I know what you mean. When it happens again, I'll teach you a simple trick so they'll leave Goldie alone."

"Thanks! How come they do that?"

"Have you ever heard of the three blind mice who hung around together?"

Johnny giggled. "Yes."

"That's what the ponies do, because they're friends. When you're on Goldie, you have to show them who's the boss."

"But how?"

"Have you ever heard the expression giddyup?"

"Yup."

"Well, you're going to practice saying that to Goldie today. And when you say it, you're going to nudge her sides with your heels. That'll make her go faster. Pretty soon she'll start to go faster every time you say the word and you won't need to use your heels. When she understands, then you wait until you're riding with the other kids. If their ponies start to crowd in on you, just call out 'giddyup' and see what happens."

"But what if that makes the other ponies go faster, too?"

Carson threw his head back and laughed, producing another cough. When it subsided, he could still hear Tracy's laughter. "That's a very astute question, partner. In all probability it will, so you'll have to ride even harder and make a lot of noise. But you'll also need to be prepared to pull on the reins so you don't lose control."

"That's going to be fun!"

Johnny bounced up and down on the seat all the way to the barn where their horses and pony were saddled. Carson parked the Jeep outside before grabbing the bags, including his own. He fastened a set behind each saddle while Bert helped Tracy and Johnny to mount.

Bert waved them off. "Have a good ride!"

"Thanks. We will!" Johnny called back. "See ya tomorrow, Bert."

"Okay, young fella."

Add another fan to Johnny Baretta's list. To charm old Bert wasn't an easy feat. So far the waitresses and desk staff, not to mention Carson's buddies, found him delightful.

Carson hadn't personally known Anthony Baretta, but he had a reputation in their division for being well liked and easy to get along with. Like father, like son.

Carson led them along a track through the sage in a northeastly direction. Johnny followed, and Tracy brought up the rear. When they'd been going for a while, he fell back alongside Johnny and told him to start working on Goldie.

The first few times the boy said giddyup, he didn't use his heels fast enough and nothing happened. Johnny's frustration started to build.

"You have to be patient and listen to Carson, honey."

"But I *am* listening, Mom."

"Sure you are," Carson encouraged him. "The trick is to use your heels at exactly the same time you call out. Try a louder voice the next time."

"What if it doesn't work?"

"Then you keep trying until it does. Did I ever tell you about the first time I learned to ride a bull?"

"No. What happened?"

"I was training for the junior bull-riding competition. It was awful. I got unseated so fast every time, I was ready to cry."

"Did you?" came the solemn question.

"Almost. But then I looked at my grandpa. He was

just standing there by the gate with a smile, telling me to try it again."

"What did you do?"

"I got so mad, I walked back behind the barrier and climbed on another bull. When the gate opened, I concentrated on what I'd learned, and guess what? I stayed on long enough for the other cowboys watching to clap."

"I bet your grandpa was happy."

"Yup, but not as happy as I was."

"I think I'll wait a little while before I try again," he announced.

Carson understood Johnny's sentiments well enough. He'd been there and done that many times before. "That's fine. We're in no hurry."

Tracy drew up along the other side of her son. "I hope you don't wait too long. We're coming to the forest."

Carson could sense her desire for Johnny to conquer this moment. It managed to fire her son who got a determined look on his cute face. All of a sudden they heard a loud giddyup rend the air and Goldie took off trotting. Johnny let out a yelp.

"Pull on the reins and she'll stop."

To Carson's delight, Johnny had the presence of mind to follow through and ended up doing everything right. He turned his pony toward them. "She *minded* me."

"Yup." Carson couldn't be more proud if Johnny were his own son. "Now she knows who's boss."

"You were amazing, honey!"

"Thanks."

When Tracy beamed like that, her beauty took Carson's breath. She stared at him through glistening eyes. "You've worked magic with him."

"He's *your* son, don't forget."

"I can't take any credit for this. His confidence level is through the roof. How do I thank you?"

"With that smile, you already have."

"Hey, you guys—aren't you coming?"

Johnny's question broke the odd stillness that had suddenly enveloped them. Both their shoulders shook with laughter at the same time. "What's the hurry?" Carson called out when he could find his voice.

"I want to keep riding."

"You mean you're not tired yet?"

"Tired? No way! Come on! Goldie wants to keep going."

"We're coming. Since you're in the lead, we'll continue to follow you."

"What if I get lost?"

"Hey, partner—we can't get lost. This is my back yard."

"Back yard!" Johnny laughed hysterically. "You're so funny, Carson."

He blinked. "No one in the world has ever said that to me before."

"Sometimes you really are," Tracy concurred. "As my son has found out, it's a very appealing side of you."

Carson felt an adrenalin rush. *Is that what you think too, Tracy?*

"Mom? How come you guys keep talking?"

He heard her clear her throat. "Because we're waiting for you to get going." She darted Carson an amused glance.

"Oh."

With less trouble than he'd demonstrated earlier, Johnny turned the palomino around and headed into the forest. The three of them were on the move once more, this time with Tracy at Carson's side. But after they got into the thick of the pines, the trail became less discernible in spots. Carson pulled alongside Johnny. His mother stayed right behind them.

"Seen any bad guys yet?"

"No, but I'm keeping a lookout."

"Got your mustang handy?"

"It's in my pocket. How far is the lake?"

"We wind up the slope for two more miles."

"What's it called?"

"I call it Secret Lake."

"Who else knows about it?"

"Only my best friends."

"You mean Ross and Buck?"

"That's right. And a few others. It's my favorite place. I can't let just anybody come up here. Otherwise it wouldn't be a secret."

Johnny looked over at him with those serious dark eyes. "Thanks for bringing me. I'm having the funnest time of my whole life."

Chapter Six

It was the second time Tracy's son had expressed the very sentiment she felt. She had to admit she was enjoying this trip a lot more than she'd anticipated. But along with this newfound excitement, her guilt was increasing.

Strictly speaking, it wasn't the guilt some war widows experienced, making them cling to the memory of their husbands. The love she and Tony shared would always be in her heart. They'd talked about the possibility of his dying, and she'd promised him she would move on if—heaven forbid—something happened to him. Since that horrible day, she'd been doing her best to make a full life for herself and Johnny.

This was a different kind of guilt, because she *didn't* feel guilty about enjoying Carson's company. To be honest, she was attracted to him. Very attracted.

Her biggest fear was that he'd already sensed it. Last night he'd sounded relieved after they'd had their talk. As he'd explained, when he and his friends had put their plan into action, they'd done it purely to brighten up the lives of a few families affected by the war.

Neither Carson nor his friends wanted or expected some love-starved woman with a child to come on to them because she'd lost her husband. The thought had to have crossed his mind when they'd first met at the airport.

According to Carson, the three men had been bachelors when they'd joined the Marines. And they were still living that lifestyle outside of this special project that was bringing so much joy to Johnny's life. Since Tracy couldn't help what they were thinking, there was no point in being embarrassed. What she needed to do was be friends with all of them, the way she was with Tony's brothers. That was going to be especially hard when she was around Carson, but she could do it. And she would!

"Mom—there's the lake!"

Johnny's exultant cry jolted her back to the moment. They'd moved on ahead of her. "Good for you for finding it! Does it look like Lake Erie with lots of barges and a lighthouse?" she teased.

"Heck, no. It's little, with pine trees all around it."

She smiled. "Can you see any fish?"

"Can you?" she heard him ask Carson. *Oh, Johnny.* Her son was so predictable.

"See all those dark things moving around?"

"Yeah."

"The lake is full of rainbow trout."

"I don't see their rainbows."

"You will when you catch one." Carson was ever the patient teacher. "We'll cook it for your dinner tonight."

"Won't there be anything else to eat?" was her son's forlorn reply.

Carson's laughter warmed new places inside her. "We've got lots of stuff."

"That's good."

Tracy drew closer to them.

"Hey—I can see some tents and a table! Someone else is camping here." He didn't sound happy about that.

Carson laughed again. "Yup. That someone is *you,* partner. Those tents have already been set up for us."

"Whoa!"

"Maybe you'd like to sleep in that three-man tent with Sam and Rachel."

"Oh, yeah. I forgot they were coming. Where will you sleep?"

"Right next to you guys in my tent."

"What about my mom?"

"There's a tent for her and one for the Harrises. The one on the end is for Buck."

"But there are six tents."

"Yup. The extra one is where we keep the food and all the supplies we'll need. After we take care of the horses, we'll fix ourselves some lunch."

"Goody."

Their entertaining conversation was music to Tracy's ears. She finally broke through the heavy cover of pines to discover a small body of deep green water bathed by the sun. "This place looks enchanted."

While Carson put out some hay and water for the horses, he slanted her a hooded look. "It is."

She felt a shiver run through her. They'd already dismounted and he'd removed the saddles and bags.

"Come over here, Mom. I'll tie your reins to this tree the way Carson showed me."

"Such wonderful service deserves a kiss." She got down off her horse and planted one on her son's cheek.

"The latrine is around the other side in the trees, away from the camping area," he informed her.

Latrine. Since their arrival in Jackson, Johnny's vocabulary must have increased by a couple of hundred words at least. He was becoming a veritable fount of knowledge.

"Thanks. I'll keep that in mind." Without being asked, Tracy picked up their bags. "I'll take these."

"Put mine in the big tent."

"Didn't you forget to say something?"

"Oh, yeah. Please. I forgot."

"I know, but it's so much nicer when you remember."

Carson's eyes smiled at her before she started walking along the tree-lined shore toward the tents pitched some distance away. She undid the tie on the screen and entered the big one where three sleeping bags and extra blankets were rolled out. It was getting hot out, but the temperature inside was still pleasant.

She emptied his saddlebag and put his things in little stacks against the side of his sleeping bag. Then she left and picked out one of the other tents for herself. It didn't take her long to unpack.

When she emerged, she discovered Carson putting out picnic food on the camp table beneath some pine boughs to give them shade. Johnny had the duty of setting up the camp chairs.

Tracy approached them and looked all around. "With the smell of the pines so strong, this is what I call heaven on earth." She eyed her son. "Do you know how lucky we are, Johnny? Can you believe Carson and his friends have gone to all this trouble for us? We're going to have to think of something really special to do for them."

"I know."

They settled down to eat.

"Guess what?" Carson said after swallowing his second roast beef sandwich. "You've already done something special."

Johnny stopped chewing on his sandwich. "No, we haven't."

"Want to bet? You accepted our invitation to come. We hoped you and your mom would like the idea." He darted her a penetrating glance. "That's all the payment we needed."

Carson.

"At first I didn't want to." Her son was nothing if not honest.

"I don't blame you. I'd have been scared to go someplace where I'd never been before. I think you were very brave to come."

"I'm not brave, but my mom is."

"She sure is." In an unexpected gesture, Carson pulled out his phone and clicked on the photo gallery. "Now take a look at this." He handed it to Johnny.

"That's me riding Goldie!"

"Yup. How many kids do you know your age who can go on a trail ride in the mountains on their own pony?" Tracy hadn't seen him take a picture. She was amazed. Had he taken one of her, too?

Johnny's brown gaze switched from the photo to study Carson. "I don't know any."

"Neither do I. So don't ever tell me Tony Baretta's son isn't brave." Carson's expression grew serious. "You're just like your dad and I'm proud to know you."

The conviction in his tone shook Tracy to the core and affected Johnny to the point of tears. They didn't fall, but they shimmered on the tips of his lashes with every heartbeat. "I'm proud of you, too. You're sick all the time and still do *everything*."

If Tracy wasn't mistaken, Carson's eyes had a suspicious sheen. As for herself, a huge lump had lodged in her throat.

"If everyone's finished eating, what do you say we put the rest of the food in the bear locker and go for a swim? Remember we have to fasten it tight. Occasionally a black bear or a grizzly forages through this area, but unlikely you'll ever see one."

Johnny looked at Tracy. "Don't worry, Mom. Carson brought bear spray. He'll keep us safe."

She lifted her gaze to a pair of blue eyes that blinded her with their intensity. "I have no doubt of it."

The three of them made short work of cleaning up and went to their respective tents to change into their bathing suits. When Johnny was dressed, he came running with his beach sandals and towel to her tent. She'd put a beach cover-up over her one-piece blue floral suit.

Before leaving Sandusky, she'd searched half a dozen shops to find something modest. Other women didn't mind being scantily clad, but she wasn't comfortable walking around like that.

Once she'd covered them in sunscreen, she grabbed her towel and they both left the tent in search of Carson. He'd beaten them to the shore and was blowing up a huge inner tube with a pump. Johnny squealed in delight.

The only thing more eye-catching than the sight of this pristine mountain lake was Carson Lundgren dressed in nothing more than his swimming trunks. Tracy had trouble not staring at such an amazing, hard-packed specimen of male beauty.

She felt his keen gaze play over her before he said, "Johnny? I want you to wear the life jacket I left on the table. Even if you're a good swimmer, I'll feel much better if you wear it while we're out here. Don't be fooled by this lake. You can only wade in a few feet, then it drops off fast to thirty feet."

Johnny's dark head swung around. "Okay." He ran over and put it on. Tracy made sure he'd fastened it correctly.

"I think we're ready!" Carson announced. He tossed the tube in the water, then dove in and came up in the center with a lopsided smile that knocked her off balance. "Come on in, and we'll go for a ride."

Johnny needed no urging and started running. Tracy threw off her cover-up and followed him in. "Oh—this water's colder than I thought!"

"It's good for you," Carson said, and then promptly coughed. The moment was so funny she was still laughing when he helped her and Johnny to grab on to the tube. Once they were all comfortable, he propelled them around.

They must have been out there close to an hour, soaking up the sun and identifying wildlife. Sometimes they swam away from the tube. Carson flew through the water like a fish and played games with them. When everyone was exhausted, they went back to shore to dry off and get a cold drink.

"I think it's time for a little rest."

"But Mom, I have to go talk to Goldie. She's missed me."

"You can see her in a little while. Come on. It's time to get out of the sun."

"What are you going to do, Carson?"

He'd been coughing. "I've got a few phone calls to make, partner. It won't be long before Buck arrives with the Harrises."

Tracy didn't know how he was able to spend so much time with them when he had the whole operation of his cattle ranch to worry about. "Thank you for another wonderful day, Carson."

He flicked her a shuttered glance. "It's only half over."

She knew that, yet the fact that he'd mentioned it filled her with fresh excitement. With an arm around Johnny, Tracy walked him to her tent, but stopped by his to get him a change of clothes. Once he was dressed, he lay down on top of her roomy sleeping bag. After she got dressed, she joined him. In two seconds, he was asleep.

Tracy lay there wondering if Carson's calls were all business. Since he'd come home from war, surely he'd been with women he'd met in Jackson or through his business contacts, even if it hadn't been an official date. That would go for his friends, too. Any woman lucky enough to capture his interest would be wondering why he hadn't been as available lately.

When she realized where her thoughts had wandered, she sat up, impatient with herself for caring what he did in his off time. She was supposed to be thinking of him as a friend, but her feelings weren't remotely like anything she felt for her brothers-in-law.

He would have been a charmer during the years he was competing in the rodeo. He had to be driving a lot of women crazy, these days, too. Carson was driving one woman crazy right here on the ranch and she didn't know what to do about it. Tracy had to admit those blue eyes and the half smile he sometimes flashed were playing havoc with her emotions.

After she'd met Tony, nothing had kept her from responding to him in an open, free way. Now, she had a son who came first in her life and the situation with Carson was so different it was almost painful. If he had feelings for her—sometimes, when he looked at her, she felt that he did—he hadn't acted on them. But then again, he was naturally kind and generous. She didn't dare read more into a smile or an intense look than was meant. He'd told her that she and Johnny were their guinea pigs.

The daunting thought occurred to her that Carson's emotions weren't invested, which explained why he never did anything overtly personal. Next month, another family devastated by the war would be arriving. He and his friends would welcome them and be as kind and attentive as they'd been to Johnny and her.

Maybe he'd meet a widow this summer who would be so desirable to him, he'd reach out to her because he couldn't help himself. Tracy groaned. What kind of woman might she be?

Tomorrow was Tuesday, and they only had four more days here. With her attraction to Carson growing, she'd found herself dreading the march of time, just like Johnny. But it suddenly dawned on her that without some signal from him, those days would seem like a lifetime.

Another worse thought intruded when she heard voices in the distance. Johnny heard them, too, and sat up, rubbing his eyes. She reached for her watch, which she'd taken off to go swimming. It was four-thirty. Buck appeared to have arrived with the others.

What if Carson had picked up on certain vibes from Tracy and had been including the Harris family in all their activities to keep everything on an even keel?

Was it true?

Maybe she was wrong, since she didn't know Carson's mind, but she cringed to think it could be a possibility.

"Hey, Johnny!" Sam was right outside her tent. "What are you doing? We're going swimming!"

"I'm coming, but I've got to get my suit back on!"

"Okay. Hurry!"

Off came his clothes. Soon he was ready. "Aren't you coming, Mom?"

"In a minute. You go on."

In case Carson was up for more play time in the lake, she decided against going swimming again. Grabbing her hairbrush and Johnny's beach towel, she left the tent and walked toward the others. Monica and Ralph waved to her. They were already in the water with the inner tube. "Come on in!"

"I just barely got out! How was the balloon ride?"

"Fantastic! You should try it before you leave the Tetons."

"Maybe I will!"

The children were clustered around Carson and Buck, who were handing out life jackets. She sat down in a camp chair, ostensibly to keep an eye on the children. But it was hard to focus when there were two tall, well-built ex-marines ready to enter the water. She finally closed her eyes and gave her damp hair a good brushing while she soaked in the heat.

THE COLOR OF Tracy's hair shimmering in the sun was indescribable. The fine strands could be real silver and gold intertwined. While the kids played with the Harrises, Carson kept his eyes above the waterline to take in the curves of her exquisitely proportioned body.

Buck emerged from the depths next to him, coughing up a storm. "I agree she's quite a sight," he whispered when he'd caught a breath. "When are you going to do something about it?"

"Is it that obvious?"

"Not to anyone but me and Ross."

"We didn't invite her family to the ranch for me to make a pass."

Buck scowled. "Hey, it's me you're talking to. I damn well know that. Tell me the truth. You haven't gotten any signals from her that she'd like you to?"

"I don't know. It's hard to read her. She's warm and friendly enough when she's with Johnny, which is most of the time."

"Maybe we need to arrange something this evening so she isn't with him. Time is fleeting. Saturday will be here before you know it."

Carson threw back his head. "Thanks for making my day, Buck."

"Just trying to help things along for a buddy."

"Sorry for snapping."

"Forget it. There's only one cure for your problem. I'll tell ghost stories in the kids' tent after everyone goes to bed. No adults allowed. While the Harrises retire to their tent, you and Tracy can sit around and talk. That ought to give you plenty of time to get creative."

"She'll probably go to her tent."

After a pause Buck said, "Like I said, get creative and follow her."

"That's been my idea since the moment we set up camp."

"Then I don't see a problem."

"I wish I didn't."

"Don't let me down, buddy. You take first watch tonight and see where it leads. Wake me up when it's my turn." Buck did a backflip away from him and swam underwater to surprise the kids.

That was easy enough for his friend to say, but Carson intended to follow through, all the same. The hourglass was emptying every second. He needed to mind his grandfather's advice when he'd been teaching Carson how to wrestle steers. "Put your fear away and seize the moment without hesitation, otherwise the opportunity is lost."

Tonight might be one of the few opportunities left to find out what was going on inside her. Armed with a plan, it helped him get through the rest of the evening.

While Carson and Buck explained why they were wearing canisters of oxygen and masks, Ralph Harris volunteered to build a small fire along the shoreline away from everyone. It would help them to avoid breathing too much smoke.

Instead of rainbow trout, they served roasted Teton hot dogs and Snake River marshmallows. The menu was a huge hit and met with Johnny's wholehearted approval.

With their meal finally over, Carson put the food away. Ralph volunteered to douse the fire and make sure there'd be no sparks. Now that it was time for bed,

Buck made his exciting announcement and the children scurried to the big tent for stories.

The Harrises eventually said good-night. Before Tracy could say the same thing, Carson told her he'd walk her to the latrine. "In case Bigfoot is lurking."

"Carson!"

He stood chuckling at a distance until she came out. "Maybe you'd better sit with me and have a soda until you're not so jumpy."

"Are you intentionally trying to frighten me?"

His pulse rate sped up. "Is it working?"

"Yes."

"That's good. I don't feel like being alone on a perfect night like this."

"It's incredible."

He liked the sound of that. They walked back to the camp in companionable silence. Carson waited for her to tell him she really was tired and needed to go to bed. Instead she sat down near him, staring out at the water.

Before dinner she'd put on a navy pullover with long sleeves over her jeans. Everything she wore suited her. Earlier, while she'd been roasting her hot dog and the flames from the fire were turning to embers, they'd cast a glow that brought out the creamy beauty of her complexion. She'd left her hair free, flowing to her shoulders. It had a lot of natural curl. He'd never met a more feminine woman.

"Tracy?"

Her gaze swerved to his. "What is it? I can tell something's on your mind."

He'd been about as subtle as a sledgehammer. "How would you like to go into Jackson with me tomorrow night?"

"You mean me and Johnny?"

"No. Just you. I want to take you dancing."

After a slight hesitation, she smiled. "I don't recall that being listed on your brochure."

He took a deep breath. Damn if it didn't always cause him to cough. "It isn't. I'm asking you out on a date, strictly off the record. If the answer's no, tell me now and we'll pretend I never brought it up."

She looked pensive. "I'm afraid I'm not a very good dancer."

Carson still hadn't been given the right answer. As far as he was concerned, this evening was definitely over. He got to his feet, too filled with disappointment to sit still. "Do I take it that's a no?"

"No!"

His heart gave a big kick at her emphatic response. "So it's a yes?"

"Yes, but let me warn you now, I'm out of practice."

"It's been a while for me, too." He studied her classic features in the near darkness. "If you remember, we listed babysitting on the brochure. Do you think Johnny could handle that?"

"I think he could, but I'd rather feel out Monica. Maybe we can trade nights. If she's willing to let Johnny stay at their cabin tomorrow night, I'll tend her children at mine the following night."

It thrilled him that Tracy was so ready with a solution. He was beginning to get the impression she wanted this date as much as he did. Otherwise, she wouldn't have agreed to go out alone with him. "Sounds like a plan that will make our little cowboys and girls happy."

A gentle laugh escaped. "Johnny really likes them."

"They're great kids." He reached for the flashlight on the table. "Plan on wearing something dressy."

"I only brought one outfit that would qualify, but I didn't think I'd wear it."

"I'll wear something a little dressier, too. Come on. It's late. I'll take you to your tent."

"I'd appreciate that." She got up and started walking. "Will you shine the light inside to make sure Bigfoot's brother isn't waiting for me?"

He smiled to himself. "I'll do that and one better. Buck and I are taking turns tonight keeping watch so everyone's safe." Once they reached her tent, he made a thorough inspection. "It's all right to go in."

As she stepped past him, their arms brushed. It was all he could do not to pull her to him.

She turned to him in the darkness. "Thank you for everything, Carson." Her voice sounded husky. "With two ex-marines guarding each other and all of us, I won't have a care in the world tonight."

He needed to get away from her *now.* "Keep the flashlight with you. If Johnny wakes up and wants you, one of us will bring him to you. See you in the morning, Tracy."

With the adrenalin pumping through him, Carson headed for the food tent and grabbed another flashlight from the box. Needing some exercise, he took a walk to check on the horses and make sure all was well.

Their little group had been making enough noise all day to scare off any bears. But on the off chance that one was hungry enough to come around and investigate, he was taking every precaution to safeguard their guests. The thought of anything happening to Tracy or

Johnny in his care was anathema to him. He'd never had such intense feelings before.

With time on his hands, he got on the phone and chatted with Ross. They talked about plans for the rest of the week. There were bookings for regular guests extending into August already. It appeared their brain-child was showing the promise of success.

This kind of news should make Carson happy. It *was* making him happy, but he had two people on his mind who were sleeping in tents very close to him. He was going out of his mind thinking about them leaving so soon and told Ross as much. That's when he heard a child's voice cry out, *"Mom—"*

It could have been any one of the three children. "Ross? One of the kids is awake. Got to go."

He took off for the bigger tent and almost ran into Buck who was holding Johnny's hand. The second the little guy saw him, he cried Carson's name and ran into his arms.

Carson got down on his haunches to hug him tight. "It's okay, Johnny. You were just having a bad dream."

"Mommy and I were at this big airport looking for you, but we couldn't find you. I kept calling for you, but you never came. Then I couldn't find my mom."

Carson looked up at Buck who'd heard everything. They'd both assumed the ghost stories had given him nightmares. Maybe they had. But Carson had featured in this one and Johnny had been looking for him.

It seemed Carson wasn't the only one hating the thought of Johnny and Tracy leaving the Tetons this coming weekend. The implication sent a shockwave through his body and wasn't lost on Buck, either.

Mercifully, the other kids stayed asleep.

"I'll take over now," Buck murmured.

Carson nodded. "Come on, Johnny. Let's go find your mom."

The boy put a trusting hand in Carson's and they walked to her tent. "Tracy?" he called to her from the opening. She stirred and sat up. "Johnny had a bad dream and wants to sleep with you."

"Oh, honey, come here." Johnny ran to her. Carson turned to leave, but Johnny's cry stopped him. "Don't go, Carson!" He sounded frantic.

"Johnny, Carson needs to go to his tent and get some sleep."

"He can sleep right here by me. Please, Mommy. I don't want him to leave."

In order to avoid a bigger disturbance he said, "Tell you what, partner. I'll stay here until you fall asleep. How's that?"

"You promise you won't go away?"

"Not until after I hear you snoring."

"I don't snore. Do I, Mom?"

She laughed softly. "Sometimes."

Tracy turned on the flashlight to find the blanket. "I'm not using this, Carson. Why don't you put this down next to Johnny." She was wearing pajamas with little footballs on them and looked adorable.

As Johnny might say, this was the funnest sleepover in the whole world.

Carson arranged the blanket into a pillow and stretched out. Their close quarters made everything cozy.

Tracy kissed her boy who'd climbed into the sleeping bag with her. "Do you want me to leave the light on?"

"Heck, no. Carson's here."

Tears stung Carson's eyes.

Tracy turned it off. "What kind of a bad dream was it?"

Johnny told her exactly what he'd told Carson.

He heard her deep sigh. "I've had dreams where I couldn't find somebody."

"You have?"

"Me, too," Carson interjected.

"Well, we're all here now and it's time to go back to sleep."

"Mom?"

"Yes?"

"I don't want to go home."

Carson's heart skipped a beat.

"Shh. We'll talk about it in the morning."

"Promise?"

"Promise."

"I love you, Mom."

"I love *you,* honey."

"Good night, Carson. I love you, too."

Carson closed his eyes tightly. "The feeling's mutual, partner. Good night." What else could he have said that wouldn't have upset Tracy?

When he'd had thoughts earlier in the day of being in the tent with her, he never dreamed he'd end up here in the middle of the night under these circumstances. In order to prove to her he wouldn't take advantage of the situation, he waited until he could tell they were asleep, then he crept out of the tent. He found Buck sitting on one of the chairs with his legs propped on another one.

"Go to bed, Buck. I'll never sleep tonight."

"Why not, besides the obvious?"

Carson brought him up to speed. "I'm afraid this plan

of ours may be backfiring big-time. We were supposed to give them a fun vacation, but now he says he doesn't want to go home. I know you're going to say he'll get over it, but until he does, Tracy's probably going to wish she'd never come."

"Speaking of Tracy, what happened out there tonight when you two were alone?"

"I asked her to go dancing with me tomorrow night. She said yes." The "yes" came out a little louder because he had to cough.

Buck moved his legs to the ground. "You weren't really surprised, were you?"

"I don't know. Ever since she got here, I've been turned inside out."

He got to his feet and stretched. "Do you wish she hadn't come?"

"If this becomes a nightmare for her because of Johnny, then yes. I have no doubt it was his father he was looking for."

"I'm sure you're right. It's only natural. But she chose to accept our invitation. There's a risk in everything and nothing's perfect in this imperfect world. You have to know they've been having a wonderful time."

"But at what cost?"

"That's your old guilt talking, Carson. You've got to stop taking on what can't be helped."

Buck was right. "I don't know how to do that."

"It's the only flaw I find in you. See you in the morning."

Chapter Seven

"Come on, honey." Johnny was slow putting on his cowboy boots this morning. "Now that we've had breakfast, they're calling us to pack up." So far he hadn't talked about his bad dream last night. That was good, because now wasn't the time for the serious discussion with him about Carson.

Johnny reached for his cowboy hat and put it on. "Do we have to go back to the ranch today?"

"Yes." She finished putting his things in the saddlebag.

"But I like it here."

"There are a lot more fun things we're going to do. Remember what Buck said while he was cooking our pancakes? Ross is taking us on a hike over in Teton Park. We haven't been there yet."

"Why isn't Carson coming with us?"

"You know why. He has business matters to take care of today."

"I'd rather stay home and ride Goldie."

Home?

"You can ride her after dinner. Here. You carry your saddlebag and I'll bring mine."

After fastening her hair back with a clip, she opened

the tent flap and they joined everyone congregated by the horses. She could hear the men coughing. Carson's black Stetson stood out as he finished saddling Goldie. He darted her a private glance before his blue gaze fell on Johnny. He took the bag from him and attached it.

"Up you go, partner." He helped him mount and handed him the reins.

"Who's going to take down our tents and stuff?"

"Some of my ranch hands. They came yesterday to set everything up for us."

"Oh."

"Remember what to do when the other ponies crowd in," he whispered. Tracy heard that and smiled.

Johnny's face brightened. "Yup."

Carson moved to Tracy's horse, Annie, who was ready to go. In a deft move he fastened Tracy's saddlebag. While she mounted, he undid the reins and put them in her hands, giving them a little squeeze.

TRACY HAD BEEN so excited about the date he'd made with her last night, she'd had trouble getting to sleep. When he'd brought Johnny to the tent in the middle of the night, his presence had made it impossible for her to settle back down. With that squeeze just now, she felt breathless.

He mounted his horse with effortless masculine precision. "Is everyone ready?"

"I am!" Sam called out.

"How about you, Rachel?"

"I've been ready for a long time." Her comment produced chuckles from everyone, including her parents.

"Then let's move out." Carson sounded like the hero in a Western film. Johnny fell in line right behind him, followed by the other kids, then the parents. Tracy stayed in front of Buck, who brought up the rear. A wagon train without a wagon. She loved it. In fact, she loved it too much. She was as bad as Johnny.

At first when they moved through the forest, she thought it was the trees making it seem darker than usual. But she soon realized clouds had moved in over the Tetons, blotting out the sun's rays. She felt the temperature drop. The sight of clouds after so many days of sunshine came as a surprise.

She dropped back to ride alongside Buck. "We had blue sky at breakfast. I can't believe how fast the weather has changed. Do you think there's going to be a storm?"

He nodded. "This cold front has moved in with more force than I'd anticipated. If it keeps up, we may not be able to go on that hike today."

Johnny wouldn't mind that at all. But he wouldn't like it if he couldn't go riding. "In that case, it'll be a good day for the children to play in the game room. A marathon Monopoly session will keep them occupied."

He laughed. "When we were young, my brothers and I used to play it all night. It drove my parents crazy."

"Where did you grow up, Buck?"

"Colorado Springs."

"I've heard it's beautiful there."

"It is, but I've decided nothing beats this place." A cough followed.

"How long do you plan to stay here?"

He flicked her an enigmatic glance. "If our business venture bears fruit, I'll build a home here and put down roots."

"What did you do before you went into the Marines?"

Buck's eyes got a faraway look. "My dad's in the construction business. Our family didn't know anything else."

"I see."

There was so much he didn't say, she heard pain and decided not to question him further. "While I have the chance, I want to thank you for all you've done to make this trip possible for Johnny and me. This is a once-in-a-lifetime adventure that so few people will ever enjoy. We won't forget your kindness and generosity for as long as we live."

"We're glad you're having such a good time. It makes everything we've done worthwhile, believe me."

While they'd been talking, they'd come out of the trees into the sagebrush. The track widened. "I'm going to ride up to Johnny and see how he's doing."

"Go right ahead. It's been a pleasure talking to you."

"For me, too, Buck."

She spurred her horse on past the others, delighted at the sight of her son moving along so comfortably on Goldie. Before he saw her, she whipped out her phone and took some more pictures of everyone. Carson was right in front of Johnny so he got into the pictures, too, without his knowledge.

As she put her phone away, she noticed the ponies edging up on Goldie. It really was funny how they wanted to be by her. In a minute they'd reached Johnny. She couldn't wait to see what would happen.

"Hey, Carson—here they come!"

His mentor moved to the side of the track to make room for him. She watched Johnny brace himself before he cried, "Giddyup!" and kicked his heels at the same time. Goldie was a smart little girl and trotted off, leaving the others behind. Sam and Rachel looked totally surprised.

Unable to help herself, Tracy urged her horse forward so she could catch up to her son. Once abreast of him she said, "Well done, cowboy."

"Did you see that, Mom?" Excitement filled his countenance.

"I sure did."

By now, Carson had caught up on his other side. "Thanks for teaching me that trick, Carson."

"Any time, partner."

Over Johnny's hat her gaze fused with Carson's. She could tell he was proud of her son. So was she. It was one of those incredible moments. "At this point I feel like we're actors in a movie on location out West."

He grinned. "We *are* out West, but instead of the Ponderosa, our star actor, Johnny Baretta, is headed with his posse for the Teton Valley Ranch on his wonder pony, Goldie!"

Johnny giggled. "You're so funny, Carson."

Oh, Carson—you're so wonderful, it hurts.

During this halcyon moment, they all heard thunder, the kind that could put a crack in those glorious mountains in the far distance. It kept echoing up and down the valley.

"Whoa!" Johnny cried out along with the other kids.

Carson whistled. "Now that's the kind of thunder that grows hair on a man's chest." Johnny burst into uproarious laughter. It set the tone for the ride in, calming any fears the children might have had. Their host turned in the saddle. "First person to reach the corral gets a banana split for lunch!"

"Goody!"

By the time the barn came into view, sheet lightning was illuminating the dark clouds that had settled in over the area. Tracy shot Carson a glance. "I've never seen anything so spectacular."

"During a storm it gets pretty exciting around here."

Almost as exciting as he was.

The first drops of rain pelted them as they rode into the barn to dismount. Bert came out of his office and helped the children down. Buck smiled at everyone. "Looks like we got home in the nick of time."

Ralph eyed the children. "I wonder who won?"

"Carson," all three kids said in unison.

He shook his head. "You were all there right behind me. I say everyone gets a banana split."

"Hooray!"

While the men removed the saddles and bridles, Johnny walked over to Carson. "Do you think the horses got scared?" Sometimes Tracy marveled over her son's sensitivity.

"After that first clap of thunder, I think they were a little fidgety, but since we didn't show any fear, they did fine out there. Tell you what. I'm going to take everyone back to the ranch house in the Jeep. But we'll have to make two trips. Why don't you kids come with me first, because I know you're hungry."

"Whoopie!"

Tracy watched them follow Carson into the drenching rain. She walked over to Ralph and Monica. This was the perfect time to talk to them in private. "Now we're alone for a minute, I have something to ask you, but please don't worry if you don't feel it's something you want to do."

When she told them, Monica's face lit up. "We were

just going to approach you about the same thing. The kids like each other and trust you."

"Johnny thinks you guys are great, too. This is perfect. I'll babysit for you tomorrow night."

"Thank you. We're dying to go into Jackson and have a little time alone."

Tracy could relate to that. She gathered the two saddlebags while they waited for Carson's return. Tonight was going to be a special time with a very special man and she planned to enjoy it to the fullest. After she and Johnny were back in Ohio, it would be a memory she would pull out and relive when the going got tough again. But she didn't want to think about the tough part right now.

CARSON HAD ONLY seen Tracy in jeans or a bathing suit. When she opened the cabin door at seven-thirty, he was treated to a vision of a different kind. With her blond hair loose, the champagne-colored skirt and gauzy blouse looked sensational on her. Soft and dreamy. Her high-heeled sandals showed off her shapely legs.

"Carson—" Her hazel eyes played over him longer than usual. "I almost didn't recognize you in a regular suit minus the boots and hat. I don't think Johnny would, either."

"A man has to be civilized around here once in a while. Are you ready?"

"Yes," she said quietly. "I'll grab my purse and jacket."

They left the cabin and he helped her into his Altima. The storm had passed, leaving everything cooler. He loved the smell of the sage after the rain. "Is Johnny all right with this?"

"I wondered about it when I broached the subject this afternoon. When he found out he'd be staying at the Harris's cabin until I got back, he didn't exactly mind we were going somewhere without him. Of course, I had to promise I'd come and get him."

"Of course." Carson started the engine and drove off. "Since you've told me how protective he can be, I guess I wondered if he put up a fuss that I'm taking you out."

"Are you kidding? The king of the cowboys?"

Her comment removed the bands constricting his lungs. The result was another bout of coughing. "After his nightmare, I worried his father was on his mind."

"I'm sure he was, subconsciously, but he didn't mention Tony at all. In fact, he hasn't talked about him once since our arrival here. That tells me you and your friends have achieved your goal to bring our family some happiness. Today made it evident that my son has come out of his shell. Your goodness and generosity are the sole reason for that. I told Buck the same thing earlier today."

Carson had noticed the two of them talking as they'd headed back to the ranch. "And what about you, Tracy? Are you enjoying yourself?"

"You know very well that question doesn't need an answer. I could never imagine myself being with another man again. Yet I found myself saying yes when you invited me out. I thought, why not? If Johnny could get on a small plane and dive-bomb into Jackson Hole, then it was time I took a risk. That should tell you a lot."

It did, but it wasn't enough. Patience had never been Carson's strong suit. "I'm taking you to the Hermitage, a French restaurant I haven't been to since my return from Maryland. It's in the Spring Creek Ranch area, a thousand feet above the valley floor.

"The view is superb. I thought you might like a change from authentic Western and enjoy some great French food along with a live band that plays a lot of romantic French songs. On Friday night after the rodeo, I'll take you and Johnny to a fun place for Western music and line dancing. Everyone gets in on the act in their duds. He'll be in his element."

He felt her eyes on him. "Be careful, Carson. You're spoiling us too much. If you treat all the families who come here at your invitation the way you're treating me and Johnny, no one will ever want to leave."

"Can I quote you on that when the time comes?" He pulled up to the crowded restaurant and turned off the engine. Luckily he'd made reservations. Even in the semidarkness, he saw color fill her cheeks.

She looked away. "You know what I meant."

"My friends and I appreciate the compliment." Levering himself from the car, he went around to help her out. The place had been built to resemble one of those religious retreats in the French Alps. He ushered her through the heavy wooden doors. The high ceilings and huge picture windows were unexpected and provided a contemporary twist.

"Carson! I couldn't believe it when I heard you'd made a reservation." A wiry older man came rushing over to the entry and kissed him on both cheeks. "Are you on leave? I haven't seen you since your *grand-père*'s funeral."

"I've left the military, Maurice, and am back for good."

"That's the best news I've heard in a long time."

His throat swelled with emotion. "It's good to see you."

"And who is this ravishing creature?"

"Please meet Tracy Baretta, one of the guests staying at the ranch with her son. Tracy, this is Maurice Chappuis, the owner."

The restaurateur's warm brown eyes studied her for a long moment. "How do you do, Tracy."

"It's very nice to meet you."

Carson would have said more, but a coughing spell stopped him. Maurice frowned. "That doesn't sound good."

"I got it when I was overseas, but I'm not contagious, so don't worry." He glanced at Tracy. "His son Jean-Paul and I were friends back in high school. Jean-Paul was a local bull riding legend. Maurice came to all our competitions. What's he up to these days?"

"Same thing as usual. Helping me here and on the ranch. Except…he got married four months ago and they're expecting!"

"You're kidding!" Carson was truly happy for him.

Maurice crossed himself. "He's off tonight. When I tell him who walked in here, he'll be overjoyed."

"Tell him to come by the ranch and bring his wife."

"I will. Now come. Sit, sit, sit. Only the best champagne in the house for you. I don't need to tell you we serve the best coq au vin in the world, and we have a new *chanteur* performing with the band. He does wonderful Charles Aznavour renditions."

"That's why we're here." He gave Maurice another hug. Seeing him like this brought the past hurtling back. Once again his guilt took over. Jean-Paul hadn't gone away. He wasn't restless, as Carson had been. Once his rodeo days were over, he'd stayed in Jackson. He'd built a life here, helping his father. Now he had a wife.

After Maurice seated Tracy, Carson took the seat opposite her at the window with its amazing view of the valley. The wine steward came over to pour them champagne. When he was gone, she eyed her dinner companion with concern.

"Maurice is wonderful, but I can tell something's wrong." Her naturally arched brows lifted. "Memories?"

He nodded soberly. "Too many. They all came rushing in at once."

"I know the feeling. When you handed that photograph to Johnny at the airport, and I saw Tony, it was like instant immersion into a former life."

"Immersion's a good word." He drank some champagne. "Mmm. You should try this. It's like velvet."

But she remained still. "You loved your grandfather, didn't you?"

"Yes."

"Then why do I sense so much sadness?"

"You know the old saying, act in haste and repent at leisure? That's me. But I don't want to talk about me tonight." He lifted his wineglass. "I'm dining with a beautiful woman and don't want anything to spoil it. Here's to an unforgettable evening."

She lifted her glass to touch his, and then sipped. "Oh—" She smiled. "That's really good."

"Isn't it?"

The waiter brought their meal and a basket of freshly baked croissants. Maurice didn't usually serve these with dinner, but he knew how much Carson loved them.

"You have to try one of these. They literally melt

in your mouth. I've eaten a dozen of them in one sitting before."

She took a bite. "I believe you."

While they ate their meal, he saw the dance band assemble across the room. A man in a turtleneck and jacket took over the mic. "Ladies and gentlemen," he said in heavily accented French. "I've been told we have a very special guest in the restaurant tonight. Monsieur Lundgren, it is up to you to choose our first number before the dancing starts."

Carson chuckled. Trust Maurice to pull this. He glanced at Tracy, whose smile haunted him. "Go on. I'm curious to know what you pick."

"How about, 'Yesterday When I Was Young'?"

Many people in the restaurant clapped because they knew the song, too. Once the man started to sing, Carson's eyes slid to Tracy's. Their eyes didn't leave each other until the singing was over.

"I first heard that song before I was sent to the hospital," he told her. "Remember the opening lines about being young and the taste of life sweet on the tongue, of treating life as if it were a foolish game?" She nodded. "All of it burned through me like a red-hot poker. That's what I'd done, and now that time was gone.

"I looked back at my own life, knowing I could never return to those times. I felt older than my grandfather who'd passed away. Opportunities had been missed. Too late I learned that the *now* of life is the essence."

Her eyes filled and she reached across the table to squeeze his hand gently.

"Let's dance." Carson stood, and reached for her to join him.

They gravitated to each other on the dance floor.

When he pulled her into his arms she whispered, "You're still young, Carson."

He drew her tighter against him without saying anything. They danced every dance. He forgot the time, the place. Carson needed the warmth of her lissome body. With each movement he inhaled her sweet fragrance and felt every breath she took.

"I need to be alone with you, Tracy. Let's get out of here." He felt a tremor shake her body as he led her back to the table. Once he'd left some bills, he ushered her out of the restaurant to the car.

A few residue clouds obscured the moon. Except for his coughing, they drove back to the ranch in silence. It was after eleven, but there was no way this evening was over. Maybe she wouldn't like it, but he pulled around to the rear of the ranch house and shut off the engine.

"This is my home. I'd like you to see how I live. I want you to come in and be with me for a while. If that doesn't—"

"It's what I'd like, too," she broke in. He sensed she wanted to be with him. What surprised him was how forthright she was. That's the way the whole night had gone.

He got out and went around to help her from the car. "The guys live upstairs. I have the back of the house to myself."

They walked down the hall to his bedroom, where Buck had done some remodeling for him. His grandfather's former room had been turned into a suite with its own sitting room and bathroom, but Carson wasn't thinking about that right now. He started to help her off with her jacket, but the moment he touched her, he couldn't help kissing the side of her neck.

"So help me, I promised myself I wouldn't do this, but I don't seem to have any control when I get close to you."

She twisted around until she faced him. That beautiful face. "Neither do I."

"Tracy—"

Carson lowered his head and covered her mouth with his own, exultant that at last he was tasting her. The singing line of her mouth had been tempting him for days. By some miracle she was kissing him back and she went on giving kiss after kiss. Like their dancing, they couldn't stop. It felt too wonderful to love this way.

He'd been empty for too many years. He wanted to go slow, but he didn't know how. She wasn't helping him. This merging of lips and bodies was so powerful, their desire for each other took on a life of its own. Carson didn't remember picking her up and carrying her to the bed. But there she was, lying on the mattress, looking up at him with a longing he could hardly credit was for him.

After crushing her mouth once more, he lifted his head, but he was out of breath. "I brought you here to... to do this...and to talk."

"I know," she half moaned. "That's why I came. We *have* to talk."

"How are we supposed to do that now? Do you have any idea how much I want to make love to you?"

"That makes two of us." Her voice trembled. "Don't hate me too much if I confess that I wanted you to kiss me to see if what I was feeling was real."

"You mean I was an experiment."

"Yes. But so was I to you—be honest about that." Her eyes beseeched him to understand. "After Tony, I—"

"You don't need to explain anything to me," he cut in. "I've been wondering about that, too, but no longer. It's real, all right." He buried his face in her fragrant hair.

"What's happened to us proves there's life after death. Until I met you, I didn't believe it. Oh, Carson." She covered his face with kisses.

HE FOUND HER mouth again, starving for her. "Now we *have* to believe it, because it's evident we're both hungry for each other. There's been an awareness between us from the first instant. Whether it's an infatuation that will burn out, only time will tell, but at least we can admit to what we're feeling right now and go on from here."

A tortured look entered her eyes. "We can't go on. This has to end tonight and you know it."

"Tonight?"

He rolled her on top of him, searching the depths of her eyes. "We've only just begun and we have three more precious days and nights together. How can you say it has to end now? How do we do that, Tracy?"

"Because we can't afford to start something we can't finish."

"Who says we can't?" he cried fiercely. "It already started Friday evening. Don't you know I don't ever want you to go home? You can't! Not when we feel this way about each other. For two people to connect the way we have is so rare, we have to hold on to it and nurture it. If I've learned nothing else, that's what war has taught me. Can you deny it?"

"Carson!" she said in genuine shock. "I couldn't possibly stay."

"That's because you're afraid."

"All right, yes. I am, for too many reasons to mention!"

"So am I. Petrified. This is new for me, too."

"We've only known each other a few days."

"That's the whole point, isn't it? How can we really get to know each other unless you stay? In order to give us a chance, I'd like you and Johnny to live in the cabin for as long as you want, until Christmas, even. That way you'll have seen all the seasons come and go except spring—which is enchanting. With weather like ours, it's important you experience it. By then, we'll know if you're ready to pack your bags or not."

She knew the "or not" meant he was talking about marriage, but he didn't say it in order not to scare her over something she wasn't ready for yet. With her, it would have to be all or nothing. He'd marry her in the morning, but he was going to give her plenty of time to get used to the idea.

Carson groaned when she started to ease herself away from him. He reached for her, but she slid to the edge of the bed and stood up. "If it were just me, I might consider staying on in Jackson at a motel for another week to see more of you. But we're talking about Johnny, too."

He got to his feet. "Exactly. He needs time to get to know the real me and see if he likes the man who's not just a cowboy. He's told me several times he doesn't want to go home. Whether he really meant it or not, he said it, and that's a start in the right direction."

She shook her head. "It just wouldn't work."

"Of course it would. We need to see where this leads."

"It might lead nowhere!" she exclaimed. "You could end up not liking me. We might find out we're not good for each other."

"Johnny may end up despising me, and you may discover you're bored and hate this lifestyle," Carson agreed. "But that's the risk we'll have to take because a fire's been lit, Tracy, and you can't ignore it."

"I'm not. I'm only trying to think with my head and not with emotions or hormones."

"That would be impossible. They all work together. I know we have to head for the Harrises' cabin, but before we walk out of here, I want you to think hard about something." He grasped her upper arms. "Will you listen?"

"Of course."

"I let my grandfather down when he was alive, but now that I'm back, I intend to keep this ranch going for my own sake as well as to honor him. The only way you and I can be together is for you to come to me. If you let fear take over, you'll be throwing away something precious. Are you willing to take that chance?"

"You make it all sound so easy, but it isn't. For one thing, I have my career."

He folded his arms so he wouldn't crush her in his arms again. "The Teton School District would welcome credentials like yours. Johnny could attend any one of six elementary schools. He'll make friends there and with the neighbors. We're only fifteen minutes away from town."

"Carson, I couldn't just stay on your property for six months."

"Then pay me rent like you do your landlord in Sandusky."

"But you built these cabins for tourists. Johnny and I would be taking up one of them. It wouldn't be fair to you and your friends after all the work you've done to make this into a dude ranch."

"I've already contacted the architect to build another one." The house of glass near the river.

"Your friends will hardly welcome the news that the family you invited here has decided to stay on. You three have started a new business together and don't need that complication."

He grimaced. "I'd hardly call you a complication, Tracy. But I know why you're throwing up all these excuses. For you to stay here will cause a major earthquake in the Baretta family. Don't bother to deny it, because I know it's true."

"They'd have a difficult time if Johnny weren't there."

"Your family could come out here for visits. They'd always be welcome."

"They're very set in their ways and don't travel often."

"What's really wrong that you're not telling me?"

She lowered her head. "They wouldn't approve."

"I get it," he fired back. "But their son has been laid to rest and their daughter-in-law has the right to get on with her life the way she sees best."

"You don't know what they're like." She raised anxious eyes to him. "My in-laws are good Catholics."

An angry laugh escaped his lips. "What would they prefer? That I fly home with you and assure them that while you're staying on my ranch, you won't be living in sin with me?"

The second she blanched, he realized his mistake

and gathered her into his arms where she fit against his as if she'd been made for him. Rocking her back and forth he whispered, "Forgive me for saying that. Already you're seeing a side of me that probably makes you glad you're leaving on Saturday. I know I sound desperate. It's because I am."

Carson found her mouth and drank deeply. He would have gone on kissing her indefinitely, but he had to cough. After it subsided he said, "Have I told you what a wonderful son you have? Last night he wanted me to stay in your tent. You have no idea what that meant to me." He lowered his mouth to kiss her again and tasted salt from her tears.

In the next instant she put her hands on his chest to stop him. "We can't do this, Carson. It's midnight. We have to go for Johnny."

He drew in his breath. "I know, but I have to have one more of these." Cupping her face in his hands, he savored another heart-stopping kiss from her lips. Her response told him things she wasn't ready to admit yet. Carson needed to be able to do this for the rest of their lives. In his gut, he knew that if she didn't end up being his wife there would be other women to provide a distraction, but he'd never marry one of them.

Ross had put it into words while they were working on the cabins in April. "You're probably one of those 'one woman' men you hear about. My great-grandfather was exactly like that. A crusty bachelor who came out to Texas from the East to find oil and make his fortune. Big business and politics were the only things on his mind.

"According to the story, he saw my great-grandmother picking bluebonnets in a field. She looked like a vision and he presented himself to her. It was history from there."

Carson had experienced a similar vision when Tracy had walked into the airline terminal. He was ready to make his own history, but he needed this woman and her son for it to happen. They made him want to be a better person because they were life to him.

Chapter Eight

"Mom? My stomach hurts."

Tracy turned in the bed to look at Johnny, who was still under his covers. Normally he was up by this time, shooting off his cap gun. "You look pale. What kind of treats did you eat last night?"

"Sam's mom made popcorn."

"Is that all you ate?"

"No. When she put me in the bedroom with Sam, he had a bag of mini chocolate bars and we ate some."

"I bet his mother didn't know about those."

"She didn't. He told me we had to keep it a secret."

"So how many did you really eat?"

"All of them."

"No wonder you're sick. Do you think you're going to throw up?"

"Yes."

She pushed the covers aside and jumped out of bed. He started running and beat her to the bathroom in time to empty his stomach. Tracy waited till he was through, then she helped him wash out his mouth.

"I still don't feel good."

"I'm not surprised. I want you to get back in bed."

"But Carson was going to take us all riding this

morning. Goldie will wonder where I am." He burst into tears, the first he'd shed since coming here.

Just the mention of Carson's name set her trembling. Last night the Harrises had left the cabin door unlocked. Carson had stolen in and brought Johnny out to the car. Her son had been sound asleep. When they reached her cabin, he'd put Johnny to bed and had left without touching her. For the rest of the night she'd ached for him until it turned into literal pain.

"I'll tell him you're not feeling well. Maybe by this afternoon you'll feel better and then we can go over to the corral."

"Will you tell him to come and see me?"

"Honey, he has other guests to take care of. In the meantime, we'll wait to see if you throw up again. If you don't, I'll get you some toast and there's Sprite in the fridge." The cabin had been stocked with enough snacks and fruit for her to skip breakfast in the dining room. "Would you like to lie down on the couch in the other room so you can watch a movie?"

"Okay."

Tracy took a blanket and pillow from his bed and tried to make him comfortable. She looked through the DVDs. "Do you want *The Hobbit* or Harry Potter?"

"I don't care."

That was his nausea talking. When it passed, then he'd ask her questions about her night out with Carson. She popped in the Harry Potter DVD.

"When are you going to call him?"

She glanced at her watch. It was quarter after eight. "In a little while. Let's give him time to eat his breakfast first." In truth she had no idea what time he ate. She'd phone him at nine.

"Don't tell Sam's mom what we did or she might get mad."

"She's so nice I'm sure she'll understand. I have to call her to let her know you won't be riding with her children this morning."

His eyes were closed. "Okay."

"I'll only be in the bedroom for a minute." She hurried in the other room and phoned the front desk. They put her call through.

"Monica? I'm glad I caught you. How are the children this morning?"

"That's funny you'd ask. Rachel's fine, but Sam says he's not feeling well."

"Neither is Johnny." In the next breath Tracy told her about the overload of chocolate.

"That little monkey of mine. I'm so sorry."

"You don't need to apologize, Monica. My son was equally guilty. I think they've learned their lesson. I just wanted you to know we won't be going riding this morning. Maybe not at all today."

"I agree we'll have to give riding a miss. I'll call Carson and let him know the situation."

Good idea.

Tracy wasn't ready to face him yet, not even over the phone. "Thank you, but don't think this changes our plan for me to tend your children. How about tomorrow night instead of tonight? Hopefully everyone will be well by then."

"That would be wonderful, if you're sure."

"Absolutely. I had a lovely time last night and want you and your husband to enjoy your evening, too. Why don't I treat tomorrow night like a special campout for the children? Our last one before we all have to leave the ranch. There's a bed for everyone here and we've got the couch. That way, you and Ralph don't have to come home until you want."

"Do you mean it?"

"Of course."

"You're one in a million, Tracy."

"So are you. We'll talk later."

After hanging up, Tracy padded into the other room. Johnny had fallen asleep again. That was good. Hopefully when he awakened, he'd feel a little better. She left the DVD on, hoping it might distract her.

Last night, while she'd been dancing with Carson, she'd wanted him to kiss her so badly, she couldn't wait to leave and go home with him. But what happened after that had shaken her world and she needed to talk to her sister-in-law, the only one who wouldn't judge her or the situation. Much as she wanted to phone Natalie, she couldn't. It wouldn't be fair to intrude on their vacation. Tracy needed to work this out on her own.

While she sat there brooding, she didn't feel like getting dressed yet. Instead she walked over to the table to make herself some coffee. It was something to do while her son slept on. Among the snacks she found a granola bar. While she ate, she sat down at the table to watch the movie and sip the hot brew.

Though she stared at the TV screen, her thoughts were full of last night's conversation with Carson and the way he made her feel while they'd kissed each other in mindless passion.

Much as she might want a repeat of that rapture for the rest of her life, Tracy couldn't just stay on here. What he'd suggested was impossible. Once she'd met Tony, the Barettas had become her whole family. They weren't simply her in-laws. With the loss of their son, they'd clung to Tracy and she to them. She didn't know what she and Johnny would have done without them.

They'd be so hurt if she told them she'd be staying on in the Tetons for a while. Her plans to visit them in Cleveland would have to be put off until later in the summer. She couldn't do that to them, no matter how much she dreaded the thought of leaving Carson.

What he'd said was true. If there was any chance that a lasting, meaningful relationship could develop, they needed to explore those feelings. Would they be as strong as their physical attraction for each other?

The way she felt right now, she couldn't imagine that attraction ever burning out, but she knew it could happen. One of the couples she and Tony had been friends with after they'd moved to Sandusky had recently divorced. They'd seemed to be so in love.

She needed to put last night's events away. For Tracy to want to be with a man she'd only just met and who lived thousands of miles away was ludicrous. The more she thought about it, the more she realized it would be the height of selfishness to stay here. Johnny might be having the time of his life on this vacation, but he needed loving family surrounding him. She couldn't keep him away from that.

Tracy had been blessed with a loving marriage to Tony. Now it was up to her to give Johnny the life they'd envisioned for their boy. One that included his favorite cousin, Cory, plus his other cousins, loving aunts and uncles, adoring grandparents. Good friends from the neighborhood and school would come with time.

From the deep fathoms of her troubling thoughts, she heard a knock on the door. Maybe it was Rachel with a message from Sam. Afraid it might wake up Johnny, she padded over to the door in her Cleveland Browns pajamas and opened it.

Bright blue eyes greeted her. "Dr. Lundgren at your service, Mrs. Baretta. My receptionist informed me I needed to make a house call on a new patient. She tells me he overdosed on Kisses. I can relate to that. In fact I'm still suffering the effects because I've become addicted to them."

Carson...

Heat swept through her body into her face.

"Hey—Carson?" Johnny called from the couch with excitement while she was trying to recover her breath.

"Yup. I've brought some stuff to make you feel better."

Johnny hurried to the door. He didn't look as pale as before. "What is it?"

Carson reached into the sack he carried. "Some Popsicles when you're ready for one."

"Thanks! I threw up this morning, but I'm feeling a little better now."

"That's good. Maybe you'd like to watch the DVDs I brought of Hoppy."

"Goody!"

Tracy was completely flustered, having been caught in her pajamas with her hair disheveled. "Well, aren't you a lucky boy. Thank you, Carson. Please come in. I'll get dressed and be out shortly." She flew through the cabin to her bedroom and shut the door.

When she emerged a few minutes later in jeans and a blouse, the two of them were on the couch. Johnny was sucking happily on a banana Popsicle while he told

Carson how he got sick. Tracy thought he might throw it up later, but at least he was taking in some liquid.

"A long time ago I remember eating too many Tootsie Rolls and got a stomachache for a whole day. I still can't eat one."

"I did the same thing on some fudge cookies," Tracy admitted.

Carson's gaze drifted over her. "Sounds like you're both chocolate addicts. By the way, I like the mother–son outfits."

Johnny spoke before she could. "My aunt Natalie gave these to us for Christmas. She and Cory have a pair, too. We love the Cleveland Browns."

"How about their quarterback, Colt McCoy?"

"Yeah." They high-fived each other.

"You're not going to leave are you?" Johnny cried when Carson unexpectedly got to his feet.

"Nope. I was going to put in one of the DVDs for you to watch."

"Good. I don't want you to go. Mom said you had a lot of other stuff to do today."

He walked over to the player. Glancing at them over his shoulder he said, "I was planning on taking you guys riding, but since that's out, I thought I'd hang out with you till you're feeling better."

"I probably won't be better all day." Her son was milking this for all it was worth.

Tracy didn't dare look at Carson or she'd burst out laughing. Instead she reached for an apple and sat down in the chair, putting her legs beneath her. In seconds he'd exchanged the DVDs in the player, and one of the old cowboy movies with the kind of music written for the early Westerns came on the screen.

"William Boyd," she said aloud. Seeing the actor's name brought back memories of the past with her parents.

Johnny frowned. "I thought his name was Hoppy."

"That's the character he plays in the film, honey."

"Oh."

"I wonder if Lucky is as cute as I remember," she teased. A little imp of mischief prompted her to see if she could get a rise out of Carson.

She wasn't disappointed when his gaze narrowed on her. "Why don't we take a vote at the end of the show?"

The by-play passed over Johnny. He moved his pillow so he could lie against Carson's leg. It was exactly the kind of thing he would do when he watched TV with Tony and got sleepy. Tracy couldn't believe how comfortable her son was with Carson, who seemed to take all this in as the natural course of events.

Before long, Hoppy and his friends came riding into town at full speed.

"There he is, riding his horse, Topper—" Carson blurted, sounding as excited as a kid. "To me, he was the greatest superhero in the world."

Johnny sat up. "But that guy in the black cowboy hat looks like a grandfather!"

Laughter burst out of Carson so hard it brought on a coughing spasm.

Tracy's shoulders shook. "He really does look old now that you think about it, but Lucky's still as cute as ever."

"That white hat's too big on him, Mom. He looks like a nerd. What's his horse's name?"

"Zipper."

Johnny giggled. As for Carson, he had a struggle to

stop laughing. "Well, Mom, I'm afraid I have to throw in my vote with Johnny. That makes two of us who disagree with you."

"You guys are just jealous."

"How come you like Hoppy so much?" Johnny's tone was serious.

She watched Carson's features sober. "I don't remember my dad. When I saw Hoppy's films, I imagined my dad being like him. A great cowboy who was really good, really courageous and always fair. My grandpa was like that, too. I was lucky to be raised by him."

"Yeah," Johnny murmured.

"You know something? You were lucky to have your father for as long as you did."

"I know."

"And now you have your grandfather."

"Yup. He's awesome. Carson? Do you miss your grandpa?"

"Yes. Very much. I bet you've missed yours this trip, too."

"Nope, 'cos he's not dead." *Shock.* "I can call him and Grandma whenever I want."

"I envy you."

Tracy felt Carson's pain. They needed to get off the subject. "You two are missing the show." She doubted anyone was really concentrating on it, but the room fell quiet until the end of the movie. When it was over, she got up to turn it off. "Are you getting hungry, Johnny?"

"No. Can I have another Popsicle?"

That was a good sign the nausea was subsiding. She picked up the paper with the sticks and threw them in the wastepaper basket, then drew another treat out of the small freezer. "Is cherry okay?"

"Yes."

He still wasn't well if this was all he could tolerate, but at least he hadn't been sick again. When she turned, she noticed Carson was already on his feet. She had a hunch he was leaving and her spirits plummeted. He looked down at Johnny.

"I hate to go, but I have to take some guests riding this afternoon. When I'm through, I'll phone to find out if you're hungry. If so, I'll bring you and your mom some dinner."

"I wish you didn't have to leave." He looked crestfallen to the point of tears.

"Can you thank him for the Popsicles and the movies?"

Johnny nodded. "Thanks, Carson."

"You're welcome." He flicked a glance to Tracy. "I'll have one of the kitchen staff bring you lunch."

"You don't have to do that. There's plenty to eat here."

"I want to do it," he insisted. "Does a club sandwich sound good?"

"Wonderful."

"Great. I'll have her bring some soda crackers, too."

There wasn't anything Carson couldn't, wouldn't or didn't do. *He* was the superhero.

After he left, gloom settled over the cabin. Johnny lay there watching cartoons while she tried to interest herself in the book she'd brought. Except for the arrival of her lunch, it turned out to be the longest day either of them had lived through in a long time.

On a happier note, by midafternoon Johnny was hungry enough to eat the crackers and drink some Sprite. Things were improving. Though neither of them said it, they were both living for the evening when Carson had promised to come back.

When he finally arrived, he brought them country-fried steak and the trimmings, plus chicken-noodle soup and toast for Johnny. The sight of him walking through the cabin door dressed in a black crew neck shirt and jeans changed the rhythm of her heart.

He'd also brought a colorful puzzle of all the planets. Johnny adored it and they worked on it until his head drooped. Tracy had been counting the minutes until she could put him into bed. The thought of being alone at last with Carson was the only thing driving her.

WITH A HEART thudding out of control, Carson sat on the couch, waiting for her. When she appeared he whispered, "Come over here."

Tracy moved toward him. He caught hold of her hand and pulled her down so she lay in his arms. The fragrance of her strawberry shampoo seduced him almost as much as the feel of her warm body cuddled up to his.

A deep sigh escaped his lips as they swept over each feature of her face. "I've been dreaming about being with you like this since you first arrived. After last night, it's a miracle I functioned at all today. You're a beautiful creature, Tracy."

She smiled. "Men always say that about a woman, but the well-kept secret is that every woman knows there's nothing more beautiful than a man who possesses all the right attributes. *You,* Carson Lundgren, were given an unfair number of them."

"As long as you think that, I'll never complain." Unable to stand it any longer, he started to devour her mouth with slow, deliberate kisses that shook them both.

He wrapped his legs around her gorgeous limbs, needing to feel every inch of her.

She explored his arms and back with growing urgency. When her hands cupped the back of his neck to bring him even closer, he realized what a sensuous woman he held in his arms. It filled him with an ecstasy he'd never known before. This was an experience he couldn't compare to anything else.

"I want to take you to bed so badly I can hardly bear it, but this isn't the place, not with Johnny sleeping in the next room."

Tracy covered his face with kisses. "It's a good thing he's nearby, because you've done something to me. I don't think I'll ever be the same, even when I'm back in Ohio."

"If your craving is as strong as mine, then you won't be going anywhere."

"You sounded fierce just now." She gave him a teasing smile before kissing him long and hard.

He finally lifted his mouth from hers. "You know why that is. We're not playing a game." A cough came out of him. "This is for real."

"Carson—" She framed his face with her hands. "I'm trying to be as honest with you as I know how to be. As you can see, I'm completely enamored with you. I spent all night asking myself questions—why this should be, and why it would happen now.

"Tony's only been gone a year. So many things have been going through my mind. Am I feeling this because this is my first experience with another man since he died and I'm missing physical fulfillment? Is this rugged Western cowboy so different from any man I've ever known, that I'm blinded by the comparison? When the newness wears off, will he be disenchanted by my Ohio roots?"

He smoothed some silvery-gold strands off her cheek. "To be brutally honest, I've been asking the same questions, and others. Why am I taken with a woman who will keep another man in her heart forever? Why have I met a woman who has a son she'll always put first? Am I crazy to want to deal with all that, knowing she's bonded to her husband's family?"

A tortured expression broke out on her face. "The way you put it, it does sound crazy. As I told you last night, you're young with your whole life ahead of you. Some single, Western woman who's never met the right man is going to come along and knock your socks off. You'll be the only man in her heart. The two of you will start a new family together."

Carson grimaced. "As long as you're playing what-if, can you imagine the irony of another widow with a child, like yourself, coming to the ranch this summer and sweeping me off my feet? A woman with the wisdom to grab at a second chance for happiness?"

Shadows darkened her eyes. "Actually, I can. I've been haunted by that very possibility since last night."

He raised himself up. "Are you willing to risk it and fly back to Ohio on Saturday, away from me? Before you find out what joy you might be depriving the three of us of?"

She shook her head. "You don't know Johnny. This trip represents a huge change for him.

"In the heat of the moment he'd agree to do whatever I wanted, but in time his true feelings will surface. When they do, it could be traumatic for him if he wants to go home because he misses the family too much, but feels guilty because he doesn't want to hurt your feelings.

"I don't question his affection for you, Carson. But he'll feel the pull of family the longer he's out here. I'd rather spare him that kind of pain."

Her words gutted him. He got up from the couch, unconsciously raking a hand through his hair. "You know your son the way I never will. I have no say when it comes to your mother's intuition. It's clear to me you've made up your mind. Have no fear I'll try to persuade you further."

Tracy looked wounded as she slid off the couch. "You know I'm right," her voice trembled.

He wheeled around. "No. I don't know that. What I do know is that when you leave, you'll be preventing us from learning the truth. For the rest of our lives we'll have that question mark hanging over us. But as we've discovered by surviving the war, life goes on."

"Carson," she pleaded.

"Carson what? You've said it all, Tracy. Now I've got to go. If Johnny feels well in the morning, bring him to the barn after breakfast. I'm driving the kids to the upper pasture. My foreman has been in touch with some other ranchers and has found a cow with a blue-eyed calf for me. I'd like one of the kids to find it."

Tears glistened in her eyes. "They'll be overjoyed."

"I still need to come up with a prize. Do you think a pair of chaps?"

She wiped the tears away with the heel of her hand. "You already know the answer to that question."

He tried to ignore her emotion. "After lunch, I'll take them horseback riding. As for Friday, I'll be doing some ranching business during the day, but Ross or Buck will take them riding for the last time. I'm still good to drive them to the rodeo on Friday evening."

"Johnny's living for it," she whispered.

"I think he'll enjoy it. On Saturday morning, I'll be running you and the Harrises to the airport in the van. With the children leaving at the same time, it should make things easier all the way around. I expect I'll see you in the morning."

Carson started for the door, but saw movement in his peripheral vision. "Don't come any closer." *Not ever again.*

He left the cabin, suppressing a cough until he got outside. When it subsided, he climbed in the Jeep without looking back. En route to Jackson, he phoned Ross and told him he was going into town in case anyone needed him.

"You sound like hell."

"That's where I am."

"If you want company, I'll tell Buck I'm joining you."

"Thanks, Ross, but I'm not fit to be around anyone."

"Tracy's still leaving on Saturday?"

"Yup."

"Sorry, bud."

"I'll live, unfortunately."

Carson hung up and continued driving to Jackson where he headed for the Aspen Cemetery. The small resting place was closed at sunset, but that didn't stop him. He pulled off the road and hopped a fence. His parents and grandparents were buried in the same plot up on the hillside near some evergreens. This was the first time he'd been here since the funeral.

The moon had come up and illuminated the double headstones. In a few strides he reached them and hunkered down to read the names and dates. *Beloved Son and Daughter* was inscribed on his parents' granite stone. It had been here for twenty-eight years. How many times had Carson come to this sacred place as a youth to talk to them?

For his grandparents, he'd had the words inscribed, *Our Last Ride Will Be to Heaven.* Carson had heard his grandfather say it often enough while he was alive. He could hear him saying it now and wept.

Finally, blinking back the tears, his gaze fell on the grassy spot next to it. One day it would be Carson's own grave. When someone buried him here, there'd only be a single headstone. That would be the end of the Lundgren line.

"Sorry, Grandpa. I finally met that woman you were asking me about. But like everything else important that happened in my life, I got there too late. Marriage isn't in my destiny. But I swear I'll take care of the ranch so you're not disappointed in me."

If the guys were still in business with him when the end came, he had no doubt they'd be married with families. He'd deed them the title and their families could carry on the Lundgren legacy. They been brought together at a low ebb in their lives and had formed an unbreakable bond.

But if it turned out they wanted and needed to go back to their former lives after this experiment was over, he'd will the property to the Chappuis family. Maurice had been like a surrogate uncle to him. Jean-Paul had been his best friend in his early days. Carson couldn't think of anyone he'd want more to inherit. No family had ever worked harder to carve out a life here. Either way, the ranch would be in the best of hands.

Having made his peace, he returned to the ranch. Two more days and she'd be gone. He would have to play the congenial host to Johnny without the boy knowing Carson's pain. The whole point of inviting their family here in the first place was to bring a little happiness into their lives. To that end he was still fully committed.

Chapter Nine

"I found one!"

From her perch on a hay bale, Tracy heard Sam's shout of delight. The calf with the blue eyes had been discovered.

Carson praised everyone for looking, but Sam was proclaimed the winner. In a few minutes Johnny came running through the herd to the truck. He'd recovered from his stomach upset but was now afflicted with another problem. When she pulled him into the truck bed, he was fighting tears.

"What's wrong, honey?" As if she didn't know.

"I wanted to find it."

"I know, but so did Rachel."

"Carson's going to give him a pair of chaps."

"Think how happy it will make him."

"But I wanted to be the one so he'd be proud of me." He broke down and flung himself at her.

With that last remark, her heart ached for him. "He's always proud of you. You know what I think? You're a little tired after being sick yesterday."

"No, I'm not."

"Then hurry and dry your eyes because everyone's coming. You don't want anyone to see how you feel.

Why don't you go over to the basket and get us both some water?"

"Okay," he muttered.

The kids came running over to the truck. Carson lifted them inside. She saw him glance at Johnny with concern, then his gaze swerved to her. It was the first time all morning he'd actually looked at her. When they'd arrived at the pasture, she'd already decided to stay put in the truck so she wouldn't have to interact with Carson any more than she had to.

When he'd left her cabin last night, she'd known he'd be keeping his distance until they left Wyoming, but this new estrangement was killing her.

Afraid he knew it, she gave Sam a hug. "Congratulations! You must have sharp eyes!"

"Yeah." He smiled. "I couldn't believe it."

"I wish I found it first," Rachel lamented.

Tracy nodded. "We all know how you feel. Better luck next time." She turned to Johnny. "Why don't you hand everyone a drink while you're at it, honey? You've all worked hard in this hot sun."

He passed the drinks around, but his face was devoid of animation.

Carson closed the tailgate. "If everyone's in, we'll head back to the ranch for lunch."

He walked around to the front, draining his water bottle. Once he'd emptied it he called out, "Catch, Johnny!" and tossed it into the back of the truck before climbing into the cab.

By some miracle her son nabbed it, causing a smile to spread on his face.

On the way back, Tracy chatted with the children about the coming sleepover. Soda was allowed, but no candy. What movie did they want to watch? What board games did they want her to choose from the game room? To her relief, Johnny started to settle down and be his friendlier self. Knowing Rachel had lost out, too, helped a little.

When Carson let them out of the back of the truck after they'd arrived in front of the ranch house, Tracy moved right with the kids and jumped down from the end before Carson could reach for her. It was a bitter-sweet relief to hurry inside with them, knowing he'd disappear for a while.

The kids had the routine down pat. Bathroom first, to wash their hands. As they emerged into the foyer a few minutes later, Tracy heard a familiar female voice call out, "Giovanni! Look at you in those cowboy clothes!"

Her mind reeled.

No-o.

It couldn't be.

But it was. No one else called him by their pet name for him.

"Grandma?"

"Yes! Grandma and Papa. Come and give us a hug. We've missed you so much!"

Tracy was so unprepared for this, she almost fainted. Johnny sounded equally shocked, but he ran to them. His grandmother kissed him several times, and then his grandfather picked him up and hugged him hard. Both of them were attractive and had dark hair with some silver showing. Sylvia was even wearing a pantsuit, something she rarely did.

It was painful for Tracy to watch the interaction, because conflicting emotions were swamping her. To see them here so removed from their world...

She didn't know what all had gone on to bring them to Wyoming when her vacation wasn't over yet, but she had a strong inkling.

Between Johnny's conversation with them on the phone the other day, and her conversation with Natalie, her in-laws were curious enough to get on a plane and come. It was totally unlike them.

She felt the other kids' eyes on her, needing an explanation. "Children? I'd like you to meet Johnny's grandparents from Ohio, Sylvia and Vincent Baretta. Dad and Mom? Please meet Rachel and Sam Harris from Florida. We've all become friends while we've been staying here."

"Oh, it's so nice to meet Johnny's friends," her mother-in-law said, patting their cheeks.

Her father-in-law still held Johnny while he reached for Tracy and kissed her. "After our talk with Giovanni the other morning, we decided to surprise you."

"You certainly did that." She still couldn't believe they'd come.

"Hi!" Monica had just appeared in the foyer with Ralph. "What's all the excitement?"

"These are my grandparents!" Johnny announced. "They came to see me ride Goldic!"

Okay. The pieces of the puzzle were starting to come together.

"Do you like my cowboy hat and boots? Carson took us to the store to get them."

Sylvia clapped her hands. "You look wonderful! Who's Carson?"

"He owns this whole ranch, Grandma. He rides bulls in the rodeo and is king of the cowboys!" Johnny's eyes shone like stars.

Tracy needed to do something quick. "Mom and Dad Baretta? Please meet Monica and Ralph Harris." They walked over and shook hands.

Monica smiled. "What a thrill for you, Johnny!"

"Yeah. Wait till I tell Carson! Let's hurry and eat. I'll take you over to the corral after lunch. He takes us riding every day! This morning he drove us to the pasture!"

"And guess what?" Rachel looked at her parents. "Sam found the blue-eyed calf."

"Yes, and Carson's going to give me a brand new pair of chaps to take home for winning."

"Good for you." Ralph patted his son on the back.

"We don't want to go home," Sam told his parents. "Carson told us about all these neat hikes we can go on in the Tetons. We just barely got here."

"I don't want to go home, either." Johnny took up the mantra. "Carson said the ponies will miss us. We can't leave them, Mom!"

Tracy heard her mother-in-law give the nervous little laugh she sometimes made when she didn't quite know what was going on. Johnny's grandfather lowered him to the floor. Still reeling, she said, "Why don't we go in the dining room for lunch, and then we can talk."

The room was fairly crowded. Tracy found two tables close together. While the Harrises took one of them, she guided her in-laws to the other. Johnny sat down between his grandparents, talking a mile a minute. Carson this and Carson that.

After their waitress took the orders, Tracy was finally able to ask a few questions. "When did you get here?"

Vincent had been quiet most of the time. "We flew

into Salt Lake from Cleveland, then caught a flight to Jackson last evening and stayed at a motel. Today we rented a car and drove over here to surprise you."

"Well, it's wonderful to see you." Her voice trembled. It really was, but she was still incredulous.

"These mountains are overpowering!" Sylvia exclaimed. "It's beautiful here, but I can tell we're in a much higher altitude."

"I love it here!" Johnny blurted. "It's my favorite place in the whole world."

Tracy saw a look of surprise in her in-laws' eyes. She had an idea they, too, were in shock over the change in their formerly withdrawn grandson. Suddenly Johnny jumped up from the table.

"Hey, Carson—" He ran over to the tall cowboy in the black Stetson and plaid shirt walking toward them and hugged him around the waist. "My grandma and grandpa came to see me. Will you take us all riding?"

"Sure I will," Tracy heard him say as if it were the most normal thing in the world that her in-laws had shown up unannounced and uninvited.

Johnny made the introductions. Vincent stood up to shake Carson's hand. "It was a great thing you and your fellow marines did, inviting Tracy and Giovanni here, Mr. Lundgren. Thank you for honoring our son this way. We're very grateful to you for showing our grandson such a good time."

"We certainly are," Sylvia chimed in.

"The honor has been all ours, Mr. and Mrs. Baretta. I'd be happy to introduce you to my business partners, but they're both out with other guests at the moment. It pleases me to tell you that Johnny has turned into quite a horseman already." He coughed. "I'll be over at the corral when you want to see him ride."

"We'll be right over after we eat."

"Please feel free to use all the facilities while you're here."

"That's very generous of you. Sylvia and I are staying in Jackson. We decided we'd join our family and take them to Yellowstone Park before we fly back home together. It will be a new adventure for all of us."

A gasp escaped Tracy's throat, causing Carson to glance at her briefly, but she couldn't read anything in those blue slits. Johnny hurried over to Tracy. He put his lips against her ear. "I don't want to go to Yellowstone."

"We'll talk about this later," she murmured. "Sit down and eat your lunch."

Carson tipped his hat, and then stopped at the Harrises' table to talk to them for a minute before he left the dining room in a few long, swift strides. Tracy's heart dropped to her feet. A subdued Johnny sat down, but he only played with his hamburger.

Sylvia patted his hand. "We got a suite with another room so you can stay with us tonight."

"We can't, Grandma. We're having a sleepover at our cabin with Rachel and Sam." This time Tracy saw definite hurt in Sylvia's eyes. Vincent's face had closed up.

"I'm afraid I promised Monica and Ralph," Tracy explained.

"They babysat me while Mom and Carson went out to dinner." Johnny was a veritable encyclopedia of information, but every word that came out of his mouth caused his grandparents grief.

"Well then, we'll have to do it on Friday night."

"But Carson's taking us to the rodeo!"

Tracy needed to put a stop to this, but didn't know how. "When are you flying back?"

"Tuesday," Vincent informed her. "If you call the airline, you can change your flight so we can all fly home together."

Johnny slumped down in his seat. "I don't want to go home."

Though she couldn't condone his behavior, she understood it. "Mom and Dad?" They looked hurt and confused. "If you'll excuse us, we'll meet you at the corral. Drive your car over to the barn. You can't miss it and we'll be waiting for you. Come on, Johnny."

He bolted out of his chair without giving his grandparents a kiss and ran over to the other kids. It wounded her for their sake, but the damage was done now. Soon the three children preceded Tracy out of the dining room. She needed a talk with her son, but this wasn't the time.

Tracy saw Carson's Jeep outside the barn before they reached the corral. Bert had already saddled the ponies. Carson came out leading Annie and Blueberry.

Tracy stood at the fence. While the children waited for Bert to help them mount, she watched Carson help Johnny. The play of male muscles in his arms and across his back held her mesmerized.

She heard the sound of a car and turned in time to see her in-laws get out and walk over to her. "You're in for a treat," she promised them. "We've done a lot of riding."

"Watch me!" Johnny called out to his grandparents.

All three children rode well, but Johnny stole the show as he walked Goldie around the corral like an old hand. She saw the pride in her in-laws' eyes. "You look wonderful!" they both called out to him. Vincent had tears in his eyes.

Johnny's face was beaming. "She's *my* pony."

"She's beautiful," Sylvia cried.

"Come on and ride, Grandpa. Carson's going to take us down to the Snake River and back."

"Why don't you go?" Tracy urged him. "You can ride the horse I've been riding. Sylvia and I will stay here until you get back." This would be a good time to feel out her mother-in-law over their unexpected arrival.

Johnny's invitation must have put Vincent in a better mood because he said, "I think I will."

"What about you, Sylvia? Maybe you'd like to ride, too?"

"Not me. You go ahead, Vincent. Tracy and I will have a good visit while you're gone."

It sounded like Sylvia wanted to talk to Tracy in private. They'd had a definite agenda in coming out here. Vincent was curious about the man who'd caused this change in his grandson. This would give him a chance to get a feel for him. They'd probably talk about the war and the circumstances leading up to Tony's death.

As for Carson, a picture was worth more than a thousands words of explanation from her. During the ride with Vincent, he'd come to know and understand better the dynamics that made up the Baretta family. He'd already learned a lot from their surprise visit.

The two men spoke for a minute before Vincent climbed in the saddle. He'd ridden horses in parades with the other firefighters and looked good up there. He always did, especially when he had to dress in his formal uniform. She realized Tony would have looked a lot like him if he'd had the opportunity to live a full life.

Oddly enough, that sharp pain at the remembrance of her husband was missing. The only pain she was feeling right now was a deep, soul-wrenching kind of pain as she watched the king of the cowboys mount his horse with effortless grace. From beneath the brim of his hat, he shot Tracy a piercing glance. "We'll be gone a couple of hours. I'll bring everyone back in the Jeep."

She took a deep breath. "We'll be waiting."

On that note he nodded and led everyone out of the corral, away from her.

This is what you wanted, Tracy, so why the anguish? Except that it wasn't what she wanted. She'd been looking forward to the ride this afternoon with each breath she took. Every second with Carson was precious until they had to leave.

When she couldn't see them anymore for the tears she was fighting, she walked toward the car. "Come on, Sylvia. I'll drive us back to our cabin and fix you a cup of coffee." Her mother-in-law was a big coffee drinker.

"I like the sound of that." Sylvia handed her the keys. "This is very beautiful country," she said as they drove through the sage. "When we saw the brochure on the internet, I couldn't appreciate it the way I do now."

"You have to be here and see those Tetons to realize the grandeur."

"You love it here as much as Johnny does, don't you?"

With that serious inflection in Sylvia's voice, it was the kind of question that deserved a totally honest answer. "Yes."

Tracy pulled the car up to the cabin and they went inside. "The bathroom is through there, Sylvia. While you freshen up, I'll fix us some coffee." Her mother-in-law liked it with cream and sugar. Tracy added a few snacks to a tray and put it on the coffee table.

A few minutes later they were both ensconced on the couch. "This is a very charming cabin, sunny. So was the dining room at the ranch house. You say this whole ranch belongs to Mr. Lundgren?"

Instead of the usual chitchat about family, Sylvia had zeroed in on Carson. Tracy couldn't say she was surprised. "Yes. The Teton Valley Ranch has been in their family since the early 1900s. His grandparents raised him here after his parents were killed. Carson's grandfather died recently and left him everything."

"Johnny told us he isn't married. He's certainly young to have so much responsibility."

Oh, Sylvia... "There's no one more capable."

"Obviously. Why does he cough so much?"

Tracy explained about him and his friends who'd met at Walter Reed. "Because of their illness, they were discharged from the military and decided to make this place into a dude ranch.

"Next month, another family they're honoring will be arriving. The plan is to take care of several more war widows with children by the time summer is over. They're quite remarkable men."

"I agree."

Tracy moistened her lips nervously. "Sylvia, why didn't you let me know you were coming?"

"I wanted to, but Vincent felt it would be more fun to surprise you. You know how much he loves Johnny. Every time he looks at him, he sees Tony. It was hard for him to see you two leave on this trip."

"And hard for you, too, I bet," Tracy added.

Sylvia teared up. "Yes, but I was glad for you to have

this opportunity and told him. He was morose after you left. It came as a shock to hear Johnny talk about this man over the phone. He didn't mention his father once."

I know.

"That upset Vincent so much, especially after we'd heard Natalie telling Sally about this exciting cowboy you met. After we got off the phone with Johnny, Vincent called to make reservations to fly out here."

It was exactly as Tracy had thought. Her father-in-law had felt threatened.

"Don't be upset with Vincent, Tracy. He's different since Tony died, because he doesn't want anything to change. He wants to be there for you and Johnny."

"I know that, Sylvia, and I love him for it."

"But you didn't like our coming here out of the blue. If you could have seen your face." She reached over to squeeze Tracy's hand. "I don't need to ask what this man means to Johnny. What I want to know is, how much does he mean to you?"

Tracy's heart was thudding so hard, she had to get up from the couch. "I— It's hard to put into words," her voice faltered.

"That means it's serious."

She wheeled around. "It could be," she answered with all the truth in her, "but I don't mean to hurt you or Dad. You know Tony was my life."

"Hey—you forget I'm a woman, too." She got to her feet. "Our son has been dead for a year. I have eyes in my head. When this tall, blue-eyed god walked toward our table in the dining room, he made *my* heart leap."

"Oh, Sylvia—" Tracy reached out and hugged her mother-in-law. She'd never loved her more than at this moment. For a few minutes they both cried. Finally

Tracy pulled away and wiped her eyes. "He's asked me to stay on so we can really get to know each other."

"Does Johnny know this?"

"No, and I don't want him to know." Having broken down this far, Tracy decided to tell Sylvia everything and ended up admitting all her reservations. "After losing Tony, if it didn't work out, Johnny could be severely damaged. I told Carson it wouldn't work and that's the way we've left it."

"If, if—" Sylvia exclaimed dramatically. "You can't worry about the ifs! Do you remember Frankie, who was killed two years ago battling that warehouse fire?"

"Yes. It was horrible."

"No one thought his wife and daughters would get over it. One of the other firefighters looked out for her, and six months later they were married and expecting a baby of their own. These things happen and they should! What if she'd said she couldn't risk it? Now she has a father for her girls and a new baby with this man she loves."

Tracy was struggling. "How do you think Frankie's parents felt about it?"

"At first they had a hard time. Now they're fine with it."

She looked at Sylvia. "Can you honestly see Vincent being fine with this? Carson's not a firefighter. His life is here, running this ranch. If I were to get to know him better, Johnny and I would have to stay out here, otherwise a relationship wouldn't be possible."

Sylvia's brows lifted. "You worry too much. Yes, Vincent is having difficulty letting go, but this situation isn't about your father-in-law or me. You let *me* worry about him. This is about *your* life and Johnny's, what's best for the two of you. In time you'll get your answer."

"You're the wisest woman I know. I love you, Sylvia."

"I love you, too. I always will. Since neither Vincent nor I have ever been to Yellowstone, he has his heart set on taking Johnny to see the Old Faithful geyser. Why don't we all leave for the park after the rodeo? He has us booked at Grant Village. That will give us Saturday, Sunday and Monday together. Then we'll drive you back here to the ranch and leave Tuesday. Perhaps by then you'll know your mind better."

It was a good plan. Three days with his grandparents, and Johnny might realize he was ready to go home to Ohio, especially when he remembered Sam and Rachel would be gone. Three days away from Carson would give Tracy some perspective, too. At the moment she had none.

"WILL YOU COME to our sleepover?"

Carson smiled at Johnny as he helped him off his pony. "I'll do better than that. I'll bring pizza for your going-away party."

Johnny frowned. "What do you mean?"

"You're leaving for Yellowstone after the rodeo, so I thought we'd celebrate tonight."

"But we'll be back."

"I don't know what your mother's plans are, Johnny." Out of the corner of his eye, he watched his grandfather dismount. Carson hated to admit it, but he was a good man who obviously adored his grandson and couldn't wait to get him home to Ohio.

Carson's gut twisted when he thought back to his

conversation with Tracy, who loved her in-laws. Their hold on her and Johnny was fairly absolute. "I'll bring enough for your grandparents, too." He turned to the others. "Let's get you guys home so you can get ready for the pizza party."

"Yay!" the others cried, but not Johnny.

Everyone got in the Jeep and they took off. He dropped Sam and Rachel at their cabin, and then headed for Tracy's. The rental car was out in front. She'd been there all afternoon with her mother-in-law. It was no accident her in-laws had decided to show up. She'd been right about Tony's family. They were very protective. *You don't have a chance in hell, Lundgren.*

Mr. Baretta sat next to Carson. When he stopped the truck, the older man turned to him. "It's been a privilege to go riding with you. I can see Johnny has been in the best of hands." He shook Carson's hand and got out to help his grandson.

Since he couldn't handle seeing Tracy right now, Carson went straight to the ranch house without looking back. He made a beeline for the kitchen and put in an order for pizza for six. While he was at it, he'd bring the chaps for Sam.

He saw Ross and Buck in the office. "I'm glad you're both here." He walked inside and shut the door.

Ross eyed him curiously. "The Harrises told us Johnny's grandparents showed up."

"You heard right."

"That's interesting," Buck muttered on a cough. "What's going on?"

"They've missed Johnny and came to get him. Under the circumstances, I need a favor."

"Anything."

"You know I'm taking the kids to the rodeo tomorrow night, but during the day I need to work with the foreman. Ross, will you take the kids riding? I'll get one of the staff to take the other guests fishing."

His dark brows furrowed. "Johnny's not going to like it. You know that."

"It's the only way to handle it. Tracy expects me to help make the parting easier for him. Her father-in-law let me know they're leaving for Yellowstone right after the rodeo and will be flying back to Salt Lake from there. I've decided that it'll be the best to say goodbye with a crowd around."

"I get it. Of course I'll do it. Did Tracy know they were coming?"

"I don't think so. It was supposed to be a surprise, but I can't be sure. It doesn't matter, does it? They're here, and Tracy will be leaving tomorrow for good."

The guys stared hard at him. "It *does* matter if she didn't want them to show up," Buck said.

"Want to make a bet? I spent part of the afternoon with Tony Baretta's father. He's a crusty fire chief from a long line of firefighters and he's tougher than nails. It kind of explains Tony," Carson bit out. A coughing spell followed. It was always worse for all of them this time of day. "I've got to get my inhaler. I'll see you guys later."

Carson went to his bedroom to medicate himself. After his shower, he left for Jackson to buy those chaps for Sam. He'd buy two more pair, for Rachel and Johnny, but he'd tell Monica and Tracy to hide them in their suitcases so they'd find them after they got home. The last thing he wanted was to take away the fun from Sam who'd been the winner.

He would miss those kids like crazy. It was then he realized what a huge transformation he'd undergone since Tracy had arrived. But he couldn't allow himself to think about that right now.

Later, as he was coming out of the Boot Corral with his purchases, he bumped into Carly Bishoff. "Hey, Carly." He tipped his hat to her. "How's the best barrel racer in Teton County? I hear you're going to win tomorrow night."

"You're planning to be there?"

"I am."

The good-looking redhead flashed him a winning smile. "I'd be a lot better if you ever gave me a call. I've been waiting since high school. Do you want to hook up after the rodeo?" She'd thrown that invitation out before, but he'd never taken her up on it.

"Why not?" he asked, shocking himself. It was his pain speaking, but he couldn't take it back. Tomorrow night he needed help, or he wouldn't get through it after Tracy and Johnny drove off.

"Did I hear you right, cowboy?"

"You sure did."

"Then you know where to find me after."

"It's a date."

He headed for his Jeep, already regretting what he'd done. She was a great girl. Hell and hell.

With the pizza order ready, he was able to pick it up and head straight for the Harrises' cabin. When he knocked on their door, Monica greeted him. He learned the kids had already gone and Ralph was in the shower. Carson was in luck.

"Will you hide these from Rachel until you get back to Florida? I'm giving Sam his prize tonight."

"She'll be thrilled!" Monica exclaimed. "Honestly, Carson, you've made this a dream vacation. We'll never forget."

"Neither will I, believe me. See you tomorrow when we all leave for the rodeo."

"We can't wait."

"Have fun tonight."

"Thanks to Tracy, we definitely will. She's a wonderful person."

She's more than that. "I couldn't agree more. Good night."

The children were running around outside shooting their cap guns when Carson pulled up to Tracy's cabin. The Barettas' rental car was parked along the side. They all came running up to the Jeep.

"Pizza delivery!" he called out.

The kids whooped it up and scrambled around to take the cartons inside.

"Just a minute, Sam," he called him back. "This present is for you." He handed him a sack with the chaps.

Sam looked inside and broke into a big smile. "Thanks, Carson! Wait till I show my parents!"

He ran into the cabin with Rachel and Johnny. Carson followed them. He needed to tell Tracy to come out to the Jeep so he could secretly give her Johnny's present, but she saved him the trouble by coming outside. For the moment, they were alone. She was so beautiful, he couldn't stop staring.

"H-Hi." She sounded out of breath. "I can't believe you brought pizza."

"It's a going-away party. What else could I do?"

Her hazel eyes went suspiciously bright. "Johnny's been worried about that."

He grimaced. "I haven't been too happy about it myself. What did you tell him?"

"Nothing I said has comforted him."

"He'll be all right once you're on the road with your in-laws. I bought him chaps, but I suggest you put them in the rental car so the other kids don't see them. He wanted to win."

"Johnny hasn't gotten over it. Do you know why? Because he wanted you to be proud of him."

His throat swelled. "He's the best, Tracy."

When she took the sack from him, he could feel her tremble. "Won't you stay and eat with us? Vincent said the ride was a special treat for him. That's all because of you."

"I'm glad, but didn't you know seven is a crowd when you're already a party of six?" he asked pointedly, half hoping she'd beg him to stay. But of course she didn't, and he would have been forced to turn her down anyway. "Ross will take the kids riding tomorrow. If you and your in-laws want to meet me in front of the ranch house at quarter after four, you can follow me to the rodeo grounds. It starts at five. Have a fun sleepover. If there's anything you need, call the desk. Good night."

Chapter Ten

If a horse had kicked her in the stomach, knocking her flat, Tracy couldn't have been more incapacitated as Carson got back in his Jeep and drove off without hesitation. She would never see him alone again. Being at the rodeo with him, surrounded by family and hundreds of other people, wasn't the same thing.

This was it! With children and in-laws to entertain, she couldn't run after him right now. And even if she could, what would she say? The talk with Sylvia had taken away a lot of her guilt to do with the family, but she was no closer to making a decision. Johnny was the key. She had to put him above every other consideration.

If she decided to stay on, how long would it be before Johnny wanted to go home? But if she went home, and he ended up grieving for Carson as well as his father, it could end up a nightmare.

In agony, she went back in the cabin to supervise the evening's activities.

Her in-laws stayed until it was time to get the children to bed. They planned to come by at ten tomorrow to take everyone fishing, including the Harris children who enjoyed Johnny's grandparents a lot. Sylvia and

Vincent really were the greatest. With so many grand-children, they'd had enough practice.

On the surface Johnny went along and entered into the fun as much as he could because he loved his grand-parents, but his heart wasn't in it. Tracy knew her son. The light Carson had put there had gone out again, because Johnny knew they would be leaving the ranch for good tomorrow.

How much could she trust it to be a crush on Carson that he'd get over in a few weeks? Or could it be the real thing? She'd been asking herself the same question where her feelings for Carson were concerned, but the answer was easy. When he'd driven away in the Jeep, she'd felt her heart go with him. Somehow during this last week he'd stolen it from her. Now that it was his, she couldn't take it back. She didn't want to.

What if Johnny were suffering the same way? Chil-dren were so open and honest. That night at the lake after Johnny's nightmare, he'd told Carson he loved him before saying good-night. At the time, she'd assumed he'd said it because his emotions were in turmoil after such a bad dream.

But now Tracy wasn't so sure. She thought back to the many times Johnny had spent with his uncles. He loved being with them and had wonderful experiences, but she couldn't recall him ever saying he *loved* them to their faces in a one-on-one situation with no one else around. Only a certain cowboy held that honor, but he was gone.

Her thoughts came full circle to that night at the lake. When Johnny's declaration of love for Carson came blurting out, she realized it had to have been born in the deepest recesses of his soul.

With that memory weighing her down, she finally got everyone to bed. They'd planned for Rachel to sleep on the couch so Johnny and Sam could share the other bedroom. But in the end, Johnny said he wanted to sleep with her.

Rachel and Sam were happy enough to share the other bedroom. Long after the lights went out and all was quiet, she heard subdued noises coming from Johnny's bed. She listened hard. He was crying.

She raised herself up on one elbow. "That's not a happy sound I can hear. Want to talk about it?"

"No."

"No? How come?"

He turned away from her. "I just don't."

"Do you wish your grandparents hadn't come?"

"No. I'm glad they came so they could see me ride Goldie."

"They're very proud of you."

"I know."

She bit her lip, loving this wonderful son of hers who was suffering a major heartache. Trying to get to the bottom of it she said, "I bet you wish your dad could see you ride."

"Grandma says he can see me from heaven."

He'd said it so matter-of-factly, Tracy didn't know what to think. "I *know* he can, and I know he's very proud of you."

"Carson says I'm a natural. What does that mean?"

They were back to Carson. "It means you look like you were born on a horse and are getting to be an expert."

"But I won't be an expert, 'cos we're leaving tomorrow and I'll never see Goldie again. I don't want to go riding with Ross tomorrow."

"Then we don't have to."

"I don't want to go to the rodeo, either."

By now she was sitting up in her bed. "Why not?"

"I just don't."

Her spirits plunged. "But Carson's taking us."

"He can take Rachel and Sam. He likes *them*."

Tracy got out of bed and climbed into his. His pillow was wet. "Okay. Tell me what's really bothering you, honey, otherwise neither of us is going to get any sleep."

Suddenly he turned toward her and hugged her while he sobbed. Great heaving sobs that shook the bed.

"Honey—" Tracy rocked him for a long time. "What's wrong? Please tell me."

"C-Carson doesn't like me, Mom."

If the moment weren't so critical, she would have laughed. "You mean because Sam won the chaps?"

"No-o." He couldn't stop crying.

"He brought you some chaps, too, but he asked me to hide them until we got back to Ohio. It's his present to you."

"I don't want them."

"Why?"

"He only did that 'cos he thinks I'm a big baby."

"Johnny—" In her shock, she realized something deeper was going on here. "How do you know he doesn't like you?"

"He's not even going to take me riding tomorrow."

"But that's because he has ranch business."

"No, he doesn't."

"Johnny Baretta—I can't believe you just said that."

"It's true, Mom. He wouldn't stay for the party. He's

glad Grandma and Grandpa came. Now he doesn't have to be with me."

Where on earth had he gotten this idea that Carson had rejected him? Carson had done everything but stand on his head to give her son the time of his life. But since her talk with Carson the other night, plus the arrival of her in-laws, he'd backed off. *All because of you, Tracy.*

Tormented with fresh guilt, she said, "What if we weren't leaving?"

"I *want* to leave."

Since when? There was something else going on here. She would get to the bottom of it if it killed her. "Tell me the truth, honey. Did Carson do something that hurt you?"

Instead of words, more sobs answered her question. She couldn't imagine what this was all about. "I have to know, Johnny." She ached for him. "Please tell me."

Tracy had to wait to get her answer. Long after the tears dried up, she heard, "W-When I told him I loved him, he didn't tell me back."

"You mean the night when we were in the tent out camping?"

"Yes."

"But he *did* tell you."

He shot up in bed. "No, he didn't!"

"Yes he did. I remember distinctly. He said, 'The feeling's mutual, partner.'"

"What does that mean?"

Good heavens! "Honey—it meant he felt the same way."

"Then why didn't he say it?"

By now she was praying for inspiration. "Maybe he thought you weren't ready to hear the exact words back.

Maybe he was afraid you only wanted to hear those words from your father."

"Why? I *love* him! Now that Dad's gone, he's my favorite person in the whole world!"

"I know that," she said in a quiet tone, too overcome to say more.

"I wish you loved him, too." Her son's voice cracked.

Her eyes widened. "You do?"

"Yes, but I know you loved Dad and always will."

She wrapped her arm around him. "I will always love your father, but that doesn't mean I can't love someone else again one day."

He jerked back to life, sending her an unmistakable message. "It doesn't?"

"No."

"Do you think you could love Carson? I know you like him because you went to dinner with him."

Oh, Johnny... "I like him a lot."

"He likes you, too. I can tell."

Her pulse was racing. "How?"

"You know. Stuff."

"What stuff?"

"He told me you were prettier than Goldie."

"He did?" A smile found its way to her lips.

"Yup. And he said you were a better mom than any woman he had ever known. He said my dad was lucky 'cos you were the kind of a woman a man wanted to marry. But he's afraid a woman wouldn't want to marry him."

Tracy had no idea all this had gone on out of her hearing. "Why would he think that?"

"'Cos he's got a disease. He says no woman wants

to marry an old war vet who goes around coughing all the time. That's not true, is it, Mom?"

"No. Of course not. Tell you what, honey. Your grandparents flew all the way out here to be with you, so let's enjoy being with them until they have to fly home to Ohio. After we see them off at the airport, we'll bring their rental car back here and surprise Carson."

"Then we don't have to go home with them?"

"No." *Absolutely not.* "But don't let Carson know what we plan to do, otherwise it won't be a surprise."

"I *know,*" he said in that unique way of his. "Oh, Mom. I love you!" He threw his arms around her once more.

After a long hug she said, "Now it's time to sleep. We'll talk some more in the morning after the kids go home."

"Okay."

They kissed good-night and she got back in her own bed, praying for morning to get here as fast as possible. She wouldn't be able to breathe until they'd come back from Yellowstone.

AFTER THE RODEO, everyone congregated in the parking lot; the Harrises, the Barettas and Carson. The dreaded time had come for everyone to say goodbye.

"Did you like the rodeo, guys?"

"Yeah!" Sam was still jumping up and down with excitement in his jeans and chaps. "Especially the bulls!"

"They're so big!" Johnny exclaimed.

Rachel smiled up at Carson. "I liked the barrel racing. That looked so fun."

"Maybe if you keep riding after you get home to Florida, you'll be able to do it one day." He looked at the Harrises. "If you'll climb in the Jeep, I'll run you back to the ranch."

The kids all said goodbye to each other. Tracy hugged the Harrises. Carson heard them exchange email addresses. Then it was time to help her and Johnny get in the back of the Barettas' rental car. They were all packed and ready for their trip to Yellowstone.

He couldn't hug Johnny the way he wanted to, not in front of everyone. Instead, he shook his hand. "It's been a pleasure getting to know the son of Tony Baretta. We had a great time together, didn't we, partner?"

"Yup." Johnny's eyes teared up, but he didn't cry. He knew his grandparents were watching and took the parting like a man. "Thanks for everything, Carson. Be sure and give Goldie some oats for me tomorrow. Tell her I'll miss her."

"I sure will. She'll miss you, too." That boy was taking a piece of him away. Carson didn't know he could love a child this much. He shut the door and walked around to say goodbye to Tracy. She'd already gotten in but hadn't closed the door yet.

Her eyes lifted to his. "We'll never forget what you've done for us, Carson. We thanked Ross and Buck earlier, but please thank them again. You and your buddies accomplished your objective to help a grieving family heal in ways you can't possibly comprehend. Our gratitude knows no bounds."

"That's good to hear and means more than you know. We had a lot of fun, too," he said on a cough. That was the understatement of all time. Carson didn't know how much more of this he could take.

He shut her door and walked to Mr. Baretta's open

window. "There's still some daylight left, Vincent. Drive safely and enjoy."

"I'm sure we will. Thank you again, Carson. This was a great thing you did for Tracy and Johnny, one they'll remember forever." The two men shook hands.

He nodded to Sylvia. "It was a real pleasure meeting Johnny's grandmother."

"We enjoyed getting to know you, too, Carson. Goodbye and thank you."

Unable to bear it, Carson headed for his Jeep. Out of the rear window of the rental car he saw Tracy's gorgeous face. Her eyes glistened with tears. As he walked around the back end he spied Johnny's soulful brown eyes staring at him through the window. Tony Baretta's eyes. He belonged to the Baretta clan. So did Tracy.

The week from heaven had turned into the lifetime from hell.

On Monday, the family went back to watch Old Faithful go off. They'd seen it the day before, but Johnny wanted to see it again.

"Whoa!" he cried out when the geyser shot up into the air. It really was fantastic. But Tracy had something else on her mind that couldn't be put off any longer. Once they returned to Grant Village, she would have to open up the discussion that wouldn't surprise Sylvia. But it was going to shock and hurt Vincent. Luckily she knew she had her mother-in-law's blessing.

They all grabbed a bite to eat and went back to their adjoining rooms. While she was alone with Johnny, she said, "I'm going to tell your grandparents we're not going back to Ohio with them. They need to know, because we need to leave for Jackson. Your grandparents will need a good night's sleep at the motel there before they fly home tomorrow."

He jumped up and down. "I can't wait to see Carson!" He hugged her so hard, he almost knocked her over.

She needed no other answer. Though his grandparents would be leaving, the only person on his mind was Carson. She couldn't wait to see him, either. After three days' deprivation, she was dying for him.

"Okay. Let's go to their room." She tapped on the door and they told her to come in.

Sylvia was resting on the bed. Vincent sat at the table, looking at a map of Yellowstone. He glanced up. "What would you two like to do now?"

"We'd like to talk to you if it's all right." That caused her mother-in-law to sit up.

Vincent smiled. "Come on in and sit down."

"Thanks. This is hard for me to say, because I love you so much and would never want to hurt you, but I can't go back to Ohio yet. Carson has asked me and Johnny to stay on so we can get to know each other better."

"He *did?*" Johnny looked shocked.

"Yes. It was the night he took me out to dinner. I didn't tell you then, because I needed time to think about it."

But happy tears were already gushing down his cheeks. "Then he really does love us!"

"Yes. I believe he does." She had a hard time swallowing. "The problem is, we've only been here a week. That's why we need more time."

Her father-in-law stared at her. "How come it's taken

until today for you to tell us? Sylvia confided in me the other day. We've been waiting."

There was a light in his eyes, making her heart beat faster.

"Why do you think we flew out here in the first place? Natalie told us you'd met a man. When Johnny got on the phone with us, we knew it was for real. We couldn't let this go on without sizing him up."

He got to his feet and came over to hug her. "Our grandson was right. Carson Lundgren is awesome. You'd be a fool not to stay. Tony's gone, and we'll love him forever, but Sylvia and I knew this day would have to come. We just didn't know you'd fall for the king of the cowboys."

"Oh, Dad!"

It was a love fest all around with Johnny hugging his grandmother.

Three hours later, Vincent drove them to the ranch house and dropped them off in front. It was almost nine in the evening. After more hugs, kisses and promises to phone, they carried their bags into the foyer. Tracy's legs were trembling so hard, she could scarcely walk. Johnny was all decked out in his cowboy stuff.

Susan was at the front desk. When she looked up, she blinked. "Hi! We all thought you'd left! Did you leave something behind?"

Yes. Our hearts.

"As a matter of fact, we did. Is Carson around?"

"He's over at the barn with the vet. One of the horses went lame this afternoon."

Johnny stared up at Tracy. "I hope it's not Goldie."

"No," Susan said. "It's not any of the ponies."

"That's good."

Tracy smiled at Susan. "Do you mind if we leave our bags out here? We won't be long."

"Of course you can. I'll put them behind the desk for now."

"Thank you." Reaching for Johnny's hand she said, "Come on, honey. Let's go find him."

They left the ranch house at a run and kept running all the way to the barn. There was an unfamiliar truck outside. The vet's most likely. The sound of coughing let her know the location of the stall before they saw the light from it.

She ventured closer, but kept out of sight. The two men were conversing. "Let's wait till they're through," she whispered to Johnny.

Their voices drifted outside the stall. "Magpie will be all right, Carson. Let her rest for a few days, and then see if her limp is improving. This capped hock isn't serious. If she gets worse, call me."

"Will do. Thanks, Jesse."

"You bet."

Tracy and Johnny stood in the shadows. They watched the other man leave the barn. Her son looked up at her with eyes that glowed in the semidarkness. "Can I tell him we're here?" he whispered.

The blood was pounding in her ears. "Tell him whatever you want, honey."

While Tracy peeked, he moved carefully until he was behind Carson who was talking to the horse and rubbing her forelock to comfort her. What a man. What a fabulous man.

"Carson?"

He spun around so fast, Johnny backed away. The look on Carson's face was one of absolute shock.

"Johnny—" Like lightning, he hunkered down in front of her son. "What are you doing here?" His voice sounded unsteady. Closer to the source of the light, Carson showed a definite pallor.

"Mom and I decided we want to stay. Grandma and Grandpa dropped us off before they went back to Jackson."

"You mean, until tomorrow?"

"No. They're going back to Ohio. We're going to stay here. Don't you want us to?"

In the next breath Carson crushed her son in his powerful arms. "Don't I *want* you to—" he cried. "Do you have any idea how much I love you and your mom?"

"We love you, too!" came Johnny's fervent cry as he wrapped his arms tightly around Carson's neck.

"Every second since the rodeo I've been praying you'd come back."

"We would have come sooner, but we had to wait till they brought us back from Yellowstone. My grandparents think you're awesome!"

Carson's eyes played over Johnny as if he couldn't believe what he was seeing or hearing. "Where's your mom?"

Her heart almost failed her. "Right here." Tracy stepped into the light. "We came as soon as we could. It's probably too early in our relationship to be saying this, but I love you, Carson. I've known it all along, but it took Johnny to say it first. You know the old saying… a child shall lead them."

His eyes burned like the blue flames in a fire. He got to his feet. "I know the saying and believe it." She heard his sharp intake of breath. "Let's go home." His voice sounded husky as he turned off the light. Sliding an arm around her shoulders, he grasped Johnny's hand and they left the barn. "If I'm dreaming this up, then we're all in it together because I'm never letting you go."

"Is anyone using our cabin?" Johnny wanted to know.

"Yes."

"Then where will we stay?"

"With me."

Tracy's joy spiked.

"You mean in the ranch house?"

"Yup."

"Goody. I love it in there, but I've never seen where you sleep."

"You're going to find out right now, but it'll be temporary because I'm building us a house in my favorite spot by the river, smack-dab in the middle of a flowering meadow."

"You are?"

"It will have a loft where you can sleep and see the Grand Teton right out your window. I was thinking of getting a dog."

Johnny squealed. "Can I have a Boston terrier? Nate has one." Tracy didn't know that. She hadn't heard the other boy's name for a long time.

"What a great choice. He can sleep with you in the loft. You'll be able to see the mountains from every window." He squeezed Tracy's hip, sending a jolt through her like a current of electricity.

The sweet smell of sage rose up from the valley floor, increasing her euphoria. The moon had come up, distilling its serene beauty over a landscape Tracy had learned to love with a fierceness that surprised her.

When they walked in the foyer, Susan jumped to her feet. "Hi, Carson. Looks like they found you."

He sent Tracy a private message. "That they did. Just so you know, they're staying with me."

"Our luggage is behind the counter," Johnny announced. "I'll get it."

Her son was acting like a man. That was Carson's influence. He carried the cases around, but held on to the shoulder bag. Carson picked them up. "Let's go, partner. You want to open that door at the end of the hall past the restrooms?"

"Sure."

Once again Carson was allowing her into his inner sanctum, but this time there was all the difference in the world, because she wouldn't be leaving it.

He led them down a hall till he came to a bedroom on his left. "In here, Johnny. This is where you and your mom will stay for now." The room was rustic and cozy with twin beds and an en suite bathroom. Carson set the bags down on the wood floor and turned to her.

"When we planned the dude ranch, we decided we'd use this guest bedroom if there was ever an overflow. Little did I know when I sent you that letter…" He couldn't finish the sentence, but he said everything with his eyes. Her emotions were so overpowering she couldn't talk, either.

"Hey, Carson—can I see your room?"

"You bet. Follow me." They went across the hall to his suite where she'd been before. Her eyes slid to the bed where the fire between them had ignited, only to be stifled. Thank heaven this was now. The thought of another separation from Carson just meant pain to her.

"This is a big room!"

"My grandparents lived in here."

"Look at all these pictures!" Johnny ran around staring at them. "Hey, Mom—here are pictures of Carson when he was little, riding a pony like me! But there's no saddle. I want to learn to ride without a saddle. That's so cool."

"We'll try it out in a few days."

"What was your pony's name?"

"Confetti, because she was spotty."

"How cute," Tracy murmured as Carson came to stand behind her. He looped his strong arms around her neck, pressing kisses into her hair. He felt so wonderful, she couldn't wait to be alone with him.

"My grandparents took pictures of me constantly. You'll see me at every gawky stage."

"These are when you were in the Marines."

"Yup. My parents' and grandparents' pictures are on the other walls."

Johnny hurried over to look at them. "Is this your dad?"

The picture he was pointing to was in an oval frame. "Yes. He was twelve there."

"You kind of look like him."

"I've been told I resemble my mother more. See their wedding picture over on the left?"

Johnny moved to get a glance. "You do look a lot like her!"

This was an exciting night, but Johnny needed to get to bed. She needed him to go to sleep because she was going to die of longing for Carson if he didn't. "Honey? I'm sure Carson will let you look at everything tomorrow. But right now it's time for bed."

"Okay." He looked at Carson. "Will you come with me and Mom?"

"I was hoping you'd ask because I'd like to do it every night from now on. Let's go, partner."

Tracy moved ahead and pulled his pajamas out of his suitcase. Once his teeth were brushed, he climbed under the covers of the twin bed nearest the bathroom. While she stood by him, Carson set Johnny's cowboy hat on the dresser and sat down at his side.

"Do you know I never thought I'd get married or have a family?"

"I know. 'Cos you're afraid you'll cough too much and a woman won't like it, but Mom says it doesn't matter to her."

Carson shot her a penetrating glance. "Then I'm the luckiest man alive." He looked back at him. "I know I'm not your father, Johnny. I could never take his place, but I want you to know I love you as much as if you were my own son."

"I love you, too." Johnny sat up and gave him another squeeze before he settled back down against the pillow.

"Okay. It's time to go to sleep now. I'll stay with you while Carson closes up the ranch house and turns out the lights." In truth, Tracy had no idea of his routine, but until her son passed out, she couldn't go into Carson's room.

He got to his feet and tousled Johnny's hair. "I know a little filly who's going to be very happy when you show up to ride her tomorrow."

"I bet she's really missed me."

"You have no idea. Goodnight, partner. See you in the morning."

Carson's gaze slid to Tracy's. His eyes blazed with the promise of what was to come.

Chapter Eleven

Carson's elation was too great. He dashed down the hall and up the stairs. After coughing his head off, he called out to the guys. They emerged from their rooms in various states of undress.

Buck stared at him as if he were seeing an apparition. "What's happened to you? I hardly recognize the walking corpse."

"You might well ask."

"Something's up." Ross walked around him. "If I didn't know better…"

He nodded to both of them. "Tracy came back tonight with Johnny. They love me. They're here to stay and her in-laws gave us their blessing."

Slow smiles broke out on their faces. They slapped him on the back. "Congratulations. When's the wedding?"

"I haven't even been alone with her yet. She's putting Johnny to bed. I've installed them in the guest bedroom across from me. After tonight I'll know our plans better."

"What in the hell are you doing up here?"

"Trying to give her time to get him to sleep. Until we can be alone, I don't dare get anywhere near her.

Besides, the three of us have a business arrangement. I don't want you to think my personal plans change anything."

Buck nodded. "We know that."

"If you want our blessing, you've got it." Ross gave him another pat on the shoulder. "Now, you've got thirty seconds to get out of here!"

Carson's eyes smarted. "Thanks, guys. I couldn't have made it out of the hospital without you."

Ross's brow quirked. "If you didn't know it yet, you saved my life with your offer to come here."

"Amen," Buck muttered. "We were dead meat when we arrived at the hospital. It took meeting you guys to make me believe there was still some hope. If Tracy's willing to take you on, inhaler and all, then you're one lucky dude."

"She's a keeper."

"She is," Carson murmured. "Unless there's a fire, I'm unavailable till morning."

He heard hoots and wolf whistles as he started down the stairs.

TRACY HEARD HIM coming and hurried out of the bedroom. Johnny had finally dropped off. When they saw each other, they both started running. He picked her up and swung her around before carrying her into his bedroom.

"I need your mouth more than I need life," he cried softly. They mouths met and clung with a refined savagery while they tried to satisfy their hunger. But it was unquenchable as they found out when they ended up on the bed.

"Oh, Tracy…" His voice was ragged. "When you

drove away the other night, I literally thought I wasn't going to make it through the night, let alone the rest of my life. Earlier, when you told me you'd be leaving after the rodeo, I happened to meet the redheaded barrel racer in town and she asked me to meet her after it was over. I told her I would because my pain was so bad.

"But I couldn't. Instead I got a message to her that something else had come up and I went on a drive in the truck. I ended up at the pasture, if you can believe it, not even realizing where I was until I got there."

"Oh, my darling." She covered his face with kisses. "Sylvia and I had an illuminating talk before we ever left for Yellowstone. She knew what was in my heart and urged me to do what I wanted. She was wonderful. But it was Johnny who turned everything around. He said he wanted to go home because you didn't love him."

"What?"

"I know. Can you believe it? But children are so literal, and when he told you he loved you in the tent, you didn't say the same words back. He decided you didn't want him around."

"I was afraid to say it back before."

"I know. You didn't want to raise any hopes with him, and I love you for that. So when I translated what you said about the feeling being mutual, he was a changed child. I told him I loved you, too, but we needed to go to the park with his grandparents and I'd have a talk with Vincent.

"As it turned out, Sylvia had already told him the truth, and he told me I'd be a fool if I didn't stay on with you. That was music to my ears. You really did win them over, and they can see how happy you make me and Johnny. But I have to tell you, you make me so happy, I'm jumping out of my skin."

"Then jump into mine, sweetheart." They kissed over and over again, long and hard, slow and gentle, still not quite believing this was happening.

"I'm the luckiest woman alive to have met you. I don't know how I could have been so blessed.

"Besides being a hero in every sense of the word, you're absolutely the most gorgeous man, you know. I haven't been able to take my eyes off you since we got here."

"Let's talk gorgeous, shall we?" He rolled over on top of her. "That day at the lake, I could have eaten you alive."

"Then we were both having the same problem. The only trouble with falling in love when you have a son who's my shadow, is finding any time alone. Even now, he's just across the hall and could wake up at any moment."

"I know that." He ran his fingers through her silky hair. "It's probably a good thing. We need a chaperone if we're going to do this thing by the book. I've decided that's exactly what we're going to do."

"Don't I have any say in it?"

"Yes. Please don't make us wait months to get married. After what we both went through during the war, life's too precious to waste time when something this fantastic comes along. *You're* fantastic, my love."

"How about a month?"

His groan came out on a cough.

"I wish we could get married tonight, but a month will give any of the family long enough to make plans if they want to fly out for the wedding. Do you think you can wait that long?"

"I can do anything as long you'll be my wife. I guess I'd better make this official. Will you marry me, Tracy? This is going to be forever."

"Yes, yes, yes! You've made me the happiest woman on earth. Last night while I was lying in bed, tossing and turning for want of you, I started imagining married life with you. I—I always wanted another baby. A little brother or sister for Johnny, but maybe I'm getting way ahead of myself. It's just that you're already the most remarkable father to Johnny. But—"

"But what?" He stifled the word with his lips. "I think you and I were having the same dream last night, but I didn't stop with one child."

"Oh, darling—" She crushed him in her arms. "Johnny's so crazy about you. To have more babies with you— Life with you is going to be glorious!" She stared into those brilliant blue eyes. "Love me, darling. I need you so badly."

"You don't know the half of it."

Hours later, they surfaced. "Did I ever tell you the advice my grandfather gave me years ago?"

"No," she whispered into his neck.

"He told me I could look at a woman, but if she wasn't available, then that was all I could do. I'm afraid that advice got thrown out the window when you walked into the terminal."

She kissed his hard jaw. "You were inspired to invite all those special families here. It's a great thing you're doing, but I honestly believe I was guided here to you."

"I know you were. When the idea first came to me

in the hospital, it came fully fledged, like some power had planted it there."

"I believe that. I wouldn't be surprised if your grandfather had a hand in it, because he could see what was coming and wanted you to find true happiness."

"Tracy…" He murmured her name over and over. "I want to believe it because I know I've found it with you."

"I feel the same way, and I know that wherever Tony is, he's happy for us, too."

He hugged her possessively. "Don't leave me yet. We have at least an hour before sunup."

"I'll only stay a little longer, because you never know about Johnny."

"Then let's go use the other twin bed in your room, so we can enjoy this precious time without worry."

But it didn't work out so well. Carson finally fell asleep, face down, but coughed enough that by six o'clock Johnny woke up and looked over at the two of them. Tracy smiled at him. "Good morning."

"Hey—did you guys stay in here with me all night?"

Carson opened one eye and turned over. "We did for part of the night. How did you sleep, partner?"

"Good." He scrambled out of bed to get his cap gun.

"Guess what? There's a ten-year-old girl staying at your old cabin named Julie."

"Did her dad die, too?"

"No. She and her parents are tourists staying for a few days. I'm going to need you to show her how to ride."

"Has she ever been on a horse?"

"I don't know. We'll have to ask Ross."

"I think she'd better ride Mitzi."

Tracy lost the battle of tears and wiped them away furiously. "Johnny? Carson and I talked everything over last night. We're going to get married in a month."

He frowned. "How come we have to wait a month?"

Carson chuckled. "Yeah, Mom," he whispered in her ear.

"To give the family time to come if they want."

"Can I call Cory and tell him?"

"Of course. You can call everyone and invite them."

Johnny walked over to their bed. "Carson?"

By the inflection in his voice, it sounded serious. Carson sat up. "What is it?"

"When you get married, can I call you Dad?"

Carson had to clear his throat several times. "I'd be honored if you did, but only if you want to."

"I do!"

"How about if after the wedding I call you son? That's how I think of you already."

"I want to be your son," he said soberly. "Can I tell Grandma and Grandpa about…well, you know."

"Of course. I want everyone to know how happy I am."

"I'm happy, too."

"Come here, Johnny, and give me a hug."

Tracy's son flew into his arms. She sat up and threw her arms around both of them. Life simply didn't get any better than this.

* * * * *

A FAMILY FOR THE RUGGED RANCHER

DONNA ALWARD

Donna Alward is a busy wife and mother of three (two daughters and the family dog), and she believes hers is the best job in the world: a combination of stay-at-home mum and romance novelist. An avid reader since childhood, Donna has always made up her own stories. She completed her arts degree in English literature in 1994, but it wasn't until 2001 that she penned her first full-length novel and found herself hooked on writing romance. In 2006, she sold her first manuscript, and now writes warm, emotional stories for Mills & Boon.

In her new home office in Nova Scotia, Donna loves being back on the east coast of Canada after nearly twelve years in Alberta, where her career began, writing about cowboys and the West. Donna's debut romance, *Hired by the Cowboy*, was awarded a Booksellers' Best Award in 2008 for Best Traditional Romance.

With the Atlantic Ocean only minutes away from her doorstep, Donna has found a fresh lake on hlife and promises even more great romances in the near future!

Donna loves to hear from readers. You can contact her through her website, www.donnaalward.com, or follow @DonnaAlward on Twitter.

CHAPTER ONE

"ARE WE HERE, Mama? Is Daddy here?"

Emily smiled, though Sam's innocent question made her heart quiver. Sam looked for Rob everywhere, never giving up hope no matter how often he was disappointed. "Yes," she replied, "we're here. But Daddy's not coming, remember? I'm here to start a brand-new job."

She touched the brake pedal as she entered the farmyard of Evans and Son. It was bigger than she'd imagined, sprawling across several acres criss-crossed with fence lines and dotted with leafy green poplar trees. She slowed as she approached the plain white two-story house that rested at the end of the drive. It was flanked on one side by a gigantic barn and on the other by a large workshop with two oversized garage doors. More outbuildings were interspersed throughout the yard, all of them tidy and well-kept. The grass around them was newly clipped and the bits of peeling paint made for a broken-in look rather than broken down.

Evans and Son looked to be doing all right in the overall scheme of things—which was more than Emily could say for her family. But she was going to change all that. Starting today.

She parked to the right of the house, inhaling deeply and letting out a slow breath, trying to steady herself. When she looked into the back seat, she saw Sam's eyes opening, taking a moment to focus and realize the vehicle had stopped.

"But I want to see Daddy."

"I know, baby." Emily told herself to be patient, he was only five. "Once we're settled, I'll help you write a letter. Maybe you can draw him a picture. What do you think?"

Sam's eyes still held that trace of confusion and sadness that had the power to hurt Emily more than anything else. Sam had been clingier than usual lately. It was hardly a surprise. She'd put the house up for sale and their things in storage. She'd announced that they were leaving the city, which also meant leaving playschool friends and everything familiar, and a five-year-old couldn't be expected to understand her reasons. But the house in Calgary held too many memories—happy and devastating by turns. Both Emily and Sam were stuck in wishing for the past—a past that was long over. Rob had moved on, withdrawing not only his financial support but, more importantly, severing emotional ties with both of them.

Emily would never understand that, especially where his son was concerned. But now it was time to let go and build a new life. One where they could be happy. One where Emily could support her son and find her own way rather than wishing for what should have been. There was a certain freedom to be found in knowing she could make her own decisions now. Her choices were hers to make and hers alone. A massive responsibility, but a liberating one, too.

She reminded herself that a happier life for the two of them was why she was here. "Wait here for just a moment while I knock on the door, okay? Then we'll get settled, I promise."

"It's quiet here."

"I know." Emily smiled, trying to be encouraging. "But there is still sound. Listen closely, Sam, and when I get back you can tell me what you heard."

Sam had only ever lived in the city, with the sounds of traffic and sirens and voices his usual background music. But Emily remembered what it was like to live outside the metropolitan area, where the morning song wasn't honking horns but birds warbling in the caragana bushes and the shush of the breeze through poplar leaves. For the first time in months, she was starting to feel hope that this was all going to turn out all right.

"Wait here, okay? Let me talk to Mr. Evans first, and then I'll come for you."

"Okay, Mama." Sam reached over and picked up his favorite storybook, the Dr. Seuss one with the tongue twisters that he'd practically memorized. Emily paused, her tender smile wavering just a little. Sometimes Sam seemed to see and understand too much. Had the breakdown of her marriage forced her son to grow up too soon?

"I won't be long, sweetie." Emily blew him a kiss, shut the car door and straightened her T-shirt, smoothing it over the hips of her denim capris. It was really important that everything got off on the right foot, so she practiced smiling, wanting it to seem natural and not show her nervousness. She climbed the few steps to the front porch, gathered her courage and rapped sharply on the door.

No one answered.

This was not a great beginning, and doubts crept in, making her wonder if it was a sign that she was making a big mistake with this whole idea. Selling the house and uprooting the two of them was a bit of a radical move, she knew that. She glanced back at the car only feet away and saw Sam's dark head still bent over his book. No, this was best. Her experience as a mom and homemaker was what made her perfect for this job, she realized. She'd loved being a stay-at-home mom, and being with Sam was the most important thing.

Maybe Mr. Evans simply hadn't heard her. She knocked

again, folding her hands. It was a bit nerve-wracking being hired for a job sight unseen. She'd interviewed at the agency but this was different. She'd have to pass Mr. Evans's tests, too. He had the final say. When was the last time she'd had a real interview? All of her résumés over the last year had been sent out without so much as a nibble in return. No one wanted to hire a lab tech who'd been out of the work force for the past five years.

She forced herself to stay calm, stave off the disappointment she felt as her second knock also went unanswered.

"Can I help you?"

The voice came from her right and her stomach twisted into knots as a man approached from the shop, wiping dirty hands on a rag. This was Mr. Evans? He looked younger than she was, for heaven's sake. He wore faded jeans and dusty roper boots, his long stride eating up the ground between them. His baseball cap shaded his eyes so that she couldn't quite see them. The dark T-shirt he wore was stained with grease, stretched taut over a muscled chest. All in all he had the look of honest work about him. And honest work ranked high on her list of attributes lately, she thought bitterly. Good looks didn't.

"I...I'm Emily Northcott. I'm here from the agency?" She hated how uncertain that sounded, so she amended, "From Maid on Demand."

There was a slight pause in his stride while Emily went back down the steps. They met at the bottom, the grass tickling Emily's toes in her sandals as she held out her hand.

The man held up his right hand. "Luke Evans. I'd better not. You don't want to get grease on your hands."

Embarrassment crept hotly up her cheeks, both because she knew she should have realized his hands would be dirty and because of his flat tone. Emily dropped her hand to her side and tried a smile. "Oh, right. I hope we…I…haven't come at a bad time."

"Just fixing some machinery in the shed. I heard the car pull up. Wasn't expecting you though."

"Didn't the agency call?"

"I'm not often in the house to answer the phone." He stated it as if it were something obvious that she'd missed.

Emily frowned. His communication skills could use some work. Didn't he have a cell phone like most normal people? Or voice mail? Or was he being deliberately difficult?

"I was specifically given today as a start date and directions to your place, Mr. Evans."

He tucked the rag into the back pocket of his jeans. "They probably called my sister. She's the one who placed the ad."

"Your sister?"

"My sister Cait. They might have tried there, but she's in the hospital."

"Oh, I'm sorry. I hope it's nothing serious." His answers were so clipped they merely prompted more questions, but his stance and attitude didn't exactly inspire her to ask them.

Finally he gave in and smiled. Just a little, and it looked like it pained him to do so. But pain or not, the look changed his face completely. The icy blue of his eyes thawed a tad and when he smiled, matching creases formed on either side of his mouth. "Nothing too serious," he replied. "She's having a baby."

The news made his smile contagious and Emily smiled back, then caught herself. She clenched her fingers, nervous all over again. She hadn't really given a thought to age…or to the fact that the rancher looking for a housekeeper might be somewhat attractive. What surprised her most was that she noticed at all. Those thoughts had no place in her head right now, considering the scars left from her last relationship and her determination not to put herself through that again.

And Evans wasn't a looker, not in a classic turn-your-head handsome sort of way. But there was something about the tilt of his smile, as though he was telling a joke. Or the way that his cornflower-blue eyes seemed to see right into her. He had inordinately pretty eyes for a man, she thought ridiculously. Had she really thought "somewhat" attractive? She swallowed. He was long, lean and muscled, and his voice held a delicious bit of grit. His strength made up for the lack of pretty. More than made up for it.

Suddenly, being a housekeeper to a single man in the middle of nowhere didn't seem like the bright idea it had been a week ago.

"The agency hired me," she repeated.

He let out a short laugh. "So you said."

Emily resisted the urge to close her eyes, wondering if he'd seen clear through to her last thoughts. Maybe the prairie could just open up and swallow her, and save her more embarrassment. "Right."

"You're able to start today?"

Hope surged as she opened her eyes and found him watching her steadily. He wasn't giving her the brush-off straight away after all. "Yes, sir." She forced a smile. "I can start today."

"Mom, can't I come out now? It's hot in here."

The nerves in Emily's stomach froze as Sam's soft voice came from the car. Luke's head swiveled in the direction of the car, and Emily gave in and sighed. Dammit. She hadn't even had a chance to talk to Evans about their arrangements or anything. A muscle ticked in Luke's jaw and he looked back at her, the smile gone now, the edges of his jaw hard and forbidding.

"My son, Sam," she said weakly.

"You have children."

"Child—just Sam. He's five and no trouble, I promise.

Good as gold." That was stretching it a bit; Sam was a typical five-year-old who was as prone to curiosity and frustrations as any child his age. She looked again at Evans and knew she had to convince him. He was the one who'd advertised. She'd gone through the agency screening and they had hired her for the job. If this didn't work out she had nowhere to go. And she wanted to stay here. She'd liked the look of the place straight off.

Another moment and he'd have her begging. She straightened her shoulders. She would not beg. Not ever again. She could always go to her parents. It wasn't what she wanted, and there'd be a fair amount of told-you-so. Her parents had never quite taken to Rob, and the divorce hadn't come as a big surprise to them. It wasn't that they didn't love her or would deny her help. It was just…

She needed to do this herself. To prove to herself she could and to be the parent that Sam deserved. She couldn't rely on other people to make this right. Not even her parents.

"Mrs. Northcott, this is a ranch, not a day care." The smile that had captivated her only moments before had disappeared, making his face a frozen mask. The warm crinkles around his lips and eyes were now frown marks and Emily felt her good intentions go spiraling down the proverbial drain.

"It's Ms.," she pointed out tartly. It wasn't her fault that there'd been a mix-up. "And Sam is five, hardly a toddler who needs following around all the time." She raised an eyebrow. "Mothers have been cleaning and cooking *and* raising children since the beginning of time, Mr. Evans."

She heard the vinegar in her voice and felt badly for speaking so sharply, but she was a package deal and the annoyance that had marked his face when he heard Sam's voice put her back up.

"I'm well aware of that. However, I didn't advertise for a family. I advertised for a housekeeper."

"Your *sister*—" she made sure to point out the distinction "—advertised with Maid on Demand Domestics. If any part of that ad wasn't clear, perhaps you need to speak to them. The agency is aware I have a son, so perhaps there was a flaw with the ad. I interviewed for the job and I got it." She lifted her chin. "Perhaps you would have been better off going without an agency?"

She knew her sharp tongue was probably shooting her chances in the foot, but she couldn't help it. She was hardly to blame. Nor would she be made to feel guilty or be bullied, not anymore. If he didn't want her services, he could just say so.

"It's not that…I tried putting an ad in the paper and around town…oh, why am I explaining this to you?" he asked, shoving his hands into his pockets despite any grease remaining on his fingers.

"If it's that you don't like children…" That would make her decision much easier. She wouldn't make Sam stay in an unfriendly environment. No job was worth that. She backed up a step and felt her hands tightening into anxious fists.

"I didn't say that." His brow wrinkled. He was clearly exasperated.

She caught a hint of desperation in his voice and thought perhaps all wasn't lost. "Then your objection to my son is…"

"Mom!" The impatient call came from the car and Emily gritted her teeth.

"Excuse me just a moment," she muttered, going to the car to speak to Sam.

It was hot inside the car, and Emily figured she had nothing to lose now. "You can get out," she said gently, opening the door. "Sorry I made you wait so long."

"Are we staying here?"

"I'm not sure."

Sam held his mother's hand…something he rarely did any more since he'd started preschool and considered himself a big boy. Perhaps Evans simply needed to meet Sam and talk to him. It had to be harder to say no to children, right? It wasn't Sam's fault his life had been turned upside down. Emily was trying to do the right thing for him. A summer in the country had sounded perfect. This place was new and different with no history, no bad memories. She just needed to show Evans that Sam would be no extra trouble.

"Mr. Evans, this is my son, Sam."

Evans never cracked a smile. "Sam."

"Sir," Sam replied. Emily was vastly proud that Sam lifted his chin the tiniest bit, though his voice was absolutely respectful.

Emily put a hand on Sam's shoulder. "The agency did know about him, Mr. Evans. I'm not trying to pull a fast one here. If it's a deal-breaker, tell me now and take it up with them. But you should know that I'm fully qualified for this job. I know how to cook and clean and garden. I'm not afraid of hard work and you won't be sorry you hired me."

He shook his head, and Emily noticed again the color of his eyes, a brilliant shade of blue that seemed to pierce straight through her. Straightforward, honest eyes. She liked that. Except for the fact that his gaze made her want to straighten her hair or fuss with the hem of her shirt. She did neither.

"I'm sorry," he replied.

That was it, then. Maybe he had a kind side somewhere but it didn't extend to giving her the job. She would not let him see the disappointment sinking through her body to her toes, making the weight of her situation that much heavier to carry. She wouldn't let it matter. She'd bounced back from worse over the last year. She'd find something else.

"I'm sorry I've taken up your time," she said politely. She took Sam's hand and turned back towards her car.

"Where are you going?"

His surprised voice made her halt and turn back. He'd taken off his cap and was now running his hand over his short-clipped hair. It was sandy-brown, she noticed. The same color as his T-shirt.

"I never said the job wasn't yours. I was apologizing."

Is that what that was? Emily wanted to ask but sensed things were at a delicate balance right now and could go either way. She simply nodded, holding her breath.

"The job description said room and board included." She was pushing it, but this had to be settled before either of them agreed to anything. She felt Sam's small hand in hers. She wanted to give him a summer like the ones she remembered. Open spaces and simple pleasures. Some peace and quiet and new adventures rather than the reminders of their once happy life as a whole family. Life wasn't going to be the same again, and Emily didn't know what to do to make it better anymore. And this farm—it was perfect. She could smell the sweet fragrance of lilacs in the air. The lawn was huge, more than big enough for a child to play. She'd glimpsed a garden on the way in, and she imagined showing Sam how to tell weeds from vegetables and picking peas and beans later in the summer when they were plump and ripe.

"I offered room and board, but only for one. Adding an extra is unexpected."

"I'll make sure he doesn't get in your way," she assured him quickly, hearing the edge of desperation in her voice, knowing she was *this* close to hearing him say yes. "And we can adjust my pay if that helps." She wished she weren't so transparent. She didn't want him to know how badly she wanted this to work out. She was willing to compromise. Was he?

Pride warred with want at this moment. She didn't want to tell Luke Evans how much it would mean for them to stay here, but seeing the look of wonder on Sam's face as he spotted a hawk circling above, following its movements until it settled on a fence post, searching for mice or prairie dogs... She'd do anything to keep that going. Even if it meant sacrificing her pride just a little bit.

"Little boys probably don't eat much. If you're sure to keep him out of the way... I have a farm to run, Ms. Northcott."

He put a slight emphasis on the Ms., but she ignored it as excitement rushed through her. He was doing it! He was giving her the job, kid and all. For the first time in five years she would be earning her own money. She was making a first step towards self-reliance, and she'd done it all on her own. Today keeping house for Luke Evans...who knew what the future would hold? She reveled in the feeling of optimism, something that had been gone for a long time. She offered a small smile and wondered what he was thinking. She would make sure he didn't regret it and that Sam would mean little disruption to his house. "You mean we can stay?"

"You're a housekeeper, aren't you? The agency did hire you."

The acid tone was back, so she merely nodded, the curl at her temple flopping.

"And you did say you could cook and clean. I'm counting on it."

She smiled at him then, a new confidence filling her heart. Lordy, he was so stern! But perhaps he could smile once in a while. Maybe she could make him. Right now she felt as though she could do anything.

"Oh, yes. That's definitely not an omission or exaggeration. I've been a stay-at-home mom since Sam was born. I promise you, Mr. Evans, I can clean, cook and do laundry with my eyes closed." She could sew, too, and make origami animals out of plain paper and construct Halloween costumes out of some cardboard, newspaper and string. The latter skills probably weren't a high priority on a ranch.

"Just remember this is a working ranch, not a summer camp. There is a lot of work to be done and a lot of machinery around. Make sure the boy doesn't cause any trouble, or go where he shouldn't be going."

"His name is Sam, and you have my word." She'd watch Sam with eyes in the back of her head if she had to. She had a job. And one where she could still be there for Sam—so important right now as he went through the stress of a family breakup.

"Then bring your things inside. I'll show you around quickly. Bear in mind I was unprepared for you, so none of the rooms are ready. You'll have to do that yourself while I fix the baler."

He was letting them stay. She knew she should just accept it and be grateful, but she also knew it was not what he'd wanted or planned, and she felt compelled to give him one more chance to be sure. "Are you certain? I don't want to put you out, Mr. Evans. It's obvious this is a surprise for you. I don't want you to feel obligated. We can find other accommodation."

He paused. "You need this job, don't you?"

He gave her a pointed look and Emily shifted her gaze to her feet. She added a mental note: not only stern but keenly sharp, too. Yes, she did need the job. Until the money went through from the sale of the house, they were on a shoe-string and even then their circumstances would be drastically changed. It was why they'd had to sell in the first place. With no money coming in and Rob neglecting to pay child support, the savings account had dried up quickly and she couldn't afford to make the mortgage payments. She couldn't hide the frayed straps of her sandals and the older model, no-frills vehicle she drove instead of the luxury sedan she'd traded in six months ago. Everything was different. It wasn't the hardest thing about the divorce, but after a while a woman couldn't ignore practicalities.

He took her silence as assent. "And I need someone to look after the house. It doesn't make sense for you to pay to stay somewhere else, and days are long here. The deal was room and board, so that's what you'll get. How much trouble can one boy be, anyway?"

CHAPTER TWO

LUKE TRIED TO keep his body relaxed as he held open the screen door, but Emily Northcott was making it difficult. Whatever she had put on for perfume that morning teased his nostrils. It was light and pretty, just like her. Her short hair was the color of mink and curled haphazardly around her face, like the hair cover models had that was meant to look deliberately casual. And she had the biggest brown eyes he'd ever seen, fringed with thick dark lashes.

When he'd first advertised for a housekeeper, Emily was not what he'd had in mind. He'd figured on someone local, someone, well, *older* to answer his ad. A motherly figure with graying hair, definitely not someone who looked like Emily. Someone who lived nearby who could arrive in the morning and leave again at dinnertime. But when his local ads had gone unanswered week after week, he'd put Cait on the job. She'd been getting so clucky and meddling as her pregnancy progressed. He'd thought it would be a good project for her and would keep her out of his hair. It was only the promise of getting outside help that had ceased her constant baking and fussing over the house. Not that he didn't need the help. He did, desperately. But having Cait underfoot all the time had been driving him crazy.

Maid on Demand had seemed like the perfect solution, anonymous and impersonal. Except now he'd ended up worse off than ever—with a beautiful woman with a family of her own, 24/7.

He should have said no, flat-out.

He'd be a bald-faced liar if he said Emily Northcott wasn't the prettiest woman to pass through his door in months. Just the scent of her put him on alert. Not that he was in the market for a girlfriend. But he was human, after all.

But what could he say? No, you can't stay because you're too pretty? Because you're too young? She couldn't be more than thirty. And then there was her son. How could he turn her away for that reason either? He'd have to be cold-hearted to use that against her. So far the boy had hardly made a peep. And it was only for a few months, after all. Once things wound down later in the fall, he'd be better able to handle things on his own.

"Have a look around," he suggested, as the screen door slapped shut behind them. "I'm going to wash up. I've had my hands inside the baler for the better part of the afternoon. Then I'll give you the nickel tour."

He left her standing in the entry hall while he went to the kitchen and turned on the tap. The whole idea of hiring help was to make his summer easier, not add more responsibility to it. But that was exactly how it felt. If she stayed, it meant two extra bodies to provide for over the next few months. Twice as many mouths to feed than he'd expected. And having that sort of responsibility—whether real or implied—was something he never wanted to do again. He liked his life plain, simple and uncomplicated. Or at least as uncomplicated as it could be considering his family circumstances.

He scrubbed the grease from his hands with the pumice paste, taking a nail brush and relentlessly applying it to his nails. The plain truth was that not one soul had applied for the job—not even a teenager looking for summer work. Cait had put the listing with the agency nearly three weeks ago.

Things were in full swing now and he needed the help. Luke was already working sun-up to sundown. The housework was falling behind, and he was tired of eating a dry sandwich when he came in at the end of the day. He was barely keeping up with the laundry, putting a load in when he was falling-down tired at night.

They could stay as long as it meant they stayed out of his way. He didn't have time for babysitting along with everything else.

When he returned from the kitchen, Emily was in the living room on the right, her fingertips running over the top of an old radio and record player that had long ceased to work and that now held a selection of family photos on its wooden cover. His heart contracted briefly, seeing her gentle hands on the heirloom, but he pushed the feeling aside and cleared his throat. "You ready?"

"This is beautiful. And very old."

He nodded. "It was my grandparents'. They used to play records on it. Some of the LPs are still inside, but the player doesn't work anymore."

"And this is your family?"

Luke stepped forward and looked at the assortment of photos. There were three graduation pictures—him and his sisters when they'd each completed twelfth grade. Cait's and Liz's wedding pictures were there as well, and baby pictures of Liz's children. Soon Cait's new baby would be featured there, too. There was a picture of three children all together, taken one golden autumn several years earlier, and in the middle sat a picture of his parents, his dad sitting down and his mom's hand on his shoulder as they smiled for the camera. The last two pictures were difficult to look at. That had been the year that everything had changed. First his mom, and then his dad.

"My sister's doing. Our parents always had pictures on here and she keeps it stocked."

He saw a wrinkle form between her eyebrows and his jaw tightened. He wasn't all that fond of the gallery of reminders, but Cait had insisted. He'd never been able to deny her anything, and he knew to take the pictures down would mean hurting Cait, and Liz, too, and he couldn't do it.

"Your dad looks very handsome. You look like him. In the jaw and the shape of your mouth."

Luke swallowed. He could correct her, but he knew in reality the handsome bit no longer applied to his father. Time and illness had leached it from his body, bit by painful bit. Luke didn't want to be like him. Not that way. Not ever. The fact that he might not have a choice was something he dealt with every single day.

"I have work to do, Ms. Northcott. Do you think we can continue the tour now?"

She turned away from the family gallery and smiled at him. He'd done his best not to encourage friendliness, so why on earth was she beaming at him? It was like a ray of sunshine warming the room when she smiled at him like that. "I'd love to," she replied.

Luke didn't answer, just turned away from the radio with a coldness that he could see succeeded in wiping the smile from her face. "Let's get a move on, then," he said over his shoulder. "So I can get back to work."

Emily scowled at his departing back. She had her work cut out for her, then. To her mind, Luke Evans had lived alone too long. His interpersonal skills certainly needed some polishing. Granted, her life hadn't been all sunshine and flowers lately, but she at least could be pleasant. She refused to let his sour attitude ruin her day.

"Do you mind if I turn the TV on for Sam? That way we

can get through faster. I don't want to hold you up." After his comment about Sam being a distraction, Emily figured this was the easiest way. After Evans was gone to the barn, she'd enlist Sam's help and they'd work together. Make it fun.

As they started up the stairs, Luke turned around and paused, his hand on the banister. "I apologize for the sorry state of the house," he said. "My sister hasn't been by in a few weeks and with haying time and the new calves…"

"Isn't that why I'm here?"

"I don't want to scare you off," he said, starting up the stairs once more. Gruff or not, Emily got the feeling that he was relieved she was there. Or at least relieved *someone* was there to do the job he required.

She followed him up, unable to avoid the sight of his bottom in the faded jeans. Two identical wear spots lightened the pockets. As he took her through the house she realized he hadn't been exaggerating. The spare rooms had a fine film of dust on the furniture. The rugs were in desperate need of a vacuuming and he'd left his shaving gear and towel on the bathroom vanity this morning, along with whiskers dotting the white porcelain of the sink. The linen closet was a jumbled mess of pillows, blankets and sheets arranged in no particular order, and the laundry basket was filled to overflowing.

The tour continued and Emily tried to be positive through it all. "The floors are gorgeous," she tried, hoping to put them on more of an even footing. "They look like the original hardwood."

"They are. And they have the scratches to prove it."

She bit back a sigh and tried again. "Scratches just add character. And the doors are solid wood rather than those hollow imitations in stores these days. Such a great color of stain."

"They need refinishing."

Emily gave up for the time being; her attempts at anything

positive were completely ineffectual. She simply followed him down the hall. The smallest bedroom was painted a pale green and had one wall on a slant with a charming oval window looking over the fields. She fell in love with it immediately. A second room was painted pink and one wall had rosebud wallpaper. A third door remained closed—she presumed it was his room. But when he opened the door to the final room she caught her breath. It must have been his parents' room, all gleaming dark wood and an ivory chenille spread. It was like stepping back in time—hooked rugs on the floor and dainty Priscilla curtains at the windows.

"What a beautiful room." She looked up at Luke and saw a muscle tick in his jaw. It was almost as if seeing it caused him pain, but why?

"It belonged to my parents," he answered, and shut the door before she could say any more.

Back in the kitchen the clean dishes were piled in the drying rack, the teetering pile a masterpiece of domestic engineering. In the partner sink, dirty dishes formed a smaller, stickier pile. The kitchen cupboards were sturdy solid oak, and Emily knew a washing with oil soap would make them gleam again. The fridge needed a good wiping down. She paused a moment to glance at the magnetic notepad stuck to the fridge door. It was simply a list of phone numbers. She frowned as she read the names *Cait* and *Liz,* wondering why he didn't simply have his sister's numbers memorized. After his brusqueness, there was no way on earth she'd ask.

Overall, the house was a throwback to what felt like a happier, simpler time. "All it needs is some love and polish, Mr. Evans. You have a beautiful home."

The tour finished, Luke cleared his throat, his feet shifting from side to side. "I really need to get back to fixing the baler. This weather isn't going to hold and I have help coming tomorrow. The job is yours, Ms. Northcott."

She grinned at him, ready to tackle the dust and cobwebs and bring the house back to its former glory "You've got a deal."

"Shouldn't we talk salary?"

A shadow dimmed her excitement, but only for a moment. "I thought that was all taken care of through the agency. Unless you've made a change regarding…" She paused, glancing down at Sam.

"One boy won't eat much. The wage stands, if it's acceptable to you."

"Agreed."

"You'll be okay to get settled then?"

"Oh, we'll be fine. Does it matter which rooms we take?"

"One of the two smaller ones at the end of the hall would probably be best for your son," he replied. "My sister Liz's pink room probably wouldn't suit him. The other is still a bit girly, but at least it's not pink. You can take the one on the other side." The master bedroom, the one that had been his parents.

"Are you sure you don't want me to take the pink room? The other is…" she paused. She remembered the look on his face when he'd opened the door, but had no idea how to ask why it hurt him so much. "The other is so big," she said.

Luke tried not to think of Emily in his parents' room, covered with the ivory chenille spread that had been on the bed as long as he could remember. He had never been able to bring himself to change rooms, instead staying in the one he'd had since childhood. Nor did he want Sam there. But Emily…somehow she fit. She'd be caring and respectful.

"The room has been empty a long time. You may as well use it. The other is so small. It's just a room, Emily. No reason why you shouldn't sleep in it."

But it wasn't "just a room", and as he looked down into her

dark gaze, he got the idea she understood even without the details.

"Mr. Evans, I don't know how to thank you. This means a lot to me…to us."

Her eyes were so earnest, and he wondered what was behind them. Clearly she was a single mom and things had to be bad if she accepted a short-term position like his and was so obviously happy about it. She hadn't even attempted to negotiate salary.

"What brought you here? I mean…you're obviously a single mother." No husband to be found and insistent on the Ms. instead of Mrs. No wedding ring either, but he saw the slight indentation on her finger where one had lived. "Recently divorced?"

The pleasant smile he'd enjoyed suddenly disappeared from her mouth. "Does it matter if I'm divorced?"

He stepped back. "Not at all. I was just curious."

"You don't strike me as the curious type."

He hoped he didn't blush. She had him dead to rights and she knew it. He had always been the stay-out-of-others'-business-and-they'll-stay-out-of-yours type.

"Pardon me," he replied coolly.

But her lack of answers only served to make him wonder more what had truly brought her here. What circumstances had led Emily Northcott and her son to his doorstep?

"Yes," she relented, "I'm divorced. Sam's father is living in British Columbia. I'm just trying to make a living and raise my son, Mr. Evans."

She was a mom. She had baggage, if the white line around her finger and the set of her lips were any indication. It all screamed *off limits* to him. He should just nod and be on his way. Instead he found himself holding out his hand, scrubbed clean of the earlier grease, with only a telltale smidge remaining in his cuticles.

"Luke. Call me Luke."

The air in the room seemed to hold for a fraction of a second as she slid her hand out of her pocket and towards his. Then he folded the slim fingers within his, the connection hitting him square in the gut. Two dots of color appeared on Emily's cheeks, and it looked as though she bit the inside of her lip.

Not just him then. As if things weren't complicated enough.

"Luke," she echoed softly, and a warning curled through him at the sound of her voice. He had to keep his distance. This was probably a huge mistake. But where would they go if he denied her the job? What were they running from? He wanted to know everything but knew that asking would only mean getting closer. And getting close—to anyone—was not an option. Not for him.

He was already in over his head. The fields and barns were the place for him, and he would let Emily Northcott sort out her own family. She could just get on with doing her job.

He had enough to handle with his own.

CHAPTER THREE

THE REST OF the day passed in a blur. Emily began her cleaning upstairs in the rooms that she and Sam would occupy. Sam helped as best as a five-year-old boy could, helping change the sheets, dusting and Emily put him to work putting his clothes in the empty dresser while she moved on to her room. It was late afternoon when she was done and continued on to the kitchen, putting the dry dishes away before tackling the new dirty ones and searching the freezer for something to make for supper. The baked pork chops, rice and vegetables were ready for six o'clock; she held the meal until six-thirty and finally ate with Sam while Luke remained conspicuously absent. It wasn't until she and Sam were picking at the blueberry cobbler she'd baked for dessert that Luke returned.

He took one look at the dirty supper dishes and his face hardened.

Emily clenched her teeth. What did he expect? They couldn't wait all night, and she'd held it as long as was prudent. As it was, the vegetables had been a little mushy and the cream of mushroom sauce on the chops had baked down too far.

"We didn't know how long you'd be," she said quietly, getting up to move the dirty dishes and to fix Luke a plate. "We decided to go ahead."

"You didn't need to wait for me at all." He went to the sink to wash his hands.

Emily bit the inside of her lip. Granted, dinnertime with the surly Luke Evans wasn't all that appealing, but it seemed rude to discount having a civil meal together at all. Still she was new here and the last thing she wanted was to get off on the wrong foot. She picked up a clean plate, filled it with food and popped it into the microwave. In her peripheral vision she could see Sam picking at his cobbler, staring into his bowl. He could sense the tension, and it made Emily even more annoyed. He'd had enough of that when things had got bad between her and Rob. The last thing she wanted was to have him in a less-than-friendly situation again.

"Eating together is a civil thing to do," she replied as the microwave beeped. "Plus the food is best when it's fresh and hot."

"You don't need to go to any bother," he replied, taking the plate and sitting down at the table. Sam's gaze darted up and then down again. Was he not even going to acknowledge her son?

Perhaps what Luke Evans needed was a refresher course in manners and common courtesy.

She resumed her seat, picked up her fork and calmly said, "I wasn't planning on running a short-order kitchen."

"I didn't realize I was nailed down to a specific dinner time. I am running a farm here, you know."

Sam's eyes were wide and he held his spoon with a purple puddle of blueberries halfway between the bowl and his mouth. Emily spared him a glance and let out a slow breath.

"Of course you are, and I did hold the meal for over half an hour. Maybe we should have simply communicated it better. Set a basic time and if you're going to be later, you can let me know."

"I'm not used to a schedule."

Emily looked at Sam and smiled. "You're excused, Sam. Why don't you go upstairs and put on your pajamas?"

Obediently Sam pushed out his chair and headed for the stairs.

Luke paused in his eating. "He listens to you well."

Now that Sam was gone Emily wasn't feeling so generous. "He has been taught some manners," she replied, the earlier softness gone from her voice. "Eating together is the civilized thing to do. Respecting that I may have gone to the trouble to cook a nice meal would go a long way. And acknowledging my son when you sit at the table would be polite, rather than acting as though he doesn't exist."

Luke's fork hit his plate. "I hired you to be a housekeeper, not Miss Manners."

"I'm big on courtesy and respect, Mr. Evans. No matter who or what the age. If you don't want to eat with us, say so now. I'll plan for Sam and I to eat by ourselves and you can reheat your meal whenever it suits you. But I'd prefer if we settled it now so we don't have any more confusion."

For several seconds the dining room was quiet, and then Luke replied, "As long as you understand there may be times when I'm in the middle of something, I will make every attempt to observe a regular dinner hour."

"I appreciate it."

"And I didn't mean to ignore your son."

"He has feelings, too, Mr. Evans. And since his father left, it is easy for him to feel slighted."

Luke picked at the mound of rice on his plate. "I didn't think of that."

"You don't know us yet," Emily responded, feeling her annoyance drain away. Luke looked suitably chastised, and she couldn't help the smile that she tried to hide. She'd seen that look on Sam's face on occasion, and it melted her anger.

"Look, I put in an effort for our first dinner here. I might have gotten a bit annoyed that you weren't here to eat it."

Luke lifted his head and met her eyes. Her heart did a weird thump, twisting and then settling down to a slightly faster rhythm, it seemed.

"I have lived alone a long time," he admitted. "I'm sorry I didn't think of it. You might need to be patient with me."

"Maybe we all need to be patient," she replied, and he smiled at her. A genuine smile, not the tense tight one from this afternoon. The twist in her heart went for another leap again and she swallowed.

"There's cobbler," she said, a peace offering.

"Thank you, Emily," he answered.

She went to the kitchen to get it, hearing the way he said her name echoing around in her brain. She'd fought her battle and won. So why did she feel as if she was in a lot of trouble?

After the supper mess was cleaned up, Luke went out to the barns and Emily put Sam to bed, following him in short order. She was exhausted. She vaguely heard the phone ringing once, but Luke answered it and the sound of the peepers and the breeze through the window lulled her back to sleep.

But the early night meant early to rise, and Emily heard Luke get up as the first pale streaks of sunlight filtered through the curtains. The floorboards creaked by the stairs and she checked her watch...did people really get up this early? She crept out of bed and tiptoed down the hall, looking in on Sam.

He looked so much younger—more innocent, if that were possible—in slumber. He wasn't a baby any longer, but it didn't change the tender feeling that rushed through her looking at his dark eyelashes and curls. He was so good, so loving. So trusting. She didn't want what had happened with his father to change that about him. It was up to her to make sure he had a good life. A happy life. She was determined. He would never doubt how much she loved him. He would always know that she would be there for him.

Back in her room, she slid into a pair of jeans and a T-shirt, moving as quietly as possible. She wanted to get an early start. Make a decent breakfast and get a load of laundry going so she could hang it out on the clothesline. The very idea was exciting, and she laughed a little at herself. Who knew something as simple as fresh-smelling clothes off the line would give her such pleasure? Despite Luke's reticence, despite getting off on the wrong foot last night at dinner, she was more convinced than ever that she'd done the right thing. She'd taken him on and he hadn't given her the boot. She'd be the best housekeeper Luke Evans ever had. And when she got her feet beneath her, it would be time to start thinking about the future.

She was beating pancake batter in a bowl when Luke returned from the barn, leaving his boots on the mat and coming into the kitchen in his stocking feet. Emily had found a cast-iron pan and it was already heating on the burner. He stopped and stared at her for a moment, long enough that she began to feel uncomfortable and her spoon moved even faster through the milky batter.

"I didn't think you'd be up yet."

"I heard you leave a while ago. I wanted to get an early start." She dropped a little butter in the pan and ladled a perfectly round pancake in the middle of it. "You're just in time for the first pancakes." She was glad he was here. Now he'd get them fresh and hot from the pan, better proof of her cooking abilities than the reheated dinner of last evening. She wasn't opposed to hard work, and it felt good having a purpose, something to do. It was just a taste of how it would feel when she got a permanent job and could provide for herself and for Sam.

"Lately I've been grabbing a bowl of cereal. Pancakes are a treat. Thank you, Emily."

His polite words nearly made her blush as she remembered how she'd taken him to task for his manners at their last meal. She focused on turning the pancake, the top perfectly golden brown. "I'm glad you get to enjoy them fresh, rather than warmed up, like last night's supper." She flipped the pancake onto a plate and began frying another. "Besides, when you sleep in you miss the best part of the day, I think."

She wanted to ask him if this was his regular breakfast time but held back, not wanting to harp on a dead topic. Still, she felt as if she should already know, which was ridiculous. How could she possibly know his routine, his preferences?

Everything about Luke Evans was throwing her off balance and she was having to think and double-think every time she wanted to ask him something, measure her words, trying hard to say the right thing and not the first thing that came to her mind.

"What time do you want lunch?"

"I'm used to just grabbing a sandwich when I come in."

She put down the spatula. "A sandwich? But a working man can't live on a sandwich for lunch!"

He laughed then, a real laugh aimed at her open-mouthed look of dismay, she realized. She picked up the spatula again, trying to ignore the light that kindled in his eyes as he laughed. When Luke was grumpy, she wished he were nicer. But when he was nice, something inside her responded and she wished for his sterner side again. She didn't want to have those sorts of reactions. She wasn't interested in romance or flirting. She didn't know how, not after so many years with one man. She was never going to put herself in a position to be hurt like that again either. She deserved more. So did Sam.

"You're making fun of me."

"You sound like my sisters. They both fuss and flutter. I haven't starved yet, though."

The awkwardness had seemed to fade away between them, but what arose in its place was a different kind of tension. It made her want to hold her breath or glance over and see if he was watching her. She couldn't help it—she did, and he was. His blue gaze was penetrating, and she had the simultaneous thoughts that his eyes were too beautiful for a man and that she wished he still wore his hat so they would be at least a bit shadowed.

She handed him the plate of pancakes, taking care to make sure their fingers never touched. "Fresh from the pan."

"They smell delicious. And about lunch… I try to come in around noon, when the boys take their break. Sometimes when I'm haying I take my lunch with me though. I'll be sure to let you know."

Emily bit her lip and turned back to her pancakes, feeling a warmth spread through her. His tone at the end had held a little hint of teasing, no malice in it at all. She could nearly hear the echo of Rob's angry voice in her head, telling her to stop nagging. She had told herself his leaving had been out of the blue, but things hadn't been right for a while before he left. He had complained about her always trying to tie him down to a schedule. She hadn't. But she'd taken pride in her "job". She loved it when they all sat down together. It had been a bone of contention between them that they didn't eat dinner as a family. Since he'd left she'd made it a point to sit with Sam over dinner and talk about their favorite parts of the day.

But Luke wasn't her family, he was her boss. "It's your house," she said quietly. "I overstepped last night. Whenever you want your meals, I'll make sure they're on the table. That *is* what you pay me for, right?"

"Are you okay?"

"Fine. Why?"

"You got all…meek all of a sudden. If you want something, Emily, just ask. If I don't like it, I'll tell you."

She swallowed. Had she become so used to tiptoeing around Rob that she'd forgotten how good honesty and straight-talking felt? She took a breath. "Okay. It would be helpful if I knew what time you'd like your meals so I can plan around them."

His chair scraped against the floor as he rose, came forward and reached around her for the maple syrup. His body was close—too close. When she sucked in a breath, she smelled the clean scent of his soap mixed with a hint of leather and horses. Oh, my. Heat crept into her cheeks.

"Was that so hard?" he asked.

Her brain scrambled to remember what they'd been talking about. Oh, yes. The timing of meals. "Um…no?"

He retrieved the syrup and moved away while Emily wilted against the counter.

"I'll try to let you know when I plan to be in," he said, pouring syrup over his pancakes. "You were right, so don't apologize. It's just business courtesy, that's all." Luke dismissed it with a wave and picked up his fork.

Just business. He was right, and Emily felt chagrined at her earlier behavior. She was far too aware of him and he was her boss. Why shouldn't she simply ask questions? She would of any other employer.

"I have to run into town this morning to pick up a part for the baler. I'll make a stop at the hospital, too, I guess. Cait and Joe had a baby girl last night. Anyway, if there's anything you need, I can get it while I'm there."

A baby! He said it as blandly as he might have said *Rain is forecast for today,* and it left Emily confused. What was she missing? She remembered the first moments of holding Sam in her arms after his birth, and despite Luke's tepid response she knew his sister and brother-in-law had to be over the moon. As brother and uncle, he should be, too. "A girl! Lovely! They must be so happy."

Luke went to the coffeepot and poured himself a cup, then took down another and held it out, asking her if she wanted some. She nodded, wondering why he wasn't excited about the baby. After his reaction to Sam yesterday, she was beginning to think her assessment that he didn't like children was dead-on. "Is everyone healthy?" she asked, hoping there were no complications.

"Oh, yes." He gave a shrug. "Another girl. That's four nieces."

"Do you have something against girls?"

The cup halted halfway to his mouth. "What? Oh, of course not. We just keep hoping for a boy. To keep the Evans and Son going, you know?"

Emily watched him as he got out juice glasses—three of them—pouring orange juice in two and leaving the third one empty but waiting. He had remembered Sam, then. At times last night and this morning it had seemed as though Luke forgot Sam was even there.

"This is the twenty-first century, Luke." She smiled at him, poured another pancake. "A girl could take over the farm as well as a boy, you know. Evans and Niece might not have the same ring to it, but I didn't have you pegged for one worrying about an heir to the empire. Besides, you might still have some big, strapping prairie boys of your own." She added the pancake to the stack on the warmer with a smile. But her teasing had backfired. He stared at her now with an expression that seemed partly hurt and partly angry.

"I don't plan on having a family," he replied, then dropped his gaze, focusing on cutting his pancakes, his knife scraping along the porcelain. Emily stared at him for a second, absolutely nonplussed, and then remembered she still had a pancake cooking and it needed to be turned if she didn't want it to burn.

He finished the meal in silence as she cooked more pancakes, stacking them until the warmer was full. The quiet stretched out uncomfortably; Emily wanted to break it somehow but after his last words she had no idea what to say that would be a good start to a conversation. He'd clearly ended the last attempt.

He finished what was on his plate and came over to the stove, standing at her elbow. She wished she could ignore him and relax, but he was six foot something of muscled man. She couldn't pretend he didn't exist. Not when all of her senses were clamoring like the bells of a five-alarm fire. She gripped the spatula tightly.

"Are there any more of those, Emily?"

She let her breath out slowly, not wanting him to sense her relief. Extra pancakes—was that all he wanted? "Take as many as you like," she replied. "I can make more for Sam when he gets up."

He lifted four from the warming tray and Emily swallowed against the lump that had formed in her throat. My, he did have a good appetite. Was there nothing about the man that wasn't big and virile? On the back of the thought came the unwanted but automatic comparison to Rob. Rob in his suits and Italian loafers and his fancy car. Rob going out the door with a travel mug and a briefcase in the morning. When those things had disappeared so abruptly from her life it had broken her heart. She'd built her whole life around their little family, loving every moment of caring for their house and watching Sam grow. She'd lost the life she'd always dreamed of and it still hurt.

But it was time to start dreaming about something new. Emily lifted her head and caught a glimpse of the wide fields out the kitchen window. The golden fields were Luke's office.

His jeans and boots and, oh, yes, the T-shirts that displayed his muscled arms were his work clothes. The prairie wind was his air conditioning and the sun his office lighting.

She smiled, knowing that the wide-open space was something she'd been missing for a long time. The memories would always be there, but they hurt less now. As she looked out over the sunny fields, she knew that leaving the city had been the right thing to do. She was moving forward with her life, and it felt good.

"What are you smiling at?" Luke asked the question from the table, but he'd put down his fork and was giving her his full attention. And the pancake batter was gone, leaving her with nothing to do to keep her hands busy. Six pancakes remained; certainly enough for her breakfast with Sam. She put down the bowl and brushed her hands on the apron she'd found in the drawer.

"I was just thinking how nice it must be to go to work in the outdoors," she replied, picking up her cooling coffee. Anything to let her hide just a little bit from Luke's penetrating gaze.

"Not so nice on rainy days, but yeah…I think I'd go crazy locked up inside all day. You strike me as the inside kind."

"What makes you say that?"

He looked down at his tanned arms and then at her pale, white limbs. Then up at her face while a small smile played with his lips.

"Okay, you're right. Sam and I made it to the park but our backyard…" She sighed. "It was very small. Sam had a little slide there, a kid-sized picnic table. That was about it."

"Boys need room to run around."

She poured herself more coffee. "Yes, I know. Suburbia wasn't always part of the plan. I did grow up with more than a postage stamp for a yard, you know. In Regina."

"You're from Regina?"

"Just outside, yes. My mom was a stay-at-home mom and my dad sold cars." Telling Luke took her back to her college days when she'd been slightly ashamed of her modest home and she realized now that Rob had never quite fit in there. Perhaps this split had always been coming, and was not as random as she thought. She'd been trying to be someone she wasn't. Maybe he had, too. Now, despite the fact that she knew there would be a certain bit of "I told you so", home didn't seem so bad. She'd been afraid of being judged, but she knew that wasn't really why she didn't want to go back. She didn't want to go back a failure. She wanted to go back when she could look her parents in the eye and say that she'd fixed it. The way they'd always seemed to fix things. If money was tight or jobs were lost, they still always seemed to manage. And they'd stayed together. Not because they had to, but because they loved each other. Emily found it so hard to live up to that kind of example.

However, she could say none of this to Luke. What would he think of her if he knew? The last thing she wanted was to lay out a list of her faults and failings.

"And what took you to Calgary?"

She simply lifted an eyebrow.

"Ah," he chuckled, understanding. "Sam's father?"

She nodded, finally taking a seat at the table and curling her hands around the mug. The sun was up over the knoll now and gleaming brightly in the kitchen. This was where the questions would end. She had no desire to tell Luke the sordid details of the split. There would be no more breakfasts for two. She was here to work. It was glorious just to be able to make her own decisions now. She just kept telling herself that. Her parents didn't know she'd had to give up her house or that she hadn't received any child support. She'd been too proud to tell them. She'd been certain she'd turn things around before they got to this point. And she would. She just needed a little more time and a solid plan.

"And you?" To keep him from prying further into her personal life, she turned the tables. "You've been here your whole life, I suppose."

"Of course."

"The girls didn't care to be farmers?"

He looked at her over the rim of his mug, his blue gaze measuring. Luke Evans was no pushover, Emily realized. He saw right through her intentions. It should have put her off, but it didn't. Everything about Luke was intelligent, decisive. It was crazily sexy.

"The 'girls', as you say, got married and started their own families. Joe manages a farm-equipment dealership—he's the proud daddy this morning. Liz's husband is a schoolteacher. They both know their way around a barn, but that's not their life now."

"So you handle this alone?" She put the mug down on the table.

"I have some hired help." His lips made a thin line and his gaze slid from hers. Subject closed.

But she pressed on. "Then what about the Evans and Son on the sign? What about your dad and mom? How long have they been gone?"

He pushed out his chair and put his mug on top of his plate, taking the stack to the cupboard next to the sink. "I've got to get going. I have to get the boys started on their own this morning so I can run into town."

Emily knew she had gone too far. Something about his parents pushed a button. She had sensed it when she'd seen their picture, when he'd looked into their empty bedroom and again just now when she'd asked about them.

"About town…you really are short of groceries. Could we

go with you? We won't take extra time. We can shop while you run your errands."

He reached for his hat and plunked it on his head. To Emily, it seemed like armor to hide behind. And it added inches to his height.

Maybe some people didn't appreciate a closet full of fresh-smelling clothes, shining floors and a good meal, but she'd bet Luke would. She'd bet anything that he'd grown up exactly that way. His sisters had moved on, apparently to fulfilling, happy lives. Why hadn't Luke? Not that the farm wasn't successful. But it felt like a piece of the puzzle was missing.

"I can't expect you to cook without food, I suppose," he replied. "Be ready about nine, then. I need to get back as soon as I can."

"Yes, boss," she replied, putting his dishes in the sink to wash up.

It was all back to the status quo until he reached the screen door and then she heard his voice call quietly.

"Emily?"

She went to the doorway. "Yes?"

He smiled. "Good pancakes."

The screen door shut behind him, but Emily stared at it a good ten seconds before making her feet move.

Yes, indeed. She could wow Luke Evans in the kitchen. And she knew exactly what would be on the menu tonight.

CHAPTER FOUR

LUKE GAVE THE ratchet another turn and adjusted the trouble light. When had it gotten so dark? He stood back, staring at the rusted parts that made up the baler. It needed love. It needed replacing. But this repair would hold him through this season. And if things went well, he'd talk Joe into a discount and buy a new one next year.

He made a few final adjustments and straightened, rubbing the small of his back. Between the trip to town, Cait and the baler, he'd spent all of half an hour in the fields today. He frowned. It wasn't how he liked to run things. He wasn't a boss who gave orders and disappeared. Here everyone worked together and shared the load. But what could he do? He'd left the repairs until after dinner as it was, working in the dim light.

"Hi."

He spun at the sound of the small voice and saw Sam standing before him in his bare feet and a pair of cotton pajamas. The boy was cute as a bug's ear, Luke acknowledged, with his brown curls and wide chocolate eyes like his mother's. Eyes that seemed to see everything. Luke wiped his hands on a rag and tucked the end into his back pocket. "Shouldn't you be up at the house? In bed?"

A light blush darkened Sam's cheeks as his gaze skittered away for a moment. "I couldn't sleep. It's too hot."

"Your mom would open the window."

"She said she didn't want to hear a peep out of me," Sam admitted, and Luke hid a smile. Not hear a peep, so sneaking out of the house was okay?

"Then you'd better hightail it back in there, don't you think? You don't want your mom to be mad."

Sam swallowed and nodded and turned away, only to turn back again. "Why don't you like my mama?"

Luke's hands dropped to his sides as Sam asked the point-blank question. "What makes you think I don't like her?" he asked.

"Because you never said anything to her at supper. And she made veal. I helped. She only does that when it's special."

The veal had been good, as had the pasta and salad. Certainly much fancier than he was used to making for himself. "I suppose I had my head full of everything I need to do. I don't usually have company at the dinner table. I guess I'm not one for conversation."

Why on earth was he explaining this to a five-year-old boy? Besides, he knew it was a feeble excuse. He hadn't known what to say to her. He'd walked in to a house smelling of furniture polish and the fragrant lilacs she'd cut and put in one of his mother's vases she'd unearthed from somewhere. He'd instantly been transported to a time when the house had been filled with family. His mother's warm smiles. His dad's teasing. All of it had been taken from him in what felt like an instant, and he knew the chances of history repeating itself were too good to fool around with. But today he'd been taken back to a happier time.

He'd looked at Emily and felt the noose tightening. All through the meal he thought of her as she'd looked that morning as they ate alone in the quiet kitchen, with her pretty smiles and soft voice. It had felt domestic. Alarm bells had gone off like crazy in his head. He knew the signs. Watchfulness.

Blushes. He was as guilty of it as she was, and he had kept his distance ever since very deliberately. He'd had no idea what to say to her.

"I think you hurt her feelings," Sam persisted. His tone turned defensive and his brown eyes snapped. "My mama's a nice lady," he announced, lifting his chin as if daring Luke to dispute it, an action so like his mother Luke found it hard not to smile. "She cooks good and reads me stories and does all the best voices with my dinosaur puppets."

This was Luke's problem. He was too soft. He already felt sorry for the pair of them, and he didn't even really know the extent of their situation. Nor did he want to. He knew he shouldn't get involved. They were not his responsibility, and he didn't want them to be. He'd had enough responsibility to last a lifetime, and even though his sisters were on their own there was still the issue of his father's ongoing care. Emily was the housekeeper. Full stop.

Even Cait, in the first bloom of motherhood, had sensed something was up today. He'd said nothing, not wanting to mention Emily or her kid, instead dutifully admiring baby Janna. His sister was happy, but a family was not for him. So why did seeing her with Joe and her baby make him feel so empty? It was like that every time he saw Liz's girls, too. They thought he didn't particularly care for children. But the sorry truth was he knew he would never have any of his own and keeping his distance was just easier.

"I like your mom just fine, and you're right, supper was good. But my job is to fix this baler so we can roll up the hay out there and have feed for the winter."

Sam scowled. "Mama told me if we didn't stay here we had to go to Grandma and Grampa's. I don't even know what they look like."

Luke leaned against the bumper, watching Sam with keen eyes. When had she said such a thing? Before arriving or after he'd given her the job? He found the answer mattered to him. And how could Sam not know his grandparents? Regina wasn't so far from Calgary as to prevent visits.

"Oh, you must remember them."

But Sam shook his head. "My mama says they would be excited to see me because they haven't since I was a baby."

Three years. Maybe four, if what he said was true. Luke frowned. Even though he'd only known her a few days, he pictured Emily as the type to be surrounded by family. What had kept them apart?

"You should go on up to the house," he said, more firmly this time. "You don't want to get in trouble with your mom, Sam. Go on now."

Sam's lips twisted a little. "You don't like me either," he announced.

"What does it matter if I like you or not?" Luke was feeling annoyed now, having his character called out by a boy. Besides, it wasn't a matter of liking or not. It went so much deeper. Self-preservation, if it came to that. There was too much at stake for him to get all gushy over babies and such. "You get on up to bed."

Sam's little lip quivered but his eyes blazed. "That's all right. My dad doesn't like me either and my mama and I do just fine."

He spun on his toes and ran back to the house.

Luke sighed, watching him depart. He'd been sharp when he hadn't meant to be. It wasn't Sam's fault—or Emily's for that matter—that the years of stress and responsibility had worn him down. The boy had been through enough with his parents splitting up—Emily had as much as said so last night. He felt a moment of guilt, knowing Sam was feeling the loss of his father keenly. Did Sam never see him, then?

He rubbed a hand over his face, blew out a breath. Emily's domestic situation was none of his concern. Why he continually had to remind himself of that was a bit of a mystery. He turned out the trouble light and felt for a moment the satisfaction of another day done.

Followed by the heavy realization of all that remained to do tomorrow. And the day after that.

He squared his shoulders. "Suck it up, Evans," he mumbled to himself, shaking his head. Darn the two of them anyway. They'd had him thinking more over the last two days than he had in months, and not just about himself. About her, and the series of events that had landed her on his doorstep just at the moment he needed her most.

Emily was wiping up the last of the dishes and Sam was already sound asleep in bed when Luke returned to the house in the twilight. Sam had worked alongside her most of the afternoon, helping her dust the rooms and fetching things as she needed them. The bathroom fixtures shone and the floors gleamed again, and she sighed, not only from exhaustion but also from satisfaction. Sam had sometimes been more of a hindrance than a help, but it had been worth it to see the smile on his face and the pride he took in helping. It hadn't been until he'd nearly nodded off over his dinner that she'd realized he'd missed his afternoon nap.

Now he was tucked away in the small room, his dark head peaceful on the pillow. Meanwhile Emily had dishes to finish and the last of the dry sheets to put back on the spare beds before she could call it a night.

She heard Luke come in through the screen door and her heart did a little leap. It seemed so personal, having the run of his house, making herself at home. She heard the thump of his boots as he put them on the mat by the door and pictured him behind her. Now her pulse picked up as she heard his stockinged feet come closer. To her surprise he picked up the frying pan and moved to put it in the cupboard.

"Mr. Evans…you don't have to do that." She avoided his eyes as she picked up the last plate to dry.

"It's no biggie. I'm done for the day and you're not."

His shoulder was next to hers as he reached for another pot, the close contact setting off the same sparks as she'd felt at dinner. His jeans had been dirty with a smear of grease on one thigh, and his T-shirt had borne marks of his afternoon of work, but he'd gone into the downstairs bath and come to the table with clean hands and face and a few droplets of water clinging to his short hair.

It had been the wet hair that had done it. The tips were dark and glistening, and paired with the stubble on his chin it was unbelievably attractive. The economical way that he moved and how he said exactly what he meant, without any wasted words. He'd spoken to Sam only briefly during dinner, making little conversation before heading outside again. He hadn't even commented on the food, even though she'd pulled out all the stops and fussed with her favorite veal-and-pasta recipe. Emily tried not to be offended. Perhaps it was just his way. Perhaps he'd lived alone so long he wasn't used to making mealtime conversation. And that was quite sad when she thought about it.

"But our agreement…"

He put his hand on her arm and she stilled, plate in hand. She couldn't look at him. If she did, the color would seep into her cheeks. He was touching her. *Touching her,* and her skin seemed to shiver with pleasure beneath his fingers.

"Please," she said quietly. "This is my job. Let me do it."

"Pride, Emily?"

He used her first name and the sound of it, coming from his lips in the privacy of the kitchen, caused her cheeks to heat anyway. His hand slid off her arm and she realized she was holding the plate and doing nothing with it. She made a show of wiping the cloth over its surface. "Just stating the obvious."

"Who do you suppose cleans up when I'm here alone? I didn't realize putting a few things away would be a problem."

Oh, lordy. What right did she have to be territorial? "That's not what I meant," she replied hastily, putting the plate on the counter and reaching into the sink to pick up the last handful of cutlery. "Of course it's your kitchen…"

"Emily."

"You have more right to it than I do…"

She was babbling now, growing more nervous by the second as she felt his steady gaze on her. She bit down on her lip. She wouldn't say any more and make a bigger fool of herself. What did it matter if he put a dish away? She was the one caught up in a knot, determined to do everything perfectly. And why? She already knew that trying to be perfect didn't mean squat when it came down to it. She let out a slow breath, trying to relax.

"Why won't you look at me?"

She did then. She looked up into his eyes and saw that the blue irises were worried, making it impossible to maintain the distance she desired.

"You're paying me to do a job, so I should be the one to do it. If that's pride, then so be it."

"You're a stubborn woman, aren't you?"

Her lips dropped open and then she clamped them shut again, trying to think of a good reply. "I prefer determined."

"I just bet you do."

"Did you get the baler fixed?" She was desperate to change the subject, to turn the focus off herself and her failings. "I expect you'll be glad to be back in the fields tomorrow," she carried on, sorting the last of the cutlery into the drawer. The thought of the fields and waving alfalfa made her smile, gave her a sense of well-being. It had to be the peace and quiet, that was all. It had nothing to do with Luke Evans, or picturing him on top of a gigantic tractor in a dusty hat and even dustier boots.

"I can't expect the boys to handle things alone. I'll be glad to be back out with them again. I may be late for dinner tomorrow. Just so you know."

Oh, goodness, they were back to that again. She brushed her hands on her pants and inhaled, trying to appear poised. How could she explain that she'd actually enjoyed cleaning the homey farmhouse? That she'd felt more at home cooking a simple meal than she'd felt in a long time? Cooking anything elaborate for her and Sam seemed pointless, and she'd missed it.

"Thank you for letting me know. I'll plan something that keeps well, then. If you don't mind Sam and I going ahead."

"Of course not. Emily…" he paused and she gave in to temptation and looked up at him. He could look so serious, but something about his somber expression spoke to her. There was more to Luke than was on the surface. She was sure of it.

Their gazes clung for several seconds before he cleared his throat. "What I mean to say is, it is just great to have supper on the table when I come in and something better than a sandwich. It's a real nice thing to look forward to."

It was as heartfelt a comment as she'd guess Luke could come up with, and she took it to heart. She couldn't find the words to tell him that though, so she simply said, "Sam doesn't have such discerning taste. It was nice to have a reason to put together a real meal."

His gaze plumbed hers. "There was a reason I advertised for a housekeeper. The place looks great. And dinner was really good, Emily. I probably should have said so before."

She'd been slightly put out that he'd barely acknowledged

her efforts earlier, but the compliment still did its work, even though it was delayed. "I'm glad you liked it."

Why was he being nice to her now? She should be glad, relieved about all of it. But it threw her off balance. She furrowed her brow. Either she wanted his compliments and approval or she didn't. She wished she could make up her mind which.

"You're a very good cook."

"It was…"

She paused. So what if it was what she'd used to make for special occasions? She was tired of giving Rob any power. He had no business here. He had no business in her life anymore. He'd forfeited that privilege, and she'd done her share of crying about it. The only person keeping him front and center was her. "It is one of my favorites."

"So what's the story of Emily Northcott?" Luke folded up the dish towel and hung it over the door of the stove. "I mean, you must have a place in Calgary. Sam's father must be helping. Why pick a position that takes you away from home?"

Of course he'd ask right at the moment she'd decided not to mention Rob again. But the question struck a nerve. Somehow she wanted him to know. She wanted him to realize that she had tried everything she could to make things right. She already thought of him as stubborn rancher, a bit of a strong, silent type but she'd glimpsed moments of compassion, too. How would he remember her after she moved on? Not as a victim. Never that. She wanted him to see what she wanted to see in herself. Strength. Resourcefulness. Pride, but not vanity.

"I was a stay-at-home mom. Once I got pregnant and my ex started working, we agreed on a plan. I had my degree in science, and I put Rob through school by working for a laboratory. The idea was for him to start work and then he'd support me as I took my pharmacy degree. But then we had

Sam, and Rob said he would support us both. I was thrilled. Having Sam changed everything. Being his mom was the best job I'd ever had. I know it's not a job in the strict sense, but I really felt like I was doing something important, making a home for us, bringing him up. And I was thankful to have that choice. I know not everyone does."

Remembering those days stung. Rob had pretended the arrangement was perfect, but in the end it wasn't what he'd wanted. Emily had been too blind to see it until it was too late. "And then he left."

She cast a furtive look at the stairway, knowing Sam was asleep but still worried that if he woke up he'd hear her talking.

Luke followed her gaze. "You don't want him to hear us talking about it?"

Emily nodded, relieved he'd taken the hint so quickly. "He's been through enough. He's asleep, but any mention of his dad and he gets so upset."

"He thinks his dad doesn't like him."

Her head snapped around. "What?"

"He told me. He said I don't like him and his dad doesn't like him and that he does just fine." He pinned her with a steady look. "He's quite a kid, actually. But it made me wonder. Are you fine, Emily?"

She ignored the question, instead focusing on thoughts of Sam. Did he really believe that? That his father didn't like him? Sadness warred with anger at the situation. She hated that he didn't feel loved by both parents.

"I'm sorry he said that to you," she whispered, faltering for a moment, letting the despair in for just a second. Then she closed it away. There was nothing productive in feeling sorry for herself. "I'll have him apologize, Luke."

His gaze darkened and his jaw tightened. "No need. He

was just being honest. He's a good kid. You've done a good job with him. It's not easy being a single parent."

The compliment went to her heart. "Thank you. But I worry about what he's missing. If I'm enough, you know?"

"You just do the best you can."

She leaned back against the counter, looked up at Luke, wondering at the tight tone of his voice. What did he know of it? And yet she got the feeling he somehow understood. "I can't even put food on the table at the moment," she admitted.

His face flattened with alarm. "It's that bad?"

"Let's go outside," she suggested. Luke was standing too close again and she needed the fresh air and open space.

They left the porch light off to keep the Junebugs away, and Emily sat on the step, letting the first stars provide the light while they waited for last dregs of twilight to fade and the moon to rise. She had been at the ranch for two days, and the whole time Luke had felt like a boss, or like a complete stranger. But not tonight. Tonight he felt like an ally, despite the fact that they barely knew one another. It had been a long time since she'd had an ally. Since she'd had an unbiased ear to talk to.

Emily breathed in the fresh prairie air and the heavy scent of lilacs. "I love these," she said quietly. "Nothing smells better than lilacs."

Luke sat down beside her and the air warmed.

"My mother planted them," he said, putting his elbows on his knees and folding his hands. "I'm not much for flower gardens, I don't have time. But I've always tried to keep her lilacs. They smelled nice on the table tonight. Mom used to do that, too."

"What happened to her?"

"She died when I was nineteen. Brain aneurism."

Emily heard the grief in his voice even though it had to be ten years or more since her death. "I'm sorry, Luke."

He coughed. "It's all right. Right now we're talking about you. And why your ex was crazy enough to leave you and Sam and not even provide for both of you."

His words reached inside and illuminated a place that had been dark for a very long time.

"When he left, I had to start looking for work. No one wanted someone who hadn't been in the workplace for five years. Technology has changed. I had no references—the staff where I'd worked was all new. Rob hasn't paid a dime in child support." She twisted her fingers together as she looked over at Luke. "Not one."

"Surely a judge…"

Emily laughed bitterly. "Oh, yes. But it was an Alberta court and Rob moved to British Columbia. And I don't have the funds to fight him on it."

"I'm sorry. Of course you've had a difficult time of it."

She hadn't anticipated a helping hand and a caring tone. Not from a stranger. In a few stolen moments, Luke Evans had shown her more consideration than she'd had from any other quarter in several months. Then she reminded herself that she had promised to rely only on herself and she straightened her shoulders.

"It could have been worse," she admitted. "He didn't hurt us. Not physically. He just left. Said our life wasn't what he wanted and he was starting over."

"It doesn't always take punches to leave scars."

And, oh, she knew he was right. "Rob did lots of damage. They're just the kinds of scars that you can't see. I think they take longer to heal, too. The money is a practical difficulty, but the real kicker is how he has washed his hands of Sam. Sam is his son. I don't understand how a dad does that, Luke. I don't understand how I could have been so wrong. His abandonment made me question every single thing I thought I'd known about myself."

Luke was silent for a few moments. Then he said quietly, "You can't blame yourself for everything."

Emily wanted him to see she wasn't the kind of woman who let life happen to her. She was resourceful. But the kind way he was treating her was throwing her off balance. She'd wanted to create distance between them and instead she felt that he understood, perhaps even better than her friends in Calgary had. How was that possible?

The Junebugs thumped against the screen door, trying to get inside to the light that shone from the kitchen. Luke got up and brushed a hand down his jeans. "Let's walk," he suggested.

They strolled down the lane towards the road, past the mowed grass and to a cedar fence that was ornamental rather than functional. At the bottom Luke turned to her and she swallowed, feeling out of her league being alone with him like this. Unlike the fence, his appearance was for function rather than flash and just about the sexiest thing she'd ever seen, from the shorn hair to the faded jeans and dark T-shirt. The shirt clung in such a way that she could see the shape of his muscles, made strong by years of farm work. The sight of him with the moon behind him was something she knew she'd carry with her for a long time, burned on her mind as surely as the straightforward *E* of the Evans brand.

He was so completely opposite to the men she knew. It made her nervous and, at the same time, exhilarated. She told herself that after a year of being alone it was just a reaction. One that would go away as soon as she left the ranch.

"You didn't see it coming, did you?" Luke picked up the last thread of their conversation.

It hurt to talk about Rob. Not because she still loved him, but because she'd been so blind. While she wanted to blame him entirely, she couldn't help wondering if she might have done something differently. "He just announced one day that he was moving to start a new business. Said it was something he had to do for himself." She shook her head as though she still couldn't believe it. "I thought he meant he'd get started and we'd follow later. But he didn't. It wasn't just a job. He wanted his freedom and he took it."

She rubbed the toe of her sandal in the dusty dirt, making a swirly pattern that turned into a heart with a winding tail. "We had some savings that I protected once I realized what was going on. I needed to pay for housing, food. Clothing." She'd moved the savings money knowing that if Rob wanted to claim it, he'd end up creating more problems for himself. "We've been living on that while I tried to find a job to support us both."

Luke said a not-so-nice word that made Emily snort with surprised laughter.

"I called him that several times, too, over the last year. And I'll admit, I waited, thinking he'd come to his senses, that it was just a sort of crisis he'd get out of his system and we could put it all back together. But when he didn't, and the bills were piling up and the bank account dwindling, I filed for divorce and support."

"Sometimes life throws you one hell of a monkey wrench and all you can do is deal. Put one foot in front of the other," Luke replied.

Emily looked over at him, but his face was shadowed in the dark. Was that the voice of experience? His mother had passed away years ago. That must have been difficult. There was so much she didn't know about Luke Evans. On one hand she wanted to know more, to find some sort of solidarity with someone. On the other she knew she'd be better off to leave well enough alone, so she kept the questions on her tongue unsaid.

They turned and started walking back towards the house.

An owl called from a nearby line of trees and Emily jumped at the sound, chafing her arms with her hands.

"You're cold."

"No, it's good," she replied. "I needed this. I needed to get away. So did Sam. That's the real reason we left Calgary. Everything there was a reminder to Sam of our old life. He couldn't move past just wanting it back—how could he? He's not quite five. He doesn't understand. *I* don't understand. Sam just wanted Daddy to come home. He wanted family vacations and a huge pile of presents under the Christmas tree. I couldn't provide all of that on my own. Lord knows I did my best."

Emily shoved her hands into her pockets. "I'm not lazy, Luke. I applied for jobs for months. Anything I found was minimum wage or shift work or both. On minimum wage I can't afford babysitting. And shift work is horrible for finding good child care." She pursed her lips. "But this job is the best of both worlds. I get to do something I'm good at *and* be with my son. I've sold the Calgary house and I'm going to start over." She smiled, but it didn't chase away the cold. "I hope. I suppose if it doesn't work, there's always my parents. But no one wants to move back in with Mom and Dad, do they?"

Luke halted in the middle of the driveway. He looked up at the house, then up at the sky, and finally blew out a breath. She watched his Adam's apple bob as he swallowed. "It might not be so bad," he said quietly as the owl hooted. He turned to her and she felt her chest constrict beneath his gaze.

"But I don't think you'll need to worry. You strike me as the kind that always lands on her feet, Emily."

Luke studied her face as she smiled up at him. There was no denying that Emily was beautiful. But there was more. There was a quiet resolve to her that was equally attractive. She was a hard worker—he could tell that in the sheer volume of tasks she'd accomplished today. Even as her world spun out of control, she seemed in charge of it. Grounded. Calm in the middle of a storm. Sam thought the sun rose and set in her, because she put him first. He remembered the way she'd smoothed Sam's hair today, or had firmly made him mind his manners during dinner. Her kid was damned lucky.

"I hope you're not saying that just to be nice. I don't want pity, you know."

"Would I say anything for the sole purpose of being nice?" He raised an eyebrow.

"Good point." Her eyes sparkled up at him and he felt an unusual knot in his gut as her tongue wet her lips.

It was only a partial lie. He did feel sorry for her. Sorry that she'd been hurt and sorry she was having to deal with things alone. He knew all too well how that felt. To know that everything rests on your shoulders. To know that any decision you make affects others forever. He'd wished for a helping hand so many times when he was younger, first when his mom had died and then when his dad fell sick with Alzheimer's. He knew what it was to bear the weight of a family on his shoulders. In the past two days he'd questioned his sanity in letting Emily and Sam stay, but now that he knew a little more about their situation, he was glad.

And he was smart enough to know that if he told her such a thing she'd be furious. He was on good terms with their friend, Pride.

Meanwhile his body was tense just from being near her. He only wanted to help. Why then did just the soft scent of her, the sound of her voice, make his body tighten?

"If we keep on as we've started, I think we'll get along just fine," he said, thinking it sounded incredibly hokey, but he had to say something. She was a mother, for God's sake. A mother with a ton of baggage she was carrying around. The fleeting impulse to kiss her was beyond crazy. That was definitely a complication he didn't need.

"I think so, too," she agreed.

They drew nearer the house, the walk coming to an end and with it their confidences in the dark. "Thank you for telling me about your situation," he said. He looked up and thought he saw movement at the curtain of Sam's room, but in the dark he couldn't be sure. Was the boy watching them? Now that he knew more about it, he could understand Sam being mixed up and protective of his mother. Not that it excused bad behavior. There'd be no more sneaking out after bedtime.

"It was only fair. I'm a stranger, right? You agreed to this arrangement without knowing anything about me. You don't need me to bring trouble to your door. No fear of that, anyway," she said softly. "Rob doesn't care enough to come after us."

She tried to make it sound as though she didn't care, but he knew she did. He wondered what kind of man didn't love his kid enough to keep in touch, to know where they were? Luke didn't want the added responsibility of children, but if he had them, he'd do a damn sight better job of parenting than that.

He wasn't sure how a man could let his wife go either. Especially one like Emily.

"I'm sorry," he offered, and meant it.

"Me, too." She sighed in the moonlight. "One of these days you'll have to tell me your story," she suggested.

"Not likely," he replied quickly. "Not much to tell."

She laughed, and it seemed to lighten the evening. "Now why don't I believe that? You're pretty close-mouthed when it comes to your own saga." She grinned, looking impish in the moonlight. "But you have been kind and generous, letting us both stay."

"No one's ever accused me of being either," he replied, their steps slowing, scuffing along in the dirt of the driveway.

"Most would say I'm practical." He'd had to be, getting the girls the rest of the way to adulthood and making sure the farm could support them all. There hadn't been time for what most twenty-year-olds had been doing—working hard, but playing harder. It made him think of the old Bible verses from Sunday school, about leaving childish things behind.

"Do you ever wish you'd finished your degree, Emily?"

She looked up at him, putting one hand on the wood railing of the steps. "When the money was dwindling, I confess I did. But sometimes you exchange old dreams for new ones. After five years, this is what I do best. I love being home with Sam. I loved looking after my house and cooking and doing all the special things I couldn't do if I'd been working all day. I was very fortunate, you know?"

"And do you ever think of going back?"

She paused, her expression thoughtful. "Maybe. But not pharmacy. Something else. Something that uses my strengths. I guess I just don't know what that is yet."

For several seconds they stood there staring at each other. Luke's gaze dropped to her lips and then back up to her eyes. Maybe it was the moonlight, or the way her hair curled around her collar, or the soft sound of her voice that reached inside of him and made him want. And what he wanted was to kiss her—for the second time in ten minutes.

Which was absolutely plumb crazy. There were a dozen solid reasons why he shouldn't.

And he wouldn't.

But he couldn't help thinking about it just the same.

"Well, Mr. Evans, I believe we both have early starts in the morning." She turned to go up the steps. "There is a lot more to be done around here. I think tomorrow I'll examine your vegetable garden."

Lord, she had a lot of pride. But Luke understood that. It made him want to lend his assistance. "I haven't tended to the weeds in a while. The potatoes are sure to need hoeing."

He took a step forward, and his gaze dropped to her full, lush lips. He was standing in the moonlight with a beautiful woman and all he could do was talk about gardens and chores. Had it been that long since he'd dated that he had lost all concept of conversation? The moment stretched out and he leaned forward, just a bit until the floral scent he now recognized as hers filled his nostrils.

He reached out and took her fingers in his hand and felt them tremble.

This was ridiculous. She'd just got through telling him about her disintegrated marriage and he was contemplating coming on to her? He straightened, took a step back.

"It's been a long day," she whispered, pulling her fingers away and tucking them into her pockets. He heard the nervous quaver in her voice and knew she understood exactly what direction his thoughts had taken.

"I'll see you in the morning."

She went inside, closing the door quietly behind her, but for several minutes Luke sat on the porch, thinking.

How could a man just walk out on his family that way? Leave his responsibilities behind? A real man did what needed to be done. His dad had instilled that in him from the time he was younger than Sam. But just because Northcott had left his wife and kid didn't mean they were suddenly Luke's responsibility. For the last decade, he'd had the ranch to worry about, and his sisters until they'd made their way on their own. Now it was the ranch and his father's failing health. It was more than enough. He didn't need to take on any wounded strays.

He just had to remember to shut down any more thoughts

of kissing her. Uncomplicated. That was exactly how this was going to stay. And after she was gone, he'd manage on his own once more.

Just like he always did.

CHAPTER FIVE

EMILY CALLED HER parents first thing after breakfast, once Luke was out of the house and she'd sent Sam upstairs to get dressed. She kept the call brief, merely letting them know of the change of situation and a number where they could contact her.

Then she hung up, feeling like a big fat coward. Her parents had no idea how tight things had become financially, and she didn't want them to either. She knew her dad would insist on helping, something they could not afford now that he was retired. Maybe Luke was right. Maybe she did have too much pride. But there was satisfaction in knowing she was doing it herself. And refusing help also meant she was one-hundred-percent free to make her own choices. She liked that.

She liked being at the Evans ranch, too. She had a purpose, something that had seemed to be missing for too long. She hung out a load of laundry, smelling the lilacs on the air as she pinned the clothes on the line. Sam handed her the clothespins, his dark hair shining in the morning sunlight. "I like it here," she said easily, taking another of Luke's T-shirts and hanging it by the hem. "What about you, Sam?"

Sam shrugged. "It's quiet. And I haven't been able to see much."

"Maybe this afternoon we can take a walk. Search out some wildflowers and birds' nests." Emily felt a catch in her heart, wishing for a moment that he had a brother or sister to keep him company. "I can ask around about some day camps, too, if you like."

"I like the horses," Sam replied, handing her another clothespin. "Do you think I'll be able to ride one?"

Emily frowned. Sam was five and a full-grown horse was so…huge. "I don't know," she answered honestly. "Luke has quarter horses, and he's very busy."

Sam looked disappointed. "Don't worry," she added, ruffling his hair. "Once we get settled it'll all come around all right. Promise."

Sam went off to color in an activity book while Emily fussed around the kitchen, taking a tray of chicken breasts out to thaw for supper. Their conversation had made her think. Keeping Sam busy might be harder than she'd thought. She'd have to think of ways to keep him entertained. She looked at the chicken and then around at the kitchen. Luke had thanked her for the meal last night but it was clear to her that he appreciated plain cooking. Why not keep Sam occupied today by baking? He loved helping her at home. An apple cake, perhaps. And cookies. Sam loved rolling cookies.

With the house tidied and the laundry under control, Emily liked the thought of spending the day in the kitchen, mixing ingredients. She hummed a little as she got out a mixing bowl and began setting out what she'd need. She imagined Luke coming in to rich spicy smells and the smile that would turn his lips up just a bit at the edges.

Her hand stilled on a bag of sugar. Why should it matter if he smiled at her or not? Her stomach did a flutter as she remembered the way his hands had squeezed her fingers last night. He was being nice, that was all. Maybe that was it. He didn't come across as a typically nice person, so last night's chat in the dark had thrown her off balance.

She knew the recipes by heart and when Sam came back

downstairs, they began mixing, rolling and baking. The apple cake, with its topping of brown sugar and cinnamon was cooling on the stovetop and Sam took a fork and pressed on the peanut butter cookies in a crisscross pattern. She'd just sat Sam up to the table with a few warm cookies and a glass of milk when the screen door slammed. Emily pressed a hand to her belly, brushing the flour off the white-and-blue apron she'd found in a drawer. Luke was back already? And the kitchen was still a mess, with dirty dishes and flour dusting the counter surfaces!

"Luke, you here?"

The voice was male but it definitely wasn't Luke's. Emily bit down on her lip as Sam paused mid-drink and looked at her.

"Wait here," she instructed Sam, and took a breath. Whoever was there was comfortable enough to come into the house without knocking.

"Hello?" She stepped through the swinging door of the kitchen and moved towards the foyer, where she could hear footsteps. "Can I help you?"

A tower of a man came around the corner. He topped Luke by a good three inches, and Luke had to be close to six feet. Instead of Luke's uniform of jeans and T-shirts, this man wore dress trousers and a shirt and tie, and he carried a box cradled under one arm. Short-cropped walnut-brown hair and warm brown eyes assessed her. "You must be the new housekeeper," he said, but he smiled, making the to-the-point introduction friendly rather than brusque. "I'm Joe. Luke's brother-in-law."

This was Cait's husband, Emily remembered. The one who worked at the equipment dealership. "The new dad," she replied, holding out her hand. "Congratulations. I'm Emily Northcott."

His dark eyes were warm and friendly as he took her hand.

"My wife is very glad you're here at last. She was worried about her big brother managing everything." He inclined his chin for a moment. "It smells good in here."

She withdrew her hand from his, feeling unease center in her belly. When she'd met Luke and shaken his hand, there'd been a queer fluttering and the heat of his skin against hers. With Joe there was none of that. It shouldn't have been different. Luke wasn't any different. He was just a guy.

If that were true, why had she felt the curl of anticipation when the screen door had slammed?

Now his brother-in-law was here and she was feeling that she should play host. "There's coffee and warm cookies, if you'd like some," she invited.

"I wouldn't say no." He put the box on the floor by the door. "Cait in the hospital means cooking for myself right now. If you think Luke's bad in the kitchen…I think I can burn water. Cait got her mother's cooking skills, thank God."

Joe followed her into the kitchen and stopped at the sight of Sam at the table. "Your son?" he asked.

"Yes, this is Sam. Sam, this is Mr. Evans's brother-in-law, Joe."

"You're not a cowboy like Luke," Sam stated, taking the last half of his cookie and dunking it in his milk. Crumbs floated on the top of the creamy surface.

Joe looked down at himself and back up. "No, I guess you're right! I work at the tractor dealership in town."

"I could tell by your clothes."

Joe laughed while Emily resisted the compulsion to curb Sam's matter-of-fact observations.

"Believe it or not, Sam, I've done a fair share of farm jobs. Not like Luke, of course." Joe looked at Emily and winked. It was clear that Luke had already made a solid impression on her son. "But I've been known to lend a hand now and again."

"Luke has a four-wheeler and a tractor and horses. I haven't seen them yet, though. Not up close."

Sam's dark eyes were wide with honest disappointment. Emily hadn't realized that Sam had noticed all those things in addition to the horses. She wondered if she could convince Luke to take him for a ride on the quad or tractor one of these days.

She handed Joe a mug of coffee and put the cream and sugar in front of him as he sat at the table. "Is your wife coming home from the hospital soon?" She offered him a cookie.

"Maybe this afternoon."

"You must be excited."

His eyes gleamed. "We are. We've been waiting a long time for Janna to arrive. Cait has been worried about Luke, though. The ad for the housekeeper didn't get results and Cait is a mother hen. It's one less thing for her to worry about. And then I won't have to worry about *her*."

It was clear to Emily by the way Joe spoke, from the gleam in his eyes, that he loved his wife very much. It was beautiful but caused a sad pang inside her. She'd thought she had that once. Had Rob ever looked at her that way? She'd thought so. Now she wondered if her radar had been flawed all along. She wasn't sure she could ever trust her judgment again.

"Look what the cat dragged in."

Luke stood in the doorway of the kitchen, his hat in his hands and a smile of pure pleasure on his face. "How's the new father?"

"Anxious to get my family home."

"Mom and baby?" Luke stepped inside the kitchen and Emily felt the disconcerting swoop again, the one that felt like riding the roller coaster at Calaway Park. Trouble.

"Home this afternoon, I hope. I brought your parts out that

you asked for. Have a cookie, Luke. They're mighty good. I get the feeling you lucked out with your housekeeper."

"I could have come in and picked them up." Luke angled Joe a telling look. "Unless Cait sent you out here to do a little recon."

Joe didn't even look away, just smiled crookedly at Luke. "I'm not in a position to say no to that woman at the moment," he replied. "And even if I tried, she'd remind me about the twelve hours of labor she just had to endure."

Luke took a cookie from the plate and met Emily's eyes across the kitchen. It was as if an electric wire sizzled between them, and she held her breath. Last night he'd come close to kissing her. At the time she'd put it down to her own fanciful thinking in the moonlight, but she was sure of it now. With his blue gaze flashing at her, she knew she'd been right.

He bit into the cookie and a few crumbs fluttered to the floor. She watched, fascinated, as his lips closed around the sweet and his tongue snuck out to lick away the bits that clung to his bottom lip.

Oh, dear.

She suddenly realized that Joe was watching them with one eyebrow raised and she forced a smile, grabbing a dishcloth and starting to run some water into the sink. "I'm afraid the kitchen is quite a mess," she said, knowing it was inane conversation but desperately needing to fill the gap of silence. "I'd better get started on these dishes."

"And I'd better get back to town." Joe stood up, brought his cup to the sink. "Nice to meet you, Emily."

"You, too. Congratulations again." She squeezed soap into the running water. She didn't dare look at him. She'd blush, she just knew it. She'd been horribly transparent when she'd met Luke's gaze.

"Thanks for bringing the parts out," Luke said, grabbing

another cookie. "I'm heading back out, but now I can get a start on them tonight."

A start? Emily's head swiveled around to look at him. Did he work from dawn until dusk every day?

"Oh, and I brought out some rhubarb," Joe added. "Liz sent it. She said if you couldn't use it now to freeze it. I'm betting Emily could work her magic on it though."

"I can try," she said softly, watching the two of them leave the kitchen and head to the front door.

It was all so normal. A family who cared and looked after each other. Even the idea that Joe had been sent to scope her out for the family didn't really bother her. It was what families did, she supposed. When Luke needed a tractor part, his brother-in-law brought it. Cait worried about him and his other sister sent rhubarb. It was their way of showing they cared. The kind of big family she'd always wanted and had never had.

Sam hopped down from his chair and asked if he could go play in the yard. She let him go, not wanting him to see the telltale moisture gathering in her eyes. She was a good mother. She knew that. She loved Sam and had never regretted staying home with him. But who was there for her?

She scrubbed at the mixing bowl that had held the cake batter and sniffed. Suddenly she wished for an older sister or brother. Someone she might have called when her life was falling apart to reminisce with about childhood. Someone to share her hurt with—and someone to make her laugh again.

Someone like Luke, last night. He'd listened. He'd even made her laugh a little. But Luke was different. There was nothing brotherly about the way she reacted when she was near him. That frankly scared her to death.

"I thought I'd bring you the rhubarb before I headed out."

For once she hadn't heard him come back in and his deep

voice shimmered along all her nerve endings. She swallowed, hating that he'd caught her in a moment of self-pity. "Thank you, Luke. I'll make sure I do something with it right away."

"Em?"

He shortened her name and the intimate feeling of being alone with him multiplied.

"Are you okay?"

She gave a little laugh. "Oh, it's foolishness. You caught me being a little sorry for myself, that's all."

"Why?"

He took a step closer.

She could hardly breathe. "I don't know your family, but I get the sense that you all look after each other. It's nice, that's all. I don't have any brothers or sisters."

"You've handled your situation all alone, haven't you?"

"Pretty much. Friends can only take so much of hearing your troubles, you know? I'm not very much fun these days. So many of them are couples, and I was suddenly the odd man out. They were Rob's friends, too, and it is awkward if you're suddenly picking sides. It was just..."

"Easier to stay away?"

She looked up, surprised yet again that he seemed to understand so easily. "Yes, I guess so. Sometimes I miss the easygoing, fun Emily I used to be."

"Taking the responsibility of the world on your shoulders tends to have that effect," he replied, coming to her and putting his wide hands on her arms. "You are doing the best you can, right?"

She swallowed, tried to ignore the heat from his hands soaking through the cotton of her shirt. "Taking care of Sam is everything to me." She blinked, feeling herself unravel at the kind way he was looking at her. "Not being able to support us makes me feel like such a failure."

He lifted one hand and gently traced his thumb beneath her eye, lifting the moisture away from the skin. "You are not a failure, Emily. You only fail if you stop trying. And I might not know you well, but I can see you're no quitter."

It was a lifeline to cling to and she shuddered in a breath. But when she looked up into his eyes, everything seemed to drop out of her, making her feel weightless, feel that the clock on the wall had suddenly stopped ticking.

His fingers tightened on her shoulder as he drew her closer. For a few precious seconds his lips hovered only an inch from hers. Her heart hammered, wanting desperately for him to kiss her and terrified that he actually might.

Then his breath came out in a rush and he moved back, wiping a hand over his face. "What am I doing?" he asked, more to himself than to her, she realized. Her face flamed with embarrassment. He'd stepped back, but she would have kissed him. If he'd stayed there a moment longer, she would have leaned in and touched his lips with her own.

"I'm sorry." He put his hands in his pockets and the blue heat she'd seen in his eyes was cool and controlled now. "That isn't why you're here. I overstepped, Emily. It won't happen again."

Why on earth was she feeling such profound disappointment? Kissing him would complicate everything! And there was Sam to consider. What if he saw them? He still hadn't quite grasped the unalterable fact that his father wasn't coming back.

"It would be confusing to Sam if he were to see," she said quietly. "And I am not in the market for a relationship. You must know that."

"I do. Of course I do." He had the grace to look chastened. "I don't play games, Emily. I'm not interested in romance either, and I won't toy with you. What happened just now was…an aberration."

He paused, and Emily knew he was measuring his words. What was he protecting? Luke seemed fine when he was dealing with others, but when it came to himself he was irritatingly closed off. He had been open and laughing with Joe, but with her he put the walls back up. She wondered why.

"I don't understand you at all, Luke. You can be very distant, and then last night it was almost as if you were right there in my shoes. Why is that?"

He stared out the window and she wondered if he was avoiding looking at her on purpose.

"I know what it's like to have so much responsibility on your shoulders, that's all. I was only twenty when I took over this farm, and I'm the oldest. Cait and Liz were still in their teens. It's not easy being thrust into the role of primary caregiver and provider. I understand that, Emily. After last night... let's just say I want to help you get your feet beneath you again."

Emily felt her pride take a hit. Had she really seemed that desperate? "Rescuing women and puppies, is that it?"

He frowned. "It's not like that. There was no rescuing involved. I did need help. It was such a relief to come inside last night and know that the house wasn't in shambles. To have a meal hot and waiting rather than throwing something together at the last minute. Why is it so hard for you to accept that this is important? I'm not a particularly charitable man, Emily. I'm not one for pretty words."

She pondered it for a moment, not liking the answer that came to her mind.

"Don't you think what you've done has value?"

He did know how to get in a direct shot, didn't he? Emily dropped her eyes and reached for a dish towel.

"Economics, Emily. The value of something goes up when it's in short supply. Believe me, I've had to keep up with the ranch and the house and...everything else on my own. I appreciate what you've done more than you know."

She wondered what he'd really been going to say in the pause. What everything? "You're just saying that."

"Why would I?"

He came close again. Emily could feel him next to her shoulder and wanted so badly to turn into his arms. She clenched her jaw. How needy could she be, anyway? So desperate that she'd let herself be swayed by a husky voice and a pair of extraordinary blue eyes? She'd gone months without so much as a hug. Wanting to lose herself in his embrace made her weak, and she couldn't give in. Her control was barely hanging on by a thread. She was afraid of what might happen if she let herself go. At the very least, she'd make a fool of herself, especially after their protests that neither of them were interested in romance. She didn't want to look like a fool ever again.

"Did *he* tell you it wasn't important?"

Emily didn't have to ask who *he* was. She'd told Luke enough last night for him to paint a fairly accurate picture. "Staying home with Sam was a mutual decision," she whispered. "But it didn't stop him from getting in the little digs that the financial burden of the family rested on his shoulders. And he never quite saw that while I didn't carry the finances, I looked after everything else, and gladly." She swallowed. "We decided together. I did have to remind him of that on occasion."

She twisted her hands in the dish towel, knowing if she turned her head the slightest bit she'd be staring into his eyes again. The temptation was there. To see if the flare in his eyes was real. Rob hadn't appreciated her. She knew that now. He'd shouldered the financial responsibility of their family and then he'd had enough. She didn't realize how much she needed the validation until she heard it from Luke's lips—a relative stranger who seemed to appreciate her more in two short days than anyone had in years.

"There are some things you can't put a price tag on," Luke said. "He was a fool."

Emily's pulse leapt. Yes, he had been a fool. She had put everything into their family only to be discarded. She turned to Luke then, dropping the dish towel to the countertop. It was a seductive thing, to feel that she was being seen. Really seen.

"I know," she whispered. "I know it in my head. It's harder to convince my heart."

A muscle ticked in Luke's jaw as silence dropped. Emily couldn't have dragged her gaze away if she'd tried. Their gazes meshed, pulling them together even as they both held back.

"Dammit," Luke uttered, then curled his hand around the nape of her neck and moved in to kiss her.

She was vaguely aware of lifting her hands and placing them on his arms. The skin below the hem of his T-shirt sleeve was warm, covering solid muscle from his long days of manual labor. Every square inch of Luke Evans was solid, a formidable, unbreachable wall. Except his mouth. Oh, his mouth. It was incredibly mobile, slanted over hers and making her weak in the knees. He tasted like peanut butter cookies and coffee and the way he was kissing her made her feel like a strawberry, sweet and ripening on the vine in the summer sun.

His muscles relaxed against hers, but with the easing off came a new and wonderful complication: he settled into the kiss now, pulling her body flush against his, making her feel that it could go on forever and nearly wishing it would. She melted into him, resting against the solid wall of his chest, surrendering.

His cell phone rang, the holster vibrating against her hipbone. The ring tone sounded abnormally loud in the quiet kitchen and Emily staggered backwards, holding on to the counter for support. For one sublime second Luke's gaze collided with hers, hot and perhaps a little confused. Blindly he reached for the phone and then the moment disintegrated into dust as he turned his attention to the display.

Emily grabbed at the discarded dish towel and began drying dishes, wiping each one with brisk efficiency before putting it on a clean portion of countertop. What had they done? Got completely carried away, that's what, and right after they'd said they wouldn't. Heat rushed to her cheeks and flooded through her body. It had been perfectly, wonderfully glorious.

But so wrong. If he'd set out to prove a point, he'd done it. She was vulnerable. Hungry for affection. She put down a mixing bowl and dropped her forehead to her palm. She'd been weak, when only minutes before she'd determined this wouldn't happen. How could she keep the promises she'd made to herself and to Sam if she indulged in such a lack of self-control?

"I've got to get going," Luke's voice came from behind her and she straightened, stiffening her spine.

"Of course. You have work to do."

"Emily…"

That one word—her name—seemed full of unasked questions. Was he feeling as uncertain as she was?

"Luke." She said it firmly, shutting down any doubts. This couldn't happen again. Thinking about whatever chemistry was zinging between them was bad enough. Acting on it was just wrong. She had a plan. It wasn't a perfect plan, but it would be good for her son. A mother did what she had to do. That included taking this job until she could find a more permanent situation.

"I…uh…"

Her throat constricted. She couldn't bear to hear him apologize or say what a mistake it had been.

"You'd better attend to whatever that was," she said, nodding at his phone.

"We'll talk later?"

One more complicated look and he spun on his heel, heading out the door again without waiting for her to answer.

Talk? Emily put her fingers to her lips. They were still humming from the contact with his. They wouldn't talk about this at all—not if she could help it.

CHAPTER SIX

LUKE MADE THE last turn around the field, leaving a swath of sweet-smelling grass behind him and a sense of relief in its wake. The sun shone benevolently down on him right now, but by tomorrow night that would change. The forecast was for rain and thunderstorms. As long as the fine weather held out for another day the first cut would be done and baled and, most importantly, dry. If everything went on schedule. And if the repairs he'd made to the baler held. A lot of ifs.

He checked his watch. Nearly lunch. The Orrick brothers had been raking the east field and would eat their meal in their truck. Luke could have brought his lunch with him, but he looked forward to going back to the house and seeing what Emily had cooked up. Usually he appreciated the thought of peace and quiet and solitude at mealtime. But lately he'd found himself looking forward to Emily's quiet greetings and Sam's chatter.

As he turned the tractor south towards home, he frowned. This wasn't something he should let himself get used to. Cooking or not, being around Emily wasn't the best idea. Not after yesterday. What had he been thinking, kissing her like that? He'd got carried away. She'd turned those liquid brown eyes on him, so hurt and insecure. She'd hate his pity, but he was sorry that she had to carry the weight of her family on her own, knowing there was no way out from beneath the weight of responsibility. Sorry that she'd been married to a man who didn't appreciate all she did. Her lip had quivered and he'd wanted to make it up to her somehow.

Oh, who was he fooling? He touched the throttle, speeding up as he hit the straight dirt lane. He had wanted to kiss her, plain and simple. Still did, if it came to that, even though he knew it was a huge mistake. He could justify it six ways from Sunday, but the truth was she was the prettiest thing he'd laid eyes on in forever. She was out here in the middle of nowhere, but she didn't turn up her nose like so many of the girls did these days—like ranching was some sort of second-class occupation. She breathed deeply of the air, enjoying the space and freedom. And the way she touched Sam, ruffling his hair and showering him with hugs. It was the sort of affectionate touch that was second nature to a mother. The kind he'd grown up with. His mother had been firm but loving. His father, too.

Until his mother had died and everything changed.

The house was in sight, and he spied Emily and Sam in the vegetable garden. For a moment it felt so incredibly right. But then the feeling grew heavy in his chest. It couldn't be *right*. Emily was far too hurt from her divorce, no matter what she said. And Luke liked Sam but he didn't want kids. He didn't want to be married, either. The last thing he wanted was the burden of caring for a family, risking putting them through what he'd been through. Each time he visited his father he was reminded of what the future could hold for him. Seeing his dad suffer quelled any ideas Luke had about a family of his own. No, he'd run the farm and leave the marriage and kids thing to his sisters.

And no matter what Emily said, she was the marrying kind. She wasn't the kind of woman a man trifled with. She certainly wasn't the type for an eyes-open-no-strings fling. So that left them right back at boss and employee.

He pulled up to the barn and wasn't surprised to see

Sam bounding along to greet him. He was a good kid. He minded his mother and was polite and didn't get into things he shouldn't get into. "Hey, Sam."

"Luke! We're weeding your garden and I only pulled up one bean." His face fell a little. "I hope that's okay."

"One little bean plant isn't going to make any difference, don't worry," Luke assured him. The boy had clearly forgiven him for any slights made earlier as he aimed a wide smile at Luke. He noticed Sam had lost his first tooth and couldn't help but smile back at the lopsided grin. "Tooth fairy give you anything for that?"

"A dollar," Sam announced proudly.

Luke cleared his head, pushing away the earlier thoughts of kissing Emily. Sitting on a tractor for hours always gave him way too much time to think. What was he so worried about? It wasn't like he was falling in love with her or anything. It had just been a kiss. Nothing to lose sleep over.

Except he had. It had been ten past midnight when he'd checked the alarm clock last night. Replaying the taste of her, the feel of her in his arms. He walked towards the garden with Sam, watching Emily bent over the tiny green plants. His gaze dropped to the curve of her bottom and his mouth went dry. She straightened, standing up in the row of peas and put her hands on her lower back, stretching.

Little pieces of her hair curled up around the edges of one of his baseball caps, the curved brim shading her eyes from the sun. She wore cutoff denim shorts and a T-shirt the same color as the lilacs by the front verandah, the cotton hugging her ribs, emphasizing her spare figure. His gaze caught on the long length of her leg and he swallowed. It was impossible to stop thinking about yesterday when he'd held her in his arms.

"We might actually get this first cut done before the weather changes," he remarked as he approached the rows of vegetables. Now he was reduced to talking about the weather? It wasn't a good sign when he felt the need to keep things to nice, safe topics. He looked over the garden. Half of it was neatly weeded and tended, the tiny shoots healthy and green. The other half was slightly scraggly. "Thank you for doing the garden. It was on my to-do list."

"It was no trouble. The inside of the house is under control now and it was too beautiful a day to waste. I like being outside, and so does Sam. Don't you Sam?"

Sam nodded, his bangs flopping. "Yup. Mom showed me what a pea plant looks like, and a bean and the carrots, too!" He held up a small pail. "And I took the weeds to the compost pile, too."

"You're a good help," Luke said, unable to resist the boy's excitement. How often had he done this very thing? All the kids had. Working in the garden had been part of their summer chores. "I like working in the outdoors, too."

"Mom said you're too busy to take me on the tractor or anything."

Luke angled his head and looked at Sam, assessing. Sam was what, almost five? At that age, Luke had already been helping in the barns and riding on the tractor with his dad. The memories were good ones, and Sam hadn't experienced anything like that.

"I'm going to be raking hay this afternoon. You can come with me if you like."

Maybe it was a bad idea. He was trying to keep his distance and he wasn't sure Emily would appreciate him encouraging her son. But neither could he stand the thought of the boy feeling alone, left out. Luke knew that helping his dad had made him feel a part of something. The sound of the machinery, the time out of doors, the sense of accomplishment. What could it hurt, just this once?

Sam's eyes lit up and he practically bounced on his toes. "Mom? Can I?"

Emily's dark eyes were centered on him again and he felt the same tightening as he had yesterday when he'd held her body against his. Lord, she'd been sweet and soft and when he'd kissed her every single thought in his brain had gone on vacation.

"You don't have to do that, Luke. You're busy. Sam can wait for another time."

Sam's shoulders slumped in disappointment and he scuffed a toe in the dirt, the action reminiscent of his mother. Clearly Sam had wanted to go, and it was no big deal having him on the tractor with him. Hadn't the boy suffered enough disappointments lately? Luke looked at Emily, knowing she was acutely unhappy with the path her life had taken. He knew she was trying to do her best, but that cloud of unhappiness affected Sam, too. She couldn't keep him tied to her apron strings forever.

"It's just a tractor ride," he answered. "I'm going to be sitting there anyway, raking what we cut yesterday. The boys will be coming along behind, doing the baling. No reason why he shouldn't come along. It'll be a chance for him to learn something new. And give you a little time to yourself."

"Please, Mom?"

She paused.

"He'll be safe with me, Emily. I promise. You have to let go some time."

Her gaze snapped to his and her lips thinned but he held his ground. Sam was a boy. He needed freedom to play and see and do things. Luke understood Emily being protective, but an afternoon in the sun would be good for him. Luke was not her ex. If he made a promise he'd keep it. "It's only a tractor ride," he repeated.

* * *

Emily paused, taken aback by Luke's words. Was she over-protective? She didn't think so. She was only focused on Sam feeling loved and secure. His expressive eyes had looked so hurt, so broken since his father left and she'd do anything to keep that from happening again. She didn't want Sam to get any hopes up.

But perhaps Luke was right. It was just a tractor ride, after all. Didn't Sam deserve some fun? "I'll think about it over lunch." She put off a firm decision, needing him to see that she wasn't going to accept being nudged or coerced. He should have done the courtesy of asking her in private. Heavens, he'd barely said two words to Sam the first few days and now here they were, seemingly thick as thieves.

"Lunch is ready, by the way. I made chicken salad this morning and a cobbler out of that rhubarb your sister sent."

He sent her a cheeky smile from beneath his hat. "You might have to stop treating me so well. I'll get round and fat." He stuck out his stomach and Sam giggled.

Emily pressed her lips together. The man was exasperating! It was almost as if he and Sam were in cahoots together. Which was probably preferable to his taciturn moodiness the first few days, but she didn't want Sam to get too attached. He could get a good case of hero worship without much trouble. And this job wasn't permanent.

Sam bounded on ahead to wash up and Emily took off her cap and shook out her hair. She looked straight ahead as she asked, "You might have asked me first, rather than putting me on the spot."

"What? Oh, I didn't think you'd mind. He did mention something about the tractor the other day, didn't he?"

"That's not the point."

His steps halted, churning up a puff of dust. "Look, I know you're worried about him and it's something he might find fun. I don't get your problem."

She angled him a look that said *Get real.* "My problem is, he's had too many promises made to him that have been broken. Have you seen how he looks at you? Like you hung the moon and the stars. He's been missing a father figure and suddenly here you are."

Luke laughed. "I doubt it. He snuck out of bed the other night and told me off for not complimenting you on your veal."

Emily's mouth dropped open. "He what?"

"Came to the shop and told me you were a nice lady and that his dad doesn't like him and he doesn't care whether I do either. Now, normally a five-year-old boy's opinion wouldn't bother me, but it occurred to me that perhaps I hadn't been as welcoming as I might have been. Don't read too much into it. Like I said, it's just a tractor ride."

Emily folded her hands together. "I guess I can't blame him for being protective. His trust has been shaken."

"Just his?" he asked quietly, walking along beside her again. "Are you really planning never to trust anyone again?"

How could he blame her for being a little gun-shy? "Let's just say trust is a valuable commodity and it has to be earned."

"Yes, and your ex is a prime example of earning it and then abusing it. There's more to building trust than time."

His words cut her deeply. She had trusted Rob and he'd ground her faith in him beneath his heel when he left. She'd made a lot of progress since then. She'd stopped blaming herself for everything. She'd stopped feeling so desperate. She'd started focusing on the good—as much as that was possible. But trust...that was something she wasn't sure she'd ever quite accomplish again.

"If you're so smart, what else is there?" She didn't bother to keep the annoyance out of her voice. Sometimes Luke was far too sure of himself. Like he had her all figured out.

"Actions. Hell, instincts, if it comes to that."

His observations made her uncomfortable, because her instincts had told her from the beginning that Luke was a man she could trust. And he'd kept his word about everything since her arrival.

"Right now I don't put a lot of credence in my instincts."

He stopped, his boots halting in the dusty drive and she kept on a few steps until she realized he wasn't with her anymore. She looked over her shoulder at him. His eyes flashed at her. "And I've done something to...not earn your trust? Is that it?"

He had her there. And yesterday's kiss...she couldn't blame him for that either. She'd wanted it as much as he had. Not that they'd talk about it. No way.

"I'm cautious, then," she responded, as they reached the steps. "Very, very cautious."

"So can Sam come with me or not?"

She left him in the doorway taking off his boots. "I'm still thinking," she said. She'd already made up her mind that Sam could go, but she wasn't going to let Luke think he'd won so easily.

Just as they were finishing the meal, a cloud of dust announced an approaching car. They both looked out the window and Emily heard Luke's heavy sigh. "Who is it?"

"My sister, Liz."

"The rhubarb sister."

He smiled at her summary. "Yes, that's the one." Emily watched as he checked his watch and tapped his foot. "Dammit, she's got perfect timing," he muttered.

Liz parked the car in the shade of a tree and Emily felt the strange, nervous feeling she'd had yesterday meeting Joe. As though she was an imposter, a tag-along.

"I'm sorry, Emily. I think the family is curious about you, and you've been put under the microscope."

"Why would they do that?"

Luke plopped his hat on his head. "Because you're not the matronly housekeeper they expected. Because you're staying here. Because you're young and pretty." He sighed. "Because people who are married think that everyone else in the world should be married, and they feel free to stick their noses in."

Emily opened her mouth and then closed it again, unsure of how she was supposed to react to that little tidbit. It wasn't the meddling that shook her—she half expected that. It was the *young and pretty* part. She was only twenty-eight but there were days she felt ancient. And pretty...she'd been living in T-shirts and yoga pants for so long that she forgot what it was like to feel pretty.

She wouldn't dream of admitting such a thing to Luke, though. Surely his family wasn't putting the cart this much before the horse. "Married?" The thought was preposterous, and she laughed. Even if she did want to get married—which she didn't—she'd only known Luke for a few days.

He raised his right eyebrow until it nearly disappeared beneath his hat. "Ridiculous, isn't it? But I'll bet my boots Liz is here to check you out. She'll have some good excuse. But don't worry, she means well. This should be the end of it. You can thank the Lord that I don't have more sisters to interfere."

With that he went outside to greet Liz.

Liz came towards the house, carrying a blond-headed baby on her hip and with two more youngsters trailing behind. Emily bit down on her lip. She was an object of curiosity now. Yesterday's longing for siblings and a close-knit family dissipated as she realized that intimacy also meant interference. The last thing she wanted was to be scrutinized. Judged. And to come up short.

"What brings you out, Liz?" Emily heard him call out and

closed her eyes. She could do this. Liz would never know how Luke's voice gave her goose bumps or how they'd kissed until they were both out of breath. Emily fluffed her hair, smoothed her fingertips over her cheeks, and let out a calming breath.

Luke met his sister in the yard. The twin girls took off running across the lawn, burning off some stuck-in-the-car energy.

"Strawberries," Emily heard the woman say. "I brought out a flat of strawberries."

"I'm in the middle of haying. When would I have time for strawberries?"

They'd reached the porch and Emily stood just inside the screen door of the house, wanting to scuttle away but knowing how that would look—as though she was running from something. Hiding. She had nothing to hide.

"Joe told us you've finally got some help. It's about time, Luke. Joe said she's very pretty, too. You've been holding out on us, brother."

"No big surprise, Nosy Nellie. Cait put the request in at the agency, after all. You can't fool me."

Emily's cheeks flamed as Liz looked up and suddenly realized Emily was standing behind the screen door. For a second, Liz got a goofy look on her face as she realized she'd been caught. Then she replaced the look with a wide smile.

"Joe was right. You are pretty. I'm Liz, Luke's sister."

Good heavens, was everyone in Luke's family so forthright?

"Berries are in the trunk, Luke. Be a good brother."

Luke's jaw tightened as Liz smiled and adjusted the weight of the baby on her hip. Emily looked to him for guidance, but he gave none. Emily couldn't stand to be impolite, so she opened the door. "Come on in. We were just having lunch. Come have some cobbler."

Liz swept in and Emily heard Luke's boots tromp off down

the steps. First Joe and now Liz. The family obviously thought there was more to the arrangement than a simple trading of services. Which there wasn't. Much. Emily wondered how fast the telephone wires would burn up if Liz knew that they'd kissed yesterday.

"Don't mind Luke," Liz admonished, nosing around the kitchen. "He's always a bear in haying season. No time to call his own, you know? Not the biggest conversationalist either."

Emily was tempted to set Liz straight on that. Last night and just a few moments ago Luke had managed to hold his own quite well in the conversation department. She wondered how he managed that. He seemed to say a lot, but none of it really told her anything. Except that he'd been left in charge of the family at a young age.

But she did not want to open that can of worms with Luke's sister. She wasn't a busybody and knew exactly how awful it was to have people pry into her situation. She would keep the conversation impersonal. "Rain's coming, Luke said."

Great job, Em, she thought. First words she spoke and she was parroting the forecast? Perhaps she could have come up with something slightly more inspired.

Liz nodded. "He'll work until dark tonight, I expect. Good to get the first cut in though. What do you think of the house?"

Emily busied herself fixing a bowl of cobbler and ice cream for Liz. "It's charming. Much nicer than the cookie cutter houses in the city."

Liz nodded. She sat at the table and perched the baby on her knee, bouncing her a little and making the little girl giggle. "I think so, too. Luke's done some work to it since taking it over, but for the most part it looks just like it did when we were growing up. Of course, I'm living in town now. And I've got the little ones to keep me busy."

Luke came back in, carrying a wooden flat filled with boxes of crimson strawberries. "I think the twins have made a new friend," he said dryly.

Emily and Liz went to the window. Sam and Liz's blond girls were racing through the yard, playing what appeared to be a rousing game of tag.

"It's good for Sam. He hasn't spent much time with friends since…"

She stopped. Since the divorce. Since there was no longer any money for playgroups and preschool.

"He'll have to come play with the twins while you're here. It'll get them out of my hair," Liz offered freely.

Another tie to break later? Emily wasn't sure it was a good idea. But then she balanced it against Sam being alone here in an unfamiliar place and no children to play with. "That might be nice."

"Call anytime." Liz replied, putting the baby down on the floor. The little girl rocked back and forth for a minute before setting off at a steady crawl. "You and Luke could come over for dinner."

"Liz," Luke warned, and Emily had to look away. It was such an overt bit of matchmaking that she squirmed in her chair.

"What? Look, both Cait and I are thrilled you have some help at last. That's all. And Emily doesn't know a soul besides you. And we all know what great company you are."

He raised an eyebrow at her.

"I'm heading back out. The boys are going to wonder where I am. Emily, tell Sam I'll take him out with me another time. He should enjoy the girls while they're here." He put his plate in the dishwasher and cut himself a massive slice of apple cake. "For the road," he said, flashing a quick grin.

She nodded and walked with him to the door.

"Are you sure you're okay with my sister?" he asked quietly, pausing and resting his palm against the frame.

Emily forced a small laugh. "You have work to do. I'll be fine."

"She's meddling. Thinking that this is more than it is."

That should have relieved her but didn't. Would it be so awful for them to think that he liked her, for heaven's sake? Not that she wanted him to, but was it incomprehensible that he might? "Don't worry about it. And it's good for Sam to have playmates for an hour or so. He's been lonely." She paused. "Are you really going to work until dark?"

His gaze plumbed hers for a long moment. It was a simple question but brought with it a picture of how the evening would unfold...Sam in bed, darkness falling, Luke coming to the house in the twilight. All of it played out in her mind as she gazed up into his eyes. How did he feel about coming home to her at night? Was she an intrusion? A complication? Or welcome company, as he was to her, despite his sometimes prickly ways?

"Probably close to it," he finally answered. "We'll go until it starts to cool off, then there are chores here to see to. You and Sam should eat without me. Just fix me a plate."

There wasn't any reason for her to feel disappointed, but she did. After only a few days she'd gotten used to seeing him during meals. Company, whereas before mealtime had meant an empty space at the head of the table.

"I'd like to make a run into town for sugar and pectin. Anything you need?"

He shook his head. "Not that I can think of. Thanks for asking, though." He started off but turned around again. "Don't let Liz needle you into anything," he warned. "Cait's the bossy sister, but Liz has a way of getting what she wants without you even knowing how."

CHAPTER SEVEN

As EMILY WENT back inside, three sweaty heads ran past her into the house.

"Whoa, slow down!" Liz called from the kitchen, laughing as the children scrambled in demanding a snack. The baby was heading for the stairs, and, without a second thought Emily picked her up, breathing in the scent of baby powder and milk. She closed her eyes for a moment, enjoying the feel of the weight on her arm, the smell that was distinctly baby. Sam had left those baby days behind him long ago. Emily had always hoped the time would be right to have another, but it had never worked out. Now she was a little glad it hadn't. She couldn't imagine being responsible for two precious lives in her current circumstances. Knowing she would probably never have any more caused a bittersweet pang in her heart. Being a single mom was tough. She knew she wouldn't deliberately grow her family without being in a secure relationship. And after the crumbling of her marriage, she never intended to go down that road again. Still, it was hard to say goodbye to those dreams.

As she opened her eyes, blue eyes reminiscent of Luke's stared up at her and she smiled. "Let's find your mama," she murmured, and settling the baby on her hip, she entered the kitchen to find Liz mixing up lemonade and three expectant faces watching.

Liz looked so comfortable that it reminded Emily that this was Liz's childhood home. Emily was the trespasser here and she felt it acutely as she watched Liz add sugar to the lemonade then open the correct drawer for a wooden spoon. Emily envied the other woman her level of comfort with, well, everything. And yet she had to admit she was drawn to Liz's breezy ways.

"Out on the porch with you three," Liz admonished, filling three plastic cups with the drink. "One cookie each. No sneaking."

When the kids were settled on the verandah she came back to the kitchen. "Thanks for grabbing Alyssa," she said, taking the bundle from Emily's arms. "The stairs, right? It's always the stairs."

Emily couldn't help but laugh. Liz might be a bulldozer but she was a pleasant one, and it had been a long time since Emily'd had a mom-to-mom visit with anyone. She'd been too busy coping to realize she was lonely.

Compared to Luke's reticence, Liz was bubbly and open. "How is it you are so different from your brother?"

"What do you mean?" Liz asked, grabbing her purse and taking out a biscuit for the baby to gnaw on.

"Luke's so…"

Emily struggled for the right word, thinking of how Luke looked at her and seemed to get to the heart of any matter with a few simple words. Liz's keen gaze was on her now.

Instantly Emily recalled the kiss and the way he'd cupped her neck confidently in his palm. "Intense."

"Luke's too serious, but I can't blame him. It's a wonder he didn't disown the two of us." She flashed a smile that hinted at devilry. "Oh, Cait and I gave him awful trouble."

"Surely your parents…"

"Oh, this was after Mom died and Dad had to be put in the

care home. Luke was different before that happened. Always running with his guy friends, you know?"

Care home?

Luke had said so little about his upbringing. Now the bits and pieces were starting to come together. Luke had said he'd been responsible for his sisters and the farm at an early age. She tried to imagine one parent dying and the other incapacitated. What an ordeal they must have gone through. "How old were you?"

"Luke was twenty. Cait was almost seventeen and I was fifteen. Old enough to know better, really. But at that age—when you're a teenager it's 'all about me', you know? We were still in high school."

Emily did know. But she also knew that Luke would have put himself last, making sure everyone was looked after ahead of himself. She imagined him waiting up for them at night, perhaps pacing the floor with lines of worry marring his forehead. Had those days put the shadows she saw in his eyes? "And Luke?"

Liz frowned. "He didn't tell you any of this?"

"Not much. Why would he? I've only been here a few days, Liz. We haven't had heart-to-hearts."

She smiled, but once the words were out she knew they weren't exactly true. Maybe not baring of souls, but she'd told him more about her marriage than she'd told anyone. They'd had moments of closeness—up to and including the kiss that had nearly melted her socks. Not that she'd admit that to his sister.

Liz dipped into her cobbler, holding the spoon in the air. "Well, Luke should be the one to tell you, not me."

"Luke isn't exactly big on social chitchat," Emily replied, but Liz just laughed.

"He does tend to be on the serious side. You ask him,

Emily. Maybe he'll talk to you. He never talks to either of us."

Maybe Luke was just a private person, Emily thought, but didn't say. Liz was his sister. She had to know him better than most. And she did feel a little odd, talking about him when he wasn't here. As curious as she was, Liz was right. This was something Luke should tell her himself. If he ever did.

"Joe said there's something going on between you."

Emily's back straightened, pulled out of her thoughts by Liz's insinuation. The camaraderie she'd begun to feel trickled away as she remembered Luke's warning. Liz was here to check her out, and the last thing she wanted was to be judged. "You are direct, aren't you?"

Liz raised her eyebrows. "Luke's our brother. We love him. We want him to be happy."

"And that's not with me." Of course not. Emily was not a brilliant prospect in anyone's book. She was damaged goods. She didn't even have a long-term plan.

Emily went to a cupboard and found a large mixing bowl and began stemming the first box of berries. She didn't like that she'd been the topic of conversation around the family water cooler.

"I didn't say that, you did."

The berries flew from one hand to the other and pinged into the stainless-steel bowl as Emily removed the stems. "I'm a single mother with a very small income."

"Money isn't what Luke needs." Liz's voice held a tinge of condemnation. "After what Joe said, I thought maybe you realized that. I guess I was wrong."

Emily's hands fell still. She had always considered that the outside world saw only the surface. That people looked at her and automatically categorized her in little columns of pluses and minuses. Lately she was pretty sure there were more minuses than pluses. Now she wondered if that was simply her own insecurity talking. "What does Luke need?" she asked quietly, picking up another berry but plucking off the stem at a more relaxed pace.

Liz brought another box to the side of the sink. "A companion."

Emily dropped the berry in the bowl. Luke was barely thirty. He didn't need a companion. He needed a wife and partner, and she wasn't up for applying for either position. "Then he should get a dog."

Liz laughed at her dry tone. "Fine, then. He needs a helping hand. Someone willing to share the load. He's been carrying it by himself for a long time. Not that he's ever complained. Someone should shake him up a bit. Why not you?"

A helpmate. Emily knew that was what Luke's sister was getting at and it made her pause. That's what she'd tried to be for Rob and it had blown up in her face. "I'm not interested in that," she informed Liz. "Nothing against your brother. He's very nice. But I'm not looking for a boyfriend or husband. I rely on myself now, not someone else."

Liz looked at her speculatively. "No one said you didn't."

But Emily knew that's what it would mean. She had built her whole existence around someone else. Rearranging her life around Rob's schooling and then his job. Staying home with Sam. Looking after everyone's needs and sacrificing her own. It had little to do with the type of work, she realized, but with the principle behind it. How long had she been Rob's wife, Sam's mother? How long had it been since she'd been plain Emily Northcott, woman?

"Liz, I appreciate that you want your brother to be happy. But surely you can see how ridiculous it is to be discussing this. There are no romantic notions. I work for him."

"If you say so," Liz replied, but Emily knew by her deliberately casual tone that she wasn't convinced. And why should she be? It wasn't exactly true. Emily thought about Luke far too often throughout the day and then there was the kiss. She ran her tongue over her lips, remembering the taste of him there. Knowing it wasn't what she wanted and yet dying to know if he would do it again.

"Either way, can we be friends?" Liz's sandy-colored ponytail bobbed as she reached beneath the cupboard for a colander to wash the berries, completely oblivious to Emily's quandary.

Friends? The request came as a surprise after being grilled about Luke. But an offer of friendship was hard to resist. She'd felt so disconnected in recent months. All of her friends were 'before divorce' friends. There'd been no money or time for cultivating new relationships since. Liz was only looking out for her family. Emily could hardly fault her for that. If she didn't feel so uncomfortable, she might have admired her for it.

Liz reached for the teakettle and filled it with water. "Come on, Emily," she invited. "Let's have a cup of tea and a gab. The kids are playing and Luke's going to be gone for hours. With the little ones underfoot I don't get out much either. What's the harm?"

What was the harm, indeed? Emily couldn't hold out against the temptation of a social afternoon. She got out the teabags and put them on the counter. "He told me you'd bull-doze me, you know." But she smiled when she said it, holding no malice against Luke's vivacious sister. She would have done the same thing for her brother or sister, if she'd had one.

"Of course he did."

Emily lifted a finger in warning. "But leave off the match-making, okay? Luke's no more interested in me than…"

She had been going to say *than I am in him*, but she couldn't say the words because she *was* interested in him, more than she would ever admit.

"Matchmaking? Perish the thought." Liz affected an

innocent look so perfectly that Emily found herself grinning back. "Listen," Liz continued, getting out spoons. "Luke has always said he will never get married anyway. So nothing to worry about, right?"

"I'd like to make some jam out of these berries," Emily said to Liz, offering an olive branch as the kettle began to whistle, trying to ignore Liz's latest bombshell. Never get married? She forced her mind back to the present. "Where's the best place to shop for jars and pectin?"

For the next hour the baby napped, the kids played in the sunshine and Liz and Emily stemmed the remaining berries, chatting easily about lighter topics. But the whole time Emily thought of Luke and his past. She couldn't help wondering why he was determined to be alone. Had he had his heart broken? Was it any of her business to ask? If she did, would he answer? She couldn't help the sneaky suspicion that Liz's throwaway comment had been intended to do just that—make her wonder.

The farmyard was dark except for the light Emily saw coming from the machine shed. It was past ten o'clock and still Luke hadn't come in. He hadn't had any supper, either. She'd waited for him long after Sam had gone to bed, finishing up the last batch of jam and leaving it to set on the kitchen counter. She couldn't forget all that Liz had told her during their chat—and what she hadn't.

She carried a warm plate in her hands as she crossed the gravel drive. The man had to eat something. If he wouldn't come in, she'd take it to him.

She balanced the plate on one hand and opened the door to the shed. All that was visible of Luke as she entered was his legs. The rest of him was underneath her car. A long yellow cord disappeared along with the upper half of his body—a trouble light illuminating the dirty job of changing her oil.

Clanking sounds echoed on the concrete floor as he put down the filter wrench and oil began draining into the catch pan.

"Luke?"

At the sound of her voice he slid out from beneath her car, the sound of the creeper wheels grating loudly in the stillness. The rest of his legs appeared, then came his flat stomach, his broad chest and muscled arms and then his head—now devoid of hat, his hair dark with sweat in the oppressive heat of the shop. Her gaze fixed on his arms as he pushed himself up to sitting.

Emily felt a bead of perspiration form on her temple in the close atmosphere of the shop. Throughout the afternoon the heat had increased until the kids had dropped, sapped of their energy. It hadn't let up after sundown. Even the peepers were quiet tonight, and when the creeper came to a halt, the silence in the shop was deafening.

"What are you doing with my car?"

"Changing your oil. It looked like it'd been a while."

It had, but that wasn't exactly the point. "I…you…" She didn't quite know what to say that didn't sound grouchy and angry. Especially since she was both of those things. Part of it was the heat. But a bigger part was that he'd taken it upon himself to do this without even consulting her.

"You might have asked me first."

Luke shrugged. "It's just an oil change, Emily."

Pride kicked in. "And the cost of the filter, and the cost of the oil."

"If it means that much to you, I'll deduct it from your pay."

Her hand shook beneath the warm dinner plate. She didn't want to lose any of her precious paycheck right now. And if she were to lose any of it, she should be the one to say where it went.

"That really wasn't on my list of things to do with my first check, Luke." She was trying—and failing—to keep a quiver out of her voice. "It's been a long time since I had my own pay. I'd like to be the one to decide what happens to it. And besides, it's after ten o'clock. You've already spent the day outside while I was inside with Liz...."

Suddenly the lightbulb came on. "That's it, isn't it? You're avoiding me because you think Liz put a bug in my ear."

He couldn't meet her eyes. "What's on the plate?"

"I'm right!" Victorious, she let out a breath. "You can't stay out here all night, you know. And you can't avoid me forever. For what it's worth, Liz barely told me anything. You could have saved yourself the trouble."

Luke put on his most nonchalant expression. "Your oil needed changing and I wanted to do it for you. Now, are you going to share that plate or did you just bring it out here to torture me?"

He got to his feet, looking sexier than a man had a right to in dusty jeans, work boots and a grease-stained T-shirt, and she had the thought that he could change her oil or tune up her car any time.

She held out the plate. "You should have come in for supper—you've got to be exhausted. The car could have waited. I know you want to get the hay in." She tried a smile. "You have to make hay while the sun shines, I've heard."

"That's true," he said. "With this heat—we need to get it baled before the rain comes tomorrow. I'm guessing thunderstorms. And there is always the chance of hail."

"Then take a rest."

He reached for a rag and wiped his hands before taking the plate. His fingers were long and rough, with a half-healed scratch running the length of one. He made a living with his hands and hard work. There was something earthy about that and she found it incredibly attractive.

"Lasagna. And garlic bread." He stared at the contents of

the plate with undisguised pleasure. "My God, that smells awesome. Do you know how long it's been since I had lasagna?"

"That's a good thing, then?"

He went to a wheeled stool and sat down. "Oh, yeah, it's a good thing." The shop began to fill with the scent of spicy tomatoes and beef. "Pull up a pew, Emily."

There was little space to sit, so she perched on the edge of a homemade sawhorse. Luke cut into his lasagna with the side of his fork, took a bite, and closed his eyes. Emily smiled, pleased she'd made the extra effort. Luke was turning out to be a pleasure to cook for. "It was better, fresh," she apologized.

"You say that, but I doubt it," he remarked, biting into the garlic bread, flakes off the crust fluttering down to the plate. "It's perfect just the way it is. I didn't realize how hungry I was. You didn't bring any water, did you?"

"Oh! How could I have forgotten?" She reached into the pocket of her light sweater and produced a bottle of beer, so cold it was already sweating with condensation. "I thought you'd appreciate a cold one."

He stared at her as if she were a gift from the gods. "What?" she asked, smiling. "You're not difficult to read, Luke."

Well, not about food, she amended mentally. In other ways he was a definite puzzle. Emily considered for a moment that perhaps Liz's perspective on what happened and Luke's could be very different. Not that Liz had it easy. Losing a parent had to be devastating. But having to step into that role as Luke had...

Luke popped the top and took a long drink. "That is exactly what I needed." He sighed, swiping the final slice of bread along the plate to get the last of the tomato sauce. "Thanks for bringing it out. You didn't need to do that."

"It was kind of quiet in the house."

He nodded. "Yeah, it gets that way."

Emily looked down, studying her toes. Had Luke been lonely? Up until now she really hadn't thought about him living in the house all alone, but now she wondered how it must be to come home to it every day, with no one there to talk to or share the silence with. At least she had Sam.

She picked a wrench up off the tool bench and toyed with it, putting it down and picking up another. When she looked up at Luke she could tell he was gritting his teeth. He came forward and took the wrenches, placing them back on the pegboard. The whole bench was precisely arranged and Emily wondered where he inherited his penchant for neatness from. "Sorry," she murmured.

"It's all right." His voice sounded oddly strained. "I try to keep things organized so…so I can always find the size I need."

"Tools on pegboard and everything on lists." She had noticed Luke had a list for everything at the house. Phone numbers. Groceries. To-do tasks. She often did the same thing, but she thought it an unusual trait in a man. "You really are quite neat and tidy, Luke. For a guy." She attempted to lighten the strange tension that had come over the room.

"I'm a one-man show. Keeping organized saves me a lot of time," he explained. He finished putting the tools away reached for his beer, toying now with the bottle as he sipped. "You survived Liz's visit?"

"We had tea and stemmed strawberries."

"And talked about me."

Emily felt a flush creep into her cheeks. "My, don't we have an inflated opinion of ourselves."

He laughed, the sound filling the quiet shed and sending a tingle right through to her toes. Laughter had been another one of those things that had been missing for a long time. Something that slipped away so innocuously that she hadn't realized she'd missed it until hearing it again.

"Liz was sticking her nose in. If Cait didn't have a newborn at home, she would have been here, too. Be thankful they didn't tag-team you. You wouldn't have stood a chance."

Emily stared at him. He was smiling as though it was a big joke. "So it's funny that I was put under the microscope today?"

He lowered the bottle slowly. "I forgot. You don't have brothers and sisters. It's what they do. We're born to aggravate each other. I guess I'm just used to it."

"Well she wasn't aggravating *you* today, was she?" Emily's back straightened. Granted, she'd had a nice visit with his sister, but Luke didn't know that. For all he knew he'd thrown Emily to the wolves and he was relaxed as could be, smiling like a fool.

His smile slid from his lips though when she fired that question at him. "What exactly did Liz say to you, Emily?"

"Worried?" She asked it in an offhand manner, but the smile from earlier was gone. "She didn't say much. She mentioned you looking after her and Cait and how they'd been holy terrors. But really, that was all."

Luke seemed to relax, turning the bottle in his fingers. "And she said I should ask you about the rest."

The bottle stopped turning.

"Why don't you tell me about your dad, Luke?"

"There's nothing to tell." His voice was hard and his knuckles went white on the bottle.

"He's in a special-care home, right?"

His head snapped up and his blue gaze flashed at her. "Liz has a big mouth."

"Then make me understand what makes you so different from your sister. Because I'm guessing it had to do with the fact that you had to leave your childhood behind in a hurry to take over this farm."

Emily went to him and put a hand on his arm. "Please,

Luke. I shared bits of my story with you. Can't you do the same? Maybe talking about it will help."

"All the talking in the world won't change things," he bit out.

"But it might make you feel less alone," she reasoned. "I know I felt better after talking to you. What happened to your father?"

It was quiet for several seconds and Emily didn't think he was going to answer. But then his voice came, low and raspy, as if the words were struggling to get out.

"Dad had been acting weird for a while. We'd all noticed it, but after Mom died…it was clear there was more to it than simple stress forgetfulness. It wasn't until he nearly burned down the house making eggs in the middle of the night that we couldn't ignore it any more."

"What happened? What was wrong with your father?"

"Early-onset Alzheimer's. Dad's been in a care home since. Over the years it's got progressively worse. Not so much at first. Sometimes the fog would clear and we had good visits, you know? We could talk about the farm, the girls, my mom. But those times got fewer and farther between and lately… he's really gone downhill. I don't expect he's got much time left."

Emily remembered the pictures on the old radio in the living room. The first day, she'd seen Luke's face turn sad as he looked at the picture of his parents. The bedroom upstairs, with its faded doilies and chenille spread, looking lost and abandoned…she'd bet now that no one had slept there since his father had been put in care. And he had given it to her. She felt a little weird about that, but honored, too. What a heart-breaking decision to have to make about your one remaining parent.

"Liz mentioned you having power of attorney. That means the decision fell to you, didn't it?"

He lifted tortured eyes to hers. "Yes. As well as the day-to-day running of the farm, and looking after the girls."

"But surely they were grown enough to look after themselves…"

Luke laughed, but it was laced with pain. "Cooking, laundry, cleaning, yes. But at fifteen and nearly seventeen, they needed guidance. I was twenty. My prized possession was my truck. I wasn't ready to be a parent to two hormonal teenage girls. I wasn't that much older than they were and I was trying to keep them from making mistakes. Trying to make sure they finished school, had opportunities, you know?"

"And so you sacrificed yourself."

"What else could I have done? And look at them. They graduated, got jobs, met fine men and started families. You can imagine what a relief that is. Think if it were Sam."

He'd been taking on responsibility all his adult life. And she'd been whining about her problems yesterday. Luke had been so understanding. More than understanding—caring.

She had been in danger of caring right back, and this new knowledge touched her, making her respect him even more. Making her grieve a little bit for the young man who had had to grow up so quickly. "And all this while you grieved for your parents."

His eyes shone for a few moments until he blinked.

"What did you give up, Luke? You put the girls first, so what dreams did you put aside for later?"

Luke put the bottle beside the empty plate and placed his hands on his knees. "It doesn't matter now."

"I think it does. You were twenty, carefree and with your life ahead of you. That must have been cut short…"

"I worked on the farm for a year, but I'd planned on going to college. I wanted to study genetics so I could play with our breeding program. The idea of going away for a while was exciting. Even after Mom died, I only planned to stay a year to help and then I'd be off. But as things progressed with Dad, I knew I couldn't leave. My responsibility was to the family, and to abandon them would have been the height of selfishness."

He gave her a knowing look. "You know as well as I do that you put family first. You'd do it for Sam. You're doing it for him now by making a life for him. But Emily, don't give up on your dreams either. You give up on them and you'll end up old and bitter like me."

Luke got up from his stool, worry lines marring his tanned brow. He reached out for her arm, but seemed to remember the state of his hands and pulled back. Emily felt the connection just the same as if he'd touched her.

She met his gaze. The connection seemed to hum between them every time their eyes met, but she would not shy away from eye contact. She was stronger than that. "You are not old and bitter," she whispered.

"Em..."

She swallowed. Luke was standing in front of her car now, his thumbs hooked in the front pockets of his jeans. For a moment she remembered what it had been like when he'd stepped forward and kissed her, so commanding and yet gentle. There could be no more repeats of that. He was right. She couldn't give up on her dreams, even if right now that meant doing the right thing for Sam.

"Why don't you go back and get your pharmacy degree?"

She pondered the idea for a moment. "It's not what I want anymore. I have Sam now and want to be close to him. Going to school and trying to support us...he'd be in daycare more than out of it."

"What about online learning?"

The idea was interesting. "Maybe. But not pharmacy. Not now." She smiled at him. "Priorities change."

He smiled back. "Don't I know it?"

Her heart took up a strange hammering, a persistent tap like a Junebug hitting a screen door time and time again.

"Thank you for telling me, Luke. I know it couldn't have been easy."

"It wasn't. But you were right. I do feel better, I think. Liz and Cait have different memories than I do. In some ways that is good. But it's hard talking to them about it. I don't want them to feel responsible for anything, and I think they will if I let on how hard it was."

"Would you do it again?"

It was a loaded question, and one Emily had asked herself often since the disintegration of her marriage. Would she marry Rob again, knowing what she knew now? But then she thought of the good times, and about Sam, asleep in his room with the June breeze fluttering the curtain and the moon shining through the window. Nothing could take away the love she had for her boy. She knew her answer. What was Luke's?

CHAPTER EIGHT

LUKE LEANED BACK against her bumper. What in the world had possessed him to talk to Emily this way? He never opened up to anyone, not even his sisters who had been with him all the way. He kept to himself, and that was how he liked it. And then Emily had blown into his life and turned everything upside down.

She had him talking. That was more of a surprise than his reaction to her. If he wasn't careful, she'd have him wishing for all kinds of things he'd stopped wishing for years ago.

But her question stayed with him, and he looked at her, perched on the sawhorse, her cheeks flushed from the heat and her hair mussed from running her hand through it too many times. Would he do it again the same way? Sacrificing what he'd wanted to look after his sisters?

"Of course I would. They'd lost both their parents. They needed guidance and support. Who else would have stepped in?"

"What about support for you, Luke?"

Damn her eyes that seemed to see everything.

"I could say the same for you, Emily. Who is supporting you now?" She opened her mouth, but he cut her off. "Don't bother, I know the answer. No one. You're going it alone, too. What about your parents? Any other family?"

"I want to do this on my own. I need to. I know they are there if I need them."

"And then there's Sam."

Her eyes blazed and her back straightened. "Everything I do is for Sam!"

Luke smiled indulgently. "Calm down, I know that. Just as you get why I did what I had to for the girls. Choosing myself first would have been self-centered, especially when they needed me so badly."

"You're a good big brother," she murmured. "Do the girls realize how much you gave up for them?"

He shrugged. "Does it matter? They are healthy and happy and I am happy for them." He fought against the sinking feeling in his chest. He was happy for them with their strong marriages and beautiful children. He was thrilled they both had clean bills of health. He also knew that all three of them couldn't be so lucky. Not that he would wish their father's affliction on either of them. Of course not. But it stung just the same, seeing them with their picture-perfect lives and knowing the same wasn't in the cards for himself.

It was a good thing Emily's job only lasted until September. He would manage again after that. He'd put up with Cait coming and going and fussing. Getting closer to Emily wasn't an option, not when he'd just have to push her away again.

"That's all I want for Sam, too," Emily said softly. "He's essentially lost his father and his home and any place he's belonged. Kids do better in consistent environments. Yanking him from place to place isn't good for him. This is kind of like summer vacation for him. I know I've got to figure some things out and find us a more permanent situation."

"You're a good mother, Emily. Did you see his face today at the garden? He's having the time of his life. He's enjoying the outdoors, the freedom. And for all Liz's meddling, the twins are good girls. He could do worse for playmates. You're doing the right thing."

"I don't want him to get in your way, though. I know you have a farm to run. This thing about the tractor...don't feel obligated."

Luke blinked in surprise. What was it about the tractor? Was she worried he'd get hurt? Or did she just not trust him with her son? "Did I give you the idea I didn't like children, Emily?"

"Well, yes, kind of." A mosquito buzzed in front of Emily's face and she brushed it away. He couldn't tell if she were blushing or not because the heat kept her cheeks flushed, but he saw her shift her weight on the sawhorse and wondered.

"You weren't excited about the baby. In fact, you lamented the fact that the newest member of the family was another girl, and came right out and said you didn't want a family. Liz's kids were here today and you barely gave them a glance. You can't honestly say you want him underfoot," she challenged. "He would get in your way."

Luke stilled, feeling as if he'd been struck. Was it that obvious? Did Cait and Liz feel the same way? That he didn't care about their kids? He had kept his distance because it was a constant reminder of how different his life was. But he hadn't considered that they might feel slighted. Unloved. Regret sliced through him.

And he would die before explaining why to Emily. It was bad enough he'd said as much as he had.

"I never meant to give that impression. Of course there are times he needs to be at the house, but there's also no reason why he can't come with me now and again. He can play with Liz's kids. The Canada Day celebrations are soon. There'll be lots of activities for the kids. Has he ever ridden a horse?"

She shook her head.

"I'm not very good at showing my feelings, Emily. That's all. Don't take it personally."

"It is lovely here. The house is a joy and I'm loving the fresh air and freedom of it. I think Sam is, too. If he gets in the way, just tell me, Luke. He's my son, not yours. My responsibility. You don't need to feel like you have to...whatever."

Her words shouldn't have stung but they did. Yes, Sam was her son, and a reminder that Luke would never have one of his own. He would never burden a family the way he'd been burdened.

"Just enjoy the summer, Emily. Think about what you want to do when it's over. Just because I had to give up my dreams doesn't mean you have to give up yours."

The fluorescent lights hummed in the silence.

"I should go in, it's getting late."

Luke cleared his throat. "Your oil is definitely drained. I'll put on the new filter and be behind you in a few minutes." He boosted himself away from the hood of the car and reached for a plastic-wrapped cylinder on the workbench.

"Luke?"

"Yeah?"

"Could you show me how to do that sometime? How to change my oil and stuff? I'd like to be able to do it for myself."

After all they'd talked about tonight, the simple request was the thing that touched him most. She was so intent on being independent. And she trusted him. For some weird reason, she trusted him and it opened something up inside him that had been closed for a very long time.

"Next time we get a rainy day, I promise," he said. "Now get on up to the house. It's after eleven. And morning comes early."

"Yes, boss," she replied, but the tension from her face

had evaporated and she smiled as she picked up his plate and empty bottle. She paused by the door. "Luke?"

He looked up from his position on the creeper. "Em?"

"Thanks for the talk. I'll see you in the morning."

She scuttled out the door, but Luke leaned his head back, resting it on the grill of the car and closing his eyes.

Emily had snuck past almost all of his defenses tonight. And if he wasn't careful, she'd get through them all. And then where would they be?

Curses. Emily put one foot after the other going back to the house in the dark, the echo of a wrench sounding behind her in the stillness. His last word to her had been the shortened version of her name and it had sent a curl of awareness through her. She entered the dark house, left the dishes in the kitchen and felt her way up the steps, using the banister for guidance. In her room she paused, thinking about what had been said and what hadn't. Luke had held back at times, and she wondered why. Now she was more aware than ever that the two bedrooms were only short steps away from each other. She'd be beneath her sheet tonight, listening to the breeze in the trees, and he'd be just on the other side of the wall, doing the same thing.

Damn.

She could do this. She refused to fall for Luke Evans. Maybe they'd reached a new understanding of each other tonight, but that was all. She had to put Sam first, and that didn't include fooling around with the boss. What she needed to do was appreciate what was good about the situation. All the great things about living on a farm could be theirs for the next few months.

Then there was sitting across from Luke at the table, seeing his face morning, noon and night, washing his clothes, smelling the scent of his soap as she hung up his damp towel in the morning. She swallowed. That was the problem. She didn't want to be attracted to him, but she was. She couldn't not be. He was one-hundred-percent strong, virile male, hardworking and honest.

But attraction and acting on it were two very different things. As she lay in the dark, listening for him to return to the house, she thought about what he'd said about school. There was merit there. Perhaps she could talk to her parents after all. It would do Sam good to have family around him more as she got back on her feet. And with her summer's earnings she could buy a laptop and take a few courses.

She was still waiting and planning when she finally drifted off to sleep.

Luke squinted up at the sky, watching the broad roll of clouds balling up in the west. They were still a long way away, but as he wiped the sweat trickling off his brow, he knew they were thunderheads. The forecast had been right for once, though he wished it hadn't. He turned the wheel of the tractor, making one last pass with the rake, watching the Orrick boys work the baler. Hail would wreck what was cut, making it good for nothing. They'd finish, by God, before the rain came. They'd finish if it killed him.

It was a race against time and no one stopped for a lunch break as they worked, dirt mixing with sweat on their brows in the sweltering waves of heat. The thunderheads piled on top of each other, reaching to massive heights and creeping their way eastward to Brooks, Duchess and everywhere in between. He thought of Emily and Sam back at the house. He should have brought his cell. He had no doubt Em could handle a thunderstorm, but he would have liked to hear her voice, to make sure she wasn't out somewhere when the storm hit. To ask her if she'd brought in the hanging baskets. If Sam was okay.

He shook his head. When had he started to care so much? How was it that she snuck into his thoughts no matter where he was or what he was doing?

The thunder was just starting to grumble when the last bale was rolled. James and John Orrick took off their caps and wiped their foreheads, looking up at the sky. The sun still beat down relentlessly but it was coming. There was no sense denying it. "Just in time," James commented, putting his cap back on his head.

Luke scanned the field. The surface of the huge round bales would protect the hay on the inside. Nothing would be lost today. As long as it was just a thundershower. Tornadoes weren't common, but they happened now and again. And if he'd learned anything over the last nine years, it was that you simply had to accept the weather and roll with the punches. He thought of Emily and Sam again. They would be safe in the house. But he wanted to be home with them. To know they were there—warm and dry and safe. No matter how much he hadn't wanted the responsibility of them, he felt it anyway. It would have been easier if it felt like a burden, but it didn't. It felt right, and that was what had kept him up at night.

"Might as well head in, boys. Go home and shut your windows."

Everyone laughed, but it was a tight sound. The air had changed, bringing a shushing sound with it. It was a restless sound, like the wind holding its breath.

They made their way back to the farmyard. The hanging baskets were off the hooks and tucked under the porch roof, their leaves limp in the midday heat. So Emily was aware of the impending storm. Luke's stomach growled since he'd missed lunch, but at the same time a whicker sounded from the corral; Bunny and Fred and Caribou were still outside, nervous just like anyone else at the change in the air. Luke thought about letting them out into the pasture, but then scanned the clouds. If there was hail, he wanted them to be indoors. He forgot about lunch and went to put them in the barn, secured them in their stalls and soothed them with pats and fresh water. Back at the house, all was quiet. Sam was sitting at the table with a coloring book, scribbling busily at a picture of one of the latest superheroes.

Emily appeared at the dining-room door, smiling but he could see she was nervous underneath the cheerful exterior. "You're back. Did you finish?"

"Just." He turned his head towards the door. "You took down the baskets."

"Hard to miss that change in the air. I hope it's not bad. I'd hate for hail to take out the garden. Everything's just starting to come along. Not to mention crops. Do you think it'll be bad, Luke?"

He shrugged. "I hope not, but it's out of my hands. The hay's baled and the horses are in. That's about all I can do. Maybe it'll miss us altogether."

The tension left her face at his reassurances. "I wasn't sure when you'd be in. I made you a sandwich and put it in the fridge."

Luke knew Emily had never been a farm wife, so how was it she seemed to know exactly what he needed and when? He washed his hands and sank into a chair as exhaustion finally crept in now that he'd stopped. He'd been going flat-out for days now and not sleeping well at night. He hadn't visited his father in two weeks and felt guilty about it. He thought of Emily far too often and felt guilty about that as well. There was nothing to do right at this moment, though, and it all seemed to catch up with him. He drank a full glass of cool, reviving water before biting into the thick sandwich of sliced ham and cheese. As he swallowed the last bite, she quietly put a slice of rhubarb pie at his elbow.

"Thank you, Emily."

"You're welcome."

There was a low rumble of thunder in the distance, and the leaves of the poplars twisted in the breeze. He took his dirty dishes to the sink. The hot breeze from the open window hit him in the face. He closed his eyes.

"Hey, Em? I'm going to lie down for a few minutes."

She came to the door, holding a red crayon in her hand. "Are you feeling all right?"

He smiled. "Just tired. It's this heat. It just saps you."

"Okay."

He went to the living room and sank on to the plush cushions of the sofa, hanging his stocking feet over the arm. He closed his eyes. He'd get up in a few minutes, a short break was all he needed. His breaths deepened as he thought of all the little things Emily did, lifting his burdens and doing it with a smile. She had made the house like a home again, with voices and laughter and delicious smells.

It was just like it used to be, he thought as he drifted off to sleep. Like when Dad came in from a tough day and Mom met him with a kiss and a cup of coffee...

Emily heard the deep breaths coming from the living room and her hand paused, the crayon a few inches from the paper. Luke was plain worn out. She'd seen it in the dark circles beneath his eyes and the tired way he'd sunk into his chair in the kitchen. She watched Sam color a comic-book character in his coloring book and exhaled, wishing the sultry air would clear. It was close, suffocating. The leaves on the trees tossed and turned now, restless in the wind coming before the storm. The weather was as unsettled as she was. Calm on the surface but churning inside.

Emily paced a few minutes, coming to stop at the door to the living room. She looked down at Luke's face, relaxed in sleep. The scowl he wore so often was gone and his lips were open just the tiniest bit. He had long eyelashes for a man. She hadn't realized it before, but watching him sleep gave her the chance to really examine his face. He snuffled and turned his head, revealing a tiny scar just behind his left ear.

How could she make it through two more months of this if she already felt the tugs of attraction after a handful of days? There had been no repeats of the kissing scene. Not even a glance or small touch. And still he was on her mind constantly. When she lay in bed listening to the frogs or when she was mixing up batter or taking clothes off the line. She replayed the kiss over and over in her head, remembering what it was like to feel desirable. To feel her own longings, emotions she'd thought quite dead and buried. She was starting to trust Luke. The world was not full of Robs. Deep down she'd always known it, but it was easier to think that than to face the truth.

Emily swallowed. A cold puff of air came through the windows, the chill surprising her. It didn't take a genius to figure it out. She hadn't been enough to make Rob happy, and she wasn't sure she could survive failing again. She was tired of apologizing for it. He had been selfish leaving when they might have worked it out. He hadn't appreciated what he had...and now she looked down at Luke. Luke, who was so handsome he took her breath away. Luke, who had kissed her in the kitchen with his wide, strong hands framing her face and who said thank you for everything.

She turned away from Luke's sleeping form. It was impossible she was even *thinking* such a thing. She shook her head. Didn't she need to get Sam settled and her life in order first? Of course she did. She couldn't lose sight of the goal. Self-reliance came first. She'd made a promise to herself and she meant to keep it. And a promise to Sam. To even think of indulging herself in what—an affair? Luke wasn't interested in a relationship. In kids. He'd made it clear when he'd talked to her about what she was going to do when she left the ranch. Even entertaining the idea was selfish—thinking of herself rather than of what was best for Sam in the long run.

Emily had been so caught up in her thoughts that she hadn't noticed the room growing dark. What had been distant rumbling was now persistent, grumbling rolls of thunder. A flash went through the room, like a distant camera flash, and seconds later the thunder followed. She hurried to check on Sam, who had put down his crayons and stared at her with wide eyes.

"Boomers comin'?"

"I think so, honey."

Sam's dark eyes clouded with uncertainty. Her boy tried to be brave and strong, but she knew he hated thunderstorms. "Don't worry, okay? We're snug as a bug here."

Sam slid from his chair as another flash of lightning speared the sky. "I need to close the windows, Sam. It's starting to rain and I don't want things to get wet. You can come with me if you want."

But he shook his head, his hair flopping. "I'll stay here. I don't wanna go upstairs. Hurry back, Mommy."

Emily darted from room to room, shutting windows against the angry raindrops beginning to fall. Upstairs in Luke's room, the window stuck. She pushed down on the slider, making progress, but only in half-inch increments. The wind blew back the curtains, twisting them in her face as she struggled with the swollen window frame.

Just as it slid into the groove a fork of lightning jutted out of the sky, lighting up the whole house—followed by an astounding, foundation-shaking blast of thunder. The burst was so violent her heart seemed to leap and shudder before settling again into a quick, shocked rhythm.

She heard Sam scream and raced out of Luke's room to the stairs. She skidded into the dining room—no Sam. Emily pushed a hand through her hair, forcing her breath to calm. The bang had frightened her, too. "Sam?" she called, as another lightning strike and clap of thunder reverberated through the house.

"In here."

Luke's gravelly voice answered her from the living room.

She found them huddled together in a great walnut rocking chair. Luke's feet were planted square on the floor, and a terrified Sam was cradled in his arms, his bare feet resting on Luke's thigh as he curled up in Luke's lap. The strong arms she couldn't forget being around her now circled her son securely and the chair rocked ever so slightly.

The sight did something to her heart. It confirmed what she'd sensed at the beginning—Luke was a good, caring man hidden by a crusty exterior. He wasn't telling Sam that being afraid was silly or making him buck up, that it was only a little storm. He was simply holding him, comforting him. Rain started coming down in torrents now, hammering on the roof and windows so loudly it made a vibrating hum. Luke's gaze met hers, calm and accepting. Whether or not it made sense, Emily knew in that moment that this was where they were meant to be. This was where they would both put themselves back together before moving on.

"Sam," she said gently, "Mommy's here now. It's okay."

The storm raged around them, echoing through the house. Sam shook his head and only burrowed deeper into Luke's shirt.

"It's okay, Emily. He's fine where he is."

Had she really accused Luke of not liking children? The way he held Sam was strong and caring and sent a slice through her heart as sharp as a fork of lightning. Had Sam been missing the presence of a man in his life? At first she had thought it was just Rob he missed. But she could tell he missed having a man to look up to.

She knew after a year of struggling that she could do this on her own. But there was something about having Luke in her life right now that somehow divided the burden.

A terrific crash sounded, not thunder but sharper and harder, and Emily sank into a nearby chair, her hands shaking. Lightning had hit something and she didn't have the courage to peer out the window and see what. She heard Luke murmur something reassuring to Sam as his toe kept the chair in motion, rocking and soothing. Her son whom she loved more than life itself. And the man who was proving that the shell she'd built around her heart wasn't as tough as she thought.

At the same time, the house went strangely quiet as the power went out. The fridge stopped its constant hum and the clock on the DVD player went dark.

"Looks like we'll be grilling tonight," Luke said easily.

After several minutes the storm made its way east. Emily looked over at Sam. His head had drooped and Luke smiled. "He fell asleep about five minutes ago," Luke said.

"I can move him…"

"Leave him. He's comfortable."

He had to stop being so nice. It only made things more impossible. "Luke…surely you can see the problem. He already trusts you…"

"If he does, why can't you?"

"It's not that simple." She kept her voice a low murmur, needing Sam to stay asleep. "What happens in August when we have to leave, Luke? When he has to say goodbye to you? And this ranch? If he gets too attached, how can I pull him away? How can I do that to him again?"

"He's a smart kid. He knows this is temporary…"

"He's only five." She dug her fingers into the arm of the chair.

"He already loves being here," Luke argued. "So whether

you go now or in a few months, you may have that to deal
with anyway." He gave her a knowing look. "Or are we not
talking about Sam here? I think it's you. You don't want to
get attached to this place. Because you like it here."

"Of course I do…"

"And saying goodbye will be…"

She imagined driving away and watching Luke get smaller
in her rearview mirror. After only a few days, she knew she'd
miss him.

"I'm a big girl. I know how the world works."

"You sure do."

Sam let out a delicate snore. Luke's lips curved and then
he lifted his head, sharing the smile with Emily.

Something clicked inside her. Suddenly it wasn't about protecting her heart from Luke anymore. He'd already breached
the walls. She was in perilous danger of caring for him, truly
and deeply caring.

She sat for a few moments, wanting to snatch Sam away
from the security of Luke's arms, knowing it was foolish and
petty. She should have foreseen she'd get in too deep.

But this job could give her the start she needed. She only
had to keep the goal firm in her mind—a temporary retreat
to regroup and then move forward. If she did that, it would
all be fine.

She would enjoy every blessed minute she could, she decided. She'd be here when the beans ripened and the pea
pods popped in the sunshine. Sam could maybe go for that
horseback ride—maybe they both would. She could spend an
hour on the porch with a paperback while Sam played.

When she looked back at Luke, his lips had dropped open
as he dozed off, too. Seeing them sleeping together made her
feel as though she was losing Sam, even as her head told her
it was a ridiculous thought.

She had spent months worrying about the lack of a male

influence in Sam's life. Now that he had it, she wasn't sure she could resist the man—the real live cowboy, as Sam put it—who was putting stars in both their eyes.

CHAPTER NINE

FOR THE NEXT week Emily, Sam and Luke settled into a routine. Luke spent his days working the fields and Emily did the hottest work in the mornings. In the afternoon she ran errands or took time out to play with Sam, roaming the extensive yard looking for wildflowers and animal tracks. Luke made an effort to arrive for dinner and they all ate together. And as the sun sank below the prairie, Emily listened to the peepers and the breeze through the open windows of her bedroom. Luke was right next door and often she lay awake at night knowing the head of his bed was only a wall away. What was he thinking as his head lay on the pillow? There was a sense of comfort that came from knowing he was so close, but she wondered what to do with the attraction that kept simmering between them.

Because it *was* simmering. He hadn't touched her again. There hadn't been any more kisses. But the memory of the first kiss always seemed to hover between them, and every time she looked at him she felt the same jolt running from her heart down to the soles of her feet. It stood between them like an unanswered question. The only thing Emily could do was focus on her job. Feelings, attraction…it was all secondary right now. She had to keep her eye on the prize—self-reliance. She would need Luke's recommendation when she went job-hunting at the end of the summer, and she wouldn't do anything foolish to jeopardize it.

One mild evening Luke took Sam for a walk around the corral on Bunny's back, getting him used to the feel of the horse before letting Sam take the reins himself. After that, Sam was permanently smitten with both Luke and with the mare. It was all he talked about as he helped in the garden or dried the dishes, standing on a stepstool. He visited with Liz's twins one afternoon while Emily shopped for groceries. Emily had a look at the old record player and thought she might have a go at fixing it up. The cabinet was filled with old LPs. What would it be like to hear the scratchy albums again?

They all slipped into the routine so easily that it felt, to Emily at least, a little too real.

Then Luke came home with Homer.

At first Emily just heard the barking and she wrinkled her brow. Had a neighbor's dog strayed into the yard? Her heart set up a pattering, as she knew Sam would be paralyzed with fear. He'd never quite gotten over his fear of dogs since he'd nearly been attacked. She dried her hands on a tea towel and headed for the door.

Sam was making a beeline for the porch, his normally flushed cheeks pale. Emily scooped him up as Luke approached, holding a leash in his hand attached to a brown-and-white dog that limped behind.

Luke paused several feet away from the steps. Sam was clearly afraid of the new pup. It showed in the pallor of his face and how he clung to his mother.

"Sam, this is Homer."

No response. Luke's heart sank. He'd seen the dog weeks ago and had fallen in love. Oh, he knew that sounded ludicrous, but he had a soft spot for dogs and especially one like Homer, who needed a home so badly. But Homer had been in no shape to be adopted and in the hectic pace of haying season, it had gone to the back of Luke's mind. Until the veterinarian had called a few days ago. Luke had thought of Sam, too. He'd thought Homer could be a playmate. He hadn't thought about the boy being afraid.

"You don't have anything to fear from Homer," Luke said easily. He put his hand on Homer's back and the dog sat, his tongue hanging out happily. "He's the gentlest dog you'll ever meet."

Sam shook his head and clung to Emily even tighter. Luke noticed the shine of tears in her eyes and resisted the urge to sigh. He had to help the boy. Had to show him he didn't need to be afraid. He wasn't sure why, but he knew that it was important to help Sam overcome this hurdle. Maybe because he saw in Sam's eyes what he'd seen too often in his own—knowledge and understanding. Even at such a young age, Sam had been hurt and had grown—painfully—because of it. Luke couldn't fix that. But maybe he could make this better.

"We had an incident in the park last year," Emily said quietly. "Someone had their dog off leash and it started to go at Sam. I reached out and grabbed its collar." She looked down at Luke with liquid chocolate eyes. "He's been terrified ever since."

Homer whined and Luke heard distressed sounds coming from Sam's throat.

"Homer, hush."

Luke gave the firm order and the dog immediately quieted. He squatted down and put his hand on the brown-and-white fur. "Stay." He dropped the leash. Then he stood, went to Emily, reached out and touched Sam's back.

"Look at him now, Sam. Harmless as a flea." He spoke softly to the boy, knowing a gentle and steady touch was required. Sam obediently turned his head and looked at the mutt, whose tongue was hanging out in happy bliss as he panted.

Luke couldn't accomplish putting Sam at ease while he

had a death grip on his mother. "Come here, buddy," he said, and he lifted Sam right out of her arms and settled him on his hip. He half expected Sam to cry and reach for Emily, but he didn't. Knowing Sam trusted him did something to Luke's insides, something warm and expansive. Luke pointed at the dog. "Do you know what's special about Homer?"

Sam shook his head.

Luke looked over at Emily and smiled, hoping to thaw the icy wall that had suddenly formed around her. "Homer had an accident a while back. He's been at the vet's, because he was a stray and no one claimed him. A few weeks ago he was still wrapped up in bandages. You never saw a sorrier sight than that dog. He didn't even bark. He just looked up at me with his big, sad eyes."

He shifted his gaze to Sam, pleased that he had the boy's full attention. Sam's eyes were wide, listening to Luke retell the story. "Now he's healed up, but because he was hurt so badly, no one has given him a home." Luke paused, wondering if he should explain what fate would have befallen Homer had he not brought him home. "He isn't perfect, you see. But I think it doesn't matter if someone isn't perfect, don't you?"

Sam nodded. "Mama says everyone makes mistakes."

Luke swallowed. This was what he'd tried to avoid for so long, why he kept his nieces at arm's length. He was afraid of caring, and he'd been right. Holding Sam this way, hearing his sweet voice talk about his mama only reminded Luke of his vow to not have children of his own. How could he be so selfish, knowing he could pass his genes on to another generation? How could he have a family, knowing they might have to go through what he'd already suffered?

But the longing was there. It was there when he held Sam, and it was there when he looked at Emily, and if he wasn't careful it could have the power to break him.

He cleared his throat. "Dogs aren't that different from

people, you know. Give them a full belly and a little love and they're pretty contented."

Sam's shoulders relaxed and his gaze focused on Luke's face. Luke's gaze, however, fell on Emily. The ice in her gaze had melted and she was looking at him in a way that made his heart lift and thump oddly against his ribs. Lord, she was beautiful. Those big eyes that seemed to reach right in and grab a man by the pride. He realized he'd been holding his breath and staring a little too long, so he looked away and shifted Sam's weight on his hip.

"Homer won't hurt you. I promise. The biggest danger to you is that he might lick you to death." With an unprotesting Sam on his arm, he knelt before the dog. He stroked the fur reassuringly and Homer stretched a little, loving the attention. Still, Luke didn't force the issue, just let Sam watch his fingers in the dog's fur.

Sam's eyes were wide as he touched the soft coat. Soaking in the attention, Homer rolled over on to his back and presented his belly to be scratched.

That was when Sam noticed, and it all came together.

"He only has three legs!"

"Yep." Luke gave Homer's belly a scratch and the dog twisted with pleasure. "Doesn't slow him down much, though, does it? The vet told me he fetches tennis balls and who knows, maybe he can help me round up cattle if I can train him right. If you squat down like me, and hold out your hand, he can smell you. That's how you say hello."

Luke made Homer sit again and was beyond pleased when Sam followed his calm instructions. He balanced on his toes and held out his fingers, but when Homer moved to sniff he pulled them back.

Luke reassured him, wanting him to try again. They'd come this far. To stop now would mean two steps back. And Sam could do it. Luke knew he was just timid and that the worst of the fear was gone. Sam and Homer would be friends. He couldn't give the kid back what he'd lost, but he could give him this companion.

"Watch." He held out his hand and Homer gave a sniff and a lick. "Want to try again?"

He held out his fingers and Homer sniffed, licked and gave a thump of his tail.

"Give him this," Luke suggested, standing and reaching into his pocket. He took out a small dog biscuit and handed it to Sam. "Put it flat in your hand, and tell him to be gentle."

"H-Homer, gentle," Sam said, holding out his hand. Luke could see it trembled a bit, but Homer daintily took the treat and munched.

"See?"

"I did it!" Sam turned to his mother and beamed. "I did it, Mom!"

Emily smiled. "You sure did, baby," she replied. Homer barked and Sam jumped, his eyes wide again, but Luke chuckled. "That's just his way of saying thank-you," he said. He reached into his denim jacket and took out a rubber ball. "Homer, fetch," he commanded, tossing the ball, and the dog was up and off in a flash.

"Why don't you play fetch with him for a bit, Sam? Then I can talk to your mother."

Sam moved off with the dog and Luke looked up at Emily.

"I didn't know he was afraid."

"I wish you had asked, Luke. When I heard the barking, and saw Sam's face..."

"I'm sorry, Emily. Homer's been at the vet's for weeks and I couldn't stand to see him put down. Not when I could give him a good home. And I thought Sam would love him. Especially after all he's had to give up."

Was that a sheen of tears he detected in her eyes? His heart took up the odd thumping again.

"What you just did…that was great. Sam's been timid around dogs for months. Every time we meet a new dog, it's the same thing…"

Luke exhaled and smiled, until he heard the word *but*.

"But what happens when we leave, Luke? Homer is one more thing he will have to leave behind. Did you think of that?"

He hadn't, but he realized now he should have. "Take him with you."

But that was the wrong thing to say. "Take him with us? I don't know if he'd be welcome at my parents', and if Sam and I get an apartment…not everyone will accept pets. Then what happens when I'm gone to work and Sam is at school?"

Luke knew she was right. He climbed the steps and went to stand before her, needing her to understand. "Obviously I didn't think it through as well as I should have."

"I don't know how much more I can take away from him," she whispered, and he heard the catch in her voice.

He put his hand on her arm, feeling her warm skin beneath his rough fingers. "You are not taking anything away, Em. You give to him constantly. You give him love and acceptance and security. He is lucky to have you as a mother."

"You're just trying to get around me." She sniffled a little and looked away from him, but he put a finger under her chin and made her look back.

"Maybe." He felt the beginnings of a smile as he confessed. "If you'd seen Homer there, Em. He was skin and bones and bandages. Look what some love and attention accomplished. How could I just leave him there? I couldn't. I'm sorry for causing you problems, though."

"First me and Sam, now Homer. You do have a way of picking up strays, don't you?"

"Hey, you found me."

The sound of Sam's laughter drifted up over the porch and everything seemed to move in slow motion. Emily looked up into his eyes and he was helpless. "I guess I did," she murmured, and it was all he could do to keep from kissing her the way he'd been wanting to for days.

But what would it accomplish? Nothing had changed. And he wouldn't play games. It was bad enough his heart was getting involved. Acting on it was another matter entirely. It would get messy. People would get hurt. And he was kidding himself if he thought it was only Sam and Emily who'd pay the price.

Because ever since their arrival, *he*'d felt like the stray who'd been taken in. And he didn't like that feeling. He didn't like it at all.

They went to the Canada Day celebrations on the first of July and Emily finally met Luke's sister Cait and baby Janna. Unlike Liz and her bubbly nosiness, Cait was more reserved, with a warm, new-mother contented smile. Liz and her husband Paul were there with the girls, who tugged Sam along to the various games. They all ate cotton candy and hot dogs dripping with ketchup and mustard and as darkness finally fell, the three of them joined Cait, Joe, Liz, Paul and the kids on some spread-out blankets to watch the fireworks. It was impossible not to feel like a family. Like someone who belonged here. She knew it wasn't so, but it didn't stop the wishing. It would be foolish to imagine things were more than they seemed, but Emily wondered if some day she might find this somewhere, with someone.

The trouble was, she couldn't envision it at all. It was only Luke she saw in her mind and that fact bothered her more than she wanted to admit.

Emily sat cross-legged on the rough blanket, looking down

at Sam and watching his sleepy eyes droop while he valiantly struggled to keep them open. It was well past his bedtime, but he had wanted to stay and she didn't have the heart to say no. His head was cradled in her lap and she smoothed his hair away from his forehead as twilight deepened and the crowd gathered, waiting for the pyrotechnics show.

"He's tired."

Luke kept his voice low and spoke close to her ear, so close she felt the heat rise in her cheeks as the rest of her body broke out in goose bumps.

"He wouldn't miss this for the world."

"Neither would I."

Emily turned her head the slightest bit, surprised by how close Luke was when her temple nearly grazed his jaw. She knew he could be talking about the fireworks or visiting with neighbors or simply being there with his sisters and family. But Emily wanted to believe he meant being there with her and with Sam. How many times over the last week had they all been together and she'd felt the tug? A sense of déjà vu, knowing this had never happened before?

"Luke, I…" She didn't know how to tell him what was in her heart. There were times when she even felt guilty for taking a wage for the work she was doing. Not because what she did wasn't of value, but because she knew very well she was getting more than financial gain out of it. Sam was happy, she was happy, and she hadn't expected to be, not for a very long time.

There was a bang and the first jet of sparks flew upwards. Emily turned her head to the fireworks display as Sam sat bolt upright and exclaimed at the blue and purple cascade flowering in the sky. Emily heard Sam's name called and nudged him as Liz's twins gestured wildly for him to join them on their blanket just ahead. "Go on," she smiled. "You can watch with the girls. I'm right here."

Sam scooted up to the next blanket, leaving Emily alone with Luke.

Darkness formed a curtain and everyone's eyes were fixed on the dazzling display in the sky while Emily's heart thundered. Luke shifted on the blanket, moving behind her so that she could lean back against his strong shoulder to watch. She could smell the aftershave on his neck, feel the slight stubble of his chin as it rested lightly against her temple. One after another the explosions crested and expanded, a rainbow of colors, but all Emily could think about was Luke and how close he was. If he turned his head the slightest bit…if she turned hers…

His fingertips touched her cheek, and she turned her face towards the contact. Her heart stuttered when she discovered him watching her, unsmiling, his blue eyes fathomless in the dark of the evening, reflecting the bursts of fireworks but focused solely on her. Her mouth went dry, afraid he was going to kiss her and wanting him to so badly she thought she might die from it.

"Em."

In the din of the explosions she didn't hear him say her name but she saw it on his lips. Locking her gaze with his, she let herself lean more into his shoulder, the only invitation she dared permit herself. It was all he needed. His gaze burned into her for one last second before dropping to her mouth. His fingers slid slowly over her chin to cup her jaw, cradling the curve in the palm of his hand. And finally, when she thought she would surely burst into flames, he kissed her.

His lips were warm and mobile, skilled and devastating. As Emily clung to his arm with her hand, she realized that there was never anything tentative with Luke. He was always strong, always sure of himself, and it took her breath away. He was always in control, and she wondered, quite dazzled, what it would take to make him lose that control? To lose it with her?

The finale began with rapid bursts of color crashing into the air. Emily's fingers dug into the skin of his arm, and she felt the vibrations of a moan in his throat as the kiss intensified, making everything in her taut with excitement and desire.

A final bang and gasp and then there was nothing but applause from the crowd.

Luke gentled the kiss, tugging at her bottom lip with his teeth before moving away, making her whole body ache with longing. His gaze was still on her, but there was something different in it now. Heat. And, Emily thought, confusion.

She looked past him to the crowd and was mortified to see Liz, Cait and their husbands watching. Liz's mouth had dropped open and Cait's soft eyes were dark with concern. Joe and Paul simply had goofy smiles on their faces. Emily looked past them, afraid that Sam had seen the sparks going off behind him rather than above, but he and the girls were still chattering excitedly about which bursts had been their favorites and the horrendous noise.

She scrambled to her feet and straightened her blouse. Luke took his time, getting to his feet and gathering the corner of the blanket to fold it. Emily grabbed the other side to help. She had to keep her hands busy. Avoid the assessing looks from Luke's family. Why had she let herself be carried away?

But she'd created another problem. Holding her side of the blanket meant folding it into the middle, which meant meeting Luke face-to-face. There was the silent question as which of them would take the woolen fabric to fold again. Emily dropped it, letting Luke fold it into a square.

Cait and Joe took the stroller and said goodbye, but Liz— bless her—acted as if nothing had happened and stopped to ask if Sam was going to day camp in the morning. Emily, Luke and Sam followed along back to the parking lot. Sam's feet started to drag, so Luke lifted him effortlessly on his shoulders and carried him to the truck.

Sam fell asleep on the drive home.

Emily couldn't bring herself to say anything to Luke. She didn't want to ask why. She didn't want to analyze it. She was terrified to ask what it meant or if it would happen again. The radio played a quiet country-and-Western tune and she stared out the window at the inky sky and the long, flat fields shadowed by the moon. When they reached the house, Emily was first to hop out and she took Sam in her arms.

"I need to get him into bed," she whispered, unable to meet Luke's gaze. He didn't protest or stop her. They both knew she was running away from what had happened. Her arms ached under Sam's weight—when had he grown so much?—and she was out of breath by the time she got to the top of the stairs. When she finally had him tucked between the sheets, she paused. The light was on in the kitchen. Luke was waiting for her, she knew it. She hesitated, her hand on the smooth banister. If she went down, they'd have to talk, and she was afraid to talk. She was afraid of spoiling the balance they'd achieved so effortlessly during the past week. She was afraid they'd stop talking, that he'd kiss her again. And she was afraid it would go further. Much further. She imagined him carrying her to his room, imagined feeling his skin against hers....

No, it was too much. So much more than she was prepared to give. To accept.

So she went into her own room and shut the door, biting her lip as she changed into her nightgown and slid between the soft cotton sheets.

Several minutes later she heard him turn off the light as he stopped waiting. His slow steps echoed on the stairs, creaking on the tread third from the top. The steps paused beside her door as her heart pounded with fear and, Lord help her, anticipation.

Then the steps went away and she heard him go into his room. Muffled sounds as he shed his clothing—she swallowed—and the sound of the mattress settling as he got in bed, his head only inches from hers, and yet so far away.

She lay awake for a long time, replaying the kiss, listening for his footsteps, and wondering what it was she wanted—if she even knew anymore.

The morning sun was high when Luke stopped to survey the herd below. Caribou's chestnut hide gleamed in the summer sun and the gelding tossed his head, anxious to get going again. Luke had taken the morning to check fence lines of the north pasture now that he and the hands had moved the herd east to graze on fresh grass. He could have done it on the quad, but he was a horse man at heart. Spending a morning in the saddle had sounded perfect at 7:00 a.m. when the dew was still heavy on the grass.

It had given him ample time to think.

Caribou shifted restlessly and Luke let him go, moving into a trot to the dirt lane that ran between sections. What the horse needed was a good run, a chance to burn off some energy. Luke could use it, too. He was wound tighter than a spring, and it was all due to Emily. Emily with her shiny mink hair and big eyes. Emily with her soft smiles and even softer skin. His fingers tightened on the reins. He'd been a damned fool last night, kissing her at the fireworks. It was bad enough it was in public, but with his family there? It was as good as putting a stamp on her as far as they were concerned.

And that wasn't his intention. Not at all. His sisters would pester him to death wondering what was going on. If Emily was "the one". It didn't matter that he'd made it clear there would never be a Mrs. Luke Evans. It was just better that way. He never wanted to saddle a wife with an invalid.

A yellow-headed blackbird bobbed in the bushes as he passed. What had been his intention, then? Why hadn't he just left Emily alone and kept his lips to himself? He'd asked himself that question all morning and had yet to come up with an answer. What did he want from Emily? Things had not changed. It would be pointless to start anything up knowing it could go nowhere.

He was right back to where he'd started—a fool. A fool to get so wrapped up in her that he'd given in to his wants and kissed her without thinking of the repercussions. Now she wasn't even talking to him. She'd scooted up to bed last night and had avoided him this morning with the excuse of getting Sam ready for day camp. All-business Emily. She'd made her feelings perfectly clear. It was better this way, but it made him snarly just the same.

The gate was up ahead. He slowed Caribou to a walk and squinted. Emily was coming through the gap, all long, tanned legs in beige shorts and a red T-shirt. His body gave a little kick seeing her waiting for him. Her hair glinted with surprising red tints but he couldn't see her eyes behind her sunglasses. He didn't need to. He could see by the tense set of her shoulders and the line of her lips that something was wrong.

He gave the horse a nudge and cantered to the gate where she was waiting, pulling up in a cloud of dust. It had to be important if she'd come all the way out here to find him.

"What is it? What's happened?"

She looked up at him and took off her glasses.

His stomach did a slow turn. The chocolate depths of her eyes were more worried than he'd seen them. "Is it Sam?"

His question seemed to break through and she shook her head. "No, no it's not Sam. He's still at day camp with the twins." She peered up at him, hesitated, then said gently, "It's your father, Luke."

His father. All his energy seemed to sink to his feet, making them heavy but the rest of him oddly numb. "Is he gone?" His voice sounded flat and he had the strange thought that for just a few moments the birds had stopped singing in the underbrush.

"No. But Liz called and they want you to come."

Relief struck, automatically followed by dread. He had known something like this was coming and had buried himself in work to avoid thinking about it. Dad was getting frailer by the day, and it had been nearly ten years since he had gone into the home—a long time for someone with his disease. Luke knew the facts. But it didn't make it any easier.

"Okay."

"Luke?"

He stared down at her. She was biting her lip and he watched as the plump pink flesh changed shape as her teeth worried the surface.

"You don't look so good, Luke."

He didn't feel so great either.

"What can I do to help you?"

He realized that she'd walked all the way out from the house in the July heat to find him. He held out a hand. "Get on. We'll double up going back to the house."

"But I...I can't get up there."

"Sure you can. I'll take my foot out of the stirrup. Give me your hand and swing up."

A brief look of consternation overtook her face and he felt his annoyance grow. Was she so turned off by his presence that she couldn't stand to touch him now? He held out his hand. "Come on, Emily. It's the fastest way back to the house. I need to get to town."

She put her foot in the stirrup and clasped his forearm,

taking a bounce and swinging her leg over the saddle so that she was shoehorned in behind him. The stirrups were too long for her now and Luke slid the toes of his boots back through as he slid an inch forward, giving her more room. Even so, they were spooned together and he felt every shift of her body torturing him as Caribou started off at a walk.

He swallowed tightly. It had to be bad if Liz had phoned in the middle of the day.

"Where's Sam?" It didn't escape his notice that Sam was absent.

"Day camp, remember?"

He hadn't remembered, and he felt a spark of panic before telling himself to exhale and relax. It had only been a momentary thing and he was distracted. He swiveled in the saddle, half turning to meet her gaze. "Right. You would never have left him alone. I know that."

He faced front again, frowning. Emily might know about his father but she hadn't put the other pieces together. The lists, the precise order. It was all there for a reason. Just because he'd forgotten about day camp didn't mean anything except he had other things on his mind.

And yet there was always that little bit of doubt.

Her hand rested lightly on his ribs, an additional point of connection. What would it feel like for her to put her arms around him and hold him close? He wished he could know, but it was better if he didn't. He knew she still didn't understand what it all meant—to his father, to this ranch, to him. And he didn't want to explain. Right now he just needed to get to the nursing home. To see his father, the shell of a man he remembered. To hope that it was not too late.

And maybe, just maybe…there was always the forlorn hope that his dad might even recognize him one more time.

"Hang on," he said. And when her arms snaked around his middle, holding on, he felt his heart surge as he spurred the gelding into a canter and hastened their way home.

CHAPTER TEN

EMILY WRAPPED HER arms around Luke's waist, feeling the steel waves of pain and resentment binding him up in one unreachable package. His strong thighs formed a frame for hers as they headed for the farmyard and barns. She wished she could be out riding with him under different circumstances. A pleasure ride, stopping beneath the shade of a poplar or walking along the irrigation canal. She wanted the Luke of last night back, even as much as that man frightened her with the force of her feelings. The man she clung to now was in pain. She knew how that felt, and she wished she could take it away, make it better for him somehow.

He slowed the horse to a walk when the barn was in view, letting Caribou cool down. Emily said nothing as she dismounted and then he hopped down beside her. Silently they worked, removing bridle and saddle and Emily slid the blanket from the gelding's back and draped it over a rail in the tack room. He turned Caribou out into the corral and locked the gate, still saying absolutely nothing. Emily was beginning to worry. She didn't want him going to town alone. When he was about to head for the truck, she stopped him with a hand on his arm.

"Wait. We'll take my car."

"I don't want you to go."

The clipped words were not unexpected, but they stung just

the same. He had not let her in since she'd arrived at the gate so now was no different. She knew that. She also knew he needed help. Whether he realized it or not, he'd been there for her when she needed it most. She would return the favor.

"Liz is there and someone will have to pick up the kids at day camp. And you're in no shape to drive. So shut up and this once let someone do something for you."

She stood her ground, staring him down and watched him struggle. Didn't he think she could see how he always took care of everyone else? She wasn't blind. Married or not, his sisters still turned to him when they needed him. And he was there. Seeing his face when she'd told him about his dad had been all she needed. Someone had to be there for Luke.

"We're only wasting time," she said, quieter now, but no less sure of herself.

"We'll take your car but I'm driving." He gave in with a terse nod.

She could agree to that, so long as he wasn't alone. "Give me two seconds to grab my purse and keys," she replied, already dashing to the house. Liz had sounded tearful on the phone. Emily didn't want to think the worst, but she was sure that that was what Luke was thinking and getting him there as soon as possible would be best for everyone.

Liz and Cait were waiting outside the nursing home, sitting on a bench surrounded by petunias and geraniums. Baby Janna was asleep, bundled in a carrier and Liz's youngest was in a stroller, playing with a bar of brightly colored toys hooked along the top. When Luke strode up the walk, Liz rose and went to him, wrapping her arms around his neck. Cait was slower getting to her feet but when she went to Luke, he opened an arm and she slid in beneath it.

Emily blinked back tears for the trio who bonded amid so much pain. In the absence of parents, Luke had been their father figure even if he'd only been a few years older. Seeing them through to adulthood must have been so difficult, but he had done what needed to be done. Emily hung back, watching Luke give his sisters a squeeze and then asking the difficult question: "How bad?"

Liz was sniffling and Cait had to answer. "He fell last night. Nothing is broken, but the doctor says…"

Luke waited.

"He says it's time for palliative care, Luke."

Pain slashed across Luke's face, but he stood strong. "We knew this day would come, Cait."

"It doesn't make it easier."

"I know it. I want to talk to the doctor."

Emily felt so very in the way. Luke didn't need her. He had his sisters. This was a family problem and she wasn't family. Still, there had to be something she could do to help. They all needed to be with their father. She stepped up and searched Luke's eyes, then Liz's.

"I'm so sorry about your father. Is there anything I can do?"

Luke shook his head. "Thank you for asking, Emily." He seemed to think for a minute, and then leaned over and dropped a kiss on her cheek. "You've already helped so much."

Emily's cheek burned where his lips had touched it, even if it had been an impersonal peck. She had a sudden idea and turned to Liz. "Why don't you let me pick up the twins? Then you can stay as long as you need."

Liz's face relaxed and Emily felt Luke's hand at her back, a gentle contact that told her she'd said the right thing.

"If you do, take them back to my house. Paul's gone to Medicine Hat but he'll be back later to take over. It would be a godsend, Emily."

"You need to be with your father, Liz. You all do. I can

take Alyssa, too. It's no trouble. You just do what needs to be done."

Liz gave her the house key and got the car seat out of her car while Luke wrote directions to Liz's house on a slip of paper. When the baby was installed in the seat and buckled safely in, Luke stayed behind.

"Em, I don't know how to thank you." He braced a hand along the window of the open door of her car.

"It's not necessary, Luke. I'm happy to do it. Otherwise I'd just feel helpless."

"Helpless?"

How could she explain that Luke—and his family—had come to mean so much to her? That seeing him hurting caused her to have pain as well? They'd known each other such a short time. Her mother had always said she had a heart as big as all outdoors. It kept getting her into trouble. She felt things too deeply.

"You know, sitting around, waiting for news. At least this way I feel useful." She looked up, discovered he was watching her with a curious expression and dropped her lashes again before she gave away too much. "You should go. See your dad and talk to the doctor. I'll catch up with you later."

"You're right," he replied, shutting the car door as she buckled her seatbelt.

She drove away, only looking in the rearview mirror once and saw Luke going through the doors with his sisters. She was glad she could help, but she would rather be with him, sitting by his side.

But he didn't want that or else he would have asked. He hadn't even wanted her to come along. As she turned down a quiet street, she blinked a few extra times to clear the stinging. She was glad now that she hadn't gone downstairs last night.

She was falling in love with Luke Evans, and hearing him say he'd made a mistake would be more than she could take.

Paul and Liz returned just after seven-thirty. Emily had fed the kids and the twins were curled up with Sam on the sofa watching a movie—the girls in pink pajamas and Sam in the spare sweats and T-shirt that he'd carried in his backpack to camp. Alyssa was sweet-smelling from her bath and Emily nuzzled the baby's neck lightly, inhaling the scent of baby lotion as she prepared an evening bottle. Caring for four had been busy, but fun. The laughter, the pandemonium—they were things that had been missing from Emily's house, having had an only child. She had reconciled herself to knowing that the large family she'd wanted would never happen. Now she wondered if she might find a second chance someday. She had to get her life in order first, but she realized her heart was not as closed to the idea as it had once been. After her divorce, she'd been so determined never to go down that road again. Never to put Sam in the position of getting hurt. And yet here she was. And for a moment she wondered if rekindling those dreams meant she was putting her own wants ahead of the needs of her son. How did that make her any different from Rob, who had chosen his own dream ahead of his wife and son?

As she sat in a rocker and fed Alyssa, she banished the uncomfortable idea and turned her thoughts back to Luke. She couldn't stop wondering about his father and what the doctor said. How was Luke holding up? She lifted the baby to her shoulder and began rubbing her back just as Liz and Paul drove into the yard. Em's heart did a little rollover as they came in the back door. Liz looked so weary, even as she greeted Emily and smiled.

"Thank you, Emily, for watching the kids. It means so much that I could stay with Cait and Luke and Dad today."

Emily's lips curved wistfully when Alyssa put her chubby arms out for her mother and Paul went into the living room to check on the older kids. She missed the feeling of the baby's weight on her arm, and her heart warmed when Alyssa tucked her head against her mother's neck, utterly contented as she stuck two fingers in her mouth.

"It was no trouble. The kids had fun, I think. I just made spaghetti for supper. There are leftovers in the fridge for you and Paul if you're hungry. I wasn't sure if you'd have a chance to eat."

Liz's eyes filled with tears as her fingers stroked the baby's hair. "Oh, Emily, you really are wonderful. I hope you don't mind me saying... Cait and I both hope you're here to stay more permanently."

Emily's heart ached. Staying meant staying with Luke and despite last night's kiss she knew it was impossible. "My plans are still the same, Liz. But I'll be here until the end of the summer. Hopefully things will have normalized with your father by then."

"That's not what I meant," Liz said, settling Alyssa on her arm. "After last night..."

"Don't read too much into it," Emily replied lightly, though butterflies went through her stomach as the memory danced through her mind. "It was just a kiss." A kiss that hadn't been mentioned again. It was almost as if it had never happened. As if neither of the kisses had happened now that Emily thought of it. And yet, at the time they had been heart-stoppingly intimate... The way Luke looked at her, as though she was the only woman on earth. The way his fingers touched her face. She hadn't imagined the connection between them. But they had just been caught in the moment. They had to be, for him to become so distant afterwards.

"I don't think it was just a kiss."

Emily needed to change the subject and while Liz and her

husband were back home—together—Emily wondered about Luke. "Is Luke still at the home?" she asked, busying herself with putting the children's dirty glasses in the dishwasher.

"Yes, he wanted to stay with Dad."

Alone. Emily felt annoyance niggle at her. Didn't his sisters realize that Luke needed support, too? Someone should be with him. Liz and Cait didn't have to go through this alone— why should Luke?

He needed her. She wished she were stronger. She wished she could stay emotionally uninvolved. That was her problem—she let herself feel too deeply. Her heart twisted as she realized he'd supported her at a time she needed it most. She couldn't turn her back on him. But there was Sam to think of, too. She wasn't sure the care home was the place for him, not at such a time. "I'll go pick him up," Emily said, reaching for her purse. "Can I come back and pick up Sam later?"

The sound of laughter at a song in the movie echoed from the living room. Liz's keen eyes watched her closely, but for once Emily didn't care what she thought. "Why don't you let him stay here? He can have a sleepover with the girls. We've got an air mattress and sleeping bag and it'll be fun. After what you did for me today—it's the least we can do. He can go to camp with the girls in the morning and you can pick him up after."

It was a perfect solution. "If you're sure…"

"Of course I'm sure. Don't be silly."

Emily settled everything with Sam, who was overjoyed and not the least bit apprehensive about spending the night away from her.

The evening had mellowed, losing the July glare and settling into a hazy, rosy sunset as Emily drove back to the nursing home. Inside, all was quiet. Her shoes made soft sounds on the polished floor. Dialogue from a television turned low murmured from a common room and the hushed voices of staff kept the place from feeling totally empty. She got the room number from an attendant and walked down a quiet hall. When she got to the correct room on the right she peeked around the doorway.

Luke was sitting in a chair beside the hospital bed, leaning forward with his elbows on his knees, the very picture of defeat. The blinds were closed and the only light came from a tiny lamp in the corner. There was no movement from the man beneath the white-and-blue sheets, but Emily could see that Luke had his father's hand folded within his own. There were tears on Luke's face; silent ones, leaving a broken, shining trail down his tanned cheeks, and he lifted his father's hand to his lips and kissed it.

Emily backed out of the room and leaned back against the wall, pulling in a shaking breath as she struggled to hold on to her composure. Luke was the strong one. Luke didn't show emotion. The man who handled everything without complaint was *crying*.

She closed her eyes. Everything slid into place, but it wasn't a comfortable feeling. She had fallen in love. It was unexpected and unwanted, but it was undeniable. She had been attracted to him from the beginning—to his strength, to his kindness, to his generosity. But it was this human side of him, the part that crumbled apart with his father's hand in his, that toppled her over the edge. Perhaps it was the sense that he had so much love to give but spent his life alone. Or perhaps it was sensing that he needed love so desperately. That he was hungry for it and would rather starve than ask for it.

Where it would lead she had no idea, nor was tonight the time to worry about it. Tonight, other things were more important. Like the fact that Luke was alone in there. His sisters had gone home to their husbands and families, but Luke had stayed. Who was there for him? To whom could he unburden himself at the end of the day? She'd told Liz the plan was the same—that she would be leaving at the end of the summer. It was still true. Luke did not return her feelings. She wouldn't delude herself into pretending he did, or wish for what wouldn't be. A few kisses meant little in the bigger scheme of things.

She hadn't meant to fall for him, and no one could be more surprised, but she'd spent enough time lying to herself in the past few years that she knew she had to be brutally honest. The timing was horrible—her whole situation was in flux and she was coming out of a devastating divorce. But she loved him. She would not be leaving the ranch with her heart intact. There was nothing she could do about it. It was too late.

Now she had two choices. She could back away, protect herself. Leave, if it came to that. Or she could take what precious time she had to help him through this.

There really was no contest. She was tired of running away from her failures and away from memories. This time she would stand.

"You always were a sucker for punishment," she murmured to herself. She let out her breath and stepped back around the corner.

Luke held his father's hand in his. It felt small now, and he thought of being a child and putting his hand within his father's wide palm, innocent and trusting. He'd worshipped his father, wanted to do everything just like him. He'd followed him through the barns and fields, learned to ride, learned to herd cattle and work the land. As he'd grown, they'd had their differences. New things had become important.

Luke had felt the need to stretch his legs, explore new places and people as he'd become a young man. They'd argued. There'd been resentment on both sides, but none of it mattered now. The tables were perfectly turned. Luke was the parent. His father was the one with the small hand, the one relying on Luke to be strong and do the right thing for everyone.

Only there was nothing he could do. There never had been, and knowing he was helpless was almost more than he could bear. Luke pressed the frail hand to his lips and felt the tears sting behind his eyes. He let them come, sitting in the semi-darkness, away from the forlorn gazes of his sisters and the sympathetic pats from the nurses. He let grief and exhaustion have its way for once. There was no one to see. No one to witness the coming apart that had been building since that horrible night when the fire department had come and he couldn't ignore the signs any longer. No one should have to go through this…this awful watching and waiting. He would never put anyone through such an ordeal. Never.

He'd made the promise long ago, but it had come with a price. Tonight he paid that price as he sat alone, wondering why the hell it had all gone wrong and wishing, with a sinking sense of guilt, that he could turn back the clock and do things differently.

He squeezed the hand and there was no squeeze back. Luke laid his head on the edge of the bed and wept.

The fingers on his shoulder were firm and strong and he knew in an instant it was Emily. Damn her for coming and seeing him like this. He swallowed against the giant lump in his throat, choking on the futility and pain as he struggled to regain control. He swiped his hand over his face, wiping away the moisture he'd allowed himself to indulge in. But she'd seen him this way. Broken. He hated that she could see his weakness, but it came as a relief, too. It felt good to stop pretending. He didn't have to be strong for her the way he'd always had to be for Cait and Liz. With Emily he could just be Luke.

Emily stood behind him and looped her arms around his neck, pressing her lips to the top of his head in a gentle kiss.

They stayed that way for a few minutes until he regained his composure, and then he reached for her hand, tugging her to his side and pulling an empty chair over alongside his.

"You came." His voice came out rough, and he cleared this throat quietly.

"Of course I did."

"I couldn't bring myself to leave him here alone. Not yet."

Emily held his hand in hers and her thumb moved over the top of his hand, warm and reassuring. "It's okay, Luke. It's all okay."

"I've never lost it like that before."

"Then it's about time. Would you rather be alone?"

She felt as if she was holding her breath as she waited for him to answer. He could send her away right now and that would be the end of it. It would break this damnable connection that seemed to run between them. It would solve his problems where she was concerned. He was going to have to send her away some time—they had no future together. Now was probably a good time. Before things went any further.

But he gripped her fingers, needing her. Wanting her to stay with him. "No. Stay, please."

She squeezed his fingers back, saying nothing. She just sat with him. Beside him, somehow knowing exactly what he needed. Just as she'd done all day. She'd come with him to the nursing home and she'd stepped in to help instinctively, making it easier on all of them. Helping him by helping his family. Emily was weaving herself into his life without even trying. God, even now he couldn't imagine going back to the empty house without her. He'd told himself that anything more was simple physical attraction. But he'd been wrong. He was falling for her. He cared about her. And he needed her. Perhaps that was the most disturbing of all. He didn't want to need anyone.

He knew in his heart he shouldn't be letting her get this close, but tonight he didn't have the strength to push her away. He looked down at his father's still features and felt his insides quiver.

Tonight he realized that people did not have to die for you to grieve for them.

Emily had no words to make things better, so she simply sat and held his hand. After nearly an hour, and when the shadows grew long, he finally sighed and lifted his head. "I think it's time to go." He looked around suddenly. "I never even thought—Emily, where is Sam?"

Emily smiled. It was the second time today he'd asked about her son—what a change from his attitude when she'd first arrived. "It's okay. He's staying at Liz's for the night. He was very pleased to be having a sleepover. When I left them, the kids were watching a Disney movie and eating popcorn."

"You left him with my sister?"

"Shouldn't I have?" She wondered why Luke was frowning at her.

"It's just…you don't let him out of your sight. You're the mama bear."

He was right. She was protective of Sam. "You were the one who said I had to stop holding on so tight. And tonight you needed me more."

His gaze clung to hers as the softly spoken words hovered in the room. She knew he would never admit needing her, but it was true. Sam was fine. Emily knew Luke had been right all along. She'd focused solely on Sam because he was all she had. That wasn't true any longer, but would Luke let her in?

"He's such a good boy, Emily."

She picked up her purse, her throat thickening as she recalled hearing Sam's laughter mingled with Luke's as he'd ridden around the corral. "I know."

"And you're a good parent. You always put him first."

Emily looked up at him as they shut off the light. She wasn't sure he was so right about that part. Lately she'd been putting herself and her own wants ahead of those of her son. She'd bought into Luke's logic that Sam was already going to miss the farm so why not let him enjoy it? But it was really her. She didn't want to leave yet. And as much as she wanted to be there for Luke tonight, that fact niggled at her.

"So are you, Luke. You looked after your sisters. You still do. It was so clear when you saw them today. They lean on you. You are their guidepost."

He shut the door quietly behind them and held her hand as they walked down the hall. "Not many understand that. But you do."

"I hope the girls realize it, too," Emily remarked. "I think they are so used to you being their rock that they forget you're human, too."

He stopped, staring at her with surprise. "What are you saying, Emily?"

She lifted her chin and looked right in his eyes, still red-rimmed from his visit with his father. "I mean they are so used to you looking out for them that they might forget you need support, too. It goes both ways."

"They were younger than me. They didn't see things the same way I did."

Emily nodded. "Undoubtedly. Is that why you've never married? You were too busy bringing up your sisters? Too busy living up to your responsibilities to have a relationship?" She squeezed his fingers. "How much have you really sacrificed, Luke?"

His jaw tightened. "I suppose I've never met the right one."

He tried to brush off her questions, but the tense tone of his voice made the attempt fall flat. What wasn't he saying?

She might take offense if the situation were different, but they both knew she was not a girlfriend. She wasn't sure what she was to him anymore. Not yet a lover, not just an employee, more than a friend.

They exited into the warm night, into fresh air and the scent of the roses that flanked the walkway. "It's more than that, isn't it?"

He let go of her hand. "What do you mean?"

Emily paused, letting Luke carry on for a few steps until he turned as if he was wondering why she wasn't keeping up with him anymore.

"I mean, you keep people at arm's length. Oh, now and again something comes through—like seeing you with your sisters, or when you held Sam during the storm, or tonight, with your father. But the rest of the time..." She paused, searching for the right words. "You're a fortress. And you're the gatekeeper, too. You decide who is allowed in, and you only show bits of yourself when you want."

He stared at her as if she'd slapped him.

"You don't know anything about it."

"Because you haven't told me."

He scoffed, turning away. "Like you've told me everything?"

What more was there to tell? She shrugged her shoulders. "I told you that Rob left us. I told you why and what's happened since. What more do you want? Because if I tell you that his leaving destroyed my confidence, made me question every single thing about myself, whether I was a good wife or mother, what are you going to do, Luke?" His face paled and he took a step backwards. She kept her voice calm, rational. "That's it exactly. You're going to close yourself off and run away. Because you don't let anyone get close. Even when they really, really want to be."

She wanted to reach him desperately. He was right, she hadn't told him everything, but she also hadn't felt she needed to. He seemed to understand anyway, and now she'd gotten defensive and attacked him on a night when he was already dealing with so much. "Please," she whispered, and heard her voice catch. "I don't want to argue. I want to help. Please let me in."

"I can't," he murmured, turning away.

"Is it really that bad?"

"Please, Emily." He begged her now. "Can we not do this right now?" His voice cracked on the last word. "That small, frail man in there is the last parental connection I have. He doesn't even recognize me. Do you know what I could give for one more moment of clarity, one more real conversation? To have him look at me and say my name? His organs are shutting down. My father is going to die. Maybe not tonight. Or tomorrow, or next week. But soon."

He put his hand on the car-door handle and sent her a look so full of pain that it hit her like a slap. He opened the door and shot out a parting stab: "What does it say about me that I'm relieved?"

Emily had broken through. Luke had opened up. But now she only felt despair, knowing she'd only ended up causing him more pain.

CHAPTER ELEVEN

THE CAR RIDE home was interminable. Luke kept his hands on the wheel and his mouth shut. What had possessed him to say such a thing in the first place? As they turned on to the service road leading to the ranch, he sighed and thought back over the years to all the visits. All the times that his father had been lucid; Luke and the girls had been hungry for those moments when they had their father again.

Then the more frequent times when his father had been forgetful, repeating himself, focused on one tiny detail about something that happened before Luke had ever been born. Or the times Dad got so frustrated that he lashed out, mostly with hurtful words but sometimes with hands. When that happened, Luke knew that his father would never be the same. He was an angry, hostile stranger. Yet, each time Luke visited there was a tiny bit of hope that it would be a good day. The death of those hopes took their toll on a man. All the things he'd said to Em he'd never breathed to another soul. It was her. She got to him with her gentle ways and yes, even with her strength. She had no idea how strong she was.

And she had no idea how much he loved her for it. Nor would she, ever.

Luke parked the car and got out. He got as far as the steps and stopped. He couldn't go in there. Not tonight.

"Are you hungry? Did you even eat since breakfast?"

Emily's voice was quiet at his shoulder but he shook his head. He wasn't hungry. He was just...numb. He wanted to grab on to her and hold on and knew he couldn't. Not just for him, but for her. The way she turned those liquid eyes up at him damn near tore him apart. She'd kissed him back, making him want things he had decided he could never have. She made herself invaluable in a thousand different ways and each one scored his heart.

He shook his head but still couldn't make himself climb the steps.

"Luke?" The quaver in her voice registered and he turned to look at her. Her big eyes were luminous with tears...for him? The weight of carrying everyone's emotions suddenly got heavier.

"You're scaring me," she whispered.

He had to snap out of it.

"I'm sorry, Em. I just...can't go inside. I don't know why." But he did know. The memories were there. And the fears lived there, too. They lived in the clues he left himself as an early-warning system, in the shadowed corners where he told himself he could never let anyone get too close.

It had worked up until now. Until Emily.

"Then let's walk. It's a beautiful night and I don't need to stay close to the house for Sam. Let's just walk a while, okay?"

Relieved, he nodded. Walking was good. He pointed north, knowing exactly where he needed to be. Emily took his hand and he let her hold it. The link made him feel stronger. Grounded him in a world spinning out of control.

The evening was as mellow as he'd ever seen it this early in July. The wide-open sky swirled together in shades of pink, peach and lilac as the sun began to dip over the prairie. Even the green leaves on the shrubs and poplar trees seemed less brash in the evening light. The air was perfumed with fresh grass and timothy and the faintest hint of clover. Why had he ever considered leaving, as though this place wasn't enough? The ranch was in his blood. Something tightened inside him. So many things were in his blood and that was the whole problem.

He led Emily over the fields to the top of a knoll. He stopped and took a deep breath. From here they could see for miles. Evans's land went on for a huge portion of the view. This was his. His responsibility. His heritage.

His privilege.

"Oh, wow," Emily breathed, and he looked over at her. Lord, she was beautiful. He'd thought so from the first. Her hair had grown a little longer in the days she'd been here, the flirty tips of her short cut now softer around her face. She had held him together today, as much as he didn't want to admit it.

"I'm scared, Em."

Sympathy softened her face even more. "Oh, Luke. I'm sure that is hard to say."

He nodded. "It is. I don't have the luxury of being scared. I've known for a long time that this family is my responsibility, but there was always this little bit of 'not yet' as long as Dad was alive. It was easier to deny, I suppose. I'm starting to have to face the truth. It's all on me now. And I don't want to face it. I want to go back to being twenty and full of myself and with my life ahead of me. Not predetermined."

He shook his head. "I'm a selfish bastard. I've got everything I could ever want and I'm ungrateful."

"No you're not." She turned her back on the view and gripped his wrists. "I can only imagine how hard this is for you. He is your father."

"I never asked for this. We were still reeling from Mom's death and I think Dad must have had an idea that things weren't right. He and I went to the lawyer's one day and he changed his will and gave me power of attorney. He told me it was because one day the farm would be mine. I had no idea how soon…I think he knew what was coming and was preparing. He knew I would have to make the decisions when he couldn't. But putting your own father in a home…" His voice cracked. "It was hell on earth making that decision."

Remembering how ungrateful he'd been back then left a bitter taste in his mouth. "I wanted to finish school. To get away from Evans and Son like it was a foregone conclusion." He stared past Emily's shoulder at the blocks of color below: the dull green of the freshly hayed fields, the lush emerald of pasture, the golden fields of grain crops. "We had words about it."

"And he was already sick?"

"Yes." He turned his attention back to Emily, expecting to see revulsion on her face. Hell, he hated himself for ever having felt it and now saying it out loud was like admitting he was a self-absorbed kid. But her eyes were soft with understanding, and she took a step forward and wrapped her arms around his waist, resting her head on his chest.

He let his arms go around her, drawing strength from her.

"We thought he was just grieving for Mom and having difficulties. We made all sorts of excuses. It wasn't until the smoke alarms went off that we realized. The kitchen had some fire and smoke damage. That was all. But it could have been worse. He was a danger to all of us. The hardest thing I ever did was put my father in a home. Especially after the words I'd said to him. And the girls…they were dealing with teenage angst and emotions and missing our mother. I was barely more than a kid myself."

He paused, wondered how much of the truth to tell her and settled for half. "I never want to have that responsibility again. I've been son, brother, parent, breadwinner and sole operator of this ranch and that's enough for me. I raised my family and it was one hell of a painful experience. I don't want to raise another one."

She pulled away from his chest. Perhaps he hadn't shocked her before but he had now. Her face had gone white as she stared up at him. What would she say if he told her the rest?

But he couldn't bring himself to say it out loud. And what good would it do for her to know he wanted things that he could never have? It would only hurt them both further, because it was as plain as the nose on his face that she was developing feelings. That was his fault, and up to him to fix.

"I see."

He swallowed, hating the dull pain in her voice. "I thought you should know so you didn't get…" Oh, God, this was tearing him apart on top of everything else. He didn't want to hurt her. "So you didn't get your hopes up. About us."

"You mean after the kisses." She dropped her hands from his ribs as though his skin was suddenly burning her fingertips. It was what he wanted. He needed to push her away, so why did it have to hurt so much?

"I shouldn't have kissed you. Either time. I certainly didn't plan it. You're a desirable woman, Emily. Don't let that fool of an ex-husband let you think otherwise. But I'm not in the market for a wife and you should know that from the start."

She turned her back on him, staring over the naked fields now with her shoulders pulled up. He *had* hurt her. He'd only hurt her more if he kept on. The sky was a dusky shade of purple and he knew they had to be going back. Off to the east, the first howl of a coyote echoed, lonely and fierce.

Emily turned back to face him and he expected to have tears to contend with. But there were none. Her face was impassive, showing neither hurt nor pleasure. She merely lifted her eyebrows the slightest bit and replied, "Then it is a good thing that I'm not looking for a husband, either."

* * *

Emily held herself together all during the long, silent walk back to the house, all the while she called Liz to check up on Sam, and even up until she brushed her teeth and climbed under the covers of her bed. But once she put her head on the pillow, the tears came. She would not sob; she refused to let Luke know that she was crying over him. Hadn't it only been short weeks ago she'd claimed she'd hardened her heart to love? How wrong—how arrogant—she'd been. She'd had chinks in her armor and Luke had got past each one. She hadn't even recognized the feeling inside her as hope, but it had been there. She had envisioned getting on with her life. The possibility of more children, the big family she'd always longed for. Who was she kidding? She had pictured it happening with Luke. Maybe not right away. But somewhere in the back of her mind he'd emerged as her ideal.

She sniffled into her pillow, her heart hurting. Hadn't she just done the same thing as before? She had given of herself. Anyone could cook and clean, but it had been more than that. She'd done so with care, trying to make things better for Luke. It had been personal from the start. She'd been looking for his approval, she realized. Not approval of the job but approval of her. She'd set herself up for this. It wasn't all Luke's fault.

She was conscious of him lying in the next bedroom, and struggled to keep her breathing quiet. She couldn't stay here. She couldn't face him day after day, feeling the way she did, and knowing it would never go anywhere. Oh, she couldn't just pack up and leave in the morning. She would give it a few days. Let things resume some sort of normalcy, give Luke a chance to get his father settled. But it was time to go back to the old emergency plan. At least now she had an idea of what she could do. She was good at taking care of people and she loved children. She would go to her parents' place, find work as a housekeeper and look into some night courses. She could take early childhood education or perhaps even a teaching assistant course—both positions that would mean she could support Sam in all the ways that mattered.

She fluffed her pillow and let resolve flood into her. Thinking ahead felt so much better than the hurt. The idea took hold and she closed her eyes, desperate to look forward, willing sleep to come.

She had simply been lonely, thinking of herself, swept away by fancy. But she couldn't afford to think only of herself. She had Sam, and he came first. In time she'd stop caring about Luke Evans and simply thank him for showing her the way to her independence.

Sleep snuck in, merciful but bittersweet. If that were true, then why did she still feel this aching hole inside her?

CHAPTER TWELVE

JOHN EVANS WENT into the palliative care unit the following afternoon. Emily scrubbed bathrooms, brought clothes in off the line and picked Sam up from camp as Luke and his sisters spoke to the doctor and care worker. She did not offer to go with Luke and he didn't ask her. After his revelations of the night before, it seemed like an unspoken conclusion that he would handle things on his own. It felt as though they'd said all that could be said, and yet so much seemed left unspoken.

For three days Luke worked the farm, Emily fulfilled her housekeeping duties and Sam finished camp and played with Homer in the hot July evenings.

Each day tore into Emily's heart a little more. She saw Luke struggling with emotions, the wear and tear showing in the lines on his face and the weary set to his shoulders, though he never complained. He never talked to her about it either, not after that last night when he'd been so open and honest and sharing. It was, she realized, all she was going to get from him. Whatever had been between them—for his part—had run its course. It wasn't the same for her. Each bit of distance between them cut a little deeper. She was surer than ever that she had to go. It hurt too much to stay.

She waited until Sam was in bed one night before giving Luke her notice.

"Luke?"

He looked up from the magazine he was reading. A summer shower was falling and he'd turned on the lamp behind him, casting the room in a warm glow. It was so cozy here. So... right. But Luke didn't love her, and she couldn't survive staying without it. She wanted more. She needed more, deserved more...and so did Sam. If nothing else, Luke's turning her away had made her realize that she was the marrying kind. Even after the disaster of her first marriage, she still believed in it. Still believed in two people making that commitment to each other. She knew now that her words to the contrary had only been a way to cover up the pain of failing the first time.

And she was not the one who had given up. She wasn't the one who had walked away. No, it was all or nothing with her, even now. And she was asking more than Luke could give. No, it was time to cut her losses. Moving forward would be best for her and best for Sam.

"This isn't going to work. I know I should give you more notice, but..." she swallowed and gathered her strength, forcing out the next words. "Sam and I are going to leave tomorrow. We're going to my mom and dad's in Regina."

Luke's face showed nothing, until she looked into his eyes. Steely blue, they met her gaze, and there was surprise and perhaps regret. But whatever his feelings, he shuttered them away again as he folded the cover back over the magazine and put it down. "I was afraid you were going to say that."

For the briefest of moments, her heart surged, but the flare quickly died. He'd expected this. And there was nothing in either his words or his expression to tell her he was going to ask her to change her mind.

"Thank you for all you've done for us." Oh, how awful that sounded. She pushed forward. "Working for you made me see that I'm good at this. I was looking for an office job and overlooked the job I've been doing for years. What you said about school...I'm going to look into childhood education. I love children and I think I'd be good at it."

And if that meant surrounding herself with the children of others rather than her own, that was okay. She'd do the best she could and she would provide a good life for her son.

"You'll be wonderful at it, Emily." He offered her an encouraging smile. "You're a wonderful mother. Kind and patient and firm."

The words were the right ones, but the polite, friendly tone cut into her.

"Thank you." She lifted her chin. "I realized I was overlooking my skills rather than capitalizing on them."

His gaze settled on her warmly. "You've made such a difference here. Not just with what you do, but with your kindness and generosity."

Her breath seemed stuck in her chest. Really, this polite veneer was killing her. She wanted to demand that he fight for her. That he tell her he hadn't meant to slam the door on them so completely. Something to let her know that he cared, that they had a chance. But he said nothing. He was as determined as ever to keep her out.

"I need to finish packing. Excuse me, Luke."

"I'll write you a check for your wages."

How could she take money? It seemed to cheapen what they'd had. And yet what did they have, really? Some feelings and a few kisses. She had to take the money. Not just because she needed it, but because if she refused he would know. He'd know that this had gone way beyond a business arrangement and into deeply personal territory, and she'd been hurt and humiliated enough.

"Thank you, Luke."

He picked up his magazine again and Emily felt her tenuously held control shatter. Without saying another word, she left the room and went upstairs to pack her suitcase.

* * *

When her footsteps sounded on the stairs, Luke dropped the magazine and ran a rough hand over his face. Keeping up the pretense just now had damn near killed him. The last few days had been hell. Not just putting Dad in the palliative care unit, but wanting, needing Emily beside him and knowing he'd been the one to turn her away. What had he expected she'd do after his cold words? He'd thanked her and then flat-out told her they had no future. She'd answered him back in kind but he'd seen the hurt behind her eyes. He never should have hired her. Never should have kissed her. Definitely never should have fallen in love with her. She made him want things he couldn't have—the home and wife and marriage that seemed to make everything complete.

She didn't understand why he was turning her away, or that he was doing it for her own good. And she sure as hell didn't know what it was doing to him to let her go.

Marriage was enough of a risk, and Emily had already lost once. He couldn't ask her to take a gamble on him when she didn't even know the odds. And the odds had been all too clear as he watched his father slide further and further away. He could end up just like his father. Then where would Emily be? And Sam? Looking after an invalid? Making heart-breaking decisions they way he'd had to?

She didn't know what it was like. Couldn't know unless she'd been through it.

He'd heard her crying in her room. Quietly, but crying just the same, and it had taken every ounce of restraint not to go to her and tell her he didn't mean it. Her leaving came as no surprise, and he had tried his best to make it easier on her. He pushed out of the chair and went to the office, digging out the checkbook and taking a pen from the holder. His hand shook as he filled out her name and the date and the pen hovered over the amount.

How could he put a price on all she'd given to him?

In the end he figured out her wage and doubled it, then ripped it out of the book and put it in an envelope, licking and sealing the flap.

He'd check her car's oil and fluids before she left, too. He realized that he'd never made good on his promise to teach her how to do those things for herself. But he'd do them this time. Just to be sure she got to Regina okay.

And maybe one day she'd realize that letting her go was the kindest thing he could have done.

It was still raining the next morning when Emily put Sam's suitcase in the trunk. Sam wore a sullen look. "I don't want to leave the fun kids. I don't even know Grandma and Grandpa. They're old and I won't have anyone to play with. And I was teaching Homer to roll over!"

"Sam!" Emily felt her patience thin. "Your grandparents love you. And you will make new friends."

Sam got into the car without another word and Emily sighed, regretting the sharp tone. Inside her purse was the envelope Luke had given her with her pay inside. She couldn't bear to open it and see the last glorious weeks reduced to a number sign. Luke stood nearby, straight and uncompromising. But when Emily slammed the trunk shut Sam opened his door and scrambled out again, running to Luke and throwing his arms around Luke's legs.

Luke lifted him as if he weighed nothing and closed his eyes as Sam put his arms around his neck.

Emily couldn't watch. She wasn't the only one who had come to care for Luke. Sam idolized him, and would have followed him around as faithfully as Homer if Emily had allowed it. Luke had patiently taught Sam how to sit on a horse and the difference between garden plants, the taste of hay ready for cutting and how the cattle could tell a man when bad weather was imminent. He had so much to give and refused to give it.

"Bye, squirt. Be good for your mom, okay?"

"Okay, Luke. Bye."

Emily vowed not to cry, but it was a struggle. She finally met Luke's gaze and nearly crumpled at the pain in the blue depths. All he had to do was say the word and she'd stay. One word. The moment hung between them until she was sure she would break.

"Goodbye, Emily."

She hadn't truly realized what the term *stiff upper lip* meant until she forced herself to keep her own from trembling. She swallowed twice before she trusted herself to say the words, "Goodbye, Luke."

She turned to go to the driver's-side door but he spoke again. "I checked your oil and everything last night. You should be fine now."

Stop talking, she wanted to say. Didn't he know each word was like the lash of a whip? "Thank you," she murmured, her hand on the door handle.

"Emily…"

His hand closed over hers on the handle. She slowly turned and his arms cinched around her.

The light rain soaked into the cotton of his shirt, releasing the scent of his morning shower and fabric softener as he cradled her against his wide chest. She clung to him, her arms looping around his ribs, holding him close. Did this mean he'd changed his mind?

All too soon he let her go and opened her door. She stepped back, her lip quivering despite her determinations. She had to face the truth. Luke's resolve that he'd raised his family—that he didn't want the responsibility—was stronger than any feelings he had for her. Numbly she got into the car and dropped her purse on the passenger seat while Sam sat, silent, in the back.

"Be happy," Luke said, and shut her door.

She turned the key and the engine roared to life. She put it in gear and started down the driveway.

At the bottom she glanced in the rearview mirror. He was still standing in the same spot, his jeans and flannel shirt a contrast to the gray, dismal day. She snapped her gaze to the front and to the wipers that rhythmically swiped the rain from the windshield.

She had to stop looking back. From now on it was straight ahead.

Luke went back into the house once her car had disappeared from sight. He closed the door and the sound echoed through the hall. His footsteps seemed inordinately loud in the empty kitchen. He should go to the barn and tackle a few of the tasks he'd been saving for a rainy day. Instead he found himself wandering aimlessly from room to room, ending in the living room. A white square caught his eye and he went to the old stereo, picked up the piece of paper and stared at her elegant handwriting.

If he'd ever wondered if she could do everything, here was his answer. After all these years of the record player not working, she'd fixed it.

He carefully moved the picture frames from the top, stacking them to one side as he lifted the hinged cover. Memories hit him from all sides: being at his grandparents' house and hearing the old albums, then his mom and dad bringing it home and putting on the Beatles and Elvis. Those LPs were still there, but Luke flipped the switch and sent the turntable spinning, placing the needle on the album already in place.

The mellow voice of Jim Reeves singing "I Love You Because" filled the room. Oh, how he'd complained as a boy when his parents had put on the old-fashioned tunes. Now he was hit with a wave of nostalgia so strong it almost stole his breath.

And as he listened to the lyrics, he wished he could take back the words that had sent her away.

What was done was done. He'd stayed strong despite it all, loving her too much to sentence her to a life of pain and indecision. But damn, it hurt.

It hurt more than he'd ever imagined possible.

Sam held a bouquet of black-eyed Susans, daisies and cornflowers in his hand as Emily cut more stems for the bouquet. Her mother's wildflower garden was a rainbow of blooms right now, and Emily snipped a few pinky-purple cosmos blossoms to add to the mix. Sam waited patiently, but as Emily handed over the last flowers, she knew. He wasn't happy. And she knew why. Nothing had been the same since they'd left Luke's.

"What's the matter, sweetheart?" She forced a cheerful smile. "Aren't the flowers pretty for Grandma?"

"I guess," he muttered, looking at his feet rather than the profusion of flowers in his hand. Emily sighed. One of them pouting was enough.

"Grandma made cookies today. Why don't we have some once these are in water?"

He shrugged. "They're not as good as yours."

Emily knelt beside him. "I know there have been a lot of changes lately. And I know it's been tough, Sam. But Grandma and Grandpa are very nice to let us stay with them."

More than nice. They'd welcomed Emily and Sam with open arms and without the criticism Emily had expected. She'd come to realize their lack of contact over the years had been partly her fault. She'd always seemed too busy to visit and hadn't been as welcoming as she should have been. It was good to mend those fences, but it wasn't enough. Sam wasn't the only one discontented. Emily compared everything to Luke's house. Not as modern or updated as her parents' home but with far more character and redolent with decades of happy memories. The garden here was pretty, but she found herself wondering if the peas and beans were ready and if Luke was finding time to pick them. The wheat was ripening in the fields and she pictured Luke with the Orrick boys, high on a tractor amid the waving golden heads. August was waning and Labor Day approaching, and she wondered if he'd celebrate with Liz and Cait and the children. Remembering Canada Day caused such a chasm of loneliness that she caught her breath.

She thought about his father, and if he was still hanging on or if the family was grieving.

She had thought it would take time to forget about him, but forgetting had proved an impossible endeavor.

"Mom?" Sam's voice interrupted her thoughts and she forced a smile.

"What, pumpkin?"

He scowled. "You aren't supposed to call me pumpkin anymore."

"What should I call you?" She smiled. Sam was her one bright spot. She'd begun working part-time for a local agency and he met her at the door every single time she came home. He brought her books every night, first learning to read his own and then settling in for a bedtime story. He would start school soon and she was determined to sign up for her courses and find them their own place. But there were some days, like today, when she missed when he'd been a toddler, and names like pumpkin had been okay. What would she do when he was older and didn't need her anymore?

"I don't know. No baby names."

"I'll try. No promises." She grinned and ruffled his hair.

"I miss Luke. And Homer. And the horses. And the kids."

Oh, honey. She missed all those things, too, and more. Mostly Luke. She wanted to promise Sam everything would be better soon, but it seemed unfair. He was entitled to his feelings. He shouldn't be made to feel as if they were insignificant.

"Me, too, sweet…Sam," she amended, gratified when he smiled. "But we knew all along that it was temporary, remember?"

"I thought…maybe…"

"Maybe what?"

"That Luke was going to be my new dad. When he kissed you and stuff."

She felt her cheeks color. "How do you know about that?"

He shrugged again—a new favorite five-year-old gesture since his birthday. "I saw you. At the fireworks. Everyone did."

Emily stood up and took his hand, starting towards the house. "Luke and I liked each other for a while," she said, not sure what to tell him that would explain things without getting complicated. "But it wasn't like that," she finished awkwardly.

"I wish it was. I liked it there. Even better than Calgary."

They'd reached the back steps when her cell phone vibrated in her pocket. "Go inside and give these to Grandma. Bet she'll give you an extra cookie." Emily took the phone out of her pocket and her heart took a leap as she saw Luke's name on the call display.

It vibrated in her palm, and before she could reconsider she flipped it open and answered it.

"Hello?"

"Emily?"

Oh, his voice sounded just as rough and sexy over the

phone. Her spine straightened and her fingers toyed with the hem of her top. He could still cause that nest of nerves simply from saying her name.

"Luke. Is everything okay?" She knew he'd never call unless something was wrong. He'd said all that he'd needed to say.

"Dad's gone, Emily."

His voice cracked at the end. There was a long pause while Emily wondered if he was going to continue. Her throat tightened painfully. "Are you okay, Luke?"

He cleared his throat. "I think so. I need to ask you a favor."

Anything. She almost said it, hating herself for being so easy even if it was only on the inside. Her fingers gripped the phone so tightly her knuckles cramped. "What is it?"

"Can you come?"

Her knees wobbled and she sat down on the back steps, the cool cement pricking into her bare legs. "You want me to come for the funeral?"

"Yes. And to talk."

Her breath caught in her chest. She hadn't thought she'd ever hear his voice again, let alone see him. But she couldn't get her hopes up. "Talk about what?"

"There were things I should have said but didn't."

"You seemed to say enough." He had been the one to turn her away, and now he expected her to come when he crooked his finger? She knew it was a difficult time for him and she wanted to help, but she refused to put herself in the position of being hurt again.

"I know, and I need to explain."

"I don't know…" She wanted to be there for him, but the wounds were still too fresh. She was still too close to be objective.

"The service is the day after tomorrow. If you can't get away, I'll come to you afterwards. Give me your address."

Come here? Impossible. As kind as her parents had been, Emily had glossed over her pain at leaving Alberta. She'd let them believe she was so down because of her divorce—they had no idea she'd been foolish enough to have her heart broken all over again. Luke showing up here would create all sorts of problems. Especially considering what Sam had just said.

"No, I'll come," she decided. If it was that crucial, she'd take a day and go.

"Thank you, Emily. It means a lot."

What was she doing? Setting herself up for another round of hurt? Getting over him was taking too long. Maybe they would be better this way. Despite what had happened, it felt as if they'd left loose ends. Maybe they needed to tie those off. Cauterize the wound so she could finally heal.

"I'm sorry about your dad," she said quietly, pressing the phone to her ear, not wanting the conversation to end so soon. Lord, she *had* missed him. The line went quiet again and she thought she heard him take a shaking breath. Her heart quaked. She had so many things she wanted to say, and her one regret over all these weeks was that she'd never told him exactly how she felt. Would it have made a difference if he'd known she was in love with him?

"We'll talk about it when you get here," he replied.

After the phone went dead, Emily sat on the steps a long time. She was going back. The memory of his face swam through her mind, scowling, smiling, and that intense, heart-stopping gaze he gave her just before he kissed her. She would see him the day after tomorrow.

If nothing else, she would tell him how she felt. How his dismissal of her had cut her to the bone. And then she would let him go once and for all.

CHAPTER THIRTEEN

EMILY TURNED UP THE drive at half past twelve. The midday
sun scorched down and Emily noticed the petunias in the
baskets were drooping, in need of a good deadheading and
watering. Luke's truck sat in the drive, and the field equipment
was lined up in a mournful row next to the barn. The farm
work had ceased for today, a sad and respectful silence for the
man who had started it all and passed it on to his son.

His son. Luke stepped through the screen door and on to
the porch as she parked. He rested one hand on the railing
post while Emily tried to calm both the excitement of seeing
him again and the sadness of knowing the reason why he'd
traded in his jeans and T-shirts for a suit. Black trousers fitted
his long legs and the white shirt emphasized the leanness of
his hips and the breadth of his shoulders. The gray tie was
off-center and her lips curved up the tiniest bit. Luke was the
kind of man who would hate being bundled up in a tie.

She stepped out of the car. Her shoes made little grinding
noises on the gravel as she walked to the house. Luke waited
as she put her shaking hand on the railing and climbed the
steps to the porch.

God, how she'd missed him. She faced him, drinking in
every detail of his features. Regular Luke was irresistible.
But this dressed-up Luke felt different and exciting. He'd had
a haircut recently—a razor-thin white line marked the path

of his new hairline. His mouth, the crisply etched lips that remained unsmiling, and his eyes. She stopped at his eyes. She had expected pain and sadness. But what she saw there gave her heart a still-familiar kick. Heat. And desire.

"You look beautiful," he said quietly. He reached out and took a few strands of her hair in his fingers. "You let your hair grow."

She reached up and touched the dark strands without thinking. When she realized what she was doing she dropped her hand to her side again. "I felt like a change." She meant to speak clearly but it came out as a ragged whisper. If she reacted like this now, how would they make it through a whole afternoon?

"Emily…"

She waited. As the seconds passed, she wondered how long before they would have to leave for the church. He'd said he wanted to talk to her, but they wouldn't have much time. Surely he had to be there early. To be with his sisters. To say goodbye. With every second that slid past she felt Luke sliding away as well.

Luke drew in his eyebrows and pushed away from the post. Emily took a step forward and put her hand on his forearm. Her fingers clenched the fine white fabric and she got a little thrill as the muscle hardened beneath her touch.

"Why is it so hard to say what I need to say?" he wondered aloud, putting his hand over hers. "I've said it a million times in my head, Em. Over and over again since you left."

Emily looked up. In her heels she was only a few inches shorter than he was and impulsively she tipped up her face, touching her lips to his. "Then just tell me," she whispered, meeting his gaze evenly. "I came all this way…"

"Yes, you did." He smiled a little then. "You were always there when I needed you, Em. Right from the start. Until I sent you away. I kept looking for your car to drive up the lane because somehow you always seemed to know what I needed. But you didn't come."

"You made it all too clear in those last hours that I wasn't needed at all."

"It's completely my fault." He cupped her jaw with a wide hand. "I'm the one who forced you to leave."

"You didn't force me anywhere. I left because you made it clear you were not interested in pursuing anything further. And because my own feelings were already involved."

She could give him that much. She did want to tell him how she felt, but he was the one who had asked her here. He was the one who'd said he had something to tell her. Whatever it was, she wanted him to get it off his chest.

His gaze warmed as he looked down at her. "I know they were," he said quietly. "It was why I needed to stop what was happening between us before it went too far. I needed to push you away so I didn't have to face things. I didn't tell you everything, Em, that night on the hill. I held back the real reason why I promised never to let myself get too close to anyone. And I hurt you because I was too afraid to say it out loud. If I didn't say it, there was still part of me that could deny it."

"Then tell me now," she replied, gripping his hand, drawing it down to her side. "I'm here. I'm listening."

"It's more than I deserve."

"It's not. You gave me—us—so much while we were here." Emily took a deep breath, gathering her courage. "I fell in love with you, Luke."

The blue depths of his eyes got suddenly bright. "Don't say that, Em…"

"And as often as you looked for me to come back, I waited for the phone to ring. Hoping it would be you. I promised myself if I got another chance, I'd tell you how I felt. Because you need to understand. I vowed I would never love anyone again after what I'd been through. I swore I would never put

Sam through anything like that ever again. And I fell for you so hard, so fast, it was terrifying."

He pulled her close, his hands encircling her back and she closed her eyes. For weeks she'd despaired of ever feeling his arms around her again. Now she hung on as if she would never let go.

All too soon he pushed her away. "I can't," he said, running a hand over his closely cropped hair. "I can't do this. Please Em...let's sit."

She sat on the plush cushion of the porch swing, the springs creaking as he sat beside her and put his elbows on his knees. It had taken all she had to say the words and she was glad she had. For a brief, beautiful moment she had thought it was all going to be okay. But he kept pushing her away because of this...something that he still kept hidden inside. "I think you'd better just come out with it," she suggested. "Whatever it is, I can take it, Luke."

"Did you know there's a hereditary component to Dad's disease?"

Light began to glimmer as she realized what he was saying, and what he wasn't. Why hadn't she considered he'd be afraid he'd get it, too? "No. No, I didn't know that. It must be a worry for you."

Luke twisted his fingers around and around. "Sometimes early onset is completely random. But sometimes it's not. My father was fifty-three, Emily. At a time when my friends' fathers were going to graduations and giving away brides, my dad was forgetting who his children were, getting lost on roads he'd travelled most of his life. He should never have been around machinery or livestock—looking back, it's amazing something didn't go drastically wrong sooner. He could have killed us all that night if the smoke detectors hadn't been working. And I bore the brunt of it, don't you see? I resented it and felt guilty about it. Now he's gone, and it's a relief. Not because I wanted him to die, but because..."

His voice broke. "Because he was already gone and we simply spent the last years hoping for crumbs. That might be me down the road, and I won't do that to a family. I won't put them through what I went through. The pain and guilt and awful duty of caring for someone like that."

"Luke..."

"No, let me finish. I didn't turn you away because I didn't care about you. It's because I care too much to see you destroyed by having to go through what I went through."

She swallowed against the lump in her throat. He wasn't saying he didn't love her. He was putting her first, trying to keep her safe, and it made her want to weep. "Shouldn't that be my choice, Luke?"

"You don't know what you're asking." His voice was suddenly sharp and his eyes glittered at her. "Emily..." He put his head in his hands for a moment, taking a deep breath, collecting himself.

"How can you say no to something when you aren't even sure?" She felt him slipping away and fought to keep him there, in the moment with her. "There are no guarantees in this life, Luke. Are you willing to sacrifice your happiness for something that might or might not happen?" She paused. Put her hand on his knee and squeezed. "Are you willing to sacrifice *my* happiness, and Sam's? Because we both love you. We love you and we love this farm."

"Don't make it any harder than it has to be."

"Too late." She surprised herself with the strength of her voice. "It's already done. Look at me."

His gaze struck hers and she forged ahead. "You cannot keep me from loving you, Luke. I already do. Turning me away now won't prevent me from being hurt."

"I'm doing this for you!" Luke sprang off the seat and

went to the verandah railing, gripping it with his fingers. "I'm thirty years old. I might only have a few years left before symptoms…before…"

He turned his head away, unable to voice the possibilities.

He was terrified. Emily understood that now. He'd been through hell and he was making decisions based on that fear. She could understand that so well. Heck, she'd been there just a few months ago. So afraid of being hurt again that she was prepared to spend the rest of her life alone. But Luke had changed that for her. She went to him and touched his arm, pressing her cheek against his shoulder blade.

"You're afraid. I know you think that by sacrificing yourself you're keeping others from being hurt. I know what it is to be scared. When I left Calgary, I swore I would never fall in love again. That I would never make myself that vulnerable. The sudden loss of my marriage did a number on me. I blamed myself. I thought I wasn't good enough. And then I met you. You don't think I'm still scared?" She gave a little laugh. "You talked to me about dreams, but it isn't easy to follow dreams, especially when you have a five-year-old boy depending on you to keep his world safe and happy. I felt like every time I hoped for something more I was being self-indulgent. Not putting Sam first." She turned him around so he was facing her. "I was so scared to love you that I packed up and left. But I'm not leaving now, Luke. I'm sticking around. Nothing changed in my heart when I left except that you were here and I was there. I refuse to let you sacrifice your life for me."

"You don't know what it means," he repeated. "Dad was early onset. We were told long ago that there is a fifty-fifty chance that we kids have the genetic mutation."

Fifty-fifty. For a moment Emily quailed. It was difficult odds.

"And have you been tested?"

He shook his head, staring out over the lawn that was starting to brown in the late summer heat. "The girls did. Their risk is low. They married and had the children…"

A muscle ticked in his jaw. "How could I marry, knowing I might pass this on to my own children? To give them a life sentence like that?"

"Then why not be tested?"

He shook his head. "And what? What if I have the gene? I'd spend every day wondering how old I'd be when I started showing symptoms. I'd question every time I forgot the smallest detail, wondering if this was the beginning. I can't live that way, waiting for the other shoe to drop."

Tears gathered in Emily's eyes. Suddenly everything made sense. The absolute precision of the tools in the workshop, each piece hung on exactly the right peg. The list he kept on the fridge with the pay and work schedule. It had seemed obsessively organized at the time, but now she understood. It was his safeguard. An early-warning system, a way to keep him on track just in case.

He said knowing would make him question. But not knowing was doing the exact same thing.

"You already are," she whispered. "All the things in the house, just so. Numbers and to-do lists and having everything in a specific place…"

"I knew that if something was out of place, and I couldn't remember putting it there…"

Silence dropped like an anvil.

"You are already living the disease, Luke." The look of utter shock that blanked his face made her smile. She grabbed his hands and squeezed them. "Don't you understand? You are so afraid of dying that you stopped living. You're already second-guessing everything and missing out on what might be the happiest time of your life. Love, Luke. A wife and children. Laughter and happiness. You have given your family all of yourself. What is left for you?"

"I don't know."

"If there wasn't this disease hanging over your head, what would you do?"

"But there is…"

"Forget it for a minute. If you were free of it…"

Luke looked down into her glowing face and felt something he hadn't felt in over a decade—hope. He had been so afraid. Hell, he still was. But her question penetrated the wall he'd built around himself. If there was no chance of being ill? It was an easy answer.

"I'd ask you to marry me."

She hadn't expected that response, he realized, as her face paled and she dropped her hands from his arms.

He glanced at his watch, knowing he didn't have much time. Liz and Cait expected him to be there soon and this might be his only chance to say what he needed to say. He'd wanted to make her understand that his reasons went far deeper than not wanting responsibility. Her ex-husband had destroyed so much of her confidence. If he could only give her one thing, it was that he wanted her to know that this was about him. That she had so much to offer someone.

But she was making him want things he'd convinced himself he'd never have. More than want. It was so close he could see it all within his reach.

"It occurs to me that in less than an hour from now I'm going to bury my father. And if I continue the way I'm going, I'm going to bury myself right with him, aren't I?"

She nodded ever so slightly.

"You are the strongest woman I have ever met, Emily Northcott. No woman in her right mind would choose this. You should be running right now."

"But I'm not."

"No, you're not." His heart contracted as he realized the gift she'd truly given him. "You were strong for me when I wasn't strong enough for myself. And I love you. But it doesn't change the facts."

"Then take the test."

"As long as I don't, there's still hope…"

And as long as he didn't, it would hang like a noose around his neck, slowly tightening. They both knew it.

"If I took the test…if it came back positive…would you promise to leave me?"

When he looked down at her face there were tracks of tears marring her makeup. "No," she whispered. "I would not make such a promise. I would stay with you. No matter what the test says."

"I don't want this for you…"

"When you love someone you love all of them. Even the bits that aren't perfect." She smiled, though her lower lip quivered. "You know that, Luke. You knew it when you took in Homer. When you took in two lost strays like Sam and me."

"You should have more children," he continued, quite desperate now. "I know you want them. You said so when you talked about going back to school. I can't put this on another generation, Emily."

"Then you'd better have the test. Because you deserve to be a father, Luke. If not to your own…" she smiled up at him wistfully. "Sam adores you."

"You're asking me to make this permanent?"

"Yes. Yes I am. Either way. Unless you didn't mean it when you said you loved me…"

Luke gripped her shoulders. "I love you more than I thought I could ever love anyone!"

She smiled at him so sweetly he gathered her up in his arms and held on. "Damn, what did I ever do to deserve you?" His voice was ragged. Was it really possible? Could he possibly have a normal life? A wife and the son he'd always wanted? Sam was a gift. The son of his heart if not genetics. Over the last weeks, Luke had found himself listening for Sam's laugh and missing it terribly. It had seemed that he should be there, playing with Homer, asking questions at the dinner table, tagging at Luke's heels in the barn.

"Even considering this feels so selfish," he admitted, pressing his lips to her hair.

"I know. Don't you think I've felt it, too? But you deserve a chance at happiness, Luke. We both do. And I'll be beside you every step of the way. If you'll let me."

"You aren't afraid?"

"Of course I'm afraid. But you healed me, Luke. You made me see I still believed in love. In marriage. I want to grow old with you. And if that isn't possible…I'll take whatever time God gives us."

She was right. He knew if he'd asked his parents, they would have said the same thing even had they known how their lives would be cut short. They had loved each other with a steadfastness that had been beautiful. Cait had found Joe and Liz had found Paul. Their relationships hadn't always been easy. And neither was his with Emily. But he loved her. He wanted to spend his life with her. And if he were ever going to be selfish in his life, he figured he might as well make it count.

"What about school? Your job? I know your independence is important to you. I would never want to take that away from you, Em. Don't get me wrong. I want to love you and provide for you and protect you. But I also want you to be your own person. To be happy. Whatever you want to do, the choice is ultimately yours."

He knelt on one knee on the porch, clasping her hand in

his. "So will you marry me, Emily? Marry me and let me be a father to Sam and bring a family home to this ranch?"

Her bottom lip wobbled and he squeezed her fingers. "Everything else we'll figure out as we go along. I will spend every moment making sure you don't regret it. No one will love you harder than me, Em."

"Oh, Lord, I know that!" She knelt in front of him, pressing her palm to his.

"Do you mean it? Really mean it?"

He nodded. "Every word. Marry me, Emily." He smiled. The weight that he'd carried for nearly as long as he could remember lifted. He pulled her close and kissed her, tasting lipstick and tears.

She nodded as he drew back and touched her lips with his thumb.

The phone rang and Luke knew they were running late. But for once his family would have to wait. He let it ring, waiting for Emily's answer.

"Yes, I'll marry you," she whispered, and then her smile blossomed. "As soon as it can be arranged."

EPILOGUE

THE DRIZZLY AUTUMN day couldn't dampen the celebratory mood as the Evans extended family exited the church. First Liz and her brood, dressed all in pink. Then Joe, holding a squirming Janna in his arms and Cait with a hand over her slightly rounded belly. Emily's parents, beaming with pride and squiring a handsome Sam in a new suit between them. And finally, Luke and Emily, grinning from ear to ear. Baby Elina was nestled in Emily's arm, the heirloom Evans christening gown draped over Emily's wrist.

Back at the farm Emily, Liz and Cait laid out food buffet style. Once the kids had filled their plates, the adults followed while Elina was changed into a frilly pink dress and passed between grandparents, aunts and uncles.

Emily and Luke stole a private moment in the kitchen while Liz and Cait flipped through the family albums, the music from the old stereo creating a joyful noise throughout the house.

"Happy anniversary," Emily whispered.

"I first kissed you in this very spot. Do you remember?" Luke pressed his forehead to hers and Emily closed her eyes, wondering how on earth she'd ended up so blissfully happy.

"You cursed before you did it, you know. You were reluctant about everything…"

"Then I am a very lucky man that you persevered."

"I knew a good thing when I saw it."

"I love you, Emily. And our children."

Today the minister had performed two baptisms. Not just baby Elina in her silk-and-lace gown, but also Sam, who hadn't been baptized as a baby. Today Luke had claimed both children, even though the adoption of Sam had gone through months earlier.

"I love you, too. Are you ever going to kiss me though? We're sure to be interrupted at any moment."

He was laughing as he pressed his lips to hers, holding her close. She gave back equally, twining her arms around his neck and standing on tiptoe.

"Hey, Dad, can I change out of this suit and show the girls the new kittens?"

Sam's voice announced his arrival in the kitchen and Luke muttered a light curse as Emily laughed and loosened her arms.

"Oh. Yuck," Sam said.

"Yes, go change," Luke said. "And be smart. We'll both get in trouble if the twins get their dresses dirty."

"Yes, sir."

The swinging door flapped shut as Sam ran out.

"He called me Dad." There was a note of wonder in Luke's voice and Emily smiled.

"Em…when I think of all you've given me…I never would have had the courage to take the test if it hadn't been for you. Suddenly I had more to gain than I had to lose."

"And was it worth it?"

"You'd better believe it," he replied confidently. "I never thought I'd have this. Never thought I'd have love, and a family of my own. I know there are no guarantees, even if it did come back negative. I'm going to grab every last drop of happiness I can."

Emily's heart was so full she couldn't hold it all in any

longer. "Hey, Luke, you know how we talked about the big family I always wanted?"

He raised his eyebrows as a slow smile curved up his cheek. "You thinking of trying again?"

She grinned back. "I think it's too late for that," she answered.

He reached out and took her hand. "Oh, Emily."

"Do you suppose we'll break the girl streak this time?" she asked.

"Who cares?" He raised their joined hands and kissed her thumb. "Every day with our family is a gift, and perfect—just the way it is."

THE MAN WHO
HAD EVERYTHING

CHRISTINE RIMMER

For all you MONTANA fans.
You are the very best!

Christine Rimmer came to her profession the long way around. She tried everything from acting to teaching to telephone sales. Now she's finally found work that suits her perfectly. She insists she never had a problem keeping a job—she was merely gaining 'life experience' for her future as a novelist. Christine lives with her family in Oregon. Visit her at christinerimmer.com.

Chapter One

Grant Clifton set out that sunny Sunday afternoon with the best of intentions.

He meant for Stephanie Julen and her mom, Marie, to know of his plans good and early, so they could start getting used to the idea. He had it all laid out in his mind, just how he'd tell them.

First, he would remind them that you can't hold on to the past forever. That sometimes you've got to let go of what used to be, let the wave of progress and prosperity take you. Dump the excess baggage and move on.

In his own life, Grant was doing exactly that. And loving every minute of it. He would make Steph and

Marie understand that it was time for them to move on, too.

Since the sun was shining bright and proud in the wide Montana sky, Grant called down to the stables and had one of the grooms tack up Titan, the big black gelding he rode whenever he got the chance—which wasn't all that often lately. He worked behind a desk now. His days as a rancher were behind him.

In his private suite of rooms on-site at the Thunder Canyon Resort, he changed into Wranglers and boots and a plain blue chambray shirt. When he got to the stables, Titan was ready to go. The gelding whickered in greeting and tossed his fine black head, eager to be off. The groom loaned Grant a spare hat and he grinned to himself as he rode out.

A Clifton without a battered straw Resistol close at hand to stave off the glare of the summer sun? His dad would never approve.

Fact was, John Clifton probably wouldn't have approved of a lot of things lately. Too bad. Grant settled the hat lower on his brow and refused to let his grin fade as he let Titan have his head and the horse took off at a gallop.

On Titan's strong back, the ride to the house at Clifton's Pride Ranch took about an hour. Once he'd left the sprawling resort behind, Grant rode cross-country, stopping now and then to open a gate, going back and closing it once his horse went through.

In the distance, the high mountains still bore their white

caps. And the grasses, which would be fading to gold soon enough, lay green and lush beneath the gelding's hooves, rippling in the ever-present Montana wind.

As Titan ambled up and down the cuts and draws, Grant rehearsed what he would say. Yeah, he knew Steph and her mom would be disappointed. But he would remind them that he would always take care of them. He would make sure they had work when they left the ranch. That much would never change: He would watch out for them.

In no time, it seemed, he reached Clifton land.

He took a couple of dirt roads he knew of and then approached another pasture gate, patiently shutting it behind him once his horse went through. A few cows, lying down near the fence, got up from their grassy bed and looked at him expectantly. He tipped his borrowed hat at them, mounted up again and rode on.

Ahead, cottonwoods loomed, lush and green, lining the banks of Cottonwood Creek. They seemed taller and thicker than he remembered, obscuring the creek completely now. Grant clicked his tongue and urged the horse onward, his mind on getting it over with, getting Steph and her mom together and breaking the news that he'd had a great offer and he was selling Clifton's Pride.

The horse mounted a grassy slope and carried him in beneath the screen of wind-ruffled trees, where the ground was mossy and soft and Titan's hooves hardly made a sound. Grant could smell water, hear the soft gurgling of the creek not far ahead. He topped another slight rise and the creek lay below, crystal clear and inviting.

But it wasn't the sight of the creek that stole the breath from Grant Clifton's lungs.

He drew on the reins without thinking. Soundlessly Titan came to a stop.

A woman stood at creekside. A naked woman. Beads of water gleamed on her golden skin and her hair, clinging in soaked tendrils to her shoulders, dripped a shining wet trail down the center of her slim, straight back.

She faced the opposite bank. As he stared, she lifted both hands and smoothed her hair, cupping the delicate shape of her skull, catching the wet strands at her nape, wringing gently, so that more water trickled in little gleaming trails along that amazing back, between those two little dimples that rode the base of her spine...

Grant's gaze followed the path of the water. Sweet Lord. The lower he looked, the harder he lusted. He sat frozen in place astride the gelding, feeling the blood pool hot in his groin, his pulse pounding so deep and hungry and loud, he was surprised the woman didn't hear it and turn.

What the hell was she doing there, naked beneath the cottonwoods on Clifton land?

Not that he planned to ask. Not right now.

He would have smiled—if only if he hadn't been aching so bad with desire. Make no mistake. He'd find out who she was one way or another. He'd get to know her. Well.

But now would probably be a bad time to introduce himself.

Light as a breath, he laid the reins to Titan's neck. The horse started to turn—and the woman raised her slim arms to the sky and let out a laugh, a sound all at once free and husky and glorious.

His mind reeled. He knew that laugh.

Steph's laugh.

Grant drew the horse up short again.

Impossible.

This beautiful, naked stranger, fully a woman... *Steph?*

His head spun with denials. Stephanie Julen was hardly more than a kid, she was like a little sister to him, she was...

Twenty-one.

Damn it. Couldn't be. No way.

The woman who couldn't be Steph laughed again, and then, without warning, in midlaugh, she turned.

And she saw him there, frozen in place, at the top of the bank. The green eyes that always looked at him with trust and admiration widened in shock as she formed his name on a low cry.

"Grant?" Frantic, she tried to cover herself, one hand to her small, perfect breasts, the other to the patch of dark gold curls between her smooth, amazing thighs. "Oh, God..."

At least he had the presence of mind to lay the reins

at the horse's neck again and, that time, to follow through.

Once he faced the way he'd come, he called over his shoulder, "Get dressed." He kept his voice as calm and level as possible, given his own stunned, disbelieving state of arousal. "Ride on back to the house with me…"

Behind him, she was dead silent—except for a low, agonized groan.

"Come on." He kept his gaze resolutely front and he forced all hint of gruffness from his tone. "It's okay." He spoke gently. Soothingly. "I'm sorry I…surprised you."

Behind him, down the bank, he heard frenzied rustling sounds as she scrambled to get into her clothes. He waited, taking slow breaths, knowing he had to be calm and unruffled, totally unconcerned, in order to put her at ease again.

At ease. Damn. Didn't he wish?

Within a couple of minutes that only *seemed* to last for eternity, he heard the soft thuds of hooves behind him. She came up beside him mounted on her favorite mare, Trixiebelle.

Unbelievable. He'd been so busy gaping at her naked backside and planning how he would get her into his bed, he hadn't even noticed she had her horse down there by the creek with her.

Titan chuffed in greeting and Trixiebelle snorted a response.

Grant put on a smile and turned it on Steph, not

allowing it to waver, even as another bolt of lust went zinging through him.

Her clothes were as wet as the rest of her. Her shirt clung to the fine, sleek curves he'd never noticed till moments ago—curves that from this afternoon onward would remain seared into his brain.

Impossible. Wanting Steph. It had to be illegal. Or, at the very least, immoral.

Didn't it?

Her hair hung in damp ropes on her shoulders and her sweet, innocent face was flaming red. "How long were you..." Her voice faltered. She swallowed and made herself finish. "...watching me?"

"I wasn't," he baldly lied, somehow managing to keep his easy smile in place at the same time. "I'd just topped the rise when you saw me." He turned Titan again and started down the bank to creekside. She followed.

Since she would know the best place to cross, he pulled back once they reached the bank and signaled her to take the lead.

All too aware of the man behind her, Steph rode Trixiebelle into the shallows. Once on the other side, they climbed the far bank and emerged from under the dappling shade of the cottonwoods into open pasture. Grant caught up with her and rode at her side.

She didn't look at him. She couldn't bear to meet his eyes right yet—and if only her silly cheeks would stop blushing.

Really. It wasn't *that* big a deal.

Okay, it was embarrassing. Way embarrassing. She'd never in a million years expected Grant to appear on horseback out of nowhere during the rare moment she'd chosen to indulge herself in a quick, *private* skinny-dip.

He had to know she hadn't expected him—or anyone, for that matter—didn't he?

After all, he hardly ever came to the ranch anymore. In the six months since he'd hired her to take over the job of foreman, this was the first time she'd seen him out on the land. As a rule, when he did drop by, he always stuck to the roads and arrived at the ranch house in that fancy black Range Rover of his.

Grant didn't have time for the ranch these days. He was too busy at the resort. In two short years, he's gone from sales associate to comanager. And he played as hard as he worked. Not a lot of nights went by that he didn't have some new out-of-town beauty hanging on his arm. The women loved him. He was thirty-two, single and getting rich fast.

Steph dared to slide him a glance. He was looking straight ahead.

He was also way too handsome. Always had been. His profile could take a girl's breath away: that sculpted nose, that fine mouth, that firm jaw. He was six foot four, lean, rangy and muscular—all at the same time. She had no doubt he'd seen a lot of naked women. To him, a naked female wouldn't be anything new.

She felt a stab of pure green jealousy as she thought of

all those beautiful women he dated. Stephanie had loved Grant Clifton with all of her yearning heart since she was five years old. Of course, she knew he would never return her love. He cared for her. A lot. But not in *that* way.

And she was okay with that…

Or so she kept telling herself.

And what do you know? She wasn't blushing anymore. Her heart had stopped jumping around in her chest like a spooked jackrabbit and her pulse had even slowed a tad. Maybe hopeless blazing jealousy had its uses, after all.

So all right. He'd seen her naked. Best to get over it. Let it go. Move on.

But for some idiotic reason, she couldn't stop herself from launching into a totally lame explanation. "Me and Rufus pulled a cow out of that pond in the far pasture…"

Rufus Dale had been the top hand on Clifton's Pride for as long as Steph could remember. He'd stepped up to run things when Grant started working at the resort. But arthritis had forced the old cowboy to slow down *and* given Steph her chance to take over for him.

She babbled on, "I sent him on back to the bunkhouse. You know how he gets these days. He hates that he can't do all the things that used to be so easy for him."

Grant didn't say anything. He didn't look at her, either. Was he mad at her, after all, for being out there in the altogether where anyone could ride up on her?

She tried again. "I was covered in mud. I got to the

creek and it was just too darn tempting. I jumped in with my clothes on, to rinse everything off at once and, well, then I was all soggy—like now." She cast a rueful glance down at her wet shirt and jeans. "And it's a warm day and I couldn't help thinking how *good* the water would feel without... uh. Well, you know."

He grunted. Didn't he? Hadn't that been a grunt she heard?

"Uh, Grant?"

A grunt. A definite grunt. One with sort of a question mark at the end of it.

"I really didn't expect anyone to ride by. I truly didn't..."

"Steph."

She gulped. "Yeah?"

A pause. Her dread increased. Was he irritated? Amused? What? She just couldn't tell.

Then he actually looked at her again and gave her one of those gorgeous heartbreaker smiles of his. "Don't sweat it, okay? I know the feeling."

She felt her mouth bloom wide in a giant smile. "You do?" God. She sounded like such a dumb, innocent kid...

But he was nice about it. He was *always* nice. "Oh, yeah. Nothin' like a cold, clear creek on a hot day."

She clicked her tongue at Trixiebelle, who was showing more interest in cropping grass than in moving it along. "Well," she said, and couldn't think of a single clever thing to say. She finished lamely, "Good..."

They rode in silence the rest of the way. Stephanie tried to concentrate on the beauty of the green, rolling land around them and not to think about how he really must be irritated with her no matter how hard he tried to ease her embarrassment. He was so quiet, so reluctant to turn her way.

Bart, the old spotted hound, came out to meet them when they got to the house. He wiggled in delight, whining for attention from his old master.

Grant dismounted and took a moment to greet him, "There's a good boy." He gave the dog a nice scratch behind the ear.

Rufus emerged from the tack room as they walked their horses into the barn. He shook Grant's hand in greeting and then started giving orders.

"Go on in the house, you two. Leave the horses to me. I'm still good for a few things around here, you know."

So they thanked him and headed across the open dirt yard to the plain, white-shingled, two-story house. On the wide front porch, Steph paused to pull off her muddy boots.

Inside, the old wood floors had a warm scuffed gleam and a short walk through the front hall past the simple oak staircase led them to the kitchen in back.

Marie Julen had the oven door open. She pulled a sheet of cookies out and set it on a rack to cool. And then she turned, her face breaking into a welcoming grin at the sight of Grant. "Well, look what the cat drug in."

Grant grinned. "Sure does smell good in here."

"Get over here, you."

In two long strides, he was across the room, grabbing Steph's mom in a hug. When he pulled back, he held her by her plump shoulders. "You bake those cookies just for me?"

She grinned up at him. "Well, of course I did—even though I had no idea at all that you were coming to visit today." She sent Steph a knowing look, taking in her soggy clothes and wet hair. "I'm guessing that cow is now safely out of the pond."

Steph nodded. "And I really need a shower—hey!" She faked a warning look at Grant, who'd already grabbed a couple of cookies. "Leave some for me."

"I'm makin' no promises." He winked at her when he said it and she dared to hope that the awkwardness between them was past.

She turned for the stairs as her mom tempted him with her fine cooking. "Pot roast for dinner."

Stephanie's heart lifted as she heard him answer, "Sounds too good to pass up. I'll stay."

Grant was downright relieved when Steph went upstairs.

He needed a little time to collect himself, to get used to the idea that she'd somehow grown up right under his nose, to get over his shock at how damn beautiful she was.

How could she have changed so much, so fast?

Shouldn't he have noticed she was becoming a woman—a beautiful woman—before now?

He needed to stop thinking about her. He needed to remember his purpose here today. It wasn't going to be easy, telling them about the sale.

But then again, now he'd said he'd stay for dinner, there was no big rush to get into it. He'd break the news during the meal. That way Rufus and the other hand, Jim Baylis, would be there, too. He could tell them all at once, answer whatever questions they had right then and there, *and* reassure them that he'd find other work for all of them.

Steph already gave riding lessons at the resort, by appointment only. He was thinking he could get her something full-time at the stables. And maybe he could arrange to get Marie something where there would be cooking involved. Not at the resort, but possibly in town. She did love to cook and she was damn good at it, too.

He washed his hands in the sink and took a seat at the kitchen table. Marie, as usual, read his mind.

"Beer?"

"You bet."

She set the frosty bottle in front of him and then went back to the oven to take a peek at the other sheet of cookies she had baking in there. A born ranch wife, Marie loved taking care of the house and keeping the hands fed and happy. When she was needed, she would get out with the rest of them and drive cattle to higher summer pastures or work the chutes at branding time.

As he watched her bustling about, he couldn't help comparing mother to daughter. Steph had inherited Marie's light hair and green eyes, but she'd got her height and build from her dad. Andre Julen had been as tall and lean as Marie was short and round.

When Grant was growing up, the Julens had owned and worked the next ranch over, the Triple J. Marie and Grant's mom, Helen, were the best of friends. So were Andre and John. Grant's sister, Elise, and Steph used to play together, running up and down the stairs, giggling and whispering little-girl secrets while their mothers sat at the table where Grant sat now. Marie and Helen would drink strong black coffee and share gossip while they did the mending or snapped the beans for dinner.

Helen and Elise Clifton lived in Billings now. They'd signed over control of the ranch to him, though they still shared in any profits—including the big windfall that would come with the sale. His mom and sister seemed happy in Billings.

Marie and Steph, though....

For them, losing the Triple J six years ago had been like losing a husband and a father all over again. They were ranch folk to the bone....

"I heard that resort of yours is full up for the Fourth of July." Marie put the lid back on the cast-iron pot.

The Fourth was three days away, on Wednesday. Grant tipped his beer at Marie. "You bet we are." Teasing her, he quoted from a recent brochure. "Treat yourself to magnificent mountain views, sumptuous luxury, and thrilling recreation at Thunder Canyon Resort." He brought his beer to his heart and really hammed it up. "You've come to us for the best in winter sports and entertainment. Now, you're invited to explore our winding mountain trails, weaving in and out of lush forests, dotted with cascading streams." He paused, dramatically, then announced, "Thunder Canyon Resort. The ultimate vacation or conference spot—peaceful, refreshing, with an endless variety of activities. Come to relax. Come to party. We offer fun and excitement, rejuvenation of mind, body and soul in a majestic setting, year-round."

Marie laughed and clapped her hands and joked, "Sign me up."

He shrugged. "I admit, after Independence Day, things'll slow down. But hey. We're doing all right— and Marie, you've got to quit calling it *my* resort." Grant did have shares in the partnership, but the resort had started out as the dream child of the most powerful family in the area, the Douglases.

"They're lucky to have you working with them," Marie declared, loyal as the second mom she'd always been to him.

He thought about the sale of the ranch again. And hated himself a little. But he'd made his decision. He was never coming back here and neither were his mom or Elise. For the old man's sake, he'd given Clifton's Pride his best shot, but he wasn't a rancher and he never

would be. Better to get out while a great offer was
dangling right in front of his nose.

Marie added, "Everyone knows it was your idea to
keep the resort open year-round. 'Nother beer?"

Grant thanked her, but decided to stroll on out to the
barn and have a few words with Rufus instead.

The grizzled cowboy sat on a bale of hay, his hat
beside him, rolling a cancer stick in those stiff, knobby
hands of his.

"Try not to burn the barn down while you're killin'
yourself with that thing," Grant advised.

Rufus only grunted and stuck the rolled cigarette
behind his ear. "You leavin' already? I just took the
saddle off your horse." Stiffly, shaking his gray head,
he started to rise.

Grant waved him back down. "I'm staying for
dinner."

"Smart thinkin'. That Marie, she can cook." Rufus
nodded sagely as he settled back on the bale. "Pot
roast, I hear."

"That is the rumor…"

The old cowboy took the cigarette from behind his ear,
shook his head at it and stuck it back there without
lighting it. "She's doin' just fine, in case you wanted to
know."

Grant knew exactly who *she* was. But for some
reason he refused to examine too closely, he played it
dumb. "Who? Marie?"

"No," Rufus said with great patience. "Not Marie. I

mean little Stephanie—who ain't so little as she used to be, in case you didn't notice."

Grant ordered the image of her glorious bare backside to get the hell out of his mind and played it noncommittal with a deceptively easy shrug. "Yeah. Seems like only yesterday she was running around the yard in pigtails."

"She's a born rancher, that gal. Works hard. Loves every minute of it. And smart as a whip. You keep her on as top hand, I got a feeling she'll shock us all and make this ranch a profitable operation."

Clifton's Pride turning a profit?

Now, that *would* be an accomplishment. Even John Clifton, who'd given it his all, hadn't really managed to do that. Somehow, the Cliftons always got by. But a profit?

Not a chance. And for seven years after his dad's tragic death, Grant had tried his damnedest to make a success of the place himself. Same old, same old. Somehow he stayed afloat. Barely. But that was the best he ever did.

It had been the same when Rufus took over. The ranch had yet to go under, but it was no moneymaker and Grant didn't believe it ever would be.

He sent Rufus a narrow-eyed look and muttered darkly, "You weren't thrilled in the least when I hired her on to take over for you. And now, all of a sudden, you're her biggest booster?"

Rufus picked up his hat and hit it on his thigh. "It's true. I had my doubts about her runnin' things. But I'm a man who's willing to give credit where credit is due. That girl has got gumption. She's got stamina. She knows what she's doin'. She also has ideas and they are good ones."

"Damn, Rufus. You're starting to scare me. I don't think I've ever seen you so gung ho about anyone—or anything—in all the years you been working here."

Rufus chortled and said something else.

But Grant didn't hear a word of it. He just happened to glance toward the wide-open doors that led to the yard.

He saw Steph.

Steph. In clean Wranglers, fresh boots and a little red shirt that clung to those fine slender curves he'd only that very day realized she had. Her golden hair hung, dry now, sleek and shining as pure silk, to her shoulders.

And those slim hips of hers? They swayed easy.

She tempted him with every step and all she was doing was walking toward him.

Grant watched her coming, struck dumb all over again by how beautiful she was. His breath was all tangled up in his throat and his heart was doing something impossible inside his chest and all of a sudden his jeans were too damn tight.

Damn. He was making a total fool of himself.

All Rufus had to do was look down to see how sweet, innocent, smart-as-a-whip Stephanie affected the boss.

How in the hell, Grant wondered, could this be happening to him?

Chapter Two

Stephanie entered the barn, the bright sun outside lighting her gold hair from behind, creating a halo around her suddenly shadowed face. Grant, his senses spinning, somehow managed to get his boots under him and rise from the bale.

She came right for them. "Hey, you two. Mom said I'd find you out here." She reached him, slid her warm, callused hand into his and flashed him a smile. "C'mon. Got some things I want to show you."

Prickles of awareness seemed to shoot up his arm from the hand she was clutching. Her scent taunted him: shampoo, sunshine and sweetness. It took a serious effort of will not to yank her close and slam his mouth down on hers—with Rufus sitting right there, fingering that cigarette he hadn't quite gotten around to lighting yet.

This is bad. This is...not like me, Grant reminded himself.

And it wasn't. Not like him in the least.

Yeah. All right. He knew that in town, folks considered him something of a ladies' man.

And he did like a pretty woman. What man didn't? But he never obsessed over any of them, never got tongue-tied as a green kid in their presence.

Not until today, anyway.

Stephanie. Of all the women in the world...

By some minor miracle, he found his voice. "Show me what?"

"You'll see." She beamed up at him, those shining eyes green as a matched pair of four-leaf clovers. "Come on." She tugged on his hand.

He let her pull him along, vaguely aware of a chuckle from Rufus behind them and the hissing snap as the cowboy struck a match.

Inside, she led him to the office, which was off the entry hall, not far from the front door. She tugged him over to the desk and pushed him down into the worn leather swivel chair that used to be his dad's.

He sent her a wary glance. "What's this about?"

"You'll see." She turned on the new computer she'd asked him to buy for her when she started in as top hand.

"What?" he demanded, his senses so full of her, he thought he'd explode.

"Don't be so impatient. Give it a chance to boot up." She leaned over his chair, her gaze on the computer screen, that fragrant hair swinging forward. He watched, transfixed, as she tucked that golden hank of loose hair back behind her ear. He stared at her profile and longed to reach up and run the back of his hand down the smooth golden skin of her throat, to get a fistful of that shining hair and bring it to his mouth so he could feel the silkiness against his lips. "There," she announced. By then, she had her hand on the mouse. She started clicking. "Look at that." She beamed with pride.

He tore his hungry gaze from her face and made himself look at the monitor. "Okay. A spreadsheet."

She laughed. The musical sound seemed to shiver all through him. "Oh, come on. Who's got the fancy business degree from UM? Not me, that's for sure." She pointed. "Look. That's a lot of calves, wouldn't you say? And look at the totals in the yearling column. They're high. I think it's going to be a fine year."

He peered closer at the spreadsheet, frowning. She was right. The yearling count *was* pretty high. He muttered gruffly, "Not bad…"

"I'm working on making sure they're all nice and fat come shipping day. And as far as the calves? I think the total is high there because of that new feed mixture I gave their mamas before calving time. Healthy cows make healthy calves." She laughed again. "Well, duh.

As if you didn't know. And you just watch. Next year, when those calves are ready for market, they'll be weighing in at close to seven hundred pounds each—which is really what I'm leading up to here. Yeah, my new feed mixture is looking like a real success. But bottom line? Winter feeding is expensive. Not only because of all the hay we have to put up, but also in the labor-intensive work of caring for and feeding our pregnant cows in the winter months when the feed has got be brought to them. If you really stop and think about it, *we* work for the cows. My idea is to start letting our cows work for us, letting them find their own feed, which they would do, if there was any available during the winter months…"

He watched her mouth move and kept thinking about what it might feel like under his. What it might *taste* like…

She gave him a big smile. "There are changes going on in the industry, Grant. Ranchers are learning that just because a thing has always been done a certain way doesn't automatically mean it's the best, most efficient and profitable way. What I'm getting to here is that lots of ranchers now are switching from spring to summer calving. And you know what?"

He cleared his throat. "Uh. What?"

"It's working for them, Grant. Matching the nutritional needs of the herd to the forage available can cut production costs and improve profitabil…" Her sweet, husky voice trialed off. "Grant? You with me here?"

"Yeah."

"You seem…distracted."

"No. Really. I'm not."

She leaned in a little closer to him, a tiny frown forming between her smooth brows, the amazing scent of her taunting him even more cruelly that a moment before. "Is it…" She spoke so softly, almost shyly, the savvy ranch foreman suddenly replaced by a nervous young girl. "…about earlier?"

He flat out could not think. His mind was one big ball of mush. "Uh. Earlier?"

A flush swept up her satiny throat and stained her cheeks a tempting pink. "Um. You know. At the creek…" Her gold-tipped lashes swept down. And she swore. A very bad word.

It shocked him enough that he let out a laugh. "Steph. Shame on you."

With a low, frustrated sound, she straightened and stepped back. He felt equal parts relief and despair—relief that she was far enough away he wasn't quite so tempted to grab her. Despair that the delicious smell of her no longer swam all around him.

"Damn it," she said a much milder oath that time. "I am so…dumb. Just…really, completely childish and dumb."

"Uh. Steph."

"What?" She glared at him.

"What are you talking about?"

She flung out a hand. "Oh, please. You know exactly what I'm talking about."

"Er. I do?"

"I keep…beating this silly dead horse to death over and over again. It's just not that huge a deal that you saw me naked, right?" She looked at him pleadingly.

For her sake—and his—he told a whopper of a lie. "No. Not at all. Not a huge deal at all."

"Exactly. It's no big deal and I need to act like a grown-up and let it go. But no. Every time you look at me funny, I'm just sure you're thinking how annoyed or amused or…*whatever* you are at me and it gets me all…flustered and I instantly start babbling away about the whole stupid thing all over again. Oh, I just… Will somebody shoot me? Please. Will somebody just put me clean out of my misery?"

He rose. "Steph."

She put up a hand. "Oh, wait. I know you're going to say something nice. That's how you are. Always so good. So understanding. So…um…" Her eyes widened as he did exactly what he shouldn't do and closed the distance between them. "Wonderful…" she whispered. "Just a wonderful man."

Getting close again was bad enough. But the last thing he ought to do was to put his hands on her. He knew that. He did.

So why the hell was he reaching out and clasping her shoulders?

Damn. Her bones felt so delicate. And the warm silk of her skin where the red shirt ended and her flesh began…

There were no words for that, for the miracle of her skin under his hands. There was nothing.

But the scent of her, the *feel* of her…

She swallowed. "Grant?"

He remembered to speak. "I'm not that wonderful. Take my word for it."

"Oh, Grant…"

"And I want you to know…" The thing was, he could stand here holding her shoulders and looking in her shining eyes for the next decade or so. Just stand here and stare at that dimple in her chin, at her slightly parted lips, her clover-green eyes…

"What?" she asked.

He frowned and, like an idiot, he parroted, "What?"

"You want me to know, what?" Wildly she scanned his face.

And he had no idea what. Not a hint. Not a clue.

And something was happening. Something was changing.

Something about Steph. She was…suddenly different. All at once her nervousness, her girlish embarrassment, had vanished.

Now, he looked down at a woman, a beautiful woman, a woman sure of what she wanted.

"Oh, Grant…" They were the same words she'd said not a minute before.

The same.

And yet totally different.

She lifted her hands and rested them on his chest and before he could remember that he should stop her, she slid them up to encircle his neck.

He shouldn't be doing this, shouldn't be standing here way too close to her, shouldn't be looking down at that mouth of hers, thinking how he'd like nothing better than to cover it with his own.

He shouldn't...

"Oh, Grant. Oh, yeah." And she lifted up on tiptoe and pressed that soft, wide mouth to his.

Chapter Three

More things he shouldn't be doing…

He shouldn't be wrapping his arms around her and pulling her close, shouldn't be easing his tongue between those softly parted lips of hers. Shouldn't be sweeping his tongue over the eager surface of hers. Shouldn't be finding the taste of her even sweeter than he'd dared to imagine.

Shouldn't be.

But he was.

He ran an eager hand down the curve of her back and cupped her firm, sleek bottom, pulling her up and into him, nice and tight. So she could feel exactly how she affected him…

Wrong, he thought.

Shouldn't...

But that didn't stop him. He kissed those soft-sighing lips of hers and when she sighed again, he kissed her some more.

She didn't seem to mind.

Far from it. She kissed him right back.

It was good. The best. Better than the best. He didn't want it ever to end.

But he knew that it had to. Exerting a superhuman effort of will, he lifted his mouth from hers.

There was a moment. Breath held. They stared at each other. Her eyes were greener than ever, her lips slightly swollen from that kiss he shouldn't have shared with her.

"I'm sorry," he said, and clasped her shoulders again to put her gently away from him. "I don't know what the hell my problem is. I shouldn't have done that."

And she smiled, a smile that trembled a little at first, and then grew wider. A smile that became so bright, it blinded him. "Oh, yeah," she said. "You should have. And I'm real glad you did."

For the first time ever, Marie's famous pot roast had no taste.

Not to Grant, anyway. The last thing he could think about that evening was food.

In his mind, there was only Steph: her smile, her laughter, the memory of her kiss, the look in her eyes across the table whenever their glances happened to meet.

He had a really big problem here and he knew it. He

kept almost forgetting *who* she was, kept losing sight of the fact that he was sworn to look out for her, that he could never, *ever* hurt her, that the last thing he would ever do was to take her to bed.

He was all wrong for her and he knew it. She was a find-the-right-guy-and-marry-him kind of girl. An innocent in her heart. Hell. He was reasonably sure she was still a virgin.

A virgin. Oh God.

Grant didn't go out with virgins.

And wasn't up for the whole marriage-and-family deal. Not now. Not ever.

And even if she didn't expect him to marry her, a girl like Steph would at least want something approximating what women liked to call a *relationship*. Grant didn't have *relationships*.

When it came to women, he liked things free and easy, fun and open-ended.

And sitting at the dinner table that evening, he felt trapped. Boxed in by his own burning lust for sweet little Stephanie Julen.

He needed to stay away from her. Oh, yeah. Since he couldn't keep his hands off her once he got close, the solution was simple: He would keep his distance. Yeah. That should work. If he just stayed away…

He poked more food he didn't taste into his mouth and resolutely chewed.

Marie asked, "Grant, are you feeling all right?"

He swallowed. Hard. "Uh, yeah. I'm just fine."

"You're looking a little strange. Is the pot roast okay?"

"The best. As always."

Rufus let loose with one of those low, knowing chortles of his. Grant sent him a dark look.

The old cowboy shrugged. "Hell, Marie. This is the best you ever made. Nothin' wrong with this here pot roast, nosirree. It's tender and juicy. Perfect in every way. Just like the potatoes and the carrots and these rolls of yours that are fluffy as little pillows. Uh-uh. If the boss has got a problem, it's not with the food." He forked up a big bite and stuffed it into his mouth.

"I don't know what you're talking about, old man. I've got no problem at all." Grant scowled at Rufus for all he was worth.

"Hear that?" Rufus grinned good and wide. "Boss says he ain't got a problem." He raised his beer. "I'll drink to that."

Grant looked away from the old man—and saw that Jim, the new hand, was staring at Steph. Grant resisted the urge to tell the fool to get his eyes back in his head where they belonged.

After all, who was he to tell Jim not to look at Steph? The cowhand seemed like a nice enough guy. Steph had mentioned after she hired him that he was a good worker. Rufus said he kept his area of the bunkhouse clean and in order. Maybe Jim was hoping to settle down, find himself a suitable woman and ask her to be his wife. If so, he'd be a lot better match for Steph than Grant ever would.

But Steph wasn't looking at the hired hand. Steph

was looking at *him*. And every time she looked at him, he wanted to jump up and grab her and carry her off someplace nice and private, someplace where he could peel off that red shirt and those snug jeans and have another long look at what he'd seen down by the creek.

He covered pretty well, he thought. Except for Rufus's sly remarks and the occasional shining glance from Steph, they all kind of carried on as usual.

There was pie and ice cream after the meal. Grant dutifully packed it away. And then, at last, Marie started clearing off.

"It was great, Marie. Thanks." He slid his napkin in at the side of his plate and pushed back his chair. "And it's an hour's ride back to the resort. I think I'd better get moving."

Rufus grunted. "Your horse is ready to go. Tacked him up before I came in to eat."

"'Preciate that." He pushed his chair under the table, and turned for the entry hall. The hat he'd borrowed waited on the peg by the front door. He grabbed it, yanked the door back and fled.

Too bad Steph was right behind him.

She caught up with him out on the porch. He didn't know what the hell to say to her. So he said nothing. She didn't seem to mind, just strolled along at his side across the yard to the post beside the barn where Rufus had hitched Titan.

As they reached the big gelding, she spoke. "Nice out now. Cooling off a little..."

The sun was just sliding behind the mountains, but it would be a while yet till dark. "Yeah," he said, without actually looking at her. "Nice." He took the reins and mounted. Then he made the mistake of glancing down at her.

She smiled. That wide, glowing, happy smile. Something tightened in his chest.

"How about a picnic?" she asked. "I can't tomorrow. We've got too many fences that need fixing around here—not to mention a couple of ditches that have to be burned out so those fat yearlings I've been bragging on won't die of thirst. But I could get away Tuesday. Say, noon? I'll meet you out by that big, dead cottonwood over in the Danvers pasture." He'd ridden by that tree earlier on his way to the ranch. Once, it had been on Triple J land. She asked, "You know where I mean?"

Tell her how you just can't make it. "Yeah. I know."

"It's about midway between here and the resort, so it won't take you all that long to get there. Over the fence from that pasture is Parks Service land and some nice shade trees. I'll bring the blanket and Mom's cold chicken. And the beer."

Tell her no, you can't make it. Tell her it's just not possible. Tell her now.

"All right. Noon on Tuesday," he heard himself say.

"Good night, Grant." She stepped back.

He tipped his hat and turned his horse to go.

The whole ride back, he called himself a hundred kinds of damn fool. Now, he'd have to call her. Tell her how something had come up and he just couldn't make it on Tuesday, no way.

He was so busy stewing over how he shouldn't have kissed her, shouldn't have agreed to any damn picnic, that he didn't even think about what he'd forgotten to do until he was back in his suite at the resort, changing his clothes. He stopped with one leg out of his Wranglers and gaped at his image in the wall-to-wall mirror of his dressing area.

He'd never told them he was selling the ranch.

"Mom?" Steph leaned in the archway from the front hall.

Marie looked up from her mending and smiled a tired smile. She took off the dimestore glasses she wore for close work and rubbed the bridge of her nose. In the pool of light cast by the lamp, her round face looked shadowed and lined, older than her forty-nine years. "Off to bed?"

"Mmm-hmm." It wasn't quite nine yet, but Steph— and her mother, too—would be up and working long before first light. "Just wanted to say good-night."

Marie set her mending in her lap and reached to pat the arm of the sofa a few feet from her favorite chair. "Sit a minute."

Something in her mother's tone alerted Steph. "What's wrong?"

"Come on. Just sit with me. Not for long…"

Reluctantly, sensing she wasn't going to like what

her mother had to say, Steph left the archway. She took the spot at the end of the sofa. "What is it?"

Suddenly Marie just had to take a couple more stitches in the sock she was mending. Steph stared at her bent head, feeling fondness mixed with apprehension. She loved and respected her mother. Most of the time, the two of them saw eye to eye.

But tonight, Steph had a feeling they were about to disagree.

At last, Marie looked up again. "You and Grant got something going on between you?"

Steph couldn't hide her trembling smile. "Oh, I hope so."

Marie stitched some more. Then, abruptly, she lowered her work to her lap again. "He's far from ready to settle down."

"I know, Mom."

"You two want different things from life."

"True. But…you never know how things might turn out."

Her mother shook her head. "You should see yourself. Pink cheeks and stars in your eyes…"

"Is that so bad?"

"You watch your heart, honey."

"Oh, Mom. There's nothing to watch. My heart belongs to him and it always has."

Grant had meetings all day Monday. From concierge to housekeeping to the AspenGlow Spa to food service to sales to public relations—and more—Grant was responsible for overseeing it all.

The longest meeting was first thing. From nine until eleven-thirty, he pored over plans for the projected 18-hole, par seventy-two championship golf course, which was still in the early stages of development, with construction scheduled to begin next summer.

At eleven forty-five, he met with his assistant to go over the calendar for the week. After that, he *could* have stolen a few minutes to call the ranch and tell them about the sale.

But no. It really wasn't the kind of news he wanted to deliver in a phone call. He felt he owed it to the hands and Steph and her mom to give it to them face-to-face. And there was just no opportunity for that, not that day.

True, he had no appointments that evening. He could make the time to drive out there after six. And maybe he should…

But the more he thought about it, the more it seemed best to clear his calendar for a few hours Tuesday afternoon and meet Steph for that picnic as planned. He could tell her then. And after he told her, he could ride back to the ranch with her and share the news with the rest of them.

In the meantime, he needed to prove to himself that what had happened the day before was not going to happen again. He needed to be sure that yesterday was just…some kind of fluke. A strange, over-the-top reaction to seeing Steph naked down by the creek, an offshoot of the sudden realization that she wasn't a kid anymore.

Now that he had some distance from the situation, he knew there was really nothing to worry about. Steph might be all grown-up, but she was still like a sister to him. A sister. Nothing more.

And there were a whole lot of pretty women in the world. A nice romantic evening with a fun, friendly gorgeous female would do the trick, put things firmly back into perspective for him.

As luck would have it, just such a woman called while he was in the first of his afternoon meetings. She left him a message in voice mail. She lived in San Diego and had come for the skiing in January when they'd hooked up. He'd enjoyed every moment he'd spent with her.

"I had such a great time last winter," her recorded voice teased, "I decided to try my luck over the Fourth. I'm up in the Thunder Ridge condos with a girlfriend. Give me a buzz when you get in. I can't wait to see you. *All* of you…"

He returned her call and set up a date for that night. His receptionist beeped him just as he was saying goodbye.

He hung up and punched the other line. "What?"

"Eva Post's on two."

Eva was his realtor. "Eva. Hey."

"Grant. I've got the offer. It's exactly as promised. The acceptance deadline is tomorrow at five, so we need to get together. We'll go over all the points in detail, as a matter of course, before you sign. But I guarantee you're going to be very happy. They're giving you everything you asked for."

"What about the closing date?"

"September first. The buyer was hoping we could make it sooner, but I explained that you needed time to shut your operation down."

"September first…" It was a reasonable date and he knew it. But still, it seemed like no time at all.

"No worries, I promise," Eva coaxed. "It's in the contract that you can take whatever time you need over the next *six* months to sell off the stock and equipment. As long as the main house, the bunkhouse and the foreman's cottage are ready for the buyer to move in by nine-one, she's happy."

She was Melanie McFarlane, an Easterner who'd shown up in town a few weeks ago and was staying in the main lodge at the resort. Melanie came from money. She had a degree in hotel management and she was buying Clifton's Pride as an "investment," she said. She planned to make the place into a guest ranch.

Grant's father would never have allowed such a thing. But John Clifton was dead. The price was more than right and Melanie's financing was rock-solid.

The only problem: Grant's concern for his people. Damn it, he should have carried through yesterday as planned, not let himself get side-tracked by the new, grown-up Steph. It was plain wrong for him to sell Clifton's Pride out from under them before he'd even *told* them he was doing it. And as things stood now, he wouldn't be telling them until tomorrow afternoon.

Eva asked, "How about four o'clock? You can come out to my office, or I can come to you."

"Four o'clock...today?"

"Not working for you?"

"How about tomorrow? Late afternoon. Say, four-thirty?"

"That's cutting it right down to the wire," the realtor warned. He said nothing. After a moment, she let it go. "My office?" she suggested.

"No. Mine."

The realtor agreed and said goodbye.

It would work out fine, Grant promised himself. He'd tell Steph and the others the news tomorrow—and return to the office to sign the papers afterward.

Grant's date sent him a sultry look from under her thick black lashes. They stood at the door to her friend's condo. From her expression, he had a pretty good idea what was coming next.

And it was.

"My roommate's away for the night," she said. "Come in for a drink? Just so happens I've got a magnum of Cristal chilling." He saw her expectations in her dark eyes. They'd had one fine time last January. Lots of laughs and some good, hot sex. She had every reason to assume it would be the same tonight.

He'd *planned* for it to be the same tonight.

But since yesterday, nothing seemed to be going as he planned.

Through drinks in the resort's lounge and dinner in the Gallatin Room, he kept wondering what the hell he was doing there. Wondering made him distracted and that caused long, awkward lags in the conversation. She'd asked him three or four times if he was all right.

He'd sworn he was fine, but they both knew the night was one big loser. Surprising, now he thought about it, that she'd even bothered to invite him in. He wished she hadn't—not now that he realized he just couldn't give her what she wanted from him.

So much for putting things back in perspective with the help of a fun, friendly, gorgeous gal.

"Thanks," he said. "But I've got an early meeting tomorrow."

She blinked. But she recovered quickly. He knew what she was thinking: If he was fool enough to turn her down, it was *his* loss. She moved close and he got a whiff of her perfume. Musky. Exotic. A scent he'd found damn sexy last winter.

Hell. He still found it sexy. Just...not for him.

She touched his cheek, her hand smooth and cool. He thought of Steph's hand—sun-warmed, rough with calluses—and it hit him like a mule kick to the gut.

All his denials meant exactly nothing.

He wanted Steph so bad, it was causing him to do the strangest things—like forgetting to tell her he was selling the ranch she loved so damn much. Like turning

down a hot night with a fine, sexy woman, an experienced woman who knew a lot of really impressive, in-
ventive ways to please a man...

He was in big trouble and he didn't know what to
do about it.

"'Night, then," his date said, and went in.

He returned to his offices in the resort's corporate
headquarters down the hill from main lodge. There was
always plenty of work to catch up on and he didn't feel
a whole lot like sleeping anyway.

By the next morning, Grant had himself convinced
all over again that he really had no problem when it
came to Stephanie. No problem at all.

He would meet her at noon, as agreed. He'd feel
what he'd always felt toward her before Sunday:
fondness and protectiveness—along with some serious
apprehension, which was only natural since she was
bound to be upset when she learned about the sale of
Clifton's Pride.

Riley Douglas, who was technically comanager of
the resort, but who had a lot of irons in the fire and pretty
much left the job to Grant, came by at nine. Grant brought
him up to speed on the progress with the golf course.
Then they discussed the pros and cons of opening a third
full-service restaurant at the main lodge. They already
had the upscale Gallatin Room and the Grubstake, where
you could get a great burger and all-day breakfast. Grant
thought they needed something in the middle range.

Riley agreed. "Come up with a few specifics—like who, what, how and how much. Then we'll bring it before the board."

Grant asked after Caleb, Riley's dad. The resort had been Caleb's brainchild. The wealthy rancher had provided the land, put together the investor group and overseen the original project's development. Without the drive and influence of Caleb Douglas, the resort wouldn't exist—let alone been a raging success from the day it opened for business last November.

Riley shook his head. "Sad to say my dad is gettin' old, slowing down a little…"

"Give him my best, will you—and your mom, too?"

Riley promised that he would.

After Riley took off, there were a couple of food service issues to settle and some calls to return. Grant had the decks more or less cleared by eleven and at eleven-twenty he was mounted on Titan and headed for the Danvers pasture.

Once he left the stable yard behind, he urged the horse to a gallop, all too aware of a certain rising feeling in his chest, an eagerness in his blood.

Steph was there, waiting on Trixiebelle, beside the twisted old cottonwood in the pasture that had once been part of her father's land. He saw her and his heart started pounding hard and deep and needful. Heat streaked through him, searing as it went.

Trixiebelle danced to the side as he rode up. With a

horsewoman's sure skill, Steph calmed the mare. Her strong, capable hand on the horse's neck, she beamed him a wide, happy smile—a smile that made his head spin and his blood race even faster through his veins.

Damn. She was beautiful. So beautiful, it hurt. Her hat hung down her back and her hair, pulled loosely into a single braid, caught the sun in golden gleams. And those eyes...

Green as spring grass.

"Come on," she said, and pointed to a stand of birch trees maybe a quarter of a mile away. "Over there." She turned the horse and took off.

Hopelessly ensnared, forgetting everything but the color of her eyes and the way her hair shone like a handful of nuggets in the sunlight, he followed.

Chapter Four

Steph spread the blanket in the dappled shade of the trees.

She had plans for today. Big ones. Romantic ones. Plans that involved slow, lazy kisses and tender, arousing caresses.

And, just maybe, even more.

Funny, but she wasn't the least bit nervous. She *was* excited. Kind of tingly all over. Her heart felt full to bursting.

At last. After all these years of loving Grant Clifton and knowing his feelings for her were strictly the brotherly kind, she saw her chance with him.

And she was taking that chance, going all the way

with it. No matter what anyone thought. No matter what her mother said.

"Here we go." He was back with the rocks she'd sent him to find. He knelt and placed four nice, big flat ones, each on a corner of the blanket to hold it in place against the ever-present wind.

"Great." She sent him a glance that lingered a little too long. Heat arced between them. He was the one who looked away, rising again and stepping back.

Oh, yes. She was certain. He wanted her and she did have a chance with him.

No, she wasn't quite so naive as her mom seemed to think. She didn't imagine that Grant loved her. Uh-uh. He did not. And as dewy-eyed as she was feeling, she intended to remember that. He thought she was innocent. But she wasn't—not in her heart. Not in her tough and pragmatic rancher's mind.

Stephanie Julen was a realist and she knew what Grant felt for her: He wanted her. A lot. He wanted her—and he didn't *want* to want her. He'd always considered it his job to protect her.

And now he intended to protect her from himself.

She was a whole lot more woman than he realized, however. And as a woman, she would do all in her power to see that he put those noble intentions aside and got what he wanted. After all, it was only what *she* wanted, too.

It had taken her a while to catch on, painful hours on Sunday—between the time he found her at the creek and the kiss they shared in the office. She'd been so sure he was mad at her or shocked or disgusted or something else equally upsetting.

But eventually, she'd figured it out. That strange look in his eyes every time he glanced her way…why, it was a *hungry* look.

And if she'd had a single doubt that he desired her, the kiss had burned all uncertainty clean away.

Oh, that kiss. He'd kissed her as if he wanted to gobble her right up.

And, well, Steph wouldn't mind at all being gobbled. Not as long as it was Grant doing the gobbling. Oh, my, yes. She got chills all through her every time she thought about that kiss, about the hard, strong feel of his body pressed close to hers, about the way he'd swept his big hand down and cupped her bottom and pressed her closer still.

She'd felt what she did to him then, oh, yes, she had. She'd felt what he wanted to do to *her.* She'd felt it and known that she was getting her chance with him. At last.

No regrets, she promised herself. She would take things with Grant as they came. Ride this wild horse and just hope against hope that maybe she'd manage to stay on.

He was a good man. And a generous one. A protector of the weak and the needy. A man you could count on when you were down.

But he was not looking for a wife. What did he need with a lifetime commitment, or even a steady girl? The women flocked to him and he seemed to thoroughly enjoy his bachelor lifestyle.

Stephanie really hoped she could make him see that even a man who had everything needed the right woman to stand by his side. But she wasn't counting on anything. She had no expectations of how it would all work out.

He stood back, watching from under the brim of his hat, as she went to where they'd hobbled the horses and began taking their lunch from the insulated saddlebags. She glanced over her shoulder, sent him another smile and thrilled to the lovely flare of heat that sparked in his eyes.

"I couldn't resist the urge to race you over here," she said. "And that means the beer is nothing but foam about now. You'll have to wait for it."

"It's fine," he said, his voice low and a little bit ragged.

"I've got lemonade, though."

"I love lemonade."

She laughed. "No, you don't. But until the beer settles, lemonade is what you're getting." She unloaded the plastic jar of lemonade, the food and the forks and paper goods, taking way too much pleasure out of knowing that he watched every move she made—hungrily, like some big mountain lion stretched out on a tree limb, his tail flicking lazily, eyeing his dinner. She loved knowing it wasn't just her mom's cold chicken he was hungry for.

Once she had all the food out, she dropped to the blanket and took off her boots.

"What are you doing?" he growled.

She had to cover a laugh. For a ladies' man, he sure was acting edgy and nervous today. She wiggled her stocking foot at him and answered in an easy tone. "Just getting comfortable." She set her boots in the grass, tucked her legs to the side and patted the empty space next to her. "Come on. Let's eat."

He approached with caution and again, she had to hide a smile. But when he reached her, he turned, dropped to the edge of the blanket—and took off his own boots. She watched the muscles in his back bunch and stretch beneath the worn fabric of his old Western shirt and felt a heat down low in her belly, a sort of melting, lazy sensation. She wanted...

His mouth on hers. His knowing hands stroking her body.

Whoa, girl. Slow down a little. All in good time.

He set the boots away from the blanket, set his hat on them and faced her, drawing his long legs up, sitting cross-legged. She served him: a paper cup of lemonade, a breast and a drumstick, a mound of potato salad, a buttered roll and some carrot sticks. Over the years, she'd watched him eat hundreds of times. She knew how much food he liked, what parts of the chicken he preferred.

"It's good," he said, as he dug in.

She was filling her own plate from the plastic containers. "Oh, yeah." She tasted the potato salad. "Mmm. My mom. She sure can cook."

He waved the drumstick at her. "You mean you didn't fry this chicken yourself?"

She laughed, glad that he seemed to be relaxing a little. "Don't worry. I wouldn't do that to you." She knew how to cook. Marie had insisted on teaching her the basics, at least. But she was always much too impatient to hang around the kitchen. She wanted to be out the door and on the back of a horse. So her biscuits ended up gooey in the center and half the time her chicken got charred. "I know my limitations. I'm a rancher, not a ranch wife."

He set the chicken leg back on his plate. Suddenly he seemed kind of thoughtful. "You're happy, huh? Working cattle? Up before dawn to get the chores done, freezing your butt off all winter, dripping sweat while you fix fences and burn out ditches in the blazing summer sun?"

She tipped her head to the side and studied his face. "What kind of question is that? You know me. Does a dog have fleas? Do bats fly?"

He frowned. But when he spoke, his voice sounded offhand. "Just making sure you remember there are other options for you."

"Too bad there's nothing else I want to do."

"But there are other things you *could* do. As I recall, you got As and Bs in high school."

"I'll have you know I got straight As."

"I'm impressed."

"I did my best in school. That doesn't mean I

enjoyed being there." She wouldn't have gone past the eighth grade if her mom and Grant hadn't insisted she get her diploma. And she still believed she could have held on to the Triple J, if only she'd been able to work full-time, instead of spending five days out of seven at Thunder Canyon High.

He advised in a weary tone, "You scrunch up your face like that, it might get stuck."

"Hah," she said. "You sound like Mom."

He chuckled. "Just don't be bitter. Believe me, it was the best thing. You'd have regretted not finishing high school."

"No. I wouldn't have. But it's okay—and I'm *not* bitter." She wrinkled her nose at him again. "Well, not much, anyway…"

He ate half of his flaky, perfect dinner roll. She chomped a carrot stick and got to work on a tender, crispy-skinned thigh. Eventually he said, "What I was trying to tell you is that I'm doin' pretty well now. I could help you out, if you decided you might want to give college a try…"

Emotion tightened her throat. Not because she felt she'd missed out on college, not because she wanted it. She didn't. Not in the least.

It was just that he was always so good to her, so generous. "Oh, Grant. Thank you. But no. I'm pretty much a self-starter. If I need to know something, I find a way to learn it. I never had a yen for any formal higher education. All I've ever wanted was a chance to do exactly what I'm doing now."

"I see." His voice was flat. He set his plate down beside him, only half-finished.

Distress made a leaden sensation in her stomach. "Okay. I don't get it. What did I say?"

He stared at her for a long, strange moment. And then he shrugged and picked up his plate again. "It's nothing."

"Are you sure?"

"Absolutely."

"But you—"

"No buts, Steph. I am positive to the millionth degree." He grinned as he said it.

She grunted. "Oh, very funny."

The Christmas she was seven, five years before their dads were killed, her mom had tried to talk her into asking Santa for one of those fancy American Girl dolls, the kind that came with a whole perfect miniature wardrobe—and a doll-size trunk to put all those fine clothes in.

Steph had sworn that a doll was the last thing she needed. She wanted a pony more than anything. She knew she was old enough for a horse of her own.

Grant, a high-school senior that year, had been over at the house, for some reason long lost to her now. She'd been following her mom around the kitchen, arguing endlessly, "I mean it, Mama. Don't you get me any doll. I don't want a doll and if you get me one I'll rip its head off. I need my own horse. I got work to do. Just ask Daddy. He'll tell you I'm his best helper and his best helper needs a horse."

Grant had stuck his head in from the living room to tease, "Oh, come on, Steffie, you know you want a pretty little doll."

She still remembered whipping around to glare at him, shaking a finger as she lectured him, "Do not call me Steffie. And I don't want any doll."

"You sure?"

"I am positive, Grant Clifton," she'd smartly informed him. "Positive to the millionth degree."

Now, he lifted his drumstick to her in a salute. "You were one feisty kid."

She faked a groan. "Oh, please. Feisty? Not me. I was a *practical* kid. And I got my first horse that Christmas, if you recall."

Malomar, her sweet-natured bay mare, had ended up sold at auction with the rest of the Triple J stock. It was one of her saddest memories: her mare being led into that horse trailer, the trailer kicking up dust as it rolled away.

That memory, somehow, was almost as bad as seeing her dad's lifeless body with that big red hole in the side of his head on the day that he died. The death of a parent was an enormous and terrible thing—too terrible in some ways for a young mind to comprehend. But the end of her life as she'd known and loved it?

That had been horrible, too. And by then, three years after her dad died, she'd been old enough to understand what was happening when she watched Malomar being taken away.

But she wasn't dwelling on any sad memories today. Uh-uh. She had the man she loved sitting right beside her, and he was finally seeing her as a woman grown. She fully intended to enjoy every minute of this afternoon.

They ate in silence for a little while, finishing off their drumsticks and potato salad, sipping their lemonade.

Finally Grant said, "I remember that you got your horse that Christmas, just like you wanted—and promptly fell off her and broke your collarbone."

She confessed, "It's true. I was never what you'd call a cautious kid."

"Uh-uh. You were brave and bold and nobody ever told you what to do." Those sky-blue eyes of his gleamed at her. She saw admiration in them.

For the fearless kid she'd once been? Or the woman she was now?

Or maybe…both? Her heart skipped a beat at the thought.

And then he was frowning again. "Look. Steph. There's something I really have to—"

"Oh, don't," she cried before he could finish.

Now he seemed puzzled. "Don't?"

"That's right. Don't. I know just what you're going to say and I don't want to hear it, okay?"

He actually gulped. "Er, you *know?*"

She set her plate aside and wiped her hands on a paper towel. "Of course, I know. How could I not?

Something like this, a woman always knows. I admit, you had me wondering at first. But I got the message eventually. Really, it's all just so…perfectly obvious."

"Obvious." He gaped at her.

"Yes."

He set his own plate down. And he knocked back the rest of his lemonade, crushing the paper cup in his big fist when he finished. And he swore under his breath. "Steph."

"Yeah?"

"What, exactly, are you talking about?"

Should she say it right out? Probably not. Her mom always used to tell her that men didn't like it when a woman got too direct, when a woman dared to take the lead in an obvious way.

But her mom was from a different generation, after all. From a time when women were expected to wait around for men to make the first move.

Thank God it wasn't like that anymore.

But still, what if she spooked him by laying it right out there, bold as you please? She didn't want to scare him off.

A sudden gust of wind stirred the trees around them and tried to blow the paper plates away, with only chicken bones to hold them down.

"Oops." Swiftly she gathered up the remains of their meal, stuffed it in the trash bag she'd brought and weighted the bag down with a rock. "There," she said unnecessarily when that job was done. He was sitting so still, watching her, kind of narrow-eyed, waiting for her to explain herself.

She stalled some more. "Hey. Want a beer?" She started to rise.

"Stay here." He reached for his boots. "I can get it." He pulled on his boots and grabbed the trash bag from under the rock. "You want one?"

She didn't much care for beer. "No."

She watched him go to the horses, something inside her kind of aching in a joyous way. His shoulders were so broad, his waist so hard and narrow. And he truly did have one fine butt.

And how could she tell him—that she knew he wanted her though he didn't *want* to want her? How could she make him understand that she didn't expect anything from him?

Except maybe his kisses and his eager embrace. Just this…wonder. And this joy.

And as for the rest? Well, why not just let the rest take care of itself?

He stuffed the trash in the saddlebags, got a beer and returned to her. She stewed some more over what to say to him as he set the can on one of the rocks and pulled off his boots all over again. He popped the tab and took a long drink. She watched his Adam's apple bounce up and down and continued her internal debate: What to say?

How to say it?

Finally he set down what was left of the beer. "Well?"

"Um. Yeah. Okay. I..." The words were right there, inside her mind, so clear. *I know that you're attracted to me, but you're thinking it's not right because you're not looking for anything permanent. You're telling yourself you won't take advantage of me. But oh, please. Take advantage. Take advantage right now....*

So clear. And so much easier to *think* than to actually say.

"What?" His gaze locked on hers. "Say it."

"It's...a beautiful day, don't you think?" Oh, Lord. How lame could she get?

"Steph..." His eyes said he couldn't make up his mind between reaching out and grabbing her—or jumping up and running clean away from her as fast as he could go.

"A beautiful day..." She said those lame words again and that time, she swayed toward him. He stiffened. She landed against his chest and looked up at him longingly. "And it's just you and me, all alone on this blanket under the trees..." She put her hand over his heart. Oh, it felt so good. So perfect, just leaning against him. Her breath was all knotted up in her throat. She wanted to stay right where she was, forever, yet she was absolutely certain that any second now, he would push her away.

But he didn't. With a low groan, he gathered her close. "Damn it, Steph."

She laid a finger against his wonderful mouth. "Shh. Okay? Just...shh."

He stared down at her. She could feel the warmth and the strength of him, the shape of him, so hard and manly. And cradled close against him like this, she could feel his heart, too, beating away in there, firm and deep. He said gruffly, "I can't...think, when I touch you."

"Good," she told him, feeling braver now, her love and her yearning leading her on. "Because you don't need to think. I don't *want* you to think."

His lip twitched. It was almost a smile. "Always so damn sure of yourself."

"Oh, no," she cried. "I'm not sure of myself at all. But I am sure about how I feel. Sure about...what I want."

"This is crazy." But his arms tightened around her.

"Oh, no. Not crazy. Right. Exactly right."

"You smell like sunshine," he whispered, the sound rough, as if it hurt him, just to get those words out. "And the way you feel, in my arms, when I touch you..."

"Just kiss me," she whispered back, lifting her mouth to him. "Just kiss me and the rest will take care of itself."

"Shouldn't..." The single word came out on another groan.

"Oh, yes. You should..." So...heady. This magic. This power she was finding she had over him. The magic of wanting. The power of desire.

Who knew it could be like this between a man and woman? She never would have guessed. Every nerve in her body seemed to be singing. She was shivery— but with wonderful, heavy, lazy heat.

"Damn. You're killing me, you know that?"

"Oh, Grant…"

He took her by the arms then, and she was sure all over again that he would set her away from him.

But in the end, he only grabbed her closer as his warm mouth swooped down and covered hers.

Oh, it was amazing. Her senses swam at the feel of him, pressing her close, his hands stroking her back as his tongue traced the seam where her lips met. With a sigh, she let them part for him.

He speared his tongue inside. She sucked on it, boldly, and when he retreated, she followed him, into the warm, hot cave beyond those wonderful lips of his.

She clutched his shoulders as he guided her down onto the blanket. He kissed her more deeply, still, his tongue delving in, sweeping along the edges of her teeth, stroking her own tongue in a long, wet glide.

Oh, it was heaven.

Just as she'd dreamed it might be.

His hand cupped her breast. Beneath her shirt and bra, her nipple hardened, aching. She moaned and lifted her body toward him, wanting more.

Wanting everything. Ready to have it all, at last, right there, on that blanket, in the lovely, shadowed, private place beneath the birch trees…

To have it all with Grant, as she'd always dreamed. To be fully a woman at last, with the only man she'd ever loved.

He kissed her chin, nipping it, whispering her name

against her eager flesh. He kissed the side of her neck, opening his mouth there, licking her skin, making her shiver in the most delicious way...

He kissed the hollow of her throat and she stretched her neck back, spearing her fingers into his hair, cupping his head and cradling him close, urging him to kiss her some more, to keep on kissing her.

To never stop.

"Oh, Grant," she whispered, "Oh, Grant. Yes. Please. Yes..."

His warm hand trailed downward. She wanted... more.

To be closer, to have his hand *there,* where she was aching and yearning, hot and eager. To have *him,* completely. To *be* with him in the most passionate, intimate way.

She moaned his name again.

And then, out of nowhere, for no reason at all...he tore himself away from her. With a low groan, and a guttural, "No!" he was gone.

"Grant?" She opened her eyes to see him sitting back on his bent legs, his strong hands on his knees, face flushed, mouth swollen, eyes heavy with the same need that made her legs and arms feel weighted, that made her body so lazy and hungry and hot. She lifted yearning arms to him. "Come back here. Back here to me..."

He swore. "No. This is all wrong. I didn't come here for this."

"But I don't…"

"Damn it, Steph. Listen. Listen to me."

Stunned, punch-drunk with longing, she dragged herself to a sitting position. "I don't understand. What's the matter? What happened?"

He rocked back on his stocking feet and rose above her. She stared up at him, so tall and strong, glaring down at her, the leaves of the birches rustling above his head, the blue, clear sky beyond…

A sudden chill swept through her. She wrapped her arms around herself against a cold that came from deep inside. "What? Say it. Whatever it is, just please, say it. Now."

And at last, he did. "I came out here to tell you I'm selling Clifton's Pride."

Chapter Five

Grant stared down into her flushed, bewildered face. Right then, there were no words to describe how thoroughly he despised himself. As he watched, the hectic color drained from her cheeks and her mouth formed a round, shocked O.

On a husk of breath, she pleaded, "No..."

He forced a nod. "Yeah. It's true. I'm selling the ranch."

She gaped some more, then whispered, "When?"

"I'm signing the contract today, at four-thirty."

She swallowed, caught her upper lip between her teeth, worried it, let it go. "Today."

"That's right."

"When...do we have to be out?"

"By the end of August. The new owner wants to take possession September first."

She seemed to consider that for a moment. "Not quite two months, then... Who?"

"What?"

"Who will be the new owner?"

"Her name's Melanie McFarlane. From out of town. She wants to make it a guest ranch."

"A guest ranch," she repeated as if the very words made her sick.

Grant felt like something squirming and loathsome, something you'd find buried in sour soil under a giant rock. He made himself confess the rest. "I meant to tell you Sunday," he said, as if that mattered. As if that made any difference at all.

"Oh," she said. "You meant to tell us. But you... forgot?"

"I was...distracted."

Color stained her cheeks again and he knew that *she* knew why he hadn't. Because he'd seen her down by the creek, seen her as a woman for the first time. Because his senses, his mind, all of him, had been filled with her. No room left to remember what he *should* have done.

She hitched in a hard breath. "Distracted. By me?"

"Yeah."

"And again, today, right? It's all my fault..."

"I didn't say that. Of course, it's not your fault."

"You met me here to tell me you were selling the ranch. And I *distracted* you again."

"No. Wait. You're getting it all wrong. There's no excuse for my not telling you. I know there's not. I'm not blaming you."

She only stared at him. And he saw it all, his own complete culpability, right there in her upturned face, in those amazing leaf-green eyes of hers: the kiss on Sunday. And worse than that, what he'd almost done just now, out in the open beneath birches, where anyone might ride by and see them. He'd been too busy kissing her to tell her the thing she most needed to know, too absorbed in the feel and the taste of her, too stupefied by his own lust for her, to be straight with her.

His throat felt like two angry hands were squeezing it. Still, roughly, he made himself say the things he'd planned to say before he made such a complete mockery of her innocent trust in him. "It's time to move on. To let go of the past. The world is changing, Steph. The day of the small, family ranch is over. Thunder Canyon isn't the sleepy mountain town it once was. Growth and change are inevitable and we all need to get with the program, we need to—"

She put up a hand. "Wait."

"Uh. What?"

"Don't give me a load of that *progress* crap, please. The last couple of years, it's about *all* I've heard. I don't need to hear anymore. Bottom line is you're selling Clifton's Pride. I get it. It's your ranch, after all, and your choice to make. You can let that buyer of yours turn a fine working ranch into some silly show-place where city people can play at being cowboys if you want to."

He winced. "Look. What matters is, you're going to be okay. I'll see to it, I swear to you, we'll get you a good job. Your mom, too…and I meant what I said about college. If you think you might change your mind, now you'll be leaving the ranch, I'll be glad to foot the bill…"

She just sat there, staring up at him. It was damned unnerving. He couldn't tell what she might be thinking—he only knew it wasn't good.

After the silence stretched out for way too long, she finally asked, "Well. Are you done?"

"I…" Hell. What more was there to say? "Yeah. I'm done."

"Great." She grabbed her boots from the edge of the blanket and yanked them on. Then she settled her hat on her head, gathered her legs under her and stood.

"Put your boots on," she said in a voice so controlled it made him want to grab her and shake her and beg her to yell at him, to go ahead and get it out, tell him exactly what she thought of him. After all, it couldn't be worse than what he thought of himself.

But he didn't grab her. He knew if he did, he'd only try to kiss her again.

God. He was low. *Lower* than low.

He sat, put his hat on and then his boots.

She asked in a tone that was heartbreakingly civil, "Now, would you please get off the blanket so I can roll it up?"

He glanced at his Rolex. There was time—to ride to the ranch, say what needed saying—and get back to his office by four-thirty to meet Eva. He grabbed his beer and gulped the rest of it down, then shook out the can and crushed it.

She took it from him and put it in her saddlebags. He rolled the blanket. She took that from him, too, and tied it behind her saddle.

They mounted up.

"See you tomorrow," she said, her clean-scrubbed, beautiful face absolutely expressionless.

"Uh. Tomorrow?"

She looked at him as if she wondered where he'd put his brains. "It's the Fourth, remember? The parade?"

That's right. Every year, the town put on an Independence Day parade. They'd both agreed to ride the resort's float. Terrific. Another opportunity for her to treat him like the pond scum he was. "Of course, I remember."

Something flashed in her eyes. He couldn't read the emotion. Anger? Hurt? Some bleak combination of both? He didn't know.

He felt like a stranger, an interloper, someone evil and cruel. And still, even now, when she looked at him as if she didn't know him, didn't *want* to know him, *he* only wanted to drag her right off that mare of hers and into his hungry arms. He wanted to touch her all over, to take off her shirt and her jeans and her boots, to strip her naked and finish what they'd started a little while ago.

She tightened her knees on Trixiebelle and off she went. Grant shook himself and urged Titan to follow.

Steph reined in and leveled a far too patient look at him. "In case you've forgotten, the resort's that way."

"I'm going with you."

She blew out a hard breath. "Haven't you done enough?"

"I have to tell them."

"No, you don't. I'll do it."

"No. That wouldn't be right."

Her glance slid away. He knew what she was thinking—after the way he'd behaved, he had no place talking about what was right. But in the end, she only said, "Suit yourself," and clicked her tongue for Trixiebelle to get moving again.

At the ranch, she went on in the barn to unsaddle the mare. Grant watched her go. She hadn't said a word to him the whole ride.

He hitched Titan to the rail by the front porch and mounted the steps.

Inside, he followed his nose to the kitchen where something wonderful was in the oven and Marie stood at the peninsula of counter between the kitchen and the breakfast area, rolling out dough for pies. Sliced apples, dusted in sugar and cinnamon, waited in a bowl nearby.

He forced a hearty tone. "How come it always smells so good in here?"

She stopped rolling and grinned at him. She had flour on her nose. "Stick around awhile and you just might get yourself a warm piece of pie."

He hadn't bothered hanging his hat by the door. Instead he held it in his hands. Which seemed sadly fitting. He fiddled with the tattered brim. "Believe me, I'm tempted. But I've got to get back…"

Marie tipped her head to the side and frowned. "Okay. What's the matter? You got a look like someone just shot your best mule."

He swore.

She plunked the rolling pin down and wiped her hands on the apron she'd tied over her jeans. "I'll get you a beer…"

"No, thanks. Marie, I've got something I have to say."

She made a small sound of mingled distress and expectation.

And he went ahead and told her, flat out. "I'm selling the ranch. You'll all have to be out by the thirty-first of August."

What had he imagined? That she'd go all to pieces? Not Marie Julen. Like her daughter, she was stronger and tougher than that.

"Well," she said evenly, after a moment. "All right." And she picked up the rolling pin again and got back to work rolling out that pie dough.

He stood there in the doorway from the central hall and wondered what to do next.

Marie glanced his way again. "Grant. It's okay. It's not the end of the world. Things change. Life goes on."

He almost laughed. "That's what *I* was going to say to *you*."

She pointed her rolling pin at the table. "Will you sit down, please? You're making me nervous, looming there in the doorway like that."

"No, I really have to get back."

"Good enough, then."

But he just stood there and watched her plump, clever hands as she carefully folded the circle of flattened pie dough into quarters, lifted it off the floured board and gently set it in the waiting pie pan.

He remembered that he'd offered her no reassurances. "Marie, I promise you. I'll see you're taken care of."

"Well, of course you will." She opened the folded crust, shaped it to fit the sides of the pan and took up a rolling cutter.

He watched her expertly trim the excess crust from the edge, turning the pan in a circle as she worked. "There'll be another job, a good job," he vowed. "I was thinking you might want to be cooking, maybe something in town, at a coffee shop, something like that…"

She had a second crust ready and took the cutter to it, sectioning it into strips to make one of those fancy lattice-type top crusts that always made her pies stand out for looks, as well as flavor. "Grant." She spoke chidingly, her skilled, swift hands continuing their work. "Stop beating yourself up. We'll be fine. Don't worry."

"I told Steph."

Those busy hands hesitated—but only for a second. "Ah."

"I don't think she's ever going to forgive me."

"You give her time, she'll be okay."

"Damn it, Marie. I don't know about that."

Behind him, down at the other end of the central hall, he heard the front door open. Steph. Her footsteps approached.

He made himself turn to face her, found her mouth set in a stern line and her eyes flat, giving him nothing.

"Did you tell her?" she asked.

Marie said sweetly, "Yes, he did." A glance back over his shoulder showed him she hadn't even looked up from laying the strips of dough in a crosswise pattern onto a floured sheet of aluminum foil.

"You leaving, then?" Steph said. It wasn't really a question.

The thing was, even while she was looking at him with those dead eyes, he still wanted to reach for her, haul her up close, breathe in the warm, sweet scent of her hair, feel her body snug and soft all along the length of his. He wanted to lower his head and crush his mouth to those unwilling lips—until she sighed and opened for him.

But of course, he did no such thing. He said, "I have to talk to Rufus and Jim."

"Don't worry. I already told them."

"Great," he said, guiltily tamping down a flare of resentment at her for taking a job that should have been his. "Still, I want to have a few words with them."

"They're in the barn."

"Well. All right, then." He hit his hat on his thigh. "See you later, Marie."

Marie sent him a smile as loving and warm as any she'd ever bestowed on him. "Ride safe, now."

"I will. He nodded at the cold-eyed woman standing beside him. "Steph."

"Grant." She said his name as if it made a bad taste in her mouth.

In the barn, he reassured Rufus and Jim that he'd find other jobs for them. Jim nodded and thanked him.

Rufus said, "Hell, boy. I know you'll take care of us. Haven't you always?" He *didn't* say anything about how John Clifton was probably rolling over in his grave at the thought that his own son planned to sell the ranch he'd sweated blood over, the ranch that had been in the Clifton family for five generations.

Grant was damn grateful for Rufus's silence on that subject.

He tipped his hat at the cowboys and left the barn. Out in the sun, Titan was waiting, hitched where he'd left him. He mounted up and got the hell out of there.

* * *

Grant rode Titan harder than he should have. He reached the resort in forty minutes. He turned the lathered horse over to the head groom and went up to the lodge. In his suite, he showered and changed into business clothes and went down the hill to the office complex.

Once he'd settled behind his desk, he called his assistant in. She gave him his messages, reminding him that he had an important dinner that night with two of the resort's main backers.

He hadn't forgotten. "Drinks in the Lounge at seven-thirty. Dinner at eight in the Gallatin Room. Right?"

She smiled and nodded. "You have some voice mail, too."

"I'll check it now."

She left him. He played through his voice mail. Nothing urgent. He checked e-mail—or at least, he brought up his e-mail program and stared at the screen.

Really, though, all he saw was Steph. Her sweet, open face, smiling up at him, eyes shining with admiration and trust. And the way she'd looked Sunday, right after he kissed her, soft mouth red and swollen, eyes full of dreams…

Did she hate him now? Was she ever going to forgive him for the way he'd behaved, for selling off Clifton's Pride when she was so happy there?

He tried to tell himself that maybe, if she hated him, that would be for the best. If she hated him, she'd stay clear of him. It would be a hell of a lot easier to keep his hands off her if she refused to come near him. She'd be safe from him.

He wanted that. He did. He wanted to...protect her from himself—and any other guys like him. From guys who didn't want to get serious. Guys who would steal her tender innocence and then, in the end, walk away and leave her hurting.

The phone rang. He let his assistant answer, but took it when she buzzed him to tell him it was Caleb Douglas.

Since failing health had pretty much forced him to retire, Caleb was at loose ends a lot of the time. Grant listened to the old guy ramble on for a while before finally cutting the monologue short, saying he had a meeting he had to get to.

After the call from Caleb, he took calls from a tour packager and from Arletta Hall. In her fifties, Arletta owned a gift shop in town. She reminded him that he was expected to be at the big parking lot on the corner of North Main and Cedar Street the next day at 11:00 a.m. sharp.

He promised he'd be there, rigged out in the costume she'd dropped off at the concierge for him last Friday, ready to climb on the float and smile and wave his way down Main Street.

"Does it fit all right?" Arletta fussed.

"It's fine," he replied automatically, though he'd yet to take it out of the box she'd delivered it in.

Arletta wanted him to know how pleased she was that he'd allowed her to take charge of the resort's float. "Honored," she declared. "I am honored. And those young people you sent to help me have done an excellent job. I think you'll be pleased with the results."

He thanked her for everything, but she kept on talking. About how well the float had turned out and how excited she was for him to see it, what a big day tomorrow was going to be, what with so many events planned.

"Truly, Grant, I believe this will be the most exciting Fourth of July our town has ever seen. Every hotel and motel is full, and the merchants are doing a record business—including Yours Truly, and I'm just pleased as punch about that, I don't mind telling you. Why, we're a boomtown all over again, aren't we? And so much of it is due to you and the Douglases. That resort of yours has been a real shot in the arm to our economy. We get tourists year-round now…" She yammered on.

When she finally had to stop for a breath, he thanked her for her kind words and gently reminded her that it wasn't *his* resort—and he really did have to go.

"Oh, well. I know, don't I, how busy you are? I understand. No problem. No problem at all."

"See you tomorrow, Arletta."

"Don't forget now. Eleven sharp."

"I'll be there."

"In costume."

"Yes. In costume."

She finally said goodbye, just as his assistant buzzed to tell him that Eva Post had arrived.

"Send her in."

"Grant. Hello." A handsome woman of forty or so, Eva wore a trim gray pantsuit and bloodred lipstick. She carried one of those soft, oversize briefcases. Grant rose to greet her. They shook hands and he indicated one of the leather armchairs opposite his desk.

Eva sat and unzipped her briefcase. She pulled out a folder.

Grant saw that folder clutched in her slim hand with its long, red fingernails and something inside him rebelled.

Sternly he reminded himself of all the reasons he was selling. It made absolutely no sense for him to hold on to a ranch he didn't need, a ranch that never more than broke even, a ranch that stood for the past when Grant was the kind of man who looked toward the future.

But those reasons? They didn't mean squat.

It was no good. He couldn't do it.

"Hold on," he said.

She paused, the folder still in her hand, and sent him a baffled look. "Excuse me?"

"I'm sorry. I've changed my mind. I won't be selling Clifton's Pride, after all."

Chapter Six

Eva Post stared at him as if he'd gone stark-raving out of his mind.

And damn it. Maybe he had.

She tried a laugh. "You're joking."

"No. I'm not." What the hell? He couldn't quite believe it himself. But still, it was true.

He couldn't sell Clifton's Pride. He just…couldn't do it. Period. End of story.

Eva took a moment to collect herself. She set the folder on the edge of his desk and bent to prop her briefcase against her chair. Then she sat up straight again and folded her hands in her lap.

Cautiously she inquired, "Is there…something about

this deal you're not satisfied with? I assure you, Grant, the terms are exactly as we discussed."

"It's not the terms. The terms are fine. More than fair."

"Well, then, what's holding you back?"

He remembered the expression on Steph's face just before he left her that day. She'd looked at him as if she didn't know him at all—as if she didn't *care* to know him.

That hurt. That really got to him. Steph's respect meant a lot to him. It cut him to the core to think he'd lost it.

But losing Steph's high regard wasn't all of it.

He told Eva, "The offer was *too* good, really."

She looked at him as if he made no sense at all. And when she spoke, her tone was patronizing. "Grant. Please. If the offer's too good, why are you telling me you're turning it down?"

"What I meant was, the offer was so good, I jumped at it without thinking it through, without stopping to realize that I really *can't* sell."

"Why not?"

He'd said enough. He stood and held out his hand. "I apologize again for wasting your time." In actuality, he hadn't wasted all that much of Eva's time. He hadn't asked her to represent him until after Melanie had put the offer on the table. "But I'm not selling and that's the end of it."

Eva rose and they shook. He walked her to the door.

Before she went out, she turned and gave it one more try. "You have to realize that Ms. McFarlane is actively seeking the right property for her needs. If you don't respond to this offer and she finds something else that suits her requirements—"

"Eva." He almost smiled. "Why am I getting the feeling you still can't believe I just changed my mind?"

She pursed that red, red mouth. "I doubt you'll get this kind of deal from anyone else."

"I'm sure I won't. But the truth is, I wasn't looking to sell in the first place. Melanie approached *me*."

The realtor refused to believe he meant what he said. "This is a good deal. A terrific deal."

"It sure is. But that doesn't change the fact that I'm passing it up."

An hour after Grant showed Eva out, Melanie McFarlane called. He knew he owed the woman some kind of explanation for backing out of their deal. Too bad he didn't have one—nothing anyone else, particularly an eager and generous buyer, would understand.

Still, she deserved to hear it straight from his own mouth. He took the call.

Melanie wasted no time on idle chitchat. "My real estate agent talked to *your* real estate agent a few minutes ago. What's going on, Grant? I thought we had a contract."

He apologized for waffling on her and then told her what he'd told Eva: that he regretted any inconvenience he'd caused her, but he'd changed his mind.

Melanie McFarlane was a damned determined woman. "Change it back," she said cheerfully in that brisk New England accent of hers. "What do you need with a ranch? You've got your hands full at the resort and you know it."

"Sorry," he said again. "I know I've inconvenienced you and I regret that. But I'm giving it to you straight here. I'm not selling."

Melanie kept talking. "Your realtor implied there might be some chance you'll be ready to sell, after all, in the near future."

"My realtor, understandably, hates to lose a sale. But she's mistaken. I won't change my mind. And again, I apologize for this. I never should have told you I'd be willing to sell."

"You're serious. I can't believe this."

He did understand her disappointment. Clifton's Pride would be a fine site for a guest ranch. It had a number of interesting, not-too-challenging trails, perfect for novice riders. It was picturesque, with varied terrain and spectacular mountain views. Most important, the ranch house and outbuildings were right off the main highway. To make a go of a guest ranch, access was key. Visitors needed to be able to get there with relative ease.

She demanded, "Is it the price?"

"No."

"I can talk to my banker. I might be willing to up the offer, if that's what it's going to take."

"I'm sorry. I'm not selling."

A deadly silence. Then, "Until I find something else, the offer remains open. I like to think I have good instincts, and right now I have a feeling you'll come to your senses—soon, I hope. When you do, let me know." The line went dead.

Grant hung up and scrubbed his hands down his face. He hoped he hadn't made an enemy of the McFarlane woman. In the resort business, a man did his best to get along with everyone. And she *was* a McFarlane. Her family owned the world-famous McFarlane Hotels.

No, he didn't blame her for being furious with him. Hell. He was furious with himself. He should never have agreed to sell to her in the first place.

He buzzed his assistant and told her to send flowers and a fruit basket up to Melanie's suite, rattling off another apology to go on the card.

After that, well, he hoped Melanie McFarlane would find another suitable property real damn soon and quit waiting around for him to change his mind.

Grant said good-night to the investor group at a little after eleven and went to his suite.

He started to change into an old pair of sweats, thinking he'd have a drink or two, watch the late news and hope that the alcohol would ease him to sleep. But then, what do you know?

He ended up reaching for his Wranglers instead.

The stables were closed at that time of night. He

could have dragged the head groom from sleep with a call. There were, after all, certain privileges that went with being the boss—among them, the right to inconvenience the help.

But as much as the idea of a midnight horseback ride appealed to his troubled mind right then, the Range Rover was faster. And he didn't have to wake anybody to get to it, since it was always ready and waiting in his private space in the main lodge's underground garage.

He made it to the ranch house in twenty minutes flat, pulling into the circular dirt driveway, cutting his engine and dousing the headlights as he rolled up opposite the porch.

For a minute or two, he just sat there, staring at the darkened house where he'd grown up, at the small pool of brightness cast by the porch light, at the bugs recklessly hurling themselves against the bare bulb beneath the plain tin fixture. Bart appeared from the shadows at the end of the porch, tail wagging, sniffing the air in a hopeful way. Never had been much of a guard dog, that mutt.

Grant got out of the vehicle. He shut the car door as quietly as he could and went to sit on the steps with the old dog. Bart sniffed at him a bit and then flopped down beside him, yawning hugely and resting his head on his front paws with a low, contented whine. Grant petted the dog as he pondered what exactly he hoped to accomplish, showing up there in the middle of the night when the house was shut up tight and all sane ranch folk were sound asleep in their beds.

Rufus emerged from the bunkhouse across the yard, long johns showing up ghostly white through the shadows, the dark length of a shotgun visible in his right hand. Grant gave him a wave. After a second or two, Rufus waved in return and went back inside.

More time went by. Five minutes? Ten? Grant didn't bother to check his watch. He just sat there with Bart, his arms looped around his spread knees, knowing that eventually the door behind him would open and a soft, husky voice would ask him what he was doing there.

It happened, finally: the click of the lock and the soft creak of the door as she pulled it inward. Then another, louder creaking as she came through the screen. She shut it with care. Bare feet brushing lightly on the porch boards, she approached and sat beside him.

He didn't look at her. Not at first. There was her scent on the night and the warmth of her body next to his. It was more than enough.

She spoke first. "So…what's up?"

He looked down at her slender feet. "You forgot your slippers."

She made a small sound. It might have been a chuckle. Then she said, "Mom lectured me."

"For what?"

"She told me I was too hard on you. She said Clifton's Pride is your place to sell as you see fit, that you've always been so good to us and I should be more grateful."

He shrugged, looking out at the night again, listening to the long, lost wail of a lone coyote somewhere out there in the dark. On his other side, Bart stirred, woofed softly, then dropped his head back on his paws again. "You tell her how I laid you down on that blanket and kissed you—how I almost did a whole lot more than just kissing?"

She made a sound that could only be called a snort. "Oh, please. She's my mom. Some things a mom doesn't need to know—and besides, Grant Clifton, you weren't the only one doing the kissing. You weren't the only one who wanted to do a whole lot more."

He looked at her then. So beautiful, it pierced him right to the core, her gold hair tangled, eyes a little droopy from sleep, wearing an old sweater over a skimpy pajama top, and wrinkled pajama bottoms printed with sunflowers. "Feisty," he said.

She snorted again. "I am not—and never have been—feisty."

"Right."

"Next you'll be calling me spunky."

"Never."

"You call me spunky, I'm out of here."

"I won't call you spunky. Ever." He raised a hand, palm out. "I swear it."

"See that you don't—and I guess I might as well tell you the rest of what Mom said."

He looked out at the dark yard again. "Guess you might as well."

"She said she can see how it would be hard for you

to tell us how you're selling the ranch, because you care about us and you don't want us hurting and you know how much we've loved being here. Mom says I should look in my heart and find a little kindness and understanding there. And you know what?" She waited till he turned his gaze her way and arched a brow. "Now I've had a little time to stew over it, I think Mom's right. I really hate when that happens."

He wanted to touch her—to reach out and smooth her hair, maybe guide a few wild strands behind her ear, to brush her cheek with the back of his hand.

But he didn't. He knew one touch would never be enough.

She said, "See, all I've ever wanted is my own ranch to run. I kind of let myself forget that this place isn't mine, you know?"

"I know."

"So…forgive me for being so thoughtless and cruel to you?" She stuck out a hand. "Shake on it."

He took her hand. Mistake. Because then, he couldn't stop himself from turning it over and pressing a kiss in the warm, callused heart of her palm.

"Oh, Grant…" she whispered on an indrawn breath.

He made himself release her. It was a real hard thing to do. "There's nothing to forgive."

"Oh. See, now. Of course, you would say that."

"I'm not just saying it. It's the truth."

She started arguing. "But—"

"Wait."

"What?"

"Steph…" He sought the words—and found them, somehow. "I'm never going to be…the right guy for you. Whatever we might have together, it wouldn't be a forever kind of thing. I just…don't want that."

"That?" She looked confused.

He elaborated, "I don't want marriage. Kids. All that. I'm not…my dad, you know?"

"I never thought you were."

"What I mean is, I'm not like him. I'm not…the salt of the earth. Not a family man. What I want, it's not what you want. When I was a kid, I thought it was. I told myself all I needed in life was a chance to walk in my dad's big, muddy boots. But that was a lie. A lie to please him—and to please me, too, I suppose. Because I loved him and wished I *could* be like him. Because the world is built on men like him."

"He was a fine man."

"Yeah. The best. But I'm not him and I never will be. I'm…restless inside, you know? I want to be out there, mixing it up, meeting new people, making things happen. I always knew, deep down, that I had more talent for business than for running cattle. I loved every minute of business school—the whole time telling myself and my dad that I planned to use what I'd learned to help keep Clifton's Pride in the black. But what I really wanted, what I dreamed of, is what I have now. I like the fast life. I like the progress a few around these parts hate. I enjoy my designer suits and high-powered meetings. I like making money. I like being single. And I plan to stay that way."

She considered his words, her elbow braced on her knee and her chin cradled on her hand. Then she nodded. "Okay."

It was a damn sight removed from what he'd expected her to say. "Okay?" he demanded. "That's all. Okay?"

"Yeah," she said, with another strong nod. "Okay. I don't want you to be anybody you don't *want* to be. And don't assume you know what *I* want. I might end up surprising you."

He had a very scary feeling she just might. And he wanted to kiss her. Damned if he didn't *always* want to kiss her lately. Kiss her, and a whole lot more.

"So we understand each other, then?" he asked, thinking that he didn't understand a thing.

"You bet."

"And I've got to go." *Because if I don't, I'm going to lay you down right here on the front porch, take off that sweater and that tiny little top and those sunflower pj's and finish what I started this afternoon...*

"See you tomorrow, then," she said, with just a hint of a smile in the corners of that mouth he was aching to kiss.

He stood and started walking, putting her behind him where she couldn't see the bulge at the zipper of his jeans. He got in the Range Rover and started it up, leaning out the window before he drove away.

By then, she stood on the top step, arms wrapped

around herself, looking so sweet and pretty, it took all the will he possessed not to jump down from the car again and grab her tight in his arms.

"I changed my mind," he said over the low rumble of the engine.

She grinned wide. "What? You mean you're going to come back here and kiss me, after all?"

Her words sent another bolt of heat straight to his groin. "Don't tempt me."

"Oh, get over yourself."

He told her then, flat out. "I turned down that offer. I'm not selling Clifton's Pride."

She gasped then. And she looked at him with such hope. With such gratitude and joy. Like he was Santa come with Christmas on the Fourth of July. "You're serious."

"As a bad case of hoof and mouth."

"Oh, Grant. Are you sure?"

"I am."

She shut her eyes, sucked in a long breath, and then asked, as if it pained her to do it, "It's not... because of how mean I was to you, not because of the hard things I said about turning Clifton's Pride into a dude ranch?"

He answered truthfully. "That was part of it, yeah. But not all. I don't know exactly why I changed my mind. I just know that, when it came time to sign on the dotted line, I couldn't do it."

She hugged herself tighter, rubbing her arms against

the nighttime chill. "I'm glad. It's selfish and I know it. But, Grant, I'm so glad."

He found himself wishing he *could* be the man for her. That man would be one lucky sonofagun. And he was going to hate that man when he started coming around. He'd be hard-pressed not to beat the poor guy to a bloody pulp just for living, just for being what Grant could never be.

He brought it back around to business. "You said you could make this place turn a profit. Rufus seems to think you can, too."

"It'll take time. But, yeah. I'm gonna do it. You just watch me."

"Oh, I will." He put the Range Rover in gear and drove away, sticking a hand out the window to give her a last wave, watching her in his rearview mirror as he rolled around the circle and headed for the highway.

During the drive back to the resort, he almost let himself wonder, what their lives might have been…

If things had gone on the way they'd started out. If the Julens still owned the Triple J and Grant still worked Clifton's Pride at his father's side. If Marie and Grant's mom still sat at the kitchen table together in the long summer afternoons.

If Andre Julen and John Clifton hadn't been murdered in cold blood out by the Callister Breaks nine years ago.

Chapter Seven

The dream was always the same—and much too real. It was like living that dark day all over again.

It started with Grant and Steph on horseback, just the way it had been that Saturday in September almost nine years ago. It was well past noon, the sun arcing toward the western mountains. Well past noon and cool out, rain on the way, clouds boiling up ahead of them to the northeast, rolling on down from Canada.

Steph, on Malomar, her hat down her back and her pigtails tied with green ribbons, was babbling away about how much she hated school. Grant rode along in silence, almost wishing he was twelve again like the mouthy kid beside him. Twelve. Oh, yeah, with years of the school she so despised ahead of him.

He'd graduated from UM the year before. He was a rancher full-time now. And he had an ache inside him, an ache that got worse every day. He missed the excitement and challenge of being out among other people more, of rubbing elbows with the rest of the world.

Steph stopped babbling long enough that he turned to look at her.

"You didn't hear a word I said," she accused.

"Sure I did."

"Repeat it to me."

"Don't be a snot. I got your meaning. It's not like I haven't heard it a hundred times before. You hate school, but your dad and mom want you to go, to be with other kids, get yourself a little social interaction, learn to get along with different folks. But you'd rather be driving the yearlings to market. You'd eat dust, working the drag gladly, if only your folks would give you a break and your mom would homeschool you, so you could spend more time on a horse."

"I'm not a snot." She laid on the preteen nobility good and heavy. "And I am so sorry to bore you."

"Steph. Don't sulk, okay?"

"Oh, fine." She was a good-natured kid at heart and couldn't ever hold on to a pout all that long. She flipped a braid back over her shoulder and sent him a grin. "And okay. I guess you *were* listening. Pretty much." She pointed at the rising black clouds. "Storm coming."

"Oh, yeah." The wind held that metallic smell of bad weather on the way.

Ahead, erupting from the rolling prairie, a series of sharp outcroppings appeared: the Callister Breaks, a kind of minibadlands, an ancient fault area of sharp-faced low cliffs, dry ravines and gullies. The Breaks lay half on Clifton's Pride and half on the Triple J.

"Wonder what they're up to?" Steph asked no one in particular. "They should have been home hours ago…"

Their dads had headed out together at daybreak from the Clifton place to check on the mineral barrels in the most distant pastures. They took one of the Clifton pickups, the bed packed with halved fifty-gallon drums filled with a molasses-sweetened mineral supplement that the cattle lapped up.

The two men had said they'd be back at the Clifton house by noon. It was almost three now…

Grant and Steph rode on as the sky grew darker.

"We don't come up on them soon," Grant said as they crested a rise, "we'll have to head back or take cover."

And that was when Steph pointed. "Look…"

Down there in the next ravine was the pickup, half the full barrels traded out for empty ones, both cab doors hanging open.

Grant's heart lurched up and lodged in his throat. "Stay here," he told her.

But she didn't. She urged Malomar to a gallop and

down they went. They raced to the abandoned pickup, and past it, up the next rise, as lightning split the sky and thunder rolled across the land.

Below, they saw two familiar figures, tied together, heads drooping, not moving…

And the tire tracks of pickups and trailers and even an abandoned panel from a portable chute.

"Rustlers!" Steph cried.

The sky opened up and the rain poured down.

"Wait here," he commanded. Even from that distance, he could see the blood.

But she no more obeyed him that time than she had the time before. The rain beat at their faces, soaking them to the skin in an instant, as they raced toward the two still figures on the wet ground below.

After that, the dream had no coherence—just as the rest of that day, when it happened, had none.

It was all brutal images.

Two dead men who had once been their fathers, tied together, the blood on the ground mixing with the pelting rain, so the mud ran rusty. He dismounted first and went to them.

Steph cried silently, tears running down soft cheeks already soaked with rain. "Daddy…" She whispered the word, but it echoed in his head, raw and ragged, gaining volume until it was loud as a shout. "Oh, Daddy, oh, no…"

And she was off Malomar before he could order her to stay in the saddle. She knelt in the mud and the blood, taking her dad's hanging head in her arms, pulling him close so his blood smeared her shirt.

Grant left her there. He took his rifle from his saddle holster, mounted up and went hunting. He didn't go far. Out of that ravine, and into the next one.

Just over the rise from where their fathers sat, murdered, bleeding out on the muddy ground, he found a man. Gutshot. Dying. John Clifton and Andre Julen hadn't gone easily. They'd taken at least one of their murderers down with them.

Grant knelt in the driving rain, took the dying man's head in his lap.

"Names. I want names," he commanded. "They left you here, didn't they, to die? Tell me who they are and you get even, at least. You get to know you died doing one thing right."

And the man whispered. Two names.

Grant left him there, moaning, pleading for help that was bound to be too long in coming, for rescue that would only happen too late. He checked out that ravine, found no one else. In his head was a roaring sound, louder than the thunder that rolled across the land—a roaring, and one word, repeating, over and over in an endless loop.

No, no, no, no….

He saw himself returning to Steph, to the bodies that once had been fine men.

She'd cut the ropes that bound his father to hers. She sat between them, there in the mud, holding one up on either side of her, her braids soaked through, caked with mud and the dead men's blood, one green ribbon gone, the other no more than a straggling wet string.

"I didn't want them tied," she told him, eyes wild as the storm that raged around them. "They would hate that, being tied. But they were falling over. They shouldn't be left to lie there in the mud…"

He knew he should dismount, get down to her, where he could pull her free of death, and hold her. That he needed to tell her some nice lies, to reassure her that it would be all right. Because that was what a man did at a time like this, he looked after the young ones and the females. And Steph was both.

But as he sat there astride his horse, looking down at her in the mud, before he could act on what he knew he should do, she looked up at him and she said, "Get the pickup. I'll wait here. I'll wait with them…"

"Steph—"

"Get it."

"You sure?"

She nodded. Lightning turned everything bright white. "Just go on." Thunder cracked, so loud it sounded like it was inside his head. She commanded, "You get it. Get the pickup now."

Time jumped. They were lurching through the mud in the pickup, the two dead men in the bed in back. Steph sagged against the window on the passenger side, covered in mud and their fathers' blood. She had her eyes closed. She opened them and glanced his way. He thought that he'd never seen eyes so old.

And then, with only a sigh, she shut them again.

And all at once he stood in the front room of the ranch house, holding his mother as she sobbed in his arms, calling for his father, yelling at God to please, please take her, too...

Grant lurched up from the pillows. The breath soughed in and out of him, loud and hard. He stared into the darkness, he whispered, "No..."

It took a few minutes. It always did.

He sat, staring, shivering, panting as if he'd run a long race, shaking his head, repeating that one word, "No, no, no, no," as, slowly, the past receded and he came to know where he was. Slowly he realized that it was over—long over, that terrible day nine years ago.

Eventually he reached for the bedside lamp. The light popped on and he blinked against the sudden brightness. He was covered in sweat.

For several more minutes once the light was on, he sat there, unmoving, staring in the general direction of the dark plasma television screen mounted on the opposite wall.

He reminded himself of the things he always forced himself to recall when the dream came to him: that it had all happened years ago, that he'd caught up with the other two rustlers himself and seen that they paid for what they'd done.

Things had been made about as right as they could be made, he told himself. There was nothing to do but let it go, forget the past.

Still, though, occasionally, less and less often as the years passed, the dream came to him. He would live that awful day again.

And maybe, he thought for the first time as he sat in his king-size bed, satin sheets soaked through with his sweat, staring at nothing…

Maybe that was right. Good.

Maybe it wasn't bad to have to remember the brutal murder of two good men. To remember how senseless it was. How cruel and random.

Maybe now and then, it was right and fitting to take a minute to mourn for John Clifton and Andre Julen and all that had been lost with them.

To live again his mother's grief and pain.

And to remember Steph. Twelve years old. Taking it on the chin, stalwart as any man. Propping up the dead men with her own young body.

Steph.

Brave and solid as they come on the day her daddy died.

Chapter Eight

The offices were formally closed the next day for the holiday. Grant went down there anyway. He had a few calls to make and some e-mails to return.

Then there was an issue with the concierge. He dealt with that. And head of housekeeping needed a little support with an angry guest who felt her room had not been properly made up and refused to be pacified until she'd talked with the manager. He gave the guest a free night and let the supervisor deal with the employee in question.

It was ten-thirty when he got back to his suite and dragged out the big box Arletta Hall had dropped off last week, the one with his costume inside. He took off the lid and stared down at a pair of ancient, battered boots, a grimy bandanna, an ugly floppy hat and some dirty pink long johns.

He was supposed to be a gold miner—a tribute not only to Thunder Canyon's first gold rush over a century before, but also to the gold fever that had struck two years ago, when somebody found a nugget in an abandoned mine shaft after a local kid fell in there during a snowstorm and the whole town went wild looking for him.

All right. Maybe old-time miners did run around in dirty long johns. Maybe they were too wild with gold fever to bother wearing pants. But the damn thing was a little *too* authentic. It actually had one of those button flaps in back so a man wouldn't have to pull them down when he paid a visit to the outhouse. And in front, well, if he wore that thing by itself around Steph, no one would have any doubt about how glad he was to see her.

Something had to be done. And fast.

Arletta's chunky charm bracelet clattered as she put her hands together and moaned in dismay. "Jeans? But I really don't think jeans are the look we should be going for…"

Behind him, Grant heard a low, husky chuckle and knew it was coming from Steph. "They're *old,* these jeans," he reasoned. "Nice and faded and worn." He'd borrowed them from the groom at the stables, the same one who always had a hat to loan. "And I want to be a more *responsible* kind of gold miner. You know, a guy who remembers to put on his pants in the morning."

"Oh. Well. I just don't think we want to go this way…." Arletta moaned some more, all fluttery indecision. Townspeople milled around them, busy getting ready to play their own parts in the parade.

Grant leaned down to whisper in the shopkeeper's pink ear—she was a tiny little skinny thing, no more than four feet tall and she smelled like baby powder. "Listen, Arletta," he whispered low. "If you think I'm running around in dirty long johns with no pants, you'll have to find yourself another prospector…"

"Oh, dear Lord. No. We can't have that." She sucked it up. At last. "It's all right. Those jeans will just have to do."

He gave her a grin. "Arletta, you're the best."

"Oh. My." She simpered up at him. "You charmer, you…" She tugged on the dirty bandanna around his neck. "There. That's better. And the hat looks just great, I must say—and tell me now. What do you think of the float?"

They turned to admire it together. It consisted of a papier-mâché mountain topped with sparkly cotton snow. A miniature prairie lay below, complete with split rail fences, a creek made of crinkled up aluminum foil, a couple of homemade cottonwoods and some papier-mâché livestock happily munching away at the AstroTurf grass. There was also a log cabin trailing a construction paper cloud of smoke from the chimney and, clinging to the side of the mountain, a miniature replica of the resort's sprawling main lodge. A sparkly rainbow bearing the glittery words, Thunder Canyon Resort, arched over the whole creation.

Grant swept off his hat and held it to his chest. "Magnificent," he solemnly intoned.

Arletta did more simpering. "Oh, I am so pleased you think so." She grabbed a gold pan from a pile of props and also a baseball-size hunk of papier-mâché, spray-painted gold. "Here you go. Your gold pan and your nugget."

He hefted the hunk of papier-mâché. "Hey. With a nugget this size, I don't need this damn gold pan. In fact, I think I'll just head over to the Hitching Post right now and order a round of drinks for everyone, on me. Isn't that what miners do when they make a big strike, head for the bar and get seriously hammered?"

"You are such a kidder," giggled Arletta. Then she chided, "The gold pan is part of the costume—and you can join your rowdy friends at the Hitching Post later. After the parade."

He pretended to look crestfallen. "Yes, ma'am."

"Now, we have to get you in place. And Stephanie, too…" She signaled Steph, who waited a few yards away, wearing a leather cowgirl outfit with a short skirt and a tooled jacket, both skirt and jacket heavy on the leather fringe. Fancy red boots and a big white hat completed the costume. She had Trixiebelle with her, all tacked up in a red and white saddle, with bridle to match. It was a real Dale Evans-style getup. And she looked damn cute in it.

"This way, you two…" Arletta instructed.

The shopkeeper showed them where they were supposed to stand. Trixiebelle, a real trouper, didn't balk once as Steph led her up onto the float and into position and then swung herself into the saddle before Grant could jump up there and offer to help.

As if a skilled horsewoman liked Steph needed a hand up. She'd laugh at him if he offered. And she'd probably suspect that he was only trying to get a look under that short skirt, anyway.

Get a look under her skirt?

Where the hell had that come from?

He was thirty-two years old, for crying out loud. Far past the age when a guy tried to find ways to sneak a peek up a girl's skirt.

"Grant. Are you with me here?" Arletta was frowning, looking slightly miffed. "I need your full attention, now."

He shook himself and tried to appear alert. "You got it."

She pointed. "Stand there."

He took his place by the crinkled foil stream and Arletta stood back to study the picture they made. "Hmm," she said, somehow managing to be both thoughtful and agitated at the same time. "Hmm… oh, no. Oh, my…"

"What?" Grant demanded, beginning to worry that his fly might be open.

"It's too spotty."

Grant cast a quick glance Steph's way. He could tell she was trying real hard not to laugh. "Uh…spotty?" he carefully inquired.

Arletta frowned with great seriousness. "Yes. The composition. It's simply not…pulled together."

The high school band had started to play at the front of the line. "I think we're going to be rolling in a minute or two here," he warned.

"You're right. Action must be taken." Arletta started pointing again. "Grant. Lean that pan against the rail fence. And go stand by the horse—yes. Right there. At the head. Stephanie, let him hold the reins." Steph muffled a snort of amusement as she handed them over. "Much better, yes…." Arletta kept rattling off instructions. "Grant, you'll have to wave with that nugget, hold it up nice and high so everyone can see you've really struck it rich. Do it."

He waved with the fake nugget.

"Oh, yes. That's it. And Stephanie, take off your hat, wave with it. Big smiles, both of you. Big, big smiles." Grant smiled for all he was worth. Evidently Steph, mounted behind, was doing the same. Because Arletta clapped her hands and cried out gleefully, "Exactly! We've got it. That's perfect! Wonderful! Just right!"

And just in time, too. The float gave a lurch and started moving—slowly, like a big ocean liner inching from port. They pulled away from Arletta, who continued to gesture wildly and rattle off instructions. "Wave,

Grant! That's it. Wave that nugget. Smiling, you two. Don't forget. Smiling, smiling! That's the way…"

He felt the toe of Steph's fancy boot gently nudge him in the middle of the back.

"What?" he growled out of the corner of his mouth as he waved his nugget high and proud.

She nudged him again, but she didn't say a word. He glanced back at her and she was waving that big hat of hers, smiling wide at the crowds that lined the covered sidewalks to either side. People cheered and stomped in appreciation and kids ran out in the street to grab the candy and bubble gum the driver of the truck that pulled the float was tossing in handfuls out his open window.

Up ahead, the band played "Yankee Doodle Dandy." Grant looked out at the crowd and thought that he'd never seen so many people crowding the streets of his town.

This Thunder Canyon Fourth of July Parade was the biggest one ever, by far.

Even in that silly miner's getup, with the fake nugget in his hand, Grant felt a surge of real pride—that his town was growing. Thriving. That *he* was a part of Thunder Canyon's new prosperity. That his own efforts had contributed, at least a little, to the boom that had started with a modern-day gold rush and continued with the swift and rousing success of the Thunder Canyon Resort.

Chapter Nine

As the float rolled down Main Street, past the charming century-old brick buildings and covered sidewalks of Thunder Canyon's Old Town, Steph waved her hat wildly—and planned her next move with Grant.

Her mom wouldn't have approved of her scheming in the least. Partly because Marie Julen was a woman who found scheming beneath her—and partly because she remained doubtful about her daughter's decision to grab her chance with Grant while she could.

Too bad. Steph was all grown-up now, old enough to make her own decisions. Yeah, she and Grant had had a rough patch in their new relationship when he'd considered selling the ranch. But they'd gotten through that. Things were looking up in big way.

And today was a day tailor-made to suit her plans. A great opportunity for the two of them to be together, to enjoy each other's company. To have a little fun.

The celebrations would continue all day and into the night. There would be the annual races, right there on Main Street. And after the races, over at the fairgrounds, the big Independence Day Rodeo. She planned to sit next to Grant for the rodeo—except during the barrel races where she was a contestant.

She figured she could leave him on his own while she competed. By then, he'd feel duty-bound to root for her while she raced—especially since the resort was her sponsor and had paid a pretty penny for her top-of-the-line gear.

After the rodeo, she'd get him to take her to dinner. And after dinner, the big Independence Day dance.

She just had to make sure that, when the parade was over, Grant didn't get away.

The problem was Trixiebelle. She needed to get the mare back to her trailer and over to the fairgrounds for the rodeo. But if she took the time do all that, she just knew Grant would find some way to disappear on her. It never paid to give a skittish man the time to have second thoughts. To keep him with her for the day, she'd have to stay close at his side from the moment the float pulled to a stop.

She *needed* someone to take care of Trixiebelle—
and what do you know? As the float finished its ride
down Main and turned into the parking lot of a local
motel called the Wander-On Inn, she spotted Rufus and
Jim. The hands stood right there on the sidewalk, at the
edge of the lot.

She waved at them and shouted, "Rufus! Hey, meet
us when this thing comes to a stop!"

Rufus pulled a sour face, but he and Jim were there
waiting when she led Trixiebelle down off the float.
Arletta, who'd somehow managed to race down Main
through the packed crowds and was waiting when the
parade trailed into the motel lot, had cornered Grant
again and was gushing all over him.

Great.

She had a minute or two, at least, before he'd have
time to make his escape.

"Rufus—"

The old cowboy grunted. "You say my name that
way, gal, and I know I'm about to be gettin' my orders."

"I just wonder if you'd mind taking Trixiebelle back
to the parking lot at Cedar Street? Her trailer's there,
hitched to my pickup, along with my racing costume
and barrel saddle. If you could—"

"Hell. Why not?" He knew where to meet her and
what time. He rattled them off. "Right?"

"Thanks."

"No thanks are needed—and you better hurry. Looks
like your gold miner's gettin' away."

She laughed and paused long enough to kiss his grizzled cheek. "You know too much, you realize that."

"I'm arthritic, not blind. Best get a move on." Beside him, Jim was looking at the ground.

Steph knew the hand was kind of sweet on her, but she'd never encouraged him. She'd always kept things strictly professional between them.

Now, when he finally glanced up, she gave him a quick, no-nonsense nod—not ignoring him, but not encouraging him, either—and then whirled, her mind instantly back on the man who filled her heart. Grant was heading off into the crowd.

"Hey, Mr. Miner!"

He stopped. Turned.

She stuck out a hip and propped a fist on it. "Buy a girl a drink?"

He grunted. "It's barely noon."

She hurried to catch up and looped her arm with his. "A root beer will do." She linked her arm with his. "Love that hat." It was leather, floppy and silly and it made her smile. And he was so big and tall and handsome, even in his pink long-john shirt and dirty bandanna. Just looking up at him had her heart beating faster. He was her favorite cowboy and he always had been.

He groused, "As a matter of fact, I was just thinking about where I could go to change." The good news was he made no effort to pull away from her. In fact, he looked down at her as if he never wanted to leave her side—and hated himself because of it.

She could almost feel sorry for him. If she wasn't so dang happy to be the object of his guilty lust. "You can't change your clothes."

"Why the hell not?"

"Well, if *you* change, then *I'll* change. You know you'd hate that."

A smile tried to tug at the edges of his scowl. "Okay. I admit it. You look damn cute in that skirt."

"Thank you." She shook the arm that wasn't clutching his, making the fringe dance. "It's this fringe, right? You just love a lot of fringe on a woman."

"Er...that's it. The fringe."

The loudspeakers over by the grandstand in front of the town hall crackled to life and over the noise of the crowd, they heard the voice of the honorable Philo T. Brookhurst, town mayor. "Folks, step back off the street now. Time to cordon off Main from South Main to Nugget. We're gearing up fast for the annual Thunder Canyon Races. Get your kids ready to win a twenty-dollar prize."

She let go of his arm and grabbed his hand. "Come on. The toddlers run first. They're always so cute, the way they forget where they're going and wander off in all directions. Let's get us a good spot."

She hauled him along behind her, weaving her way through the crowd. He didn't try to protest, so she figured she had him—for the moment anyway.

And she did. She had him.

He stayed close at her side. He bought her that root beer and they watched the races, every one of them, from the plump toddlers on up to the final race for "octogenarians and above." A ninety-five-year-old woman won that one. She held up her twenty-dollar prize and let out a whoop you could hear all the way to Billings. Then the old gal threw her arms around the mayor's thick neck and planted a big smacker right on his handlebar moustache.

Steph leaned close to Grant and teased in a whisper, "Now *that* is a feisty woman."

"Yeah." He sent her a smoldering look, one that strayed to her mouth. She wished with all her heart that he would kiss her. Right there on Main Street, with the whole town watching. But he didn't. He only whispered back, "Damn spunky, and that is no lie."

After the races, Steph gave Grant no time to start making those see-you-later noises. She asked him for a ride over to the fairgrounds. After all, she told him sweetly, Rufus had taken her pickup to pull Trixiebelle's trailer over there for her.

What could he say? He would never leave her stranded without a ride.

He'd parked his black Range Rover behind the town hall.

"Very nice," she told him, once she'd climbed up into the plush embrace of the leather passenger seat. She sniffed the air. "Mmm. Smells like money in here."

"Smart aleck," he muttered as he stuck the key into the ignition. Before he could turn it over, she reached across and laid her hand on his.

114   THE MAN WHO HAD EVERYTHING

Heat. Oh, she did love the feel of that. Every time she touched him, a jolt of something hot and bright went zipping all through her body. Making her grin. Making her shiver in the most delightful way.

"Steph," he warned, low and rough.

She leaned closer. "Kiss me."

He was looking at her mouth again. "You're just asking for trouble, you know that?"

"Uh-uh. I'm not…"

"Oh, no?"

"What I'm asking for is a kiss." She dared to let her fingers trail up his arm. Amazing, that arm. So warm and hard and muscular beneath the grimy pink sleeve of his long johns.

"A kiss?" he repeated, still staring at her mouth.

"Yeah. A long, slow, wet one." She brushed the side of his neck with her forefinger and felt a shudder go through him. "That's what I want. And I know that *you* know the kind I mean…"

He said her name again, this time kind of desperately.

"Oh, yeah," she whispered as he leaned in that extra fraction of an inch and pressed his lips to hers.

Oh, my. He tasted so good. She opened her mouth and sucked his tongue inside, throwing her arms around him, letting out a moan of pure joy.

He stopped it much too soon. Taking her by the elbows, he peeled her off him and held her at arm's length.

She tried to look innocent. "What? You don't like kissing me?"

He said something under his breath, a very bad word. "You know I do. And if you keep this up…"

"What? You'll make love to me? Oh, now wouldn't that be horrible?"

"You're just a kid and you—"

She swore then, a word every bit as bad as the one he'd used. "Maybe you'd like to see my driver's license. It's got my birthday right on there, in case you forgot how old I am."

"You know what I mean. You don't…date a lot."

Gently she pulled free of his grip. "And you do. I know that. I'm not some dreamy fool, though you keep trying to convince yourself I am."

He actually looked flustered, his face red and his blue eyes full of tender indecision. "I…meant what I said last night, that's all. It wouldn't last. And you'd end up hating me. I couldn't take that."

She held his eyes and banished all hint of teasing from her tone as she told him, "No matter what happens, Grant, I'll never hate you."

"You say that now…"

"Because it's true." She hooked her seat belt. When he didn't move, she slanted him another glance. "Come on. Let's go. The barrel race is up first. I have to track Rufus down and get my horse."

For a moment, she thought he'd say more. But then he only swore again and reached for the key to start the engine.

* * *

She lost the barrel race.

Got too close to the second barrel, knocked it clean over. And that was it. The five-second penalty for tipping a barrel took her right out of the running in a race where the difference between first and second place was in fractions of a second.

She gave Trixiebelle an apple and handed her over to Rufus, who said he'd see to getting her home. "Jim can take the other truck back and I'll take yours." He shook a gnarled finger at her. "You watch yourself now. Don't go stealin' some innocent cowboy's heart…"

With teasing solemnity, she vowed, "You know I would never do any such thing." The ranch hand snorted and waved her away and she went to find Grant, who'd saved her a place in the stands.

He threw an arm around her and pulled her close. "Hey, tough luck. At least *we* know you're the best."

She thought that she wouldn't mind losing every race she entered, if it meant Grant would put his arm around her and tell her how great she was. "Truth is, I'm thinking my barrel racing days are over. I just don't have the time to practice like I used to. After all, I've got a ranch to run—not to mention teaching the occasional resort-happy tenderfoot how to stay in the saddle."

He looked at her admiringly. "You're a good sport, Steph. Always have been."

It wasn't the kind of compliment the average woman

could appreciate. But Steph recognized high praise when she heard it.

He sat right there at her side through the whole rodeo, from roping to calf wresting, bareback and bronc riding and bull riding, too. It was a dream of a day and she never wanted it to end.

They were back at his four-by-four at a little before five. "Take me to dinner," she commanded.

"This is getting damn dangerous," he said.

But he didn't say no.

He drove to a friendly Italian place he liked in New Town, east of the historic area around Main. He said they'd never get seats anywhere in Old Town, where all the restaurants would be packed with tourists and folks down from the resort, looking for a little taste of Thunder Canyon hospitality.

They shared a bottle of Chianti and she told him more about her plans for improvements at Clifton's Pride. He talked about the new golf course that a world-famous golf pro was designing for the resort, about his ideas for further expansion, about how much he loved the work he was doing.

She grinned across the table at him. "You don't have to say how much you love your work. It's right there in your eyes every time you mention it."

He teased, "Are you telling me I'm boring you?"

"Uh-uh. Not in the least. I like to see you happy, with your eyes shining, all full of your big plans."

He leaned close again. "You do, huh?"

"I do." She raised her wineglass. He touched his against it.

When he set the glass down, he said, "This is nice."

And she nodded. "Yeah. It is. Real nice."

"Too nice…" His tone had turned bleak.

And after that, he grew quiet. Oh, he was kind and gentle as ever. If she asked a question, he answered it. He wasn't rude or anything.

But she knew what had happened. He'd caught himself having a good time with her—in a man-and-woman kind of way.

And that scared him to death.

"I'm taking you home now," he said, when they left the restaurant. His strong jaw was set. It was a statement of purpose from which she knew he would not waver.

Steph didn't argue. She could see it in his eyes: She'd gotten as far as she was going to get with him that day.

Grant let Steph off in front of the ranch house. She leaned on her door and got out with no fanfare.

"Thanks," she said. "I had a great time."

He nodded. She shut the door. He waited, the engine idling, until she went inside.

And then he sat there a moment longer, wishing she was still in the passenger seat beside him, cursing himself for a long-gone fool.

He headed back to town. He wasn't ready yet to return to the resort, where he was the boss with all that being the boss entailed.

Steph's scent lingered, very faint and very tempting, in the car. Or maybe not. Maybe he only imagined it. But whether he could actually still smell her or not, he found himself breathing through his nose, just to get another whiff of her.

This was beyond bad. He'd spent practically the whole day with her. He still didn't quite know how that had happened. Somehow, every time he'd told himself he needed to cut the contact short, she would look at him with those green eyes.

And he would be lost.

He had to face it, he supposed: Steph Julen had it all. The total package.

There was not only her scent and her sweet, clean-scrubbed face and fine, slim body. There was also that husky, humor-filled voice of hers. There was how smart she was, how charming. How *good*.

She was a good person. He wanted the best for her. Even more so now, when he was finally realizing what a terrific woman she'd become.

At the corner where Thunder Canyon Road turned sharply east and became Main, across from the Wander-On Inn, the Hitching Post loomed. The big brick building was famous in Thunder Canyon history, as it had once been The Shady Lady Saloon, the town's most notorious watering hole, run by the mysterious Shady Lady herself, Lily Divine, back in the 1890s.

Grant turned into the lot, which was packed. But

luck was with him. He found a space in the last row as a muddy pickup slid out and drove away.

Inside, the place was jumping. The jukebox played country-western at full volume. Grant knew that later in the evening a local band would be taking the stage at the far end of the barnlike space.

One side was a restaurant, the other the bar, with no wall to separate the two. Grant stuck to the bar side, elbowing his way up through the crowd and sliding onto a stool as another man vacated it.

The portrait on the wall behind the bar was of a well-endowed blond beauty, resting seductively on a red-velvet chaise lounge, wearing nothing but pearls and a few bits of almost-transparent black fabric strategically placed to hint at more than they revealed. The lady was none other than the notorious Lily herself and that painting had hung in the exact same spot over a century before when she owned and ran the place.

The bartender, who knew Grant's drink of choice, set a Maker's Mark with ice before him. Grant dropped his silly miner's hat on the bar, put a few bills down beside it and toasted the Shady Lady just as a deep voice behind him said, "Well, if it isn't the local Golden Boy."

He turned to face Russ Chilton, his best friend since kindergarten. "Hey, Russ." He spoke with a wary smile. In the past couple of years, things had changed between him and Russ—and not for the good. "How you doin'?"

"I've been better." Russ looked around discontentedly. "Kinda crowded in here. Hell, it's crowded all over town. Too crowded, if you ask me."

Grant raised his glass to the other man. "The merchants like it."

"Anything for a buck, right?"

Grant considered trying to lighten the mood with a joking remark about progress, about how change was the only constant. But he decided against it. Lately, it was damn near impossible to lighten Russ's mood. Especially if the subject was progress or change. The man was a rancher, bred in the bone. He liked wide open spaces and wanted Thunder Canyon to go back the way it used to be.

Russ spoke again. "Saw you in the parade—you and Steph Julen." His dark eyes shone with disapproval. Like Grant, Russ had always been protective of Steph, especially after she lost her dad so young.

"Yeah." Grant said the single word cautiously. He had a feeling he wasn't going to like where Russ was going with this. He tried for a little old-time camaraderie. "Come on. Let me buy you a—"

Russ cut him off. "I saw you with her at the races, too. And at the rodeo."

So much for playing it friendly. "Okay, Russ. What are you getting at?"

Russ leaned in and spoke so no one else in the crowded bar would hear. "Steph's a good kid."

"Yeah. She is. So what?"

"You got no need to mess with her. You got the

women waiting in line the way I hear it. Why you want to go and hurt a nice kid like her?"

Russ's words hit their mark and Grant longed to deliver a nice, clean punch to the rancher's square jaw, even though all Russ had done was to tell it hard and true.

But somehow, though his adrenaline spiked, Grant held it together and asked flatly, "That all?"

Russ grunted. "Yeah. That's all."

"Well, all right then." With a curt nod, Grant turned his back on his lifelong best friend.

He sipped his whiskey and counted to ten. In the big mirrors on either side of the Shady Lady's portrait, he saw Russ walk away. Good.

The bartender set a second drink in front of him and tipped his head at a lean, dark-haired man down at the end of the bar. "This one's on the doc."

The doc was Marshall Cates, another of Grant's buddies from way back. Marshall used to practice at Thunder Canyon General, but since his specialty was sports medicine, Grant had lured him to work at the resort by offering a nice, fat salary and a boatload of benefits, including points in the corporation. So now, Marshall was on call to treat the injuries and illnesses of the resort's pampered guests.

Grant signaled him over.

"Russ been giving you grief?" the doctor asked as he eased in beside Grant.

"No more than usual."

Marshall chuckled. "Don't listen to him. He's livin' in the past."

"Whatever you say, Doc."

Marshall sipped his drink, nice and slow, then he looked at his glass as if admiring the amber color of the whiskey within. "I, on the other hand, appreciate the finer things in life and enjoy the fact that I can more than afford them these days."

"Well, good," said Grant.

The two men clinked their glasses. Marshall offered the toast. "To high times and pretty women."

"I'll drink to that."

Grant hung around at the Hitching Post for a while. Marshall's "little" brothers, the twins Matthew and Marlon, came in. They were just twenty-one, old enough to drink and make trouble—though around town, folks always said that the Cates boys were *born* making trouble. They had the trademark Cates dark hair and eyes and killer smiles. Grant stood them both a drink and listened to them go on about college life— they'd be headed into their senior year in the fall.

Mitchell Cates showed up, too. He was thirty and owned his own farm and ranch equipment company. Mitch had been as wild as any of the Cates boys during his teen years. Nowadays, though, he was kind of quiet most of the time. Women liked Mitch just fine, but Marshall was the charmer in the family. The doc always had a pretty woman on his arm—especially since he'd started practicing up at the resort.

Another old buddy, Dax Traub, who owned the local

motorcycle shop, came in. The men commandeered a table and Mitchell bought them all another round.

At a little after nine, the twins headed over to the town hall where the annual Independence Day dance was underway in the main reception room on the ground floor. By then, Grant had had just enough to drink that he knew he wouldn't be getting behind the wheel of his Range Rover—not for a couple of hours, anyway.

He walked up Main to the hall. It wasn't that far and the fresh air kind of cleared his head.

The hall was packed. Up on the stage at the far end, a local band played a fast number good and loud. Grant stood on the sidelines, tapping his foot, telling himself that he wasn't looking around for Steph.

No way would she be there. Right? If she'd been planning to go to the dance, she would have mentioned it earlier. Wouldn't she?

Grant swore under his breath as he watched the fast-stepping, tightly packed dancers.

Okay. The truth was, he didn't have a clue what Steph might do. Not anymore. She was…a whole new person lately.

All woman. Fascinating. Dangerous to his peace of mind in a way no other woman ever had been. So beautiful that just looking at her caused an ache deep down inside him.

He still wanted to protect her—no matter what Russ might think. He *cared* for her. A lot.

He would give just about anything to get her off his

mind. And damn it, he was trying to stay clear of her, to forget about her. Not to think about her all the time.

Too bad all that trying wasn't working in the least.

He stood there staring blindly into the crush of dancers, the day he'd just spent with her replaying in his head: the way she'd looked in her fringed cowgirl getup, astride Trixiebelle on the float; the feel of her boot nudging him in the back, making him grin in spite of himself.

Her golden hair flying out under her hat as she ran those barrels—and her good attitude when she lost. Her face across the table from him in the restaurant...

All of it. Every minute of the day they'd spent together.

He hated that it was over. He wanted to live it all over again.

"Hey, cowboy. How 'bout a dance?" Cute Lizbeth Stanton, the town flirt who worked for Grant as head bartender in the lounge at the resort, fluttered her long eyelashes at him.

The band had finished that fast number and started in on a slow one. Why not? If he couldn't dance with Steph, he might as well take a turn around the floor with curvy little Lizbeth.

"Sure." He took her in his arms.

She joked and teased through the whole dance. He teased her right back. They always played it that way with each other, though it had never gone any further than kidding around between them. The spark, somehow, just wasn't there.

When the dance was over, she frowned up at him. "You okay, Grant?"

He lied and said he was fine and Marshall appeared out of the crowd. Lizbeth turned her wide smile on the doctor and they danced away together as the band started up yet again.

By eleven, Grant had gotten out on the floor with a number of pretty women. He felt thoroughly sober. And disgustingly depressed.

He walked back to the Hitching Post and got his car and returned to the resort, where he stood on his balcony and watched contraband bottle rockets shoot up into the star-thick Montana sky.

At a little after midnight, he went back inside.

But it was no good. He knew he wouldn't be able to sleep.

He knew what he wanted. What he needed. He reminded himself, repeatedly, that he wasn't going to get it. He *had* to work off some of the tension.

Maybe a long midnight ride would relax him a little. Wear him out. Ease his nerves and his yearning for a woman he knew he had no right to touch.

In the stables, a sleepy groom emerged to greet him. He sent the man back to his bed and tacked up Titan himself.

By twelve-thirty, he was on his way. The three-quarter moon, turning back around from fullness, burnished the open land in silver, lighting his way. Now and then, in the distance, he heard the sharp explosions of home fireworks, saw the occasional small multicolored starburst break wide-open in the sky.

He rode faster than he should have—at night, when the gullies and draws are shadowed, a horse can easily loose its footing. But some angel must have been there with him, perched on his shoulder. He arrived in the deserted yard of the Clifton's Pride ranch house without mishap at twenty after one.

He looked around at the dark circle of buildings and wondered what the hell he was doing there. It was not right—not right in the least, that he'd come.

Bart stood on the top porch step, hopefully wagging his tail and Rufus emerged from the bunkhouse with his shotgun, as he had the night before. The old cowboy spotted Grant, waved and went back inside.

What now?

Stupid question. He should turn the horse around and head back the way he'd come.

But he didn't. He let Titan have his head. The gelding wandered toward the barn. And Grant let that happen. When the horse reached the barn doors, he dismounted, opened them and flipped the switch on the wall just inside.

The single bare bulb in the rafters came on. He led the horse in, shut the doors and removed both saddle and bridle, not bothering to carry them into the tack room, just setting them on a hay bale, the saddle blanket, too. Since the gelding wasn't lathered up, Grant let him loose in the paddock behind the barn without brushing him down.

He pulled the paddock doors shut and rested his forehead against the rough wood, wondering what the hell he was doing there.

Behind him, at the opposite end of the barn, the doors to the yard creaked—and creaked again.

"Grant."

That was all it took: his name from her lips and he knew. He'd been expecting her. Deep down, he'd *willed* her to come to him.

He turned.

She stood just inside the doors, all that amazing gold hair sleep-tangled around her unforgettable face, wearing plaid pajama bottoms, a green tank top, boots and a sweater so big it seemed to swallow her slim frame.

"What are you doing here?" All sleepy and droopy-eyed, she was, hands down, the most beautiful creature he'd ever seen.

In long strides, he reached her. She lifted that angel's face to his.

What could he say? What could he do?

He was lost and he knew it, lost by his own choice, by his own will to come here in spite of his constant vows to the contrary.

There was nothing to say, no denial powerful enough to tear him away from her.

Not now. Not tonight.

A hard, strangled sound escaped him. He reached for her. She came to him with a soft, tender sigh.

He lowered his head and took her mouth.

She melted into him, lifting her soft arms to clasp his neck. He lifted her booted feet off the straw-scattered plank floor and carried her, still kissing her, into the tack room.

Chapter Ten

Steph could hardly believe this was happening—at last.

After all the long years of dreaming, of hoping, of wishing that maybe someday, somehow, this man would see her as a woman, would long for her the way she longed for him, that he would reach for her. That he would kiss her so deep and touch her all over.

Just the way he was doing now.

He kicked the tack room door shut with his boot. And slowly, he let her slide to the floor.

"You sure?" The two words came out rough and full of something that sounded almost like pain.

She nodded. She'd never been so sure about anything in her whole life.

The moon shone in the small window on the side wall, more than enough to see by, silvering the space that smelled of leather and straw and clean sweat. Two-by-fours projected from the plank walls, hung with saddles. Bridles hung on iron hooks, reins trailing like black ribbons in the moonlight.

There was a woodstove on a platform in the corner, cold now, but necessary in the long Montana winters. There were stools and a couple of rough benches.

And saddle blankets, some hanging where they'd dried, others folded and stacked neatly on the end of a bench.

Steph went for those blankets. He let her go reluctantly and then he just stood there, like a man in a trance, as she made them a bed on the floor.

Rising, she went to him and took his hand.

"Steph."

"Mmm?"

He asked again, "Are you *sure?*"

"I am," she answered. "So sure. So very, very sure."

Silly man. He should have known her better, should have known that she wouldn't be here, in the moonlit dark with him, if she didn't know in her bones that she wanted this.

Longed for it.

Ached for it, even.

His big, warm hands touched her face, cradling it like a chalice. She offered her lips and he drank from them, those long fingers of his gliding down the sides of her neck, rousing a trail of heated sensation as they went. He dipped his thumbs into the hollow of her throat and a moan rose from her, echoing so strangely inside her head as he eased his hands under her old cardigan. Fingers skimming her eager flesh, he pushed the sweater off her shoulders.

She caught it as it fell, tossed it toward a bench and didn't really care if it landed where she threw it. Because by then, he was cupping her breasts, one in each hand, his hot palms engulfing them. She moaned again then, into his open mouth. He took the sound into him, the way he had taken her tongue, so deep into the wet cave beyond his parted lips.

He sucked her tongue, rhythmically, as he rubbed her nipples, catching them between his thumbs and fore-fingers right through the fabric of her top, rolling them until they were so hard…

Hard and aching, yearning. Throbbing. In the most wonderful, exciting way.

Her arms felt heavy and between her legs there was heaviness, too. And wetness. Her body wept, hungry for him, though all he'd done was take her mouth, carry her in here, caress her breasts…

She couldn't resist touching him, her hands skimming downward over his hips. She clutched his hard, muscled thighs sheathed in denim. She caressed him and he pressed himself against her, seeming to like what she was doing, seeming to urge her to do more.

She dared. Oh, yes. She dared. She might be new at

this, but she had a bright and curious mind, an eagerness for sensation. And no fear.

Not with Grant. He was, after all, the man she'd
always dreamed of knowing in this special way, the
only man for her.

By then, he had his hands up under her top and he
was touching her bare skin, bringing more moans from
her, more sounds that came of their own accord and
spoke of her eagerness, of how much she liked every
kiss.

Every caress, every tender, needful groan.

She dared some more. To touch him, to lay her hand
over the bulge beneath his zipper. He moaned hard
when she did that. She sucked that sound into herself.

And then he was taking her arms, guiding them up
so they were over her head. In matching long, firm
strokes, he caressed his way back down, over her raised
forearms, her elbows, her upper arms. She shivered
with heat, she reveled in each touch.

He had to stop kissing her long enough to whip the
top over her head and off. But that only took a second.
Then his mouth was hard on hers again.

And she was in heaven, she was just…lost in a sea
of warm, shivery sensation.

In her secret imaginings, she'd always pictured
herself undressing him while he undressed her. Her
fantasies of making love with him had always pro-
ceeded in a certain…erotic sequence: Her shirt, his
shirt. His boots, hers…

When she'd lie in her bed alone, enjoying her waking dreams of him, they would always take turns, uncovering each other.

But now, in real life, everything was so much more intense. Wilder. There was no time for order, no taking turns.

He gave her no chance to slowly peel his clothes away, to reveal by sweet degrees the hard flesh of the man beneath. He was a man on a mission and she found she was only too happy to let him lead the way.

Once he had her shirt off, he went for her pajama bottoms. He shoved them down as he lowered that dark gold head of his and took her breast in his mouth.

Oh. My. She clutched his head close to her, little pleading sounds escaping her parted lips. He sucked her nipple, working his teeth so gently against it and she felt a kind of…pulling, a shimmering erotic tug all the way down in the feminine heart of herself, in that wet, hot place that was yearning to be filled with him.

She cradled his head and arched her chest, lifting her breasts to him, eager for more, as his hungry hands caressed her, stroking the skin over her ribs, clutching her bottom, gliding around over the curve of her hips and inward.

Oh, this…

This was better. More intense. Sweeter than her virgin fantasies. He parted the damp curls between her thighs and he dipped a finger into her wetness.

She still had her boots on. And when he'd shoved

CHRISTINE RIMMER135

her pajamas down, they'd gotten hung up at her ankles, hobbling her, preventing her from spreading her legs as wide as she wanted to. She opened as best she could for him.

And she lifted her hips to him, awash in pleasure, eager for more. More of his endless, deep kisses, his caresses, the things he could do with that bad tongue of his, the way his fingers seemed to know exactly the right spot to touch, to stroke, to rub in little circles until she was crying out, begging him.

"Oh, yes, Grant. Like that. More. Oh. Yes. Please…"

Something happened then. A hot bud of something formed within her. As she begged him to keep touching her, keep rubbing her right there—oh, yes, right there…

That bud became a burning, moist flower, one that burst into sudden bloom.

The hot blooming spread all through her, raying out from the spot where he stroked her. A scream boiled up from her throat—too loud, she knew it, but she couldn't seem to stop herself. He lifted his head from her breast and covered her mouth with his, muffling the racket she was making.

Somewhere way back in her mind she was glad he moved to quiet her.

They didn't need company. Uh-uh. She didn't want her mom or Rufus to come nosing around, wondering what all the shouting was about.

Oh, it was just amazing. She was…swept away.

Carried off into ecstasy in a lovely, hot sensation of blooming, her body shuddering with joy, all loose and so gloriously, completely alive.

She opened her eyes.

Well, how had that happened? She was down on the blankets.

He must have lowered her there while the blooming was ending, while she was screaming her excitement into his mouth. She lay back on the scratchy wool, raising her arms, feeling strangely luxurious, running her fingers through her snarled-up hair, stunned with delight at what had just happened.

Time drifted away. She shut her eyes on a sigh, only stirring when he touched her again. He murmured soft reassurances as he pulled off her boots and got rid of her pj's. She was so glad for that, to have her feet and ankles bare at last, like the rest of her. She wanted nothing to bind her, nothing to get in the way of the next pleasure he might bring.

He touched her again—there—where she was so wet and so sensitive. She moaned and moved her hips, easing her legs wider, now that no pajamas reined her in. He touched her, stroking her...

And then his mouth was there.

Oh. Well. Who knew?

Who would have guessed it was going to feel like this? She was swollen and so wet and still yearning, even though a few minutes ago, she'd thought she was finished. Fulfilled. Content.

But now, the pleasure was rising again, her body reaching for more, yearning for…

Everything. Whatever he could give her. Whatever he could teach her. Whatever he would share.

She whispered his name, she told him yes, as she tossed her head on the blanket, her eyes drifting open so she stared, dazed and amazed, at the moon-silvered room, at the saddles hanging on the walls, the benches, the plank ceiling overhead.

He was…doing things. Wonderful things, with that hot, wet tongue of his. She could hardly believe it, the wonder. Of this.

The blooming happened again. Hotter, deeper, more consuming than the first time. She cried out as she had before and he reached up a hand to cover her mouth, to silence her cries of pleasure. She smelled her own arousal on his fingers as the wonder crested.

Oh, the way he kissed her, kept on kissing her, right there, in the perfect spot. It felt so fine, she reveled in it, opening her knees wider, lifting her legs, bracing her feet on his broad bare shoulders…

Bare?

With a gasp of surprise, she raised her head and looked down at him, amazed to find he was naked as she. When had that happened? He'd managed, somehow, to get out of his jeans and boots and shirt, all without her even noticing.

Oh, she was far gone on this, on what he was doing

to her. Far gone and more, to have missed the lovely moments when he stripped off all his clothes.

But then again, well, she'd get herself a good long look at him later. When she wasn't so excited. When her body wasn't thrumming with a hunger so fine.

What mattered right now was the feel of his flesh against hers, the heat of him, the hardness.

And her head was just too heavy to hold up. She let it drop to the blanket again, shut her eyes, moaned her willingness, her joy—and his name.

And then he was kissing his way up her body. He lingered to lick her belly, low down, to nibble the sensitive skin over her hip bones.

She lifted her head again on a moan. He was up on his knees, and she saw him…that part of him. So big. So…ready for her. She wondered what virgins probably always wondered: if he was going to fit, and how much it might hurt when he did.

But even as she wondered those things, they really didn't matter. She'd worked around large animals most of her life. She knew that nature had a way of making a fit—no matter how impossible such a thing might seem.

And oh, he was beautiful. His strong body, the muscles flexing. His tanned skin silvery in the moonlight. And that part of him she yearned for? It was beautifully formed, ropy with veins that were visible even beneath the sheath of the condom he wore.

A condom?

Again, he'd surprised her, providing protection without her even realizing he was doing it.

And of course, knowing him, he would always carry protection. Given all the pretty women up at the resort, he'd need to be…prepared. At all times.

He glanced up then. Their eyes met. His gleamed hard and hungry. With a surrendering sigh, she let her head drop, shut her eyes once again—and opened them a moment later as he licked her chin in one long, wet stroke.

He said her name. "Steph…" As if it were the only name that mattered.

All the barriers were down then. She looked into those blue, blue eyes of his. And saw what *could* be, what they could have together. All they might share.

Heaven. Oh, yeah. A little bit of heaven right here on earth.

She felt the rough hairs on his muscled thighs, rubbing the inside of *her* thighs. And the nudge of heated hardness right *there,* where she wanted him, right where he'd been kissing her. Where she was dripping wet and swollen, yearning all over again, in spite of the two times he'd taken her to the finish already.

He braced his big arms on either side of her and he pushed in. She moaned. It hurt. But the pain was delicious in a strange way, her nerve endings so sensitized from his attention, she only wanted more.

She wanted…

To be his in the fullest way.

To feel him, inside her, stretching her, making her give and open for him.

"Don't want...to hurt you..." He growled the words, low. Sweat beaded his brow and the strong muscles in his shoulders bunched with his effort to go easy, to take her slow.

She wrapped her legs around him, opening herself wider. "Now, Grant," she commanded. The command melted, became a breathless plea, "Just...oh, please. Now."

With a deep groan, he thrust in, his hand automatically covering her mouth to muffle her long, sharp cry.

It hurt. But not as much as it pleasured. She moaned and she pulled him down to her, so she could feel the hot, sweat-slick weight of him, the crisp hair on his chest rubbing her nipples, driving her higher, to a fever pitch.

He was still.

She held him. Close. Tight. She took long, slow, hungry breaths and she felt herself relaxing, her inner muscles giving, making more room.

For him. To be hers...

He moved. Another hard thrust.

She groaned low, felt her body opening, taking him deeper.

And deeper still.

He claimed her mouth, his tongue delving in. She sucked it as she surged up to meet him.

"Yeah," he whispered against her parted lips. "Move with me. Oh, yeah. Like that. Like that..."

And from then on, she was lost. More lost than ever. Lost in a way that meant she was also found.

She was a river, flowing all around him as he moved in a slow, hot, hard glide. He was within her and the scent of him was all around her.

There was nothing.

But this. The two of them.

Rising.

His mouth on hers, drinking her cries as the dark flower of fulfillment burst wide into full bloom yet again.

Chapter Eleven

Grant nuzzled her sweet-smelling hair, thinking how he only had one condom left, wishing he had more, but a guy can only fit so many of the damn things in a wallet—and was he crazy?

Was he absolutely stark-raving out of his mind?

He shouldn't have used the first one. And yet, here he was, holding her close, feeling himself stirring all over again, planning to use the one he had left.

Wishing he had more. A hundred of the damn things. A thousand. Wishing he could keep her here, in his arms, forever and a day. Never let her go.

Make love to her over and over. Until the end of time.

He was a real, first-class rat-bastard and that was a plain fact.

"Don't," she whispered.

They lay naked on the makeshift bed of saddle blankets, spoon-style, his body curved around her smaller one.

"Don't." She said it a second time.

He smoothed her hair back away from her ear and trailed his finger down the side of her neck. Amazing, the feel of her skin. Like the petals of some exotic, perfect flower.

"Don't what?" He lifted up on an elbow and she rolled to her back so she could see him.

Damn. He'd never get enough of just looking at her, of marveling at how the brave kid he'd known for so long had suddenly become the most tempting woman he'd ever met.

He was more than just *stirring* now. He was hard again.

She must have felt him pressing against her thigh, because she grinned. Damn knowingly. Was a virgin supposed to grin like that?

It didn't seem right, somehow, that she should be so pleased about this. Didn't virgins usually cry in a man's arms afterward? Didn't they cling and worry and fret over what they'd just done, over whether it was the right thing or not, over if they should have waited for marriage? Or for a different kind of guy?

He'd always heard virgins did things like that. It was

one of the many reasons he'd been real careful to avoid them. With a virgin, a man was bound to feel responsible.

Then again, Steph didn't need to cry and carry on over the loss of her innocence. He already felt responsible for Steph, and he always would.

She was a part of him in a way that had nothing to do with the two of them, lying here in the moonlit tack room, minus all their clothes.

She was…the best of the life he'd once known. She was strong and good, a person a man could count on. She was honest. And true. Willing to work hard to make a place for herself. Expecting nothing. Giving her all.

He wasn't worthy of her and he knew it. He never should have—

"Don't beat yourself up," she chided, her mouth suddenly gone stern. "I mean it." She reached up and smoothed his forehead. "Wipe that frown off your face. It was wonderful. It was…what I wanted. What I've dreamed of. Don't you go and start making it…less."

"Did I hurt you?" There was blood on the blanket. Not much, but still…

She caught his chin in her hand. "Listen."

"What?"

"Yes. It hurt a little. So what? That hurt was nothing, only a moment. The rest felt so good. I'm serious. You will never know how good…"

He pressed his forehead to hers. "Oh, yeah. I know."

That grin was tugging at her mouth again. "Yeah?"

"Yeah."

"Whew. Well. Considering you did all the work so I would get so much pleasure, that's pretty nice. I mean, if it felt good to you, too."

Good? Understatement of the decade. "It did."

She snuggled in against him and his arousal hardened even more. "Well, okay then." She giggled.

"Something's funny?"

Her head was tucked in the curve of his shoulder. She tipped it back and met his gaze again. He saw the naughty gleam in her eyes. "I think you'd like to be feeling good…again." Her hand closed around him.

He groaned. "Oh, yeah. I would…"

"You'll have to tell me how to do this." She gave an experimental tug that sent a bolt of white-hot lightning zapping along every nerve. "I'm not the least experienced." She squeezed. He groaned again. She licked her lips. He knew she did that on purpose.

"It's fine," he muttered roughly. "You're doing just fine…"

They didn't use the second condom for a couple of hours. No need to. She was an eager lover and she wanted to try everything. He was more than happy to oblige her.

And though she amazed him, so adventurous for someone so innocent, she *was* tender after her first time. He tried to go extra easy that second time. But she wrapped herself around him and moved those fine hips so seductively, urging him to lose himself.

He did. At the end, everything flew away but the feel of her slim body beneath his, the wet, tight heat of her all around him. It was sex like he'd never known it before.

Deeper. Better. More…satisfying.

In no time, it was four in the morning. Rufus and Jim would be up and about their chores soon. Marie would be puttering around the kitchen, putting the coffee on, whipping up a big batch of breakfast biscuits.

Steph kissed his shoulder, opening her mouth a little, giving him a quick, teasing stroke of her tongue, reminding him that he still wanted her. Bad. More than ever, now he knew what he'd been missing.

He wanted to roll her right under him and bury himself in her all over again.

But the condoms were used up.

And their night was gone.

Gone, and he hadn't had enough of her. Not nearly enough. He stroked the sleek curve of her arm and wondered if he would ever be through with her, wondered if he could ever get his fill.

She nipped where she'd licked him. "I know what you're thinking, and I don't like it one bit."

He wrapped her hair around his hand, buried his face in it. It smelled so damn good. "Oh, yeah?"

She tugged on the strands. He released them. "Yeah," she said. "You're thinking it's time to go."

"Because it is."

"Stay." She clutched his arm, as if she had the strength to hold him there by physical force alone.

She couldn't.

But she had other things. A face and a body like no other. A scent that drove him wild. A kiss he'd never forget in his lifetime.

And heart. And...history.

They had history together, him and Steph. No matter what happened after this, that would never change.

He peeled her fingers away from his arm and kissed her fingertips. "I can't stay. Your mom—"

"I'm full-grown, in case you failed to notice. A woman with a right to make her own way—and her own choices."

"Marie isn't going to like it."

Steph sat up. She looked down at him, her eyes dark now, shadowed as the night itself. "Don't be a damn coward. We did what we did. It's our business and nobody else's. Can we just *not* sneak around? Can we just...stand tall?"

He caught her hand again, brought it to his lips a second time and kissed it. She allowed that, briefly. And then she pulled her fingers from his hold.

"You're something," he said. "You always were."

"I want you to come in for breakfast."

"It's a bad idea."

"Please."

"More coffee, Grant?" Marie stood over him, holding the pot.

For a split second, he just *knew* she would empty the scalding contents in his lap.

She did no such thing. But she wasn't happy with him. Oh, she acted kind as ever. She'd even hugged him when he came in from the barn.

But he'd caught the looks she gave him—and her daughter—when she thought they couldn't see. She knew what they'd been up to last night.

And she didn't like it one bit.

He nodded. "Thanks."

She filled his cup, went around and filled Rufus's and then took the pot back to the counter. Across the table, Rufus kept his attention on his plate.

Jim kept his eyes focused on his food, as well. Too focused.

Only Steph behaved as if nothing out of the ordinary had happened. She ate heartily and told the cowhands what projects she hoped to get finished today—the fences she wanted mended, the cows and calves that should be checked on because the calf wasn't eating right or the cow had been acting poorly in the past couple of days.

To Grant, the meal seemed never-ending. He ate a pile of scrambled eggs, sausage and two biscuits, shoving the food in his mouth without tasting it or wanting it. The tension around that table did nothing for a man's appetite.

Finally the hands got up and left and Marie started clearing off. Grant thanked her and made his escape.

Out in the yard, he found Titan, tacked up and waiting—courtesy of Rufus, no doubt.

"I guess a kiss goodbye would be asking too much." Steph leaned against one of the porch pillars, arms folded under those small, perfect breasts of hers, shaking her head.

Need pierced him, just from looking at her. She let her arms drop to her sides and came down into the early-morning sunlight and he wanted to reach for her so bad he could taste it. The need only got stronger the closer she came.

He waited, his hat in his hand, until she stood next to him, before he muttered, "Marie almost poured a pot of coffee on me and I think Jim hates my guts."

She wanted to touch him—as he longed to touch her. He could see that in her eyes. But she didn't. She kept her arms at her sides. "You don't know any such thing about Jim. The man does his work and keeps to himself. He never asked me out and I sure never gave him a bit of encouragement. And my mom, well, she'll get over it."

"I hope so."

Her eyes grew sad. "Okay, Grant. See you later, then."

He swore—and then he yanked her close and kissed her. Hard.

When he let her go, she told him softly, "That's better."

He put on his hat, mounted up and rode away. Fast.

"How's the new hand working out?" Marie asked.

Steph turned from the front window and the deserted

yard. Beyond the circles of light cast by the porch lamp and the lamps on the outbuildings, all was darkness.

A full week had passed since the beautiful night in the tack room. Jim had quit last Friday, collected his pay and told her he was ready to move on. Steph hadn't asked him why. She'd taken care all along not to get personal with him, and she kept things that way, right to the end. Plus, she'd learned early on that when a cowhand said he was leaving, there was no point in getting into a big discussion over it. Some men just didn't like hanging around in one place too long.

"You need a reference, let me know," she'd told him. "I've got no complaints about your work."

He'd muttered a low, "Thanks," and that was it. He was gone.

Monday, she'd hired the new hand.

She watched her mother knit. Marie could really get those knitting needles flying. She glanced up, over the top rims of her reading glasses.

Steph answered her question of a moment before. "The new man is doing fine. Works hard. Rufus says he's okay."

Marie wrapped the yarn around the needle, hooked it into the afghan she was making and wrapped again. "Haven't heard from Grant, then?" Her mother asked that one without looking up—or pausing. *Click, click, click, click*. The needles flew.

"No, Mom. I haven't."

"You were…careful?"

Steph felt the color flood her cheeks as she thought of those two condoms and how they'd used them, of everything else they'd done that wonderful night. Her cheeks flamed and she felt an ache through her whole body. An ache that had no real location, yet was as physical as a broken bone, a gunshot wound—a knife, stabbing, deep, right to the heart of her.

"Yes," she said. "We were careful."

Her mother never looked up. "It's not the end of the world, you know. Things don't work out. That's how it goes sometimes." Marie spoke gently.

"I know."

"He's a good man. A fine man. But he's not—"

"Can we just…not talk about it? Please."

The flashing needles paused—and then went on. "Of course. But I'm right here, if you change your mind and want someone to listen, after all."

"I know, Mom. Thanks."

It was almost ten. Time to turn in.

But Steph didn't feel much like sleeping. Lately the nights dragged by in an endless agony of waiting. She lay in her bed, eyes wide-open, listening. For the sound of tires crunching gravel, or a horse's hooves. Noises that meant someone had ridden into the yard.

Since the night in the tack room, those sounds never came.

She turned to leave the room.

Marie said good-night.

"'Night, Mom."

But when she got out in the hall, she detoured to her office, for no particular reason beyond her reluctance to go to bed when she knew she wouldn't sleep. She shut the door and sank into the chair behind her desk, where she stared at the dark eye of her computer monitor and wished she didn't feel so miserable.

Eventually, with a heavy sigh, she folded her arms on the desk pad and rested her head on them. As she had any number of times in the past seven days, she considered going to him.

He wanted her. Bad. She knew if she went to him, she could most likely get through to him—at least physically. Get him to reach for her. To hold her and kiss her and…

But no. For some reason, that just seemed…unfair. To herself. And to him. If they were going any further together, she wanted him willing, for pity's sake. She wanted him *glad* to be with her. She just wouldn't settle for a man who felt trapped by his own desire for her.

And really, the ache in her heart wasn't so bad in the daytime. She had lots of work to do and she kept her mind on that.

And in her practical soul, she knew that no misery lasts forever. The deepest wound either heals—or kills you.

And Stephanie Julen was not going to die. She was too tough for that.

The phone rang. She didn't even jump. It was progress, of a sort. She supposed. Up till now, every time the phone rang, her heart would leap and she would race to answer, just certain it had to be Grant calling to tell her his life was empty without her, to insist that he just *had* to see her.

Tonight, her pulse didn't even accelerate. Tonight, she calmly reached over and picked up the receiver. She put it to her ear and said pleasantly, "Clifton's Pride Ranch. Stephanie speaking."

"Steph."

Wouldn't you know? Now she'd finally stopped hoping, stopped waiting for his call, there he was on the other end of the line, saying her name in a dark, pained sort of way.

She commanded her hopeless heart not to start racing. "Hello, Grant."

There was a silence. An endless, echoing one.

Finally he spoke again. "Look. I really screwed up. I know it. I've been staying away from you, hoping that maybe…" He ran out of words.

She refused to supply them. Except to prompt, "Hoping that what?"

Another pause. At last, he tried again. "That I'd stop feeling like such a user and a jerk. That things would go back to the way they were before. That…hell. I don't know what. I only know I want you. I know if I get near you, I'll just end up thinking about ways to get you out of your clothes again."

More silence. She wanted to beg him to come to her—or tell him to wait right there. She'd break every land speed record getting to his side. And then she'd be more than happy to take her clothes off *for* him.

But in the week he'd stayed away, she *had* done some thinking.

And she'd come to the conclusion that one person can't make love—or even a love *affair*—work. As the old saying goes, it takes two.

He said, as if he'd read the direction of her thoughts, "It can't work, Steph."

"Only because you don't want it to." Her head ached, suddenly. She braced her elbow on the desk and cradled her forehead in her hand. "Listen. There's no point in this. I want to be with you. I want to…take this thing we have wherever it goes. But not if you don't want it, too. I'm not pushing you."

"I know."

"I'm not demanding anything…permanent."

"I know."

"So then, why are you avoiding me?"

"It's for the best."

Her heart did beat faster then. With anger. She quelled the fury and spoke in a level voice. "I'll tell you what…"

He made a questioning sound.

"Don't call me just to tell me how it can't go anywhere with us. I don't need to hear that again."

He swore, low, and whispered her name.

"Good night, Grant." She hung up.

Chapter Twelve

Since Steph had taken over as foreman at Clifton's Pride, she no longer gave group riding lessons at the resort. They'd hired another instructor full-time. Steph filled in for her, giving private lessons whenever the full-timer had a scheduling conflict.

Steph got a call Friday morning from the full-timer.

"I need you this afternoon," the other woman said. "First, for a half hour with a fast-talkin' guy from San Francisco. Doug Freethy's the name. Computer programmer. Never been on a horse in his life. Then there's a full hour, with a…" The instructor paused. "Ah. Here we go. Melanie McFarlane." Steph recognized the name: the woman who'd tried to buy Clifton's Pride. "Melanie says she already rides English style. Wants to learn Western." The instructor explained that when she'd spoken with each of the two students, she'd made sure they understood what to expect and what to wear. "So you won't need to make the preliminary calls. Just show up at the stables to meet the computer programmer at two."

As it turned out, the computer programmer was a big, good-looking guy more interested in flirting with his riding instructor than in learning his way around a horse. He asked Steph to dinner twice during that half hour lesson. Both times he seemed vaguely stunned that she turned him down.

"You don't know what you're missing," he told her at the end.

She gave him a pleasant smile. "Enjoy your stay in Thunder Canyon, Doug."

"I'd enjoy it a lot more if I could spend an evening with you."

Steph kept her smile in place and he finally gave up and went away.

Melanie McFarlane arrived at the stables fifteen minutes early. She'd taken the instructor's suggestions to heart and dressed appropriately in comfortable, sturdy blue jeans, a fine-looking pair of Justin boots and an aqua-blue T-shirt. She even had a nice straw Resistol on her stylishly sleek red head.

Steph didn't know what, exactly, she'd expected. But the woman was slim and attractive and seemed nice enough. She listened attentively as Steph ran down the differences between English and Western tack.

They were in the saddle and out of the stable in no time. Steph gave the other woman pointers as they rode. She learned fast. The hour passed quickly—much more so than the grueling thirty minutes Steph had endured with the date-obsessed Doug.

Back in the stables, as the lesson came to an end, Melanie said, "I confess, I had an ulterior motive for requesting this lesson."

Steph dismounted and the groom took the horse.

Melanie asked, "Did you know I plan to buy Clifton's Pride, to create a top-level guest ranch there?"

Steph patiently corrected her. "I know that Grant was going to sell to you—but he changed his mind."

The redhead took off her hat and fiddled with the crease. "I like to think positive. I'm counting on him changing his mind again—when he sees how much I'm willing to offer."

Dread made a dropping sensation in Steph's belly. Was there more going on here than she knew about? "But…he *hasn't* changed his mind again. Right?"

"Not yet. But when he does, I'm hoping you'll stay on and work for me. I'll need a wrangler, someone familiar with the ranch. Someone to give riding lessons to my guests. Seems to me you'll fill the bill perfectly. And your mother—I'll be wanting to talk to her, too. I'm going to need a really good cook. And I do my homework. I know what they say about Marie Julen's cooking. This could end up working out quite well for both of you."

Steph felt sucker-punched. "Honestly, Melanie. The way I understood it, Grant doesn't plan to sell." Her heart sank as she realized she should probably go have a talk with him, find out what this was all about. If he *was* reconsidering the idea of selling out, she needed to know.

Too bad talking with Grant was the last thing she wanted to do that day. Or any day. Not…for a while, anyway.

"I only want you to be aware of your options," Melanie said. "And I don't want anyone thinking they're out of a job. I can probably hire the two men who work for you, as well." Melanie offered her hand. "A pleasure to meet you. I mean that."

After a little stewing over what to do next, Steph went on back to the ranch. She just couldn't bear to deal with Grant for a while—not till she could talk to him without wanting to yell at him. And the more she thought about it, the more she realized she didn't need to deal with him right now.

If and when he accepted Melanie's next offer, she would hear all about it. She didn't much look forward to working on a dude ranch.

But a girl had to eat. And *if* Grant sold to Melanie, it looked like Steph, her mother and the hands would get to keep their jobs, at least.

She should be thankful for small favors, right?

The rest of the afternoon dragged by. She tried to keep her mind on her work and *off* the infuriating man who wanted her so much, he'd vanished from her life for over a week, only bothering to call once—and then just to tell her how much he regretted the one amazing night they'd had together, how guilty he felt about having made love to her.

That evening, she ended up in the living room, staring out the front window, trying not to wish that Grant would come rolling up in that fancy Range Rover of his.

"Oh, for heaven's sake," said Marie. Steph turned from the window. Her mother had dropped her knitting in her lap. "I can't stand this anymore. Go." She made shooing motions with her plump hands. "Go see him. Work it out. Somehow."

Steph gaped. "But Mom. You said—"

"Oh, what do I know? Except that I can't bear another moment of you moping around here waiting for that damn fool to finally realize he can't get along without you."

Grant stood at the burled oak bar in the Lounge, with Marshall Cates to his left and Mitchell to his right. Marshall was telling some joke about a traveling salesman. He delivered the punch line. Mitchell grunted. Lizbeth Stanton, behind the bar, let out a musical trill of laughter.

Marshall clapped Grant on the back. "Buddy. You are not laughing. What's the matter with you? You been wearing a long face for days now."

"I'm fine."

Marshall snorted. "Damn. You're gettin' more serious than Mitch." He raised his drink to his brother. "And more serious than Mitch is too damn serious, believe you me."

Grant was just about to tell the good doctor to mind his own business when he noticed Dax Traub coming in the door from main lobby. "Hey, Dax."

Dax approached, his chiseled jaw set in a grim line. Since his divorce from his high-school sweetheart, Allaire, Dax was prone to dark moods. Hell, Grant thought. Except for Marshall, all his friends looked downright bleak today. As bleak as Grant felt.

Steph's sweet image drifted into his mind. He ordered it gone.

"What's up?" Grant wrapped an arm around Dax as Mitchell slid down to the next stool to make room.

Dax shrugged. "Not a thing."

"Pour the man a drink," Grant said.

Lizbeth batted her eyelashes. "What the boss wants, the boss gets."

Grant flirted back out of habit. He sent her a slow smile. Right on cue, Lizbeth slanted him one of her practiced, flirty, come-and-get-it looks.

She set a whiskey in front of Dax. "There you go, Dax."

"Thanks," Traub muttered, hardly even looking up.

Grant got down to business. "You're the man I've been wanting to talk to."

"About what?"

"D.J."

D. J. Traub was Dax's younger brother. He'd left town a decade before, right after Dax and Allaire got married. Left and never returned, except once, for his dad's funeral.

The younger Traub brother hadn't been wasting time out there in the big, wide world. In fact, D.J. had made it big—first by creating and marketing his own brand of barbecue sauce. And then by opening a chain of restaurants, with headquarters in Atlanta. Seemed like everywhere you looked the past couple of years, you saw a D.J.'s Rib Shack. Except in D.J.'s own hometown.

"We need a Rib Shack here," said Grant. "And I don't mean just in town. I mean right here, at the resort. I've been kicking the idea around with Riley and he's in agreement. We want to add a friendly midpriced restaurant on-site. I got a hunch a Rib Shack would be perfect. Hearty Western food, great atmosphere, reasonable prices. And everybody'll love that D.J.'s one of our own."

Dax shrugged. "Maybe so. But if you're thinking somehow it'll be better for me to approach him with the idea, think again."

"Hell, Dax. He *is* your brother."

"That's right. And I haven't seen him but once in a

damn decade. You guys were good friends, back when. I'm sure he'll be happy to hear from you."

Over the years, Grant had wondered what went wrong between Dax and his brother. *Something* had. But Dax always claimed there was nothing—nothing that *he* knew about, anyway.

Grant shrugged. "All right, then. I'll get in touch with him all by my lonesome and see what I can talk him into. However the restaurant idea works out, it'd be great to see him again."

"Yeah," said Dax.

"It would," said Mitch.

Marshall raised his glass. "To D.J. Whatever the hell he might be up to down there in Atlanta."

"To D.J.," the others echoed. They lifted their glasses and drank as one to their missing comrade. Grant couldn't help wishing that Russ could be there with them, to raise his glass along with theirs.

But Russ Chilton would no more set foot in the Thunder Canyon Resort Lounge than he would move to New York City, don a suit and tie and go to work on Wall Street.

Grant plunked his empty glass on the bar. "Hey, gorgeous. 'Nother round for me and the boys."

Lizbeth, who'd been mixing umbrella drinks down at the far end of the bar, sashayed back to them. "Boss. Your wish is my command." She gave him another smoldering glance as she started pouring fresh drinks.

Marshall joked, "Whoa, Lizbeth. Send some of those hot looks *my* way."

She let loose with her flirty laugh as she refilled Grant's glass. "Sorry, Doc. I'm after the boss—and he's crazy 'bout me."

All the men laughed.

"Excuse me. Grant?"

Grant froze with his drink halfway to his lips. *Steph.*

Her husky, amazing voice came from directly behind him.

Every nerve in his body on red-alert, he shot a glance at the mirror over the bar. And there she was. Their eyes met and locked in the glass.

Heat flashed through him. He lowered his drink carefully to the surface of the bar as Marshall and the others greeted her.

"Hi, guys." She nodded at the men she'd known all her life, turning her steady gaze to the bartender. "Lizbeth. How are you?"

For once in her man-crazy life, Lizbeth looked at a loss. She might not know exactly what was happening here, but she knew *something* was. "Hey, Stephanie. So. Um. What can I get you?"

"Not a thing, thanks. Grant." Her voice was cool. Careful. Distant.

He turned on his stool. Faced her. The heat flashed higher inside him. God. The woman could drive him stark-raving out of his mind. Just by standing there in front of him in jeans and a T-shirt, her nugget-gold hair loose on her shoulders. "Steph." Merely saying her name turned him on. And *looking* at her...

That drove him wild.

The night in the tack room seemed to rise up between them—everything they'd done together, all the ways he'd touched her.

He ached to touch her again, to grab her close and slam his mouth down on hers. To strip every stitch off that slim, gorgeous body.

Right there. In the Lounge. He wanted to take her. He wanted it bad.

To have her again, touch her once more, be inside her once more—as he'd sworn to himself a thousand times now he wouldn't ever do again.

Scariest of all? A part of him didn't give a good damn that everyone would see.

He had to get her out of there. Now.

He took her arm. She stiffened—but she had sense enough not to try to pull away.

"Come on," he commanded. "Let's go someplace we can talk."

Chapter Thirteen

Grant had a hold of her arm. A tight hold.

Stunned, Steph made no attempt to pull away. What had she expected when she came to find him?

Caution, maybe. Even coldness. Some stilted reminder that they needed to keep away from each other...

But not this. Not blazing heat and urgency. And the two of them, racing out of the Lounge like a couple of crazy people, leaving all his gaping buddies behind.

He led her out into the vast, open lobby with its huge central fireplace and three-story ceiling. They crossed the gleaming inlaid floor. It seemed to take forever, to get from one side to the other of that huge room.

Were the desk clerks staring?

Oh, it seemed that way. Steph knew her face was flaming and she just knew everyone in the lobby was watching, wondering if the two of them were crazy, or what?

Keeping her arm firmly manacled in his big, warm grip, Grant turned down a wide hallway and suddenly they were walking on lush carpet, their footsteps silent as a breath. People moved past them. Some of them turned and looked. Probably because of the length of his powerful stride, the way he held on to her as if he would never let her go.

And the look of pure determination on his handsome face.

He ignored them all, turning another corner.

They were at the elevators. He punched the up arrow.

"Where are we going?" she asked, her voice small and breathless, her gaze focused straight ahead at a pair of shut elevator doors—somehow, at that moment, she just couldn't bring herself to look at his face.

"My rooms."

The doors opened. The car was empty. He walked her inside and the doors slid shut, closing them in there. Together. They glided upward.

She stared at the closed doors, heat zinging through her. Wanting him. *Needing* him. "You can let go of me now. Please."

He did as she asked, releasing her arm, dropping his hand to his side. Though he was no longer touching her, she *felt* touched. Stroked. Caressed. Her body was on fire.

For him.

She had a lot to say to him. A thousand things. She wanted to understand what it was in him, that couldn't let love in, couldn't give whatever might happen between them a chance. She wanted him to explain himself, to tell her why he found it so necessary to push her away, to keep saying no to all they might share.

That was what she'd come here for: to get it all out there at last, to come to some sort of peace with him.

Peace.

Not real likely. Not tonight.

The doors opened. "This way," he said.

His rooms were on the top floor.

In the living room, the beamed ceiling seemed miles above her head. The wall opposite the entry hall was all window. It faced Thunder Mountain, the snow on the peak blue-white beneath a canopy of stars.

"It's beautiful," she said.

He touched her. Like a blind man, seeing with his fingertips, he framed her face, traced the shape of her nose, the curve of her chin. "What's the matter with me?" The words seemed dragged up from somewhere deep inside him. "I've known you since the day you were born. But now, since that time I saw you by the creek, nothing's the same. Now, just the sight of you is enough to make me lose all control. Oh, God. And the scent of you…" He shut those haunted eyes, nuzzled her cheek, drew in a long breath through his nose.

She wanted to be firm with him. To ask him about what Melanie had told her, to chide him about flirting so blatantly with Lizbeth, to tell him she was angry with him, for cutting her off, for staying away. That she wanted—needed—to understand what drove him to shut her out, to deny her not only as his lover, but as the true friend she'd always been to him.

And yet somehow, as she stared up into his anguished eyes, all that—Melanie's insistence that she *would* buy Clifton's Pride, her own confusion, her suffering at his silence in the past week—seemed nothing. Meaningless. Of no importance at all.

Not when stacked up against the tender, hungry feel of his hands on her face, on her throat, skimming across her shoulders and down her arms….

Sex. Desire. Lust. Whatever you wanted to call it. This power, this pulse of heat and yearning between them—it was everything at that moment. Against the wonder of this, the rest was a pale shadow. Bloodless. Without form or meaning.

Or so it seemed right then.

Later, she thought. We'll deal with all the tough stuff later…

She whispered the single word aloud. "Later…"

He misunderstood. "Now," he insisted as his lips covered hers.

She didn't explain herself. It didn't matter.

He was kissing her. At last. *That* mattered.

Oh, what a kiss. *His* kiss. The *only* kiss. His mouth devoured hers and his hands were everywhere.

He took off her clothes. Got rid of his own.

They stood in the starlit night before the floor-to-ceiling window. Naked. He crushed her close in yet another stunning, soul-searing kiss.

When he lifted his head that time, she opened her eyes. They regarded each other in a breath-held stillness that seemed to crackle with energy. With heat.

For then, for that moment, they were in perfect agreement. She remembered the promise she'd made herself when this started between them: to ride this wild horse wherever it took her.

Right now, with his arms around her, his hard, hot body pressed to hers, his manhood thick and ready against her belly, his eyes burning, twin blue flames, into hers—that promise she'd made herself seemed, again, one she could easily keep.

"Steph…" He formed her name as if he had to, as if the feel of it in his mouth were a necessity to him.

"Yes," she replied, as if he'd asked a question. "Oh, Grant. Yes."

And right there, in front of the window, he dropped to his knees before her. He kissed her again. Intimately. He parted her with tender fingers, tasted her with his tongue. She cradled his head, pushing her hips toward him, urging him on.

In no time, she felt the gathering, the blooming—the

hot, lovely explosion that started where he was kissing her and spread through her whole body, so she shuddered and whimpered and cried out his name.

He rose and lifted her in his arms.

In his bedroom, he carried her to the wide bed, laid her down, took a condom from a drawer and rolled it on over himself.

And then he was with her, his body on hers, moving inside her, filling her up so fine and so deep.

When the finish cascaded through them, she wrapped her legs around him. She held on so tight...

They rested.

And then they were reaching for each other again.

She wished the things that lovers always wish for: that it could always be like this. That the night would never end.

Somewhere deep in darkness, content for the moment, satisfied, they drifted off to sleep.

Steph woke as a sliver of bright morning sun found its way through a slit in the blinds. She squinted at that gold slice of sunlight, remembering.

Last night. With Grant. She moved her hand against the satin sheets.

This was his bed. And the clock on the nightstand read...*6:30 a.m.*

Panic washed through her. She hadn't intended to stay all night. At the ranch, the workday would have started hours ago.

But then she relaxed. Her mother knew where she'd gone. And Rufus and the new man could handle things without her just this once.

With a sigh, she turned over.

And there he was. Naked beside her. As she watched, he opened his eyes.

He reached up a hand and touched her face. So lightly. As if to reassure himself that she was really there. He didn't say anything. And she found she was glad for that.

Yes, there was a lot that *needed* saying. But right now, in the early morning light, she felt much too naked, too raw. Too vulnerable.

She didn't want words filling up the silence. She just wanted…to let the silence be.

He stroked her shoulder. She turned over and snuggled back into him, loving the way his body curled around her, cradling her so intimately, so protectively.

He petted her hair, smoothing it away from her neck. And then he placed a kiss there, on the side of her throat.

She let her eyes drift closed.

They slept some more.

Later, she felt him stir. They made love again. Slowly. Lazily.

Finally, as they lay facing each other, satisfied, she dared to break the beautiful silence.

She laid her hand on the side of his face. "I saw you, last night, flirting with Lizbeth." Her thumb strayed to his lips.

He sucked it inside, stroked it with his tongue. Pleasure shimmered through her.

When he let her thumb slide free, he said, "It meant nothing. Lizbeth and I just kid around. That's as far as it goes. As it's ever gone. A few teasing remarks. A little innuendo…"

"All right."

He turned his head enough to kiss the heel of her hand. She reveled in the velvet touch of his mouth on her skin. He asked, "What does that mean, all right?"

"It means…there's nothing more to say about it. I know you. I know Lizbeth. I get what was going on. That's all."

He scraped his teeth on the place he'd just kissed, bringing more waves of lovely sensation. And he told her, "There's been no one else, since the day I saw you by the creek. I've got no interest in anyone else, not anymore."

Her heart felt lighter. "I'm glad…" She studied his face and had no idea what he might be thinking. He wasn't smiling. He looked at her steadily. She moved on to the next issue. "I gave Melanie McFarlane a riding lesson yesterday. At the end, she told me that she's determined to buy Clifton's Pride from you. That she'll be making you another offer, a bigger one. And when you sell to her, she hopes that my mom and Rufus and the new hand and I will stay on to work at her dude ranch."

"But I'm not selling to her."

"Seriously, she did mention a larger offer. And I know that the first one must have been pretty good for you to have even considered it…"

"It doesn't matter what she offers. I'm keeping Clifton's Pride. And I'll talk to her. Again. This time I'll make sure that we understand each other."

Steph hadn't realized she was holding her breath. She let it out slowly. "Good." And now came the hard part. "I'm sorry," she said. "I thought…I could just go with this, with you and me. Just kind of take it however it happened."

"But you can't."

She smiled a sad smile. "You say it like you knew that all along."

He made a low sound, something midway between a grunt and a chuckle. "Because I did."

She said, "This last week. It's been awful."

He said nothing for a moment. She waited, letting him consider his response. At last, he told her, "I thought it would be the best thing…to break it off. You know. Cut it clean. I tried to explain it on the phone. Didn't do a very good job of it."

"You seem…"

He caught her thumb between his lips again, licked the fleshy pad, let it go. "I seem what?"

"Oh, Grant. I don't know. Resigned, maybe? Yeah. That's it. You seem resigned."

He ran a finger along the outside of her arm, bringing a trail of goose bumps, sending a hot little thrill down to her core. "When I saw you last night, in the Lounge, I knew it was hopeless." Hopeless? Such a strange word to choose. "I knew I couldn't give you up."

"Give me up? You say it like you wish you could, like I'm some kind of liquor or bad drug you've gone and gotten yourself addicted to."

"Steph. What do you want me to tell you? I *do* wish I could give you up. It would be better if I could. Better if, over time, we could go back the way we used to be."

"But…it's not what it used to be. It never will be again."

"It doesn't matter, anyway. The fact is I can't. I've never felt like I feel about you."

"And that's bad?"

"I never wanted to feel this way. I like a life that's…uncomplicated, you know? I like my freedom. But I'm not free. Not anymore. Even if I managed to walk away from you, it would kill me inside. And if you found someone else…" He shook his head. "I've thought about that. A lot in the past two weeks. How you should find someone else. How it would be better for you if you did—and how, if you did, I'd spend my life hating that other man's guts and wishing him dead. For doing nothing—but loving you better than I ever could."

She sat up then, and gathered the sheet around herself. "You make it sound like such a terrible thing. To want to be with me. To miss me when we're apart."

"I'm sorry. I'm making a mess of this. As usual."

"I didn't say that…"

"Look. However I made it sound, it's…how it is. And like I said, I know how you are. You're not a woman to be taken lightly. When you give, you give it all. I won't disrespect you. Not anymore."

"Grant. No. You don't understand. You haven't disrespected me. Never. No way."

"But I know what you want. And I accept it." He reached up, hooked his hand around the back of her neck and pulled her down to him again. Eye to eye with her, he said, "We'll get married. It's the best way."

Chapter Fourteen

Surely she hadn't heard him right. "Grant?"

"What?"

"Married? Did you say…married?"

"Yeah." He kissed her cheeks, pressing his soft lips first to one and then the other. "Get together with your mom. Figure out how you want to handle it. Whatever you decide, weddingwise, it's fine with me. Make it soon, that's all I ask."

She pulled away from him and grabbed the sheet close again. Her throat had clutched up. She had to cough to clear it. "But I don't…you're not serious."

"Yeah. I am."

"Marriage? *Now?*"

He sat up, too. "Don't look so shocked. It is what you wanted, right?"

For all of my life…

But, oh. Not like this. Not so…grimly. Not as if he hated the very idea, as if he were somehow resigned to his fate.

"It's too soon," she said.

His brow creased and that mouth she loved to kiss turned down at the corners. "Too soon for what?"

"For us. To get married. We're not ready yet."

"We're as ready as we'll ever be."

"No. We're not. Two weeks ago, you thought of me as a sort of honorary kid sister. Everything's changing between us. I think that's good. It's what I've always dreamed of, longed for. But marriage…no. Uh-uh. Not yet."

He gave her a long, hooded look. "It's the words of love, right?"

"Pardon me?"

"You want me to tell you I love you. All right. I love you. I can't live without you. It's driving me crazy, wanting you all the time. Put me out of my misery. Marry me."

"Oh, Grant. Just listen to yourself. Put you out of your *misery?* Like a pony that's come up lame?"

He scowled. "I'm spilling my guts here and you're making jokes about it."

"No. I'm not. I'm just trying to get you to see. It's

not something we should rush. We need to…know each other better."

"You've known me all your life."

"Not like this. Not in a man and woman way. This is…it's like getting to know each other all over again."

He slumped back against pillows. "You're mad at me now."

"No. I swear. I'm not."

"I've made this too cut-and-dried. I'm sorry. It's difficult for me and I—"

"Grant. I'm not mad. And if I thought we were ready for marriage right now, I wouldn't care how you asked me. I'd be saying yes."

"You don't want to marry me?" He looked like she'd just dropped a boulder on his head.

"But I do."

"Then why the hell do you keep saying no?"

She took his hand. He let her have it, but his eyes were watchful, doubtful. On guard. "I'm just going to say this. Just…say it right out and clear the air, okay?"

"Damn it, Steph. What?"

She barreled into it, before she could lose her nerve. "I love you, Grant Clifton. I'm *in* love with you. I think I always have been, ever since I was kid. I never planned to tell you what was in my heart. I never figured that you would—or could—love me back. But then, after that day by the creek, after the first time you kissed me…I started to hope. All at once, you were seeing me as a woman. You wanted me. And, well, suddenly, it seemed like anything might happen. All my dreams might just come true."

"So, fine." He brought her hand to his lips and kissed the back of it. "Marry me." He licked where he'd kissed.

And she was so tempted. To do whatever he wanted. To say yes. Yes, yes, yes! To head for the altar, and work the problems out later.

But she couldn't. To her, marriage was a sacred promise. A lifetime agreement a person needed to be ready for. "Oh, why can't you see? For marriage, there has to be more than just not being able to keep our hands off each other. There has to be easiness between us. We need to be each other's best friend. There's got to be trust, a knowledge that we're in understanding with each other. About what we want out of life, about what kind of life we're going to live. You know what I mean. Your folks had it. So did mine."

He pulled his hand from hers. "It's that damn ranch, isn't it? You want me to give up the resort business and move back to Clifton's Pride."

She tamped down a surge of frustration. "No. I don't want you to give up the work you love. Why would I want that? That's not what I meant."

"Good," he growled. "Because it's not happening."

"I know that. And Grant. That you *don't* know I know that…that's why we need more time."

He stared at her. And he didn't look happy. "You're talking in circles. The truth is, you're not sure you want to marry me."

"Wrong. I'm sure. I'm just not ready."

He swore and then he swore some more. "There you go. Talking in circles, like I said. If you're not ready, it's because you're not sure."

She sat a little straighter. "This is going nowhere."

"Because you won't be straight with me."

"That's not so. And you're not going to bully me into this, so you can just save your breath on that score."

"Yes or no, Steph. It's simple. Yes or no."

She couldn't sit still. So she threw back the covers. But then she realized her clothes were in the other room. She flipped the sheet back over herself and demanded, "Are you trying to chase me away? Is that it?"

His jaw was as set as a slab of granite. "Yes or no?"

She longed to pop him a good one about then. Somehow, though, she controlled herself. The way he was acting only proved her point. But that didn't mean he would let himself see it.

His blue eyes shone hard and bright as he repeated his ultimatum. "Yes or no. Make up your mind."

Oh, she knew what he was doing. He'd boxed her in neatly: She said yes when she wasn't ready to—or she rejected him. Either way, as far as she was concerned, they would both lose.

"Yes or no."

And it came to her. A workable response. "Yes. In December."

He gaped. And then another string of swear words turned the air blue.

"Why are you swearing at me? I said yes."

"In damn December?"

"That's right. At Christmas time. It's not that long." But it *was* long enough that maybe they could work a few things out. Maybe he'd open up to her more. Maybe, by then, they would be friends again.

Oh, how she longed for that. She wanted him so bad. Just plain lusted like mad for him.

She loved him with all her yearning heart.

But he wasn't her friend anymore. And the man that she married *would* be her friend.

"December," he muttered, as if the word tasted bad in his mouth. But then he grabbed her and kissed her and she knew that though he didn't like it, he would do this her way.

That afternoon, Grant called his mother in Billings. He told her that he and Steph were getting married.

Helen Clifton congratulated him. She said, "I always had a feeling you and little Steph would get together."

"Hell, Ma. You did? You never said a word to me."

"And have you tell me I was crazy? I don't think so."

He told her they hadn't set a date yet. "Sometime in December, I think." *Unless I can get her to quit stalling and see things my way.*

"December," said his mother in a musing tone. "It's a fine month for a wedding…"

He made a low, disagreeable sound. As much as he

hated the way Steph was stalling him, he didn't want to get into it with his mom.

She said, "Keep us posted, will you?"

"We will." He dared to add, "I hope you'll come."

After a moment, she promised, "We'll be there. You and Steph. A December wedding. How could your sister and I miss that?"

He was pleased. And more than a little surprised. His mother didn't like to return to Thunder Canyon. For her, there were too many sad memories waiting there.

Grant drove out to the ranch that evening so he and Steph could tell Marie their big news.

Marie hugged them both and said she was sure they'd be really happy together. Grant had a funny feeling Steph's mom had reservations about the engagement, but she didn't say so and he had no intention of asking her what she *really* thought. Marie had two lips and a voice box and a fine command of the English language. If she had objections, it was up to her to speak them out loud and clear.

Grant didn't get it. Not any of it. Not Marie's lukewarm reaction to the news. And not Steph.

He didn't get Steph in the least. She said she loved him. That she'd *always* loved him.

But she wasn't going to marry him for months.

Damn it. Now he was resigned to being her husband, he wanted it done. He'd never been a man to drag out the inevitable.

If Marie seemed kind of lukewarm at the news, Rufus was downright ecstatic. He clapped Grant on the back and told him what a lucky man he was and then insisted Marie get out the good Scotch so they could share a toast—or three—to love and happiness.

After dinner, Grant and Steph went out and sat on the front steps in the warm evening.

He put his arm around her and she snuggled in close and he breathed in the arousing scent of her and wished they were at the resort, in his bed. Where he could touch every inch of her, bury himself inside her, hold her close to his body all night long.

He pressed his lips to her silky hair. And grumbled, "You thought about how we're gonna sleep together when we're married? I work late most nights—and you're up and in the barn at five in the morning."

"Hey."

"What?" He growled the word.

"Get that chip off your shoulder. It's all going to work out."

"It's a problem."

"We'll manage. It's less than half hour by car between here and the main lodge. Some nights I'll be there, with you. And some nights you can come here."

"Oh. Yeah. So damn simple."

She turned her head and pressed her lips against his neck, thrilling him. Her every damn touch just set him on fire. "Shh. Don't be a grump. Please."

He tipped her chin up and kissed her. Harder and

deeper than he should have maybe, considering they sat right out there on the porch where anyone might glance out a window and see what they were up to. When he finally lifted his head, she gazed at him kind of wistfully. He didn't ask her why the sad look. Hell. If he asked, she'd be sure to tell him and he might not like what she had to say.

They sat in silence for a time. Bart's back leg thumped the porch as he scratched himself behind the ear. Somewhere beyond the circle of the buildings, an owl hooted. From the bunkhouse, faintly, Grant heard music. Rufus was playing his old Johnny Cash tapes on that ancient boom box of his.

Grant wasn't going to bring Marie up—but he heard himself doing it anyway. "Your mom doesn't seem all that excited about us getting married."

Steph looked at him levelly. "I think she has doubts it's what you really want."

That irked him. "What *I* really want? I'm not the one who's put the wedding off till Christmas. You tell her that?"

"You were there. You heard what I said." He wasn't the only one who was irritated. Those green eyes flashed. "And if you've got a problem with my mom's reaction, maybe you ought to have a talk with her about it."

He realized they were on the verge of an argument. Now, how the hell had that happened? "Look. I don't want to fight."

"Could have fooled me." She muttered the words as she turned her head away.

He wanted to grab her close. Kiss her some more. But then he wouldn't want to stop with just kissing. And *then* what would they do? Head for the tack room and make love on the rough wood floor again? March upstairs together, right past Marie sitting in the living room with her knitting? He wouldn't feel right about that. It would seem…disrespectful to the woman who had been his mother's best friend. And to Steph, too, somehow.

Damn it. Why did this have to be so complicated?

Because Steph just had to wait five months before she'd wear his wedding ring.

He stood. "I think I'd better go."

She rose, too. "Good night, then." She didn't look annoyed anymore. She didn't look particularly adoring, either, like a bride-to-be ought to. What she looked was self-contained. Distant. Accepting.

He reached down and took her hand and pulled her up into the circle of his arms. She softened as he kissed her. And then she walked him the few steps to the Range Rover. He got in.

She shut the door. "Thank you for the ring." The big engagement diamond glittered on her tanned hand. He'd made a special trip to Billings that afternoon to buy it. He'd even guessed her size right. "It's beautiful," she added, sounding like she meant it. "I'll treasure it always."

He took that hand with the ring on it, turned it over and pressed a card key into her palm. "To my suite."

Her cheeks colored. With pleasure, he hoped. "Thank you."

He wanted to demand she come to him tomorrow night. But what if she said she couldn't, that she had too much work on her hands at the ranch? His pride was ragged enough, with the way she'd put off marrying him. He didn't need to know he took second place to a broken fence or a sick cow.

She stepped back from the vehicle and he drove away.

Since it was still early and he didn't much relish the thought of going back to his empty rooms at the resort, he stopped in at the Hitching Post in town.

Dax, Marshall, Mitchell, the twins and Russ were there, playing Texas hold 'em in the back. They all got together to play at least once a month, usually around the first. But with all the Independence Day hoorah that month, they'd put it off till now. Grant grabbed a chair and joined them. He won four hands in a row.

Marshall remarked that he was looking pretty grim for a guy on a winning streak.

Grant only shrugged and nudged Mitchell to his left. "Deal."

Mitch obliged. Grant tipped up the corners of his two hole cards. Big Slick—an ace and a king. His luck was holding. He bet twenty and then got two more aces on the flop. In two more rounds of betting, he coaxed more money out of them. Then, on the river, he went all in.

The rest of them folded.

He was hauling in his winnings when Russ said, "I heard you're selling Clifton's Pride."

He gave Russ a look. Not a friendly one. "Who told you that?"

Russ shrugged. "Word gets around."

Melanie McFarlane.

The woman must have been talking to more than just Steph. *Tomorrow,* Grant thought. Without fail. He would have a talk with Melanie and make certain she understood that he was never going to sell her Clifton's Pride.

He told Russ, "You heard wrong. I'm keeping the ranch."

"Well." For the first time in two years, Russ looked at him without a scowl. "Good. It's a fine spread. I'd hate to see you let it go."

"What could I do? My fiancée is set on keeping the place. And you know women. What they want, they get."

The table went dead still.

Marshall said, "What the hell? Your *fiancée?*"

Dax said, "Stephanie, right? You and Stephanie…"

Grant nodded. "That's right."

Mitchell let out a low laugh. "Damn. Never in a million years would I have guessed you'd be the first of us to tie the knot."

"Steph wants a December wedding." Grant tried not to sound as bugged as he felt over the way she'd put him off for almost half a year when, to him, the whole point of the marriage was to get things settled between them. "That's months from now. So who knows? Maybe one of you will beat me to the altar, after all."

They all laughed at that one. And Mitchell faked a threatening glare. "We're gonna have to pretend you didn't say that."

Dax grunted. "Yeah. Otherwise, we'd have to kill you."

A rumble of agreement went around the table.

"We're single men," Marshall announced to the table at large. "And we like it that way." He looked at Grant again. "You and Steph. Hell. Life is just packed with surprises, and that is no lie."

And then they were all out of their seats, even Russ, gathering around his chair, pounding him on the back and telling him what a lucky man he was, razzing him about how brave he was, taking on a woman full-time, for life.

He let it go on for a minute or two.

Then he commanded, "Enough. Take your seats. Let's get back down to business here, boys. When I head for the resort tonight, I plan on taking all your money with me."

Grant called Melanie in her rooms at nine the next morning and asked if she was free for lunch.

"I am," she answered briskly.

"The Gallatin Room at one?"

"I'll see you there."

He arrived fifteen minutes early and was waiting at a prime table by the fireplace when she arrived. She waved away an offer of a cocktail and told the waiter she'd have a Caesar salad and an iced tea.

The waiter turned to him. "Mr. Clifton?"

"The usual. Thanks, Paul."

The waiter nodded and left them, reappearing in no time with a basket of hot bread and Melanie's tea.

Grant wished for a nice, stiff whiskey. He sipped his water. "How's the property hunt going?"

She opened her designer bag and took out a pen and a small square of paper. "I've been meaning to talk to you about that."

"You have, huh? Well, I wouldn't say I'm an expert on what to buy and how much to pay, but I do know the area. I'll be glad to tell you what I've heard about any of the spreads up for sale around here."

"Grant." She said his name patiently. "Don't play me."

"Well, Melanie. I'm not the one who's doing the playing around here."

She wrote on the paper. "I'm not sure I made this clear before, but I'm financing my guest ranch project out of my own funds. Whatever you may have heard about my family money and connections, I'm on my own now. I can pay well, but my pockets are only so deep. That said, I'm determined to make a success here in Thunder Canyon. And I want Clifton's Pride. I want it a lot." Her dark eyes shone with a steely resolve.

Well, well. Melanie McFarlane might be a rich city gal, but damned if she didn't have more than her share of grit. Grant found himself believing that she would succeed at anything she set that sharp mind to.

However, she wasn't getting Clifton's Pride. "I wish you the best of luck. I'm sure you'll do just fine."

She picked up the scrap of paper and set it down again—directly in front of him. "There's my final offer. Say yes now and I'll have my realtor draw up the new contract today."

Grant glanced down and almost let out a whistle. The figure was a lot more than her first offer, and that had been a fine one. He met her eyes. "I don't know how to make this any clearer than I already have. I'm really sorry you've got your heart set on my ranch, because I meant what I said the last time we talked."

"But—"

He raised a hand. "You're wasting your breath, Melanie. I'm not selling."

"I'm sure you—"

"I'll say it again. No. No matter what you offer, I'm keeping my ranch. I've realized Clifton's Pride isn't something I can let go of, after all. Plus, my fiancée is damned fond of the place."

Melanie blinked. "Your…fiancée? I didn't know you were engaged."

"I am. To Stephanie Julen. You know, my foreman? The one you offered a job to day before yesterday?"

"Oh. Well…" The redhead swallowed. Hard.

"I'd appreciate it if you'd stop offering jobs to the people who work for me."

"I only thought it might be reassuring for them to know—"

"They don't need reassurances. They already have jobs. They work for me."

"It wasn't my intention to offend."

"I'm not offended. I'm also not selling. I'll keep my eyes and ears open for you, though, like I said I would. If I hear of something that might suit your needs, I'll let you know. *I'd* like to know that you're hearing me loud and clear this time. I'm not selling my ranch and that's my final word on the subject."

Melanie put her hands in her lap and sat very straight. After a moment, she granted him a regal nod. "All right."

"I hate to belabor this point, but I need to know for certain that you're going stop running around town telling everybody you talk to that you're buying my ranch."

"I get it. You're not selling. That's firm. And I think I've lost my appetite." She tucked her napkin in beside her untouched iced tea and rose. "Excuse me."

He watched her walk away from the table with her red head high. He still felt bad about backing out of the deal with her, especially now that he was coming to admire her gumption.

But he'd accomplished his goal with her, at least. She finally understood that she would have to look elsewhere for the property she needed to build that dude ranch of hers.

* * *

Steph surprised him that night.

She did come to see him.

In fact, she was asleep in his bed when he got up to his suite at ten. She'd left a lamp on low across the room, so he wouldn't have to stumble around in the dark.

He stood over her, captivated by the sight of her in his bed.

She lay on her side, her hand tucked under her head. He was mesmerized—by the inward curve of her waist and the smooth swell of her hip under the sheet, by the shadowed luster of her skin. Her hair, like gold silk, flowed back from her head against the white satin pillow. She was so beautiful it made a sharp ache down inside him, just to look at her.

She stirred and rolled onto her back. Her eyes opened. And she smiled. "There you are." She reached up those slim arms.

He couldn't get out of his clothes fast enough.

She held the sheet up for him, welcoming him. He went down to her softness. And she touched him, bringing a deep, hungry groan from him as her strong fingers encircled him.

Lost, he thought, as she stroked him. *I'm gone. Finished. Hers...*

She kissed him. Deeply. He surrendered to her caresses, to the giving, wet softness of her mouth under his.

When he fumbled for the condom, she got to it first. She rolled it down over him. Slowly. He groaned some more as she rose up over him, straddling him, taking him into her by slow degrees.

He looked up at her, watching her as she rode him, her body moving like a wave above him, her hair falling forward, brushing his chest when she bent down to kiss him. He wrapped his arms around her and pulled her down.

She came to him willingly, gave herself completely. Eagerly. As if surrendering to him was the most natural thing, as if giving him everything only made her *more*.

She didn't understand. It wasn't that easy for him. His whole life was changed, now, because of her.

His mind, all his senses, every beat of his heart. All of him. Hers. There would never be another for him.

He knew that now.

It wasn't what he'd wanted for himself. It scared him, to belong to someone the way he belonged to her, scared him to want someone as much as he wanted her.

What would happen if he lost her?

How would he live if she was gone?

No answer came.

And soon enough, the pleasure claimed him, pushing all the dark questions from his mind. He crushed her close and surged up into her as his climax rolled through him, stealing all thought.

Chapter Fifteen

Patience, Steph told herself. *I need to be patient with him.*

Yet as one gorgeous summer day became the next, she couldn't help getting a little discouraged. She went to him every chance she got. Most nights, she would be there, waiting, when he came to his rooms at the resort.

He made love to her with a passion and a heat that continued to astound and amaze her. And though he had a well-deserved rep as a ladies' man, she had no trouble believing that he'd put the bachelor life behind him. He wanted her and only her. She had zero complaints on that score.

But he was still angry that she insisted on waiting

until December for the wedding. Every chance he got, he tried to push her to move the date closer.

More than once, he suggested they just run off to Las Vegas.

And then she would say how she really did want to wait. And he would get surly.

She kept hoping he would...what?

Relax a little, maybe? Not be so guarded and gruff. She wasn't the kind who needed a man to talk to her constantly. She had no problem at all with silence—not as long as it was a good silence, one without anger or bitterness, one sweet and easy with mutual understanding.

She desired him, loved him, wanted to *be* with him. But more and more it seemed to her that he resented his feelings for her, that he was only with her because he couldn't stay away.

What kind of marriage would they have? Not a very good one, if things kept on like this.

Two weeks after she accepted Grant's marriage proposal, Steph went into town to run a few errands. She saw Jim Baylis outside the grocery store. He gave her a nod and she nodded back. He looked pretty scruffy, unshaven and not all that clean. She hoped he'd found other work, but no one had called her to ask her about what kind of an employee he'd been.

She almost stopped to ask him how he was doing, but he turned and walked off before she could say anything, so she just let it be.

Inside, she met up with Lizbeth Stanton in the pasta aisle.

"You're mad at me, aren't you?" Lizbeth demanded. "Just say it. Just admit that you are. I swear to God, I had no clue that you and Grant were a couple. If I had known, I would never have—"

"Lizbeth. I'm not mad. Truly."

"I just want you to know. There was never anything going on between Grant and me. Yeah, I flirted with him, but that was all. It never *went* anywhere."

"It's okay. Really."

"You're sure?"

"Lizbeth, there's no problem, take my word."

"Whew. I hate it when women hate me."

"Well, stop worrying. Because I don't hate you."

"People don't understand. Just because I make no bones about being on the lookout."

"The…lookout?"

"Yeah." She pushed her cart to the side and stepped closer, so no one but Steph would hear. "I'm looking for the right guy. I just want…to get married, you know? Settle down. Have a family. I admit that maybe I kind of hoped Grant might be the one for me. But I promise you, after I saw you and him together the other night…I'd have to be blind not to see that he's Taken. Capital T. And I can respect that, I honestly can."

Steph gave her a big smile. "Well, thank you."

"I hope you'll be real happy together."

"I know we will." The way things were going with her and Grant, Steph knew nothing of the kind. But Lizbeth Stanton didn't need to hear that.

Lizbeth frowned. "Hey. You all right?"

"Yeah. Fine. Really."

Lizbeth trilled out a laugh. "Men. They drive you crazy and break your heart. But you gotta love 'em. I mean, *somebody* has to, right?"

That night, Grant came out to the house for dinner. Over her mother's beef stew, he reported that Jim Baylis had robbed Arletta Hall's gift shop that afternoon. He'd gotten away with the contents of her cash register and what was in her safe, about two thousand dollars altogether. "And when Arletta took too long opening the safe, he shot her in the arm."

"Did they catch him?" asked the new hand.

"Not yet," Grant muttered darkly.

Steph was stunned. "I saw Jim this afternoon. Hanging around outside the Super Save Mart."

"You see him again," Grant said, "you call 911."

Marie put her hand to her throat. "What went wrong with that boy?"

"It's a damn shame," said Rufus. "He seemed like a nice enough guy. Just goes to show you never really know what goes on inside of some folks."

After the meal, the hands went back to the bunkhouse and Steph and Grant sat out on the porch in the summer dark but had nothing to say to each other.

That would have been fine. If only it had been a *good* sort of silence.

But it wasn't. Steph could feel his frustration with her. It came off his big body in waves.

How many times had she tried to bridge this strange gap between them? She only felt close to him when she was in his arms. Though talking about it hadn't worked up till then, she didn't know what else to do.

So she went ahead and gave voice to the issue that always seemed to hang in the air between them. "Rushing to get married isn't going to make everything all right."

"Stalling for months won't, either." He stared out at the shadowed yard. "Unless the real truth is, you never plan to marry me at all."

"I *do* plan to marry you." She felt like she was talking to a stone statue, to a brick wall. "But I want things to be…right between us first."

He turned his head and looked at her then. It was one of those dark, broody looks she got way too many of recently. "There's nothing wrong between us that you can't fix by saying yes now—and meaning it."

She shut her eyes, sucked in a slow breath. "I do mean it."

"So all right, then. Let's—"

"Please, Grant. Don't, okay? Just…don't."

"Fine." He stood. "Listen. I'd better get back to the resort."

She gazed up at him. "What's eating you, Grant Clifton? I really and truly want to understand. But you're just…shut up tight against me and I don't know how to get through."

He made no reply to that, only reached down, took her hand, and hauled her up into his arms. "See you tomorrow night. Come to my rooms."

"I'll be there. You know I will."

He kissed her, kind of slow at first, then more deeply. The kissing, as always, curled her toes and made smoke come out of her ears. If the rest of what they had together could be half as good as the lovemaking, she'd be one contented cowgirl.

Too soon, he was lifting his head. He said good-night and headed for the Range Rover. She dropped back to the porch step and watched him leave and wondered why she felt so lost and empty inside.

Would she ever get through to him?

She looked down at the toes of her boots and wished she knew where to go from there…

A moment later, she was on her feet. She ran inside to grab her purse and the key to her pickup.

Marie glanced up from the ironing board as she rushed past the open archway to the living room. "Where are you off to, now?"

"I want to see Russ."

"Russ Chilton? Whatever for?"

"Just a visit."

"At nine o'clock at night? It's at least a forty-minute ride to the Flying J."

"Yes, it is. So don't wait up. I'll probably be a couple

of hours." She pulled open the door and went through it before Marie could ask another question.

The lights were on in the front room of Russ's white clapboard house when Steph stopped the pickup a few yards from the front·walk. Russ must have heard her drive up. He pushed open the door as she mounted the porch steps, the light from within outlining his tall, broad-shouldered frame.

"Steph. What's going on?" The porch light shone on one side of his lean face. He was frowning, probably worried there was some kind of trouble.

Which there was—just not the kind a rancher expects when a neighbor comes calling out of nowhere that time of night. "No problem—I mean, nobody's injured or missing or anything. It's only I…"

He peered at her more closely, brows drawing together. "You okay, Steph?"

"Not really. It's about Grant…"

Without another word, he stepped back and ushered her into the house.

In the kitchen, he offered coffee and she accepted. They sat at the Formica table under the window that, in the daytime, provided a clear view of rolling open land, including both Russ's ranch and the neighboring Hopping H.

Russ set a full mug in front of her and took the chair opposite hers. "So tell me," Grant's longtime best friend said grimly, "he decided he's not ready for marriage, after all? He break your heart, Steph? If he did, I'll be glad to smash that fool's face in for you."

"Oh, Russ. Not...exactly."

Russ sipped his coffee. "Not following. He didn't *exactly* break your heart?"

"He *is* breaking my heart. But not in the way you're thinking."

"Well, then, how?"

"He's...he's mad at me all the time. He wants to run off and get married ASAP. I want to wait a little, get to know him better, as the man I love, you know?"

Russ only frowned and made a motion with his hand that she should tell him more.

"I...want some time before we rush into being husband and wife. I told him I'd marry him in December, but that's just not good enough for him. He's either broody and silent around me, or he's pressuring me to elope, claiming he wants things 'settled' between us—'settled,' he says. At the same time as he won't hardly talk to me. He's not...easy with me, Russ. He used to be my friend, you know? But that's all gone now. He wants to race off and get married. And when I won't, he's surly as a peeled rattler. I just...sometimes I wonder if he even *likes* me anymore."

"Hell, Steph. He likes you."

"I don't know..."

"He *more* than likes you. Or he wouldn't be after you to marry him, believe me. Not after what he told me when his dad died..."

Steph sat forward in her chair. "What? What did he tell you?"

"He said then that he was never getting married. He said his dad's death almost killed his mom. And he couldn't stand the thought of loving someone so much you'd want to die without them…" Russ looked at the darkened window, though all he could see was their shadowed reflections.

"Go on," she prompted. "What else? Please tell me."

Russ grunted. "You know, he's gonna be mad as hell at me for talking to you about this." He let loose with a rough, low laugh. "But then, it's not like him and me are on the best of terms lately anyway. So here's what I think, for what it's worth.

"Yeah, he's real good at running that resort. He seems to love it. But he's a man carrying around a world of guilt. He promised his dad he'd stick with Clifton's Pride. And he's broken that promise. That's gotta be tough to live with."

Steph jumped to his defense. "But he *has* stuck with Clifton's Pride. For seven years after our dads were killed, he ran the ranch himself, sweated blood over that place. And now he's got *me* to run it for him. And he ended up not being able to bring himself to sell it to that McFarlane woman, even though she offered him a big ol' potfull of money. He's kept his promise to his dad, you know he has."

But Russ shook his head. "Grant's a rancher. He's

turned his back on what he is, and that's gotta be bothering him, deep down."

Steph made an impatient sound in her throat. "Oh, come on. He hasn't turned his back on anything. He never liked ranching, he was always itching to get out in the big world. But still, he stuck with it for years after his dad died. Isn't that enough?"

"Uh-uh," said Russ. "You're not getting it."

"No. I get it. I do. But I don't see it. I mean, just because you and I can't imagine enjoying the life Grant has chosen, that doesn't make it wrong for him."

Russ wasn't convinced. "*I* think it's wrong for him. And I keep waiting for the day Grant finally comes to his senses, gives up that fast-track life he's been living and goes back to the ranch where he belongs."

Steph drove away from the Flying J with plenty to think about. In the end, she and Russ had agreed to disagree on the idea that Grant needed, more than anything, to get back to the ranch.

Steph just didn't buy that one. Exactly the opposite, in fact. She happened to be absolutely certain that Grant had finally found the right job for him.

But the guilt angle…

Yeah. Russ might have something there. Grant was the kind of man who kept his word. If he'd promised John Clifton he'd spend his life on Clifton's Pride, well, it would be bound to eat at him that he'd chosen a different path in the end.

And the part about him swearing he'd never get married…

Well, maybe that had something to do with how much trouble he seemed to be having over the idea that he was going to be a married man, after all. And if he feared losing her, well, it kind of made sense that he'd push to get that knot tied right away, to "settle" things between them, the way he kept insisting he wanted them to do.

Maybe, she thought, as she slowed for a sharp curve in the dark highway, she should change her approach here. Maybe she should take the leap and marry him now, do it his way instead of insisting that he do it hers. Maybe she should show a little faith that they were going to work things out in the end, prove to him that she was willing to—

Her thoughts hit a wall as a figure loomed up out of nowhere in the wash of her headlights. A man. Waving.

She slammed on the brakes, cranking the wheel to the side in order not to run the fool down. Tires screamed as she slid—fishtailing wildly. She turned into the slide.

And by some miracle she managed to regain control. The pickup stopped on the shoulder—facing directly back the way she'd come. Shaking, her mouth tasting of copper, she shifted into Park. After that, she gripped the steering wheel and stared through the windshield at the hard gold glow of her headlights and the darkness beyond.

Well. That had been exciting. *Too* exciting, as a matter of fact.

She blinked. *The man.*

Some guy with a breakdown, most likely, needing help. One of the long list of situations where a person wished she had a cell phone. Too bad that in most of Montana, the things rarely worked.

As her racing heartbeat slowed, she turned to get her rifle off the rack behind the seat. On a deserted highway at night, you just couldn't be too careful.

Before she could pull the weapon down, she heard the tap on the passenger side window. She glanced that way.

And saw Jim Baylis on the other side. He had an automatic pistol pointed at her face.

Chapter Sixteen

"Open this door, Steph." Jim's words were slightly muffled by the glass, but bone-chillingly clear nonetheless.

Her heart gave a thud so heavy, it felt like a fist hitting the wall of her chest. And the taste of pennies was back in her mouth. As fear tried to own her, she considered her options and found them to be severely limited.

Jim tapped the glass again with the gun. "Open it. Lean across nice and slow."

She did as he told her, not sparing so much as a longing glance for her rifle, still in the rack—so close. But totally useless to her without the precious seconds she needed to take it down and load it.

The latch gave, the door swung wide. Jim, smelling of stale sweat and seriously in need of a shave, hitched himself up into the seat and pulled the door shut. He lowered the gun. Now it was aimed at her side.

"Saw you go by an hour ago. Figured at some point, you'd have to come back this way."

Steph said nothing. Really, she couldn't think of anything to say right then that would do her a bit of good.

Jim grunted and wiped his nose on the sleeve of his dirty rawhide jacket. "Piece of crap pickup of mine broke down. So I have to say, I'm real pleased to see you." He tipped his head at the windshield. "Drive."

"Where to?"

"Thunder Canyon Resort. I got me nineteen hundred dollars from old lady Hall's safe. It's not enough. I need some *real* cash, enough for a decent truck, enough to be able to put a lot of miles between me and this town.

"So we're gonna drop in on that rich boyfriend of yours. See how much he's willin' to pay to get his fiancée back."

Twenty minutes later they were rolling up the long private driveway that led to the main lodge, the bright lights of the sprawling, multileveled structure shining up ahead.

Jim leaned across the seat and jabbed her with that gun of his. "Rufus told me Grant's got himself a fancy big apartment on the top floor of the lodge. Ain't that the life?"

Steph said nothing.

Jim laughed. "Where's the key? I heard you and him are engaged. And I know damn well he gave you a key to his place."

Still, she refused to speak, expecting any second to hear the roar of a gunshot echo through the cab, followed instantly by a hot, hard punch to her side that would bloom into agony all too soon.

She thought of her dad, suddenly, so still in the mud with that bullet hole through his head on that rainy day nine years before. Was the same thing going to happen to her?

Apparently not—at least, not right then. Jim grabbed her purse and started rifling through it. He found her wallet, took the sixty-four dollars cash she had in the billfold and then started checking out the sleeves. It only took a few seconds and he was holding up the card key. "What do you know?" He threw the purse on the floor and shoved the money in a pocket. He spotted the sign that pointed the way to underground parking. "Go that way."

She drove around the back of the main building and into the shorter, downsloping driveway that led into the parking garage. He handed her the key and she stuck it in the key reader. The striped security arm rose. Steph drove inside.

"Park by the elevators."

She found a space not far from the two sets of elevator doors and nosed the pickup into it.

"Turn off the engine and pass me the key to the truck." He didn't ask for the card key—she assumed because he was going to be too busy poking a gun in her ribs to open any doors with it. Opening doors would be her job. "I'll take that fancy diamond ring of yours, too."

Oh, how she longed to spit in his face. But she knew it was a bad time to argue with him. She had to wait for an opening. And with that gun of his pointed straight at her, now wasn't it.

She took off her ring and handed it over.

He shoved it in a pocket of his dirty jeans. "Now, Stephanie," he said. "I'm going to ask some questions and you're going to answer in a truthful way. I don't want to shoot you. It'd be a shame to put a bullet hole through you, especially considering I still got kind of a sweet spot for you, even though you never would give me the time of day. You're a fine lookin' woman and a brave one. But I'll do what I have to do to get what I need. I shot old lady Hall. And I can shoot you. See, I tried to play it straight my whole damn life. But it didn't work out for me. Now I just need cash to get me to someplace where I can start fresh. Understand?"

She nodded.

"One of those elevators over there go straight to the top?"

"No. You have to change elevators on the main floor."

"I was afraid of that." He shrugged out of his jacket, taking his time about it, careful to pass the gun from hand to hand and kept it pointed her way the whole time. He draped the jacket over his arm, masking the gun. "Okay now." He leaned on his door and pushed it open. "Come on toward me. Get out on this side."

She slid across the seat and emerged from the pickup right after him. He shoved the door shut, took her arm and guided her so she was in front of him, kind of tucking the gun against her. To anyone not looking too close, it would appear he was holding her elbow.

"Okay, Steph. Take it nice and easy. Smile and don't make any fast moves."

It all went so smoothly. The elevator opened and two men stepped out. Steph didn't recognize either of them. They nodded, neither man so much as looking twice, and got out of the car.

Jim and Steph got on.

On the main floor, they changed elevators without incident. A bellman recognized her, but only to nod and smile. She nodded back, wanting to scream, knowing if she did, she'd take a bullet for her effort. In no time they were in the second elevator, on their way up.

When the doors slid open on the fifth floor, there was no one in the hall. That was good, right? No one else needed to be hanging around Jim, with his burning need for quick cash and his loaded gun...

"Which one?" Jim demanded.

She stalled, aware of the tiny eye of the security

camera, up in the corner, hoping that maybe someone in the security center with its banks of monitors was paying attention.

More than anything, she wanted to keep Grant out of this. There was going to be big trouble—bigger even than the cold, round mouth of the pistol poking into her side—when Grant Clifton saw what Jim Baylis was up to. He would make Jim pay. Which was fine with her— she wanted Jim to pay herself.

But she couldn't bear the thought that Grant might get hurt in the process.

"Which door?" Jim shoved the gun into her side again.

She said, "He might not even be in the suite yet. Sometimes he doesn't get to his rooms until after midnight."

"No problem. I'm willing to wait. Which one?"

"At the end of the hall."

"Let's go."

Grant sat in the dark in the living room of his suite, an empty whiskey glass at his side. He was thinking about how things change.

How maybe he needed to learn to roll with the punches a little, learn to trust his woman when he knew she deserved his trust. She deserved *everything*. All he could give her, including his sorry, mixed-up heart.

No, he hadn't planned to fall in love.

But hell. It had happened. He loved Steph. And it

didn't look like that love would be going away anytime soon. In fact, it was starting to seem to him that he'd *always* loved her. He'd just been too damn stubborn and hardheaded to admit what he felt.

He loved her. He would *be* loving her until the day he died. There was no escaping his love. If he lost her, it would kill him. He'd have to learn to live all over again. Or end up like his mom, walking around with a big old empty hole where his heart used to be.

But, as of now, he *hadn't* lost her. And he wouldn't, not anytime soon, if fate would only smile on them just a little. *And* if he didn't manage to drive her away with his constant insistence that she marry him and do it now…

So maybe, the deal was to learn how to live with loving her, learn how to be a better man than he'd ever thought he'd have to be.

He didn't especially relish crawling on his hands and knees and begging her forgiveness for being a surly jerk in need of a serious attitude adjustment.

But in the end, a man had to do what a man had to do. He knew she was really torn up over him.

Would it be too damn ridiculous to go to her tonight? To ride out to the ranch right now, rouse her from bed, kiss her senseless, swear on the graves of their fathers that he could wait till December, he could do it *her* way, if only she could forgive him for being such an ass?

He shifted to rise. But a muffled, furtive sound from

the foyer of the suite had him freezing dead-still where he sat, adrenaline kicking in, lifting the short hairs on the back of his neck.

Steph stuck the card in the slot and pulled it free. The twin lights in the electronic lock blinked green. She turned the handle and the heavy door gave inward. Onto darkness. Through the archway to the living room, she could see the fat, shadowed shapes of expensive, heavily padded sofas and chairs and the big window that was the far wall, framing Thunder Mountain beyond.

Was he here, in his bed? Or safe, for the moment, downstairs in the Lounge or maybe in town at the Hitching Post with the guys?

Oh, dear Lord. Protect him. Somehow, let him be safe...

The desperate man behind her gave her yet another sharp poke with his gun. His sour breath stirred her hair as he put his mouth to her ear.

"No lights." The whisper came, low and soft. And deadly. "No sound. Real slow, we'll have us a good look around." He had the barrel of the gun at the small of her back now, and one hand manacled her arm. "Let's go."

As they tiptoed through the empty living room, then down the hallway on the right to the kitchen and the spare room, the extra bath and Grant's in-suite office, Steph formulated a two-option plan.

If Grant was in his bed, she'd make her move when they entered his bedroom. She'd probably end up taking a bullet. But if she moved fast enough, she should be able to avoid a fatal wound and warn Grant at the same time. Piece of cake.

Yeah. Right.

If the suite was empty, she'd have to wait until Grant came in. She should have a split second when they heard him open the door. An instant when Jim would glance away, distracted by the sound. It would be her chance to dive for cover. And to shout out Grant's name good and loud.

She'd been totally unresisting up till now. That should work in her favor. Jim should be lulled by her obedience, certain she was too scared to take action in her own behalf.

At least, she *hoped* he would be lulled. She had to admit he didn't *seem* at all overconfident. He moved with careful deliberation. He kept his cool. At every turn, he'd taken pains to keep that gun of his pointed right at her, to keep her close and under his physical control.

He guided her around and they went back along the darkened hallway the way they had come. At each doorway, he pulled her to a halt while he gave the shadowed room they were passing a quick second glance. He was taking nothing for granted. Damn it.

Moving silently and with caution, they crossed the dark living room again and entered the short hall that ended in one door: the door to Grant's bedroom.

The door stood wide-open, darkness beyond. The moon in the wide bedroom window gave just enough light to see that the bed was neatly made. And empty. The door to the bathroom was ajar. It was dark in there, too.

Steph stood in the doorway, staring at that empty bed, her heart knocking hard, at the same time as she felt a weakness in the pit of her stomach: relief. Grant wasn't in the apartment. He was safe for the moment.

And she would be going with option two.

Jim nudged her with the gun again, urging her into the bedroom so he could check things out. She took a step and cleared the threshold.

And all hell broke loose.

Chapter Seventeen

A dark shape erupted from just inside the doorway. Steph ducked instinctively as she heard her captor gasp in surprise. The gun went off, so loud it seemed to rip the air wide-open. A bedside lamp exploded.

The dark shape jumped on Jim.

Grant! Oh, God. Grant.

She was on the floor without knowing how she got there, scooting backward out of the way, as Grant kicked the gun from Jim's hand and took him down.

The men rolled, punching, grunting, punching some more, knocking over tables and sending stuff crashing to the hardwood floor.

The gun!

Steph had seen it spin under the bed. She went for it, flipping to her belly, going flat and sliding under there. She pulled it out and got to her feet as someone started pounding on the door of the suite.

"Security!" a deep voice shouted. How had they gotten here so quickly?

Her stunned mind caught up: Someone must have been watching the monitors in the security center after all.

She heard the door burst open. Two uniformed men ran in, pistols drawn. By then, Grant had the top position. He slammed his fist into Jim's jaw.

Jim groaned. Grant hit him again. And that was when her former kidnapper gave it up. "Hey," he moaned. "All right. It's done, I'm through."

Dawn was breaking over the mountains when they left the sheriff's station after giving their statements. Grant had a gash across the bridge of his nose and his left eye was bright purple, swollen up fat as a hen's egg.

But aside from that, they were both healthy, not a bullet hole in sight. Steph had her engagement diamond back on her ring finger where it belonged.

Grant gave her a smile. Even with the giant shiner, he was the best-looking man in Montana. "What now, my darlin'?"

My darlin'. He said it so easy and sweet. Crazy, but she felt the tears rising.

Must be some strange stress reaction. Now the danger was past, she could let herself go...

With a discreet sniff she told him, "I'd hand over a couple of prime stud bulls for a big cup of coffee, black."

"You got it."

They went to a little coffee shop in New Town. By then, they were both starving. So they took a booth and ordered breakfast.

Steph sipped her coffee and thought how good it tasted. The best coffee she'd ever had. Maybe because she'd made it through the night when for a little while there, she was sure she was a dead woman.

Surviving made the whole world seem brighter, more hopeful, full of beauty.

And love.

She gazed at the man across the booth from her. And the look in his good eye told her that everything was going to be all right between them. "We are going to have us one fine, happy life, Grant Clifton."

One corner of his mouth kicked up in that smile that lit up her world. "You better believe it—and did you call your mom yet?"

She clapped her hand over her mouth. "I completely forgot. She's going to be frantic."

"Phone's back there." He shot a thumb over his shoulder.

The sheriff had returned not only her ring, but also her wallet and her money, so she grabbed her purse, slid out of the booth and went to make the call.

She probably should have known her mom would

have already contacted the sheriff. "They told me what happened," Marie said. "I have to say, I am mightily relieved. They swore to me you were both unhurt…"

"Grant's a little beat up, but it's nothing serious. We're fine, Mom." She cradled the phone gently, let out a soft sigh as she thought of his easy smile, of the way he'd called her *darlin'*. Her heart rose up, light as a sunbeam in her chest. "We're more than fine."

Marie understood. "So. The man who's got everything has learned what he's been missing."

"Yeah. Guess so."

I'm glad for you, honey."

"Oh, Mom. I'm glad, too."

"Love is a rare and fine thing. Treasure it."

"I will, Mom. I swear."

Her Western omelet was waiting when she got back to their table. She slathered it in ketchup and dug in. They ate with gusto, in easy silence.

She thought how she'd never been so happy. Not in her whole twenty-one years of life.

Back in the Range Rover, with her belly full and the danger past, with her future looking extra rosy before her, she let her head droop against the seat rest and closed her eyes.

"Steph…" His tender voice came to her, luring her to wakefulness.

"Um?"

He kissed her, a gentle brushing of his lips against hers.

She opened her eyes and saw him, right there, so close, his dear face filling her world. "We're here?"

"Yeah. We are."

He'd parked the Range Rover out on open land. She wasn't surprised when she glanced out her side window and saw the rough, jagged outcroppings of bare rock.

The Callister Breaks.

"Oh, Grant." She touched his wonderful beard-stubbled cheek. "It's…fitting. It's right."

"I knew you'd think so. Come on."

They got out of the big vehicle and started walking, hand in hand. It wasn't far. Soon enough they stood above the place where their fathers had died.

"Beautiful here," he said.

"Yeah." She looked out at the rugged beauty of the land, at the wide sky and a hawk, soaring so high above them.

He tugged on her hand and she moved closer, into his strong, warm embrace. He said, "I dream of that day now and then. Of them, dead in the mud. Of how damn brave you were."

She felt a tear rise, spill over and slide down her cheek. "They were fine men."

"The best."

"I suppose I'd better tell you…" She felt suddenly shy. She swiped the tear away, tipped her head down.

He caught her chin and guided it upward so he

looked in her eyes again. "Anything. You can tell me anything."

So she did. "After you left last night, I went to the Flying J."

The truly amazing thing was, he instantly knew why. "Hoping Russ could tell you why I'm such a jackass?"

"Oh, more or less. I guess."

"Well. Did he?"

"He helped. Then I kind of thought of it myself. I was just putting together what I would say to you when Jim jumped out into the middle of the road in front of my pickup and I got seriously distracted for the rest of the night."

He laughed. It was a wonderful, free and easy sound. "So now you're safe and here with me, I think you should tell me what you planned to say to me."

She felt shy again. She had to clear her throat before she could begin. "Ahem. I think…you've been afraid to love me. I think it's not what you intended for yourself. I think you had some idea that if you never loved anyone too much, you wouldn't get hurt. Like your poor mom was hurt when your dad was killed."

"Ouch. You got me."

She put her hands on his chest, felt the strong, even beat of his big heart. "Not that it matters anymore, what your problem was with loving. Because all I have to do is look at you to know you've worked it out all by your lonesome."

"Naw. Not by my lonesome. Not by a long shot. You

did most of the work, just by being you. By showing me…all I was missing. All I was throwing away."

"But *you* did it. Without me explaining to you what your problem was. You figured it out."

"Yeah. Guess I did."

"Right on time, too."

"Yep. Which is why I was sitting there in the dark, not making a sound, when Jim Baylis brought you to me. At gunpoint."

A chuckle escaped her. "It did work out all right, after all, didn't it?"

"There were a few iffy moments."

"But here we are."

"Oh, yeah," he said. "Together. As we were always meant to be."

"Oh, Grant. I love how you say that."

He dipped his head and kissed her—a quick, sweet one.

When he straightened, she rested her head against his heart. "Okay," she whispered. "I'm willing now, if you still feel strongly about it. We can get married right away if that's how you want it."

"Hey. Come on. Look at me."

She raised her head. "Yeah?"

"I know. About December. You never dared to say it to me, because I think you knew I couldn't take it. But, Steph. I can take it now."

The tears were rising again. Two of them dribbled down her cheeks. Light as the touch of true love itself, he brushed them away and she asked in a trembling voice, "You're sure?"

He nodded. "You go ahead. You say it right out. We don't need to hide from the past anymore. The past has made us what we are now. The past is part of us. I'm learning that we should no more turn our backs on what came before than we should say no to the future."

She added, "Because we can have both, Grant. I know what you promised your dad. That you'd stick with Clifton's Pride, make him proud by doing right by the land. Well, if you think about it, that's exactly what you *are* doing. You turned the ranch over to me and I'll do what John Clifton wanted, I'll do it with joy in my heart and a smile on my face. And you can go ahead and be a wheeler-dealer golden boy. There's no law that says we both can't live the lives we always wanted."

The wind teased her hair. He guided a few wild strands behind her ear. "Say it. Out loud. Right here and now. About December."

"It's…when our folks were married. Remember? A double ceremony—Marie and Andre, John and Helen—they said their vows to each other just a few days before Christmas. It's always seemed to me the best time of year for a wedding."

He didn't even hesitate. "December it is, then."

"Oh, Grant. Are you sure?"

"I know what I want now, Steph. You. A lifetime with you. I don't need to rush it now. I don't need to…lock things up. December is fine with me. I can wait."

"Oh, you are just an amazing and wonderful man."

His arms tightened around her. "Prove it. With a kiss."

She lifted her mouth to him and he claimed it. All their passion was in that kiss. All their hope. Their dreams. Their commitment.

Their love.

When he lifted his head, they turned together, to look down at the place where their fathers had died.

She said, "I love you, Grant. I always have."

"I love you, too," he answered. "Always."

Above them, the hawk soared. They heard its wild, hungry cry on the wind. As one, they turned to go home.

To Clifton's Pride. Or his fancy apartment at the resort.

It didn't matter where they went.

Just as long as they were together when they got there.

* * * * *

Lynne Graham has sold 35 million books!

To settle a debt, she'll have to become his mistress...

Nikolai Drakos is determined to have his revenge against the man who destroyed his sister. So stealing his enemy's intended fiancé seems like the perfect solution! Until Nikolai discovers that woman is Ella Davies...

Read on for a tantalising excerpt from Lynne Graham's 100th book,

BOUGHT FOR THE GREEK'S REVENGE

'Mistress,' Nikolai slotted in cool as ice.

Shock had welded Ella's tongue to the roof of her mouth because he was sexually propositioning her and nothing could have prepared her for that. She wasn't drop-dead gorgeous... *he* was! Male heads didn't swivel when Ella walked down the street because she had neither the length of leg nor the curves usually deemed necessary to attract such attention. Why on earth could he be making *her* such an offer?

'But we don't even know each other,' she framed dazedly. 'You're a stranger...'

'If you live with me I won't be a stranger for long,' Nikolai pointed out with monumental calm. And the very sound of that inhuman calm and cool forced her to flip round and settle distraught eyes on his lean darkly handsome face.

'You can't be serious about this!'

'I assure you that I am deadly serious. Move in and I'll forget your family's debts.'

'But it's a *crazy* idea!' she gasped.

'It's not crazy to me,' Nikolai asserted. 'When I want anything, I go after it hard and fast.'

Her lashes dipped. Did he want her like that? Enough to track her down, buy up her father's debts, and try and buy rights to her and her body along with those debts? The very idea of that made her dizzy and plunged her brain into even greater turmoil. 'It's immoral... it's blackmail.'

'It's definitely *not* blackmail. I'm giving you the benefit of a choice you didn't have before I came through that door,' Nikolai Drakos fielded with a glittering cool. 'That choice is yours to make.'

'Like hell it is!' Ella fired back. 'It's a complete cheat of a supposed offer!'

Nikolai sent her a gleaming sideways glance. 'No the real cheat was you kissing me the way you did last year and then saying no and acting as if I had grossly insulted you,' he murmured with lethal quietness.

'You *did* insult me!' Ella flung back, her cheeks hot as fire while she wondered if her refusal that night had started off his whole chain reaction. What else could possibly be driving him?

Nikolai straightened lazily as he opened the door. 'If you take offence that easily, maybe it's just as well that the answer is no.'

Visit **www.millsandboon.co.uk/lynnegraham**
to order yours!

MILLS & BOON

MILLS & BOON®

Mills & Boon have been at the heart of romance since 1908... and while the fashions may have changed, one thing remains the same: from pulse-pounding passion to the gentlest caress, we're always known how to bring romance alive.

Now, we're delighted to present you with these irresistible illustrations, inspired by the vintage glamour of our covers. So indulge your wildest dreams and unleash your imagination as we present the most iconic Mills & Boon moments of the last century.

Visit **www.millsandboon.co.uk/ArtofRomance** to order yours!

MILLS & BOON®

Why shop at millsandboon.co.uk?

Each year, thousands of romance readers find their perfect read at millsandboon.co.uk. That's because we're passionate about bringing you the very best romantic fiction. Here are some of the advantages of shopping at www.millsandboon.co.uk:

* **Get new books first**—you'll be able to buy your favourite books one month before they hit the shops

* **Get exclusive discounts**—you'll also be able to buy our specially created monthly collections, with up to 50% off the RRP

* **Find your favourite authors**—latest news, interviews and new releases for all your favourite authors and series on our website, plus ideas for what to try next

* **Join in**—once you've bought your favourite books, don't forget to register with us to rate, review and join in the discussions

Visit **www.millsandboon.co.uk**
for all this and more today!